Praise For *The Kingdom*

Clergy who have put the fear of God in their congregations through their words and actions should read *The Kingdom* where they can learn how to put the love of God in the minds and hearts of those they serve. This is a story that goes far beyond the need for unconditional love of family. If all Americans read *The Kingdom* and embraced Tom Hardin's wisdom, we would ALL be better.

— **Mitchell Gold**, co-founder of Faith In America; editor of *Youth in Crisis*; co-founder Mitchell Gold + Bob Williams home furnishings.

A powerful story of redemption and transformation, *The Kingdom* by Tom Hardin, takes a hot-button issue of our day, makes it human, and helps us think and stretch and grow. This book is living proof that the greatest truths are found in stories.

— **Philip Gulley**, Quaker minister; author of the Harmony series, also *If The Church Were Christian*, *Front Porch Tales*, *If Grace Is True* and *If God Is Love*.

It is often painful to read beyond the blistering stigma that Tom Hardin exposes in *The Kingdom*, but one is deeply rewarded with the promise of hope and healing. It is, ultimately, a story of resurrection, and a chilling reminder of the cost of a closed heart.

— **Addison Ore**, Executive Director of Triad Health Project; freelance contributor to *Go Triad*, Greensboro, N. C

To Diane:
Thank you for your show.
You make the world a better
place for your listeners.
Tom Hardin

THE KINGDOM

A NOVEL

BY

TOM HARDIN

The Kingdom is a work of fiction. Names, characters, places, incidents,
organizations, coalitions and houses of worship are the product
of the author's imagination or are used fictitiously.
Any resemblance to actual events, locales, academic
institutions or persons, living or dead, is coincidental.

ISBN: 1478348690
ISBN-13: 9781478348696
Library of Congress Control Number: 2012914142
CreateSpace, North Charleston, SC

Acknowledgements

While *The Kingdom* is completely fictional, it is a story whose telling is long overdue. It was a labor of love with much help behind the scenes. To my immensely talented fellow writers—Mark Fleming, Cindy Cipriano, Emily Dunlap Carter, Chris Laney, Betsy Bevan and Chip Bristol—I express my deepest gratitude for their encouragement, caring support and monumental commitment to read and reread the manuscript. For their technical and legal expertise, I extend my appreciation to Magistrate Mike Williams, Detective Sergeant of Homicide Debbie Butler (Retired) of the Greensboro Police Department, and especially retired attorney and, dear and valued friend, Juanita Blackmon. To Barbara Farran whose caring patience and insight know no end. To my friends Joanna Schroeder and Wes Isley for kindly listening and advising. To professional photographer Patrick Eilers (www.patrickeilers.com) for so sensitively capturing the cover photo. To David Lojko for modeling for the cover. To Ross Holt for website design.

I particularly want to acknowledge the members and ministers of College Park: An American Baptist Church in Greensboro, North Carolina, whose love, caring, warmth and total acceptance served as an inspiration to write this novel, especially Rev. Dr. Michael Usey, a true but modest servant of God and Bible scholar, who possesses unbridled courage in the face of discrimination.

And to a host of friends and family who enrich my daily existence more than you will ever know.

I like your Christ, I do not like your Christians.

Your Christians are so unlike your Christ.

—Mahatma Gandhi

CHAPTER ONE

SUNDAY EVENING—MAY 10

A mighty sight, Reverend Matthew Winslow thought, pride coursing through him. No. It was *Almighty*. And he knew God was extremely pleased. He had to be.

Standing in front of the first pew with his back to the altar, he fed on the sight before him—the ultra-modern horseshoe-shaped Holy Bible Fellowship sanctuary and the five thousand congregants returning to their seats after intermission. "Almighty, indeed," Matthew whispered, knowing that he deserved to be proud. He had raised the millions needed for the massive building and everything in it, especially its state-of-the-art everything—audio-visual equipment, closed-circuit television cameras, two colossal screens that provided a larger-than-life view of those on the stage. Color-coordinated seats, carpet and wall coverings completed the majestic array underneath a dome ceiling. He took a deep breath. Yes, he was proud of it all, and tonight he swelled with pride over something else. Something even more important. Much more. His son, Nathaniel, was competing for the coveted title of Bible Scholar of the year and all of these people had come to witness that honor. And Nathaniel *would* win. Of that, Matthew had not a single doubt.

"Reverend Winslow." Shaken from his reverie, he turned around to the female voice and outstretched hand. "Amazing sermon at this morning's worship. Simply amazing." Average in appearance, she was neatly dressed, not overly-stylish, but her face radiated sincerity. "We thought it was just so powerful." She gestured toward the man next to her. Matthew noted his Polo shirt stretched tightly over his plump mid-section.

"Oh, thank you. Thank you so very much," Matthew said as he stepped toward her and took her hand in both of his. "I'm so glad you all were here." He turned to the man and reached over to shake hands with him. He had no idea as to their names nor did he recognize them as they returned to their seats. But he followed his father's sage advice—be overly gracious and warm toward all members.

As the lights dimmed and brightened urging the audience to be seated for the final round of the contest, Matthew shook hands with a few more members who had come to the front of the sanctuary to greet him and compliment him on his message that morning—none of whom he knew or recognized. Finally, he motioned to his wife and daughter standing in the aisle to take their seats on the front row with him. As the church's highest ranking pastor, the prominent pew was reserved for him whenever he had no part in a service or program. As the lights dimmed again, he performed a routine check of his appearance—the snugness of the knot of his powder blue, silk tie in the starched V of his collar, centering it inside the jacket of his navy blue suit. Crossing his right leg over his left knee, he pretended to pick a piece of lint from his pant leg, then calmly clasped his hands in his lap.

As if he might be praying, Matthew lifted his eyes to the massive stage where a ten foot tall antique bronze sculpture of an open Bible hung in front of soft golden drapes. "In this..." was written in raised letters on the left page and "we believe..." on the right page. "Holy Bible Fellowship" in six foot high bronze letters arced over the holy symbol with an American flag gracing one side of the stage and a Christian one the other.

His grandfather, Benjamin Garland Winslow, the church's founder, and Matthew's father, Jacob Madison Winslow, who grew the church and the academy, would both be proud. Proud of all that he had done in his seven years as lead pastor—raised the membership to nearly eight thousand, expanded the academy to over two thousand students, added the baseball stadium and soccer field and built this glorious sanctuary. And he, Reverend Matthew David Winslow, proudly stood at the helm of all of it.

Matthew dropped his gaze back to the stage which was bathed in glaring spotlights as the auditorium darkened. Except for an occasional stifled cough, all were still, eagerly anticipating the final round. He took a deep breath as he thought about his only son. A scholar—academic as well as biblical—a lettered athlete, class president, popular, clean-cut, wholesome. If there was an All-American high school senior contest, his son, Nathaniel Harris Winslow would win unanimously. And someday all of this would be his, Matthew thought, and he would carry on the traditions and greatness of Holy Bible Fellowship and Academy, all begun by his great-grandfather.

Sitting next to her husband, Miriam Winslow discreetly pulled her skirt down to properly cover her knees. Her pale yellow summer dress appropriately matched her husband's blue suit. Wearing compatible colors was something that he insisted on whenever they appeared together. With her index finger she tucked her blond hair first behind one ear, then the other. Yesterday she'd had it cut to just the middle of her neck, the length Matthew thought looked best for her role as his wife and first lady of the church. She also had it touched up to cover the latest streaks of gray, something he had done to his hair on a weekly basis.

Miriam fought to appear calm, but inside she was anxious and worried. She wanted Nathaniel to win, but what if he didn't? Not that she thought he wasn't capable. She knew he was. But losing in front of all these people. And those towering TV screens showing his face so close. He would be humiliated. And worse—much worse—so would Matthew.

Always win. Be first. Be the best in everything. That had been Matthew's mantra even before Nathaniel was in the first grade. But Nathaniel seemed to handle it, always producing the results his father expected in school and athletics. But when he started school at the Academy, Miriam had broached the topic with her husband—subtly, non-confrontationally, as she was always careful to do. "Nathaniel's still so young. I wonder if too much pressure when he's so little might not be good for him," she had said bravely. Matthew had looked directly at her with an unconvincing smile. "That's not something you need to worry about," he assured her. Still, Miriam had tried again, "I just want him to—" But he had halted her as he always did by lifting his hand. "That's not something you need be concerned with," Matthew repeated calmly with a dismissive even tone. Still, she prayed vigorously for her children everyday, but especially for Nathaniel.

Miriam turned to her right and smiled at her second child. Sarah Elizabeth wasn't as driven as her brother. She did her best, but the outcome never seemed to matter. Miriam knew that as a girl, she was not as important to her father as Nathaniel was—although there was no question of Matthew's love for his daughter.

Sarah Elizabeth responded to her mother's warmth with a strained, sincere grin. She wore her school uniform—white blouse and gray skirt. Like her mother, her blond hair fell straight and to mid-neck. She sat with her arms crossed over her abdomen, pressing lightly. She tried to do so without anyone noticing, especially her father, but sometimes the cramping was so uncomfortable. She wanted to be here for Nathaniel. She wanted him to win, but she also wanted to be at home in bed.

Behind the stage Nathaniel and the other finalist, Jason Daniels, sat waiting for the intermission to end. Each held a bottle of water. They were dressed in their school uniforms—charcoal slacks, blue Oxford shirt and black tie. Jason's shoulders were broad, his arms muscled, his jaw square. His near six foot frame sported a trim waist. His hair, dark and short but thick. Even though Nathaniel was leaner, he was just as solid, his torso filling out his shirt. He carried himself with what appeared to be quiet confidence. His recently trimmed, dark hair was perfectly combed. Both exuded distinctly handsome features. Masculine. Mature. Both enjoyed several sports and had lettered in basketball and baseball and frequently played pickup games with other guys at the Academy.

At Holy Bible Academy all high school students were paired up by their Bible teacher to quiz each other on verses. This year—their senior year—their teacher, Reverend Sessoms, had paired Nathaniel and Jason to be "Bible Buddies," mainly because they both knew the Bible backwards and forwards. "You're perfect challengers for each other," Sessoms had told them. Their weekly, hour-long Biblical testing of each other, either at Jason's house or Nathaniel's, resulted in their mastery of verses as well as a solid friendship. To Nathaniel the friendship was special, but in a way he tried desperately not to think about. A wrong way. Wrong and sinful.

"Nice drawing of the Academy's main entrance," he said, looking at the cover of the program for the competition.

"Thanks," Jason responded. "I wanted to draw all the Bible faculty for it, but Mrs. Medlin nixed that."

Nathaniel grinned. "No surprise there with your reputation for giving people big noses, elephant ears, cash register chins and pot bellies."

Jason smiled. "Yeah, well, I can't help it if she doesn't have a sense of humor." Sitting forward, he put his forearms on his thighs to speak privately while wearing a mischievous grin. "You realize we could keep this thing going all night."

Nathaniel smiled as he leaned closer. "What are you talking about?"

"If we both give the wrong answer to the same question, they have to keep going."

For a moment Nathaniel was distracted by the dark, heavy shadow of Jason's beard, even though he'd shaved.

"Keep it going so late they'd have to delay school tomorrow maybe," Jason added.

Nathaniel laughed quietly. "But we can't lie," he said, turning serious.

"I know," Jason said, sitting back in his chair. "Just trying to relieve the tension. Either way, one of our fathers is going home pissed because his son lost tonight."

The reality struck Nathaniel. His father *would* be hurt, not to mention embarrassed, and from what he knew of Jason's dad, the same would be true.

"Very well, gentlemen," Associate Pastor Richard Newland said, approaching them. "It's time for the final round." His black suit set off his thick white hair that was no doubt heavily sprayed to hold it immaculately in place.

"Good luck, buddy," Jason said quietly as they followed the minister to the stage entrance. He offered his hand.

"You, too." Nathaniel shook the warm, firm grip.

With the lights in the worship center dimmed, Pastor Newland entered the stage followed by Jason and Nathaniel. Vigorous applause greeted the three as they took their places. The moderator's podium had been moved to center stage and each of the two finalists stood at a microphone, one on each side of the podium and six feet from it.

"Ladies and gentleman," Pastor Newland said, perching his reader glasses near the end of his nose, "this is a momentous occasion; indeed the most revered tradition at Holy Bible Fellowship and Academy. Over a hundred years ago, Benjamin Garland Winslow instituted the annual Bible Scholar Competition to mark the culmination of each student's twelve years of studying the holy book. In the first grade each student is required to create a notebook of memorized verses—ten each week, including summers. For twelve years members of the Bible faculty drill pupils each day on biblical facts, on each student's verses and others that the ministerial administration deems important. Every year in May, all seniors vie for the coveted title. Benjamin Winslow, our senior pastor's grandfather, felt it was vital to require each student to demonstrate his or her commitment to God as they graduated and continued on to college. As has been true for the last eleven years, the winner will receive a full four-year scholarship to Freedom Bible University."

Matthew hid his impatience. Everyone already knows the history, he wanted to say. No need to repeat it. No need to worry about the scholarship, either, he smirked to himself. Nathaniel was definitely going to Freedom Bible University, and tuition was not going to be an issue. The university trustees and The Christian Coalition for Biblical Authority in America had already assured him of that privately—payback, as it were, for his identifying students as potential Christian attorneys and candidates for state and national offices, as well as judges and other crucial government positions. A goal of the university and the Coalition. No, the scholarship would not be important. Paramount was Nathaniel winning, just like he had almost done when he had been a senior. But that was long ago, he told himself as painful memories threatened his attention. He took an unnoticeable deep breath and let it out easily. Just get on with it.

"This is the final round," Richard Newland said as if he had heard the senior pastor. "I will ask each contestant a question. If he doesn't know the answer, the other contestant will have a chance to answer. If the second contestant doesn't know, then the competition will continue. Each will have thirty seconds to respond. As usual we will proceed in alphabetical order. Therefore, our first question is for Jason Daniels. Who took Judas' place as a disciple?"

The image of Jason's face covered the giant screen on the left side of the stage. Keeping his hands confidently by his sides, he leaned slightly toward the microphone. "Mathais."

"Correct. Nathaniel, what was Paul's profession?"

His handsome face filled the other gigantic screen, making it easy for all to inspect his clear, sparkling blue eyes. "Tent maker."

"Correct. Jason, where did Rebekah tell Jacob to run when Esau was plotting to kill him?"

"To Haran."

"Correct. Nathaniel, who was Rebekah's brother?"

"Laban."

"Correct. Jason, give the book, chapter and verse for this scripture: 'What then shall we say to this? If God is for us, who is against us?'"

Jason paused for only a moment. "Romans 8:31."

"Correct. Nathaniel, give the book chapter and verse for this scripture: 'Obey your leaders and submit to them; for they are keeping watch over your souls.'"

Nathaniel did not hesitate. "Hebrews 13:17."

"Correct."

The volley of questions and answers continued like an endless battle of ping pong—rapid fire, never breaking rhythm.

"Who was Rebekah's husband?"

"Isaac."

"What is the definition of a beatitude?"

"Supreme blessing."

For over thirty minutes Jason and Nathaniel shot back their answers with assurance. Matthew Winslow made sure his neutral facial expression remained galvanized, but with each question he hoped that Jason would falter and his son would win.

Miriam tried to remain calm. All these years when other seniors competed, she'd felt the tension. But this was her child, her son. She clenched her hands together unconsciously, praying for Nathaniel.

Sarah Elizabeth listened closely. She was proud that she knew all of the answers. Maybe she would be a finalist in two years. A girl finalist. The thought almost made her smile. She wondered if her father would be as proud of her as he was of Nathaniel—if she won.

"Nathaniel, who warred with Baasha, king of Israel throughout his reign?"

"Asa."

"Correct. Jason, what part of Asa's body became diseased in his old age?

"His feet."

"Nathaniel, who was Asa's son and succeeded him as King?"

"Jehoshaphat."

"Correct. Jason, give the book, chapter and verse for this scripture: 'For God did not give us a spirit of timidity but a spirit of power and love and self-control.'"

Jason stared through the blinding spotlights into the darkness but did not answer. His silence numbed the audience. No one moved or scarcely breathed. Was this it? The question that would decide it all? The stillness had everyone in its grasp.

Knowing that the television camera was on him, Nathaniel looked at the floor. He knew Jason had this. That same verse came up when they sat studying together on Jason's bed last Thursday. Both wearing shorts and t-shirts. Jason had known the answer immediately. He'd even stopped and brought up that odd question. "Do you think God makes us all love in the same way?" he'd asked Nathaniel. Nathaniel immediately felt uneasy. "I don't know. I never thought about it," he'd said. Jason's only response was to lie back and stare at the ceiling. Still the question plagued Nathaniel. So did Jason's occasionally bumping his bare, thickly dark haired leg against Nathaniel's bare leg that same afternoon. But what had plagued Nathaniel more—much more—was that he did not mind the contact but knew that he should.

"Jason, do you need me to repeat the scripture?" Pastor Newland asked.

Jason looked down and put his hands into his pockets.

Matthew sat rigidly still. Miss it, he thought.

"I'll have to call time, Jason, if you don't give me an answer," Pastor Newland said.

Jason leaned toward the microphone. "John 8:15."

Nathaniel continued looking at the floor. That wasn't the right answer and Jason knew it. Was he doing this to keep the competition going like he had joked?

"I'm sorry, Jason. That isn't the correct answer," the associate pastor said with solemn dramatic tension, more for his own ego than out of concern for the contestant.

There was a rustling and some gasps in the dark auditorium. Matthew took a breath. He wanted to lean forward and cheer on his son like a fan at a ball game, but he remained perfectly composed. He knew that Nathaniel knew the answer. He had quizzed him on this very verse last week. First Timothy 1:5.

"Nathaniel, I'll repeat the question. Give the book, chapter and verse for this scripture: 'For God did not give us a spirit of timidity but a spirit of power and love and self-control.' You have thirty seconds."

Nathaniel's face was on the big screen. Still, he wanted to turn and look at Jason. He wanted to know why he was throwing this. Was he expecting him to give a wrong answer, too? Was he challenging him to lie? But somehow Nathaniel knew this wasn't a prank. *One of our fathers is going home pissed.* Was he letting him win?

When his son didn't answer right away, Matthew became alarmed. What was the matter with him?

"I need to ask you for your answer," Pastor Newland said.

Outwardly Matthew showed no emotion. But inside his head he was screaming. First Timothy 1:5. Say it.

Nathaniel took a deep breath and leaned toward the microphone. "Second Timothy 1:7."

Matthew exhaled. How could he have missed it? He was livid but steeled himself not to show it. As he uncrossed his legs and crossed them again, he noticed that Jonathan Sessoms, chairman of the Bible department, and the entire Bible faculty—all seated on the front row across the aisle—were smiling and nodding proudly. Why were they reacting like that? Fury began to rise in him.

Pastor Newland, obviously pausing again for dramatic effect, removed his reader glasses and looked out at the audience. "Correct. Ladies and gentlemen, the Bible Scholar for 2008-2009 is Nathaniel Winslow."

* * *

"Almighty God, we thank you for this day and the endless opportunities to spread your gospel of love and peace to those who are so lost and so in need of knowing you." Matthew paused. "We thank you for Nathaniel's gift of Biblical knowledge and his winning tonight's competition to glorify your name."

Matthew, Miriam, Nathaniel and Sarah Elizabeth held hands in a circle in the upstairs hallway of their home as they did every night. Always in the exact same spot—the wear on the carpet greater than the usual traffic paths. They stood in the same order each night—Miriam to Matthew's right, then Nathaniel, next Sarah Elizabeth, and back to Matthew. All stood with their heads bowed reverently except for Matthew who leaned his head back as he devoutly directed the evening prayer heavenward.

"We pray that you will always guide us to the people who are lost and forlorn that we may minister to them and bring your holy word to them."

Sarah Elizabeth suddenly inhaled deeply but as softly as she could until the cramp passed.

"Keep us mindful of your word, your gospel, your safety, your love as we live our lives amid those not as fortunate to have found the way of your truth."

Miriam wished she were next to her daughter so she could gently rub her thumb over the back of her hand as minimal comfort.

"And, oh God, we pray that you will protect us this night. Provide us with the security of your love and peace as we restore our bodies in rest. Give us your holy sustenance through sleep so that we may be strong both physically and mentally to do thy will tomorrow."

Nathaniel braced himself for the prayer that he knew was sure to follow.

"Thank you, Father, for giving Nathaniel your trust tonight at this momentous competition. We are so proud of him as you must be also. Continue to bless him, granting him speed and sharpness as he plays baseball for the remainder of the school year and mental toughness to continue excelling in his classes and go on to Freedom

Bible University and come back here to serve you. Comfort Sarah Elizabeth during this time. Give her strength to get through this spell. Watch over Miriam, their mother and my wife, as she provides the daily needs for this family. We are so blessed, Father, God. Help us never to forget that. Hear us now as we each pray to you. Miriam."

Miriam raised her head slightly. "Father God, bless this family. Keep us strong as we go about doing your will. Help me to give strength and wisdom to my chil—my husband and my children."

"Sarah Elizabeth."

Sarah Elizabeth took a deep breath. "Help me, God, to be strong during these few days of discomfort. Thank you for reminding me of my place as a woman."

"Nathaniel."

Nathaniel shifted his feet slightly. "Holy God, make me strong and wise. Help me to know the right thing to do. Lead me in the right and Godly way."

"Father, hear our prayers," Matthew said. "Grant us your favor. In your blessed name we pray. Amen."

"Amen," the other family members echoed.

They all opened their eyes and dropped their hands.

"Good night," Matthew said to Sarah Elizabeth, hugging her briefly.

"Night, Dad."

Miriam followed her husband, also hugging her. "Did you have another cramp?" she asked softly.

Sarah Elizabeth nodded. "I'm going to take some Tylenol right now."

"Call me if you need me." She kissed her on the cheek.

"I will. Night, Mom."

"Son," Matthew said, offering his right hand and putting his left on Nathaniel's shoulder, "so proud of you. So proud. I knew when Jason said John, you had won."

"Thanks, Dad."

"Get a good rest tonight. Mr. Cheshire said you have an Advanced Chemistry test coming up and there's practice for Saturday's game."

"I'll be ready for both, Dad."

"I know you will." As they did every night, they shook hands firmly and at the same time used their left arms for a brief embrace.

"Good night," Miriam said, first smiling her congratulations as she held his arms, then reaching up to hug her son who was taller than she. Finally, she kissed him on his cheek.

"Night, Mom." He had always liked the way his mother held him, even when he was a child. Now he was the first to end their embraces even though he didn't truly want to. He quickly kissed her on the cheek.

"Night, Sis." He hugged Sarah Elizabeth. "Feel better," he whispered.

"Thanks. Night," she replied. Sarah Elizabeth felt a special bond with her brother. Their hugs were brief, but she knew that was the only way a brother could show affection for his sister. He had always looked out for her and, without his ever saying so, she knew he always would—a feeling that meant the world to her.

Matthew stood at the door of the master bedroom while Sarah Elizabeth and Nathaniel went to their respective rooms and closed their doors. He switched on the small lamp in the hallway and turned off the overhead light.

"Questioning Sarah Elizabeth about her cramps—I'd rather Nathaniel not hear that," he said with quiet authority after he had closed their bedroom door.

Miriam stopped folding back the comforter and sheets and looked at her husband across the bedroom. "I just wanted to be sure she was—" she began but stopped when she saw her husband gently raise his hand to silence her.

"I'd rather Nathaniel not hear it," he repeated. "That kind of discussion should be held in private between you and your daughter." He began unbuttoning his shirt. "I don't think it's spiritually healthy for a young man to hear. And," he added, "if she would take the Tylenol sooner she wouldn't experience the—so much pain."

Miriam continued folding back the sheets. She wished he would permit Sarah Elizabeth to take birth control pills to ease the cramping pains, but he had overruled that option emphatically. "I'm sorry, Matthew. I'll be more careful from now on."

He came around the bed and put his arm around her. "I know you will." He gave her a brief hug and kissed her on the forehead. "I think tonight would be a good night." It was his signal.

"Yes." She looked up at him, then smiled.

"Why don't you go into the bathroom and freshen up and I'll be waiting for you," he smiled and kissed her again.

Miriam crossed the room and went into their bathroom. After undressing she used a sanitary disposable wipe to be sure she was completely clean. She brushed her teeth and used a mouthwash, then washed her hands and face with sanitizing soap and warm water. All expectations from her husband. From the towel cabinet she chose one of her older and least favorite nightgowns, the ones she wore only when he wanted to be intimate. Not at all surprising that he wanted to have sex tonight, she thought. He usually did when he felt a measure of success.

While she was out of the room, Matthew quickly undressed and put on his pajamas. Sitting on the side of the bed, he picked up his Bible from the nightstand. How could he have not known that scripture? Second Timothy 1:7, he repeated silently. He turned to the passage and read it, as if to be sure everyone else wasn't mistaken. Nathaniel's answer was correct. He flipped back one page to First Timothy 1:5: "Whereas the aim of our charge is love that issues from a pure heart and a good conscience and sincere faith." Immediately, the memory punched him in his gut. The Bible Competition his senior year. Luke 17:21. He didn't know the verse and was eliminated with five fellow students still in the competition. For two weeks his father didn't speak to him or look at him.

16

Matthew put his Bible on the nightstand. He would never miss another one, he told himself, unaware that he was clenching his jaw. He would study his twelve notebooks and reread the whole Bible. Genesis to Revelation. It was time to do it again anyway. He sighed. Finally, the name Winslow would again be etched in the long list of Bible Scholar champions on the large plaque in the academy's front hall. His father's and Nathaniel's. He was sure both his grandfather and father would be proud.

He leaned over and set the alarm clock. When he heard Miriam opening the bathroom door, he got into bed. With his plan for reviewing the Bible decided, he was able to smile at her as she got into bed beside him.

Miriam lay on her back as he turned off the light and rolled over to her, roaming her chest with his hand. He unbuttoned her nightgown and put his hand inside, kneading her left breast. Then he kissed her, first on one cheek, then the other; next, on her mouth. Miriam as always put her arms around him but never tightly. He pulled her night gown up and moved on top of her. Within a moment he was inside her, thrusting rhythmically but not as he usually did. Tonight he was harsh, almost brutal. But she knew she could not say anything. She closed her eyes and feigned pleasure as she always did. Finally, he finished, rolled off of her and lay beside her as his breathing slowed.

"Thank you, God, for this Holy Act and for my husband," she whispered.

Matthew patted her hand and rolled onto his side, facing away from her.

Miriam sat up and pulled her nightgown down over her legs and covered herself with the sheet. She too rolled onto her side, facing away from her husband. When she was sure he was asleep, she pulled her nightgown up between her legs to wipe away his semen even though she knew he didn't want her to. As usual she began dreading the next time, hoping it wouldn't be soon.

Careful not to wake Matthew, she slowly pulled her knees toward her. Quietly she sighed and prayed for her children.

Sarah Elizabeth poured two tablets from the bottle of Tylenol. She filled her glass with water and swallowed them. She put the glass down and pressed her hands gently, then more firmly against her lower abdomen. She closed her eyes and leaned against the bathroom vanity. She wanted to pray to God to take away her misery but knew that such a prayer was unacceptable. Brushing her blond hair, she sighed and turned off the bathroom light. She sat on the edge of her bed and took her Bible from the nightstand and opened it to Leviticus 15, verse 19 and began reading softly aloud.

"When a woman has a discharge of blood which is her regular discharge from her body, she shall be in her impurity for seven days, and whoever touches her shall be unclean until the evening. And everything upon which she lies during her impurity shall be unclean; everything also upon which she sits will be unclean. And whoso-ever—" She couldn't read anymore.

Respectfully, Sarah Elizabeth closed her Bible. Her sheets were clean. She always took special care not to mess them up. She couldn't help what was happening to her. She put her Bible on the nightstand and, pressing her legs tightly together, rolled onto her bed. She fought the tears that wanted to come. It was so unfair. She tried to reason that this would be over in three more days and she would be back to normal. For three weeks. Just for three weeks. Then it would start all over, again.

Determined not to think about it, she reached for her cell phone and began texting Mike. If her father caught her, she knew he'd take her phone for a month. She'd risk it. "Saw U 2nite w/ parents. Wanted to sit w/U. CU tomorrow. Nite. SE" She turned off the sound and plugged in the charger. The Bible competition ran through her mind. What if she wound up winning when she was senior?

Nathaniel sat at his laptop, scanning emails. The number of congratulatory messages seemed endless, but he was searching for one in particular. There was one from Martha which he skimmed before continuing. When he didn't find one from Jason, he supposed he shouldn't be surprised. He debated sending him one or texting him, maybe even calling him, but he didn't want his father to hear him on the phone. He checked his own cell phone, Martha's photograph popping up first on the touch screen. He turned to her school picture on the shelf next to his desk. Her bouncing auburn hair, tiny little nose and deep brown eyes. Why? he thought. Why was he so mixed up? He turned back to his phone. More messages from friends at school—including Martha—but nothing from Jason.

He replayed in his mind the end of the competition. Both he and Jason had shaken hands with Pastor Newland, then with each other. He had looked at Jason with the one question in his mind. Why had he done this?

"Congratulations, buddy," Jason said above the din of applause. "You deserve to win. Do yourself proud at Freedom Bible."

Nathaniel had just looked at him. Then his parents and friends—Martha foremost— swarmed the stage, everyone congratulating him, and Nathaniel lost sight of Jason.

As Nathaniel turned off his computer and plugged the charger into his phone, he thought about Jason's haunting question—do you think God wants us all to love in the same way? Nathaniel battled his thoughts—at Jason's house studying and in the locker room at school, the shower—

He stood up and quickly undressed. He wasn't going to think about that. Those thoughts were unclean, stupid thoughts. He went into his bathroom and took a quick shower. Drying off, he looked at his naked body in the mirror. He thought of Jason. Naked. He clamped his eyes shut, gritted his teeth, and gripped the towel in his fists until his knuckles whitened. Why was this happening to him? He hung the towel on the rack and returned to his room. He quickly put on his sleeping shorts and t-shirt. Sitting on his bed, he took out his Bible and began turning to Leviticus but then stopped. He didn't need to read it. He knew what it said. He got down on his knees and placed his face and outstretched arms on his bed.

"Oh, God, please take these sinful thoughts out of me," he whispered into mattress. "I don't know how they got there. I don't want them. I know it's wrong, but I don't know how to get them out of my mind. I'm trying to love Martha Davies. I am. And I want to serve you, Father. Help me to be a better person. Help me not to feel all this and keep me from having those dreams about Jason and—" He halted. He couldn't say it. Not in a prayer. "And what happens when I do," he said even more softly. "I want to get married. I will get married. Someday. Help me, God. Help me be pure. I'll do whatever you ask me to do. Please, God. Amen."

He remained on his knees as he placed his hands on both sides of his head, pressing as if to squeeze out his sinful impurity. Fighting his emotions, he went into the bathroom and got a towel. He pulled back the cover and top sheet on his bed and spread the towel across the middle as he had been doing every night for the last several years. Just in case it happened again. He did not want his mother to ever see—that mess. When he lay down on the bed, he checked to be sure the towel was positioned between his waist and his knees. He pulled the top sheet over him, hoping nothing would get on it if he had a dream. He tried to sleep, but his thoughts ricocheted like a pinball game. When he went away to college in August, he would change. He knew it. He had to. And he wouldn't need to sleep with a towel underneath him anymore.

CHAPTER TWO

MONDAY—MAY 11

"How absurd," Matthew muttered with indignation, reading the morning newspaper as he sat at the breakfast table in the kitchen.

Miriam poured coffee into his cup. "What is, Matthew?" she asked with caution but also out of obligation.

He listened to be sure both children were still upstairs. "This," he said almost whispering. He held up the paper and pointed to the large heading at the bottom on the front page. "'Gays To Rally in Elmsborough,'" he read aloud in an irritated whisper. "It's a three-day series on homosexuality. I cannot believe they would put such a thing in the newspaper, much less on the front page. And I'm going to have to look at it for two more days." He shook his head. "If it weren't for having to keep up with what's happening in the community for the church's sake, I'd cancel my subscription." He continued reading. "'Gays from all over North Carolina are coming here for an all day gathering downtown on June 27.'" He read more. "And they're having a parade." Disgruntled he folded the newspaper and put it beside his plate. "Gay Pride. Why would anyone take pride in being a homosexual?"

Miriam set a plate of her husband's usual breakfast—eggs, bacon and toast—in front of him but made no comment.

"And to think how some of the so-called ministers in this city—or anywhere for that matter—welcome those people into their churches with open arms. It is beyond me." He put his napkin in his lap and tapped the paper with his index finger. "I don't want Nathaniel and Sarah Elizabeth reading this." he said. He took a sip of coffee, then sprinkled salt and pepper on his eggs.

"Nathaniel likes to look at the sports page," Miriam said carefully as she sat down with her bowl of oatmeal and coffee. She noticed a slight pain between her legs. From last night, she was sure.

"I'll bring it home tonight. He can read it then." He took several bites. "What a way to begin the day seeing that on the front page."

Miriam ate her oatmeal without speaking. She had learned to keep silent when he was upset. She knew he would write a letter to the editor as he usually did when the paper carried a significant article on one of his peevish sins.

Matthew picked up the final bit of crisp bacon and popped it into his mouth. He drained his coffee cup and blotted his mouth. "Kenneth Ward called last week to set up a meeting for today with me and Howard Carr to discuss this very matter," he said, as he stood. "Wonderful breakfast as always."

"Thank you." She smiled up at him as he pushed his chair under the table.

"I have a feeling I'm going to be involved with this all day," he said, holding up the newspaper.

"I'll see you tonight."

"Most assuredly. Have a nice day." He walked out the door into the garage.

Hearing the mechanical garage door hum open and shut, Miriam sighed and finished her oatmeal. She drank a bit of her coffee, then glanced at her watch. She was about to go to the bottom of the stairs to urge Sarah Elizabeth and Nathaniel to hurry when she heard Nathaniel's voice.

"Hurry up, Sis, if you're going with me."

Miriam stood up slowly to avoid pain and cleared the table. She went to the stove and turned on a burner to scramble two eggs for her son and put two pieces of whole wheat bread into the toaster.

Nathaniel came into the kitchen and put his book bag on the counter near the door. "Hi, Mom," he said, kissing her on the cheek.

"Morning, sweetheart. Sleep well?"

"Uh, yeah, fine."

"Not too excited still," she said, beating the eggs in a bowl.

"No, I, uh, drifted off pretty quickly." He looked around the room. "Did Dad take the paper with him?"

Miriam raised her eyebrows and nodded as she poured the eggs into the frying pan. "Yes. He said he would bring it home tonight so you could look at the sports. Sorry."

"It's okay." He opened the refrigerator and got out the pitcher of orange juice and poured a glass for himself and Sarah Elizabeth. He drank some of his standing at the refrigerator and set hers on the table. He came to the stove and grabbed the popped up toast, put it on a plate and held it out for Miriam to put two pieces of bacon and the eggs on it.

"Thanks, Mom."

"You're welcome." He sat down, sprinkled salt and pepper on his eggs and began eating. Miriam carefully sat down at her place and sipped her coffee. "How's school?"

"Fine. Getting ready for exams. You know, the usual."

"How's Martha? What's going on with her?"

"Well, she's getting all excited about the graduation banquet in two weeks. Said she's got a new outfit."

"Graduation," Miriam said, shaking her head. "Seems like yesterday you were just starting school. Now in three months you'll be leaving for college."

"Now don't go getting all soft and droopy on me, Mom," he said with a smile while eating.

Miriam smiled back. "I will if I want to." She reached over and rubbed his upper arm. "I miss having you around. You're always on the go. Now it seems like the only time I get to see you is when you're eating," she said with a tone of toying exasperation.

Nathaniel half laughed as he continued. "Because I'm always hungry—" he drank the last bit of his orange juice, "—and because you're a great cook." He swiped his mouth with his napkin and went to the refrigerator and poured himself more juice.

"Well, the eating part is true," she agreed.

"So's the great cook part."

Miriam smiled. "I just—" she began but hesitated.

Nathaniel looked at her as he sat down. "What?"

Miriam crossed her arms and leaned onto the table, looking down, still unsure. Maybe she still saw the little boy in him and wanted to protect him from all harm. She tilted her head to one side, her voice sincere. "I just want—I just want to know you're happy."

For a split second Nathaniel stopped chewing his food but did not look at her. "Sure. I'm happy." Still he avoided her eyes. "Why wouldn't I be?"

Miriam hesitated again. Finally, she shook her head and smiled. "No reason," she spoke quietly. "Just a mother watching out for her first born."

Nathaniel still did not look at her but continued eating. "I'm fine," he said just before having the last bit of toast. "Really. Everything's great." He forced a smile. "No need to worry." He stabbed the last of the eggs.

"It's a mother's prerogative."

Sarah Elizabeth walked into the kitchen. "I know. I know. I'm late. Just going to have toast and juice." She put a slice of bread in the toaster, then went to the refrigerator.

"Hey," Nathaniel said, holding up the glass of juice he had poured for her.

She closed the refrigerator door and took the glass from him. "You're such a good brother." She drank several swallows.

"I know," he said without skipping a beat.

"Don't you want something more substantial. Oatmeal?" she asked, ready to rise and fix a bowl.

"No, I'll have something more at lunch. I promise. I just don't want food right now."

"Sure?"

"Don't worry, Mom. She'll eat lunch because Mike'll be eating lunch."

Sarah Elizabeth looked at him with total disdain and disgust. "You are just pure nastiness."

"You just got through saying I'm such a good brother," Nathaniel shot back. "Can't you make up your mind?"

Miriam grinned at their banter.

The toast popped up. Sarah Elizabeth took the bread and with her free hand picked up her book bag. "Bye, Mom. I'm going to the car now so I won't be late," she said sarcastically, ignoring her brother. She kissed her mother. "See you this afternoon."

Miriam laughed. "Bye, honey."

Nathaniel stood up and retrieved his book bag. He leaned over and kissed Miriam. "Have a good day, Mom."

"Thanks, sweetheart. You, too. And be nice to your sister. She's having a hard time right now."

Nathaniel winked at her and smiled. "I will. She knows I love her."

Miriam smiled back as he followed Sarah Elizabeth to the car. She stood up with her coffee cup and watched from the kitchen window as her children drove away. *I am so lucky to—* She stopped. *We* are so lucky to have such great kids, she thought. Then she added, *God, please watch over them.*

After clearing the dishes she took a pad and pen from a drawer and returned to the table. As she sat down the dull twinge of pain reminded her again of Matthew's forcefulness. It wasn't the first time. And just as she had the other times, she recalled her sister's question of nearly twenty-five years ago—"Are you sure this is the right man for you?"

She remembered the occasion well. Matthew had just announced their engagement to her family. Immediately Carolyn had caught Miriam's eye with an expression of forced joy.

Sipping her coffee, she thought about Carolyn and her husband Jim breaking ranks with their strict religious upbringing, which became fodder for Matthew's criticism. "Not putting the Lord first in their lives is a sin," he told Miriam again and again. "Especially with children." Miriam never defended her sister but wanted to remain close. After their parents died, her obligations as Matthew's wife and her role at the church took all of her time. But Carolyn's question never went away and neither did Miriam's answer—she loved Matthew Winslow and wanted to marry him.

Miriam stared into her coffee cup as guilt began edging its way into her thoughts. Her eyes traveled to the pad and pen. Grocery list, she reminded herself. She finished her coffee and began writing.

Portraits of Benjamin Garland Winslow and Jacob Madison Winslow stared out over Matthew's tastefully decorated, contemporary office in the administrative wing of the church. Seated in a leather armchair Matthew listened to Kenneth Ward who sat on the matching sofa alongside Howard Carr. Kenneth—tall and unusually thin, mid-forties—strategically combed over his bald head the sparse, long black strands that still grew above his left ear. Hairspray lacquered it in place. The result, however, was not a distraction from his immaculate expensive navy pin-stripped suit and maroon tie. While amiable, Kenneth exuded an undeniable confidence which he made certain others noticed. As the representative of the Washington-based Christian Coalition for Biblical Authority in America he met on a regular basis with church leaders in the southeastern United States, particularly those which operated faith-based schools or academies.

Howard Carr was chairman of the Board of Trustees of Holy Bible Fellowship and Academy, a position he had held for eleven years. Scattered small, brown spots dotted his bare, pasty-white head. A thin fringe of gray circled around the back from one ear to the other. In his early sixties, Howard disguised his paunch with expensive suits, accompanied by high-priced ties, shirts and shoes. He prided himself on rules and details which he considered the cornerstone of his success as president and CEO of Elmsborough Federal Bank. He clasped his perfectly manicured fingers in his usual calm, business-like pose as he listened to Kenneth.

"We want you to preach a sermon about it," Kenneth Ward said to Matthew.

"I agree wholeheartedly," said Howard.

"Oh, I definitely will do that," Matthew responded. "Large gatherings called Gay Pride—it's frightening." He nodded toward the folded newspaper on the coffee table. "Parades are happening all over the country. And now here."

"But a sermon isn't enough," Kenneth continued.

"A letter to the editor and a call to complain to the mayor?" Matthew asked.

"Those are all good ideas," Kenneth said, "but The Coalition wants you to ask other churches to get involved—the ones you believe might be willing." He stopped and tapped his index finger on the arm of his chair for emphasis. "We want this message to reach the masses."

Matthew nodded. "Maybe invite those ministers to a meeting here and get their input." He stroked his upper lip as he thought. "And have a press conference? With them here. A real show of force."

"That would be perfect." Kenneth nodded vigorously.

"Bring in as many TV and newspaper people as we can," Howard Carr said.

"I'll call in Richard, Harry and William this morning," Matthew said. "See what ideas they can come up with."

"Absolutely," Kenneth encouraged. "Try to dwell on how all this is corrupting children and ruining families, especially with that ridiculous idea of same-sex marriage. Work AIDS into it, too. Fear is always a good tactic, carefully placed." He crossed his legs.

"It would be tempting to go overboard on this, but better to keep it very logical."

Matthew nodded. "Hate the sin, not the sinner."

"Exactly. Just as you did with the sermons on abortion and racism. And who knows, this might flush out a homosexual kid like that one last year and you can send him to that camp out West to cure him."

Matthew and Howard looked at each other. "That didn't turn out so well, unfortunately," Howard said. "The boy stayed out there for two months, came home and ran away the next day. I don't think he ever contacted his parents again."

Kenneth shook his head. "Tragic. Just tragic. Are his parents still attending? Are they likely to be against this campaign?"

"The Bakers still attend," Matthew said. "They constantly ask for prayers for Steve. So I think they'll be behind what we're doing."

"Good but keep an eye on them," Kenneth gestured to Matthew. "You know how to handle issues like this. That's why we see Holy Bible as a flagship, a model for other churches to follow." He turned to Howard. "You folks are very blessed to have Matthew."

"Oh, yes, we know that," Howard said. He pointed over his shoulder to the two portraits. "Your father and grandfather would be extremely proud of you."

"Yes, indeed they would," Kenneth said. "And the Coalition is watching you with this project. It could go a long way toward getting your Sunday services televised nationally. The more name recognition, the better."

"It's all about serving the Lord," Matthew said, trying to sound modest but also confident.

All three men stood up.

"And speaking of proud, Nathaniel was simply brilliant last night," Howard said. "I'm sure you were pleased."

"Oh, you have no idea."

"And he plays what? Basketball?" Kenneth asked.

"And baseball." Matthew beamed.

Kenneth nodded but with a frown. "Has the team improved since we last talked?"

"Gotten worse," Howard Carr said. He looked at Matthew. "I think they've only won three games this year. And one more to go this Saturday."

"As bad as last year." Kenneth thought for only a moment. "You might want to think about replacing the coach. Stansbury, right?" Matthew and Howard nodded. "Schools with losing teams don't attract well-rounded students."

"We'll definitely watch him and see how this last game turns out," Howard said, directing his remark as much to Matthew as to Kenneth.

"Too bad they all can't be as well-rounded as Nathaniel," Kenneth continued. "The folks at the Coalition are jealous that he's not a prospect for the law school at Freedom."

"Well, thank you for that," Matthew said. "But he's definitely minister material."

"He certainly impressed Dean Myers at the Divinity School at Freedom when he visited a few weeks ago. They're looking forward to having him there." He took several steps toward the door. "Another great Winslow," Kenneth said. "But what about the young man he defeated last night? Jason Daniels? Obviously smart, clean cut, athletic, well-rounded. Do you think he would make a good lawyer or even a judge?"

"Oh, absolutely," Matthew said. "He would be brilliant. I'll mention that to his father before school is out. Just to get an idea."

"Scholarships are always available for future leaders of God's army," Kenneth said.

After walking Howard and Kenneth downstairs to the main entrance, Matthew returned upstairs. "Gwen, ask Richard, Harry and William if they would step into my office," he told his secretary as he passed her desk. He went inside and began flipping through his calendar and making notes. Within a few minutes the three associates came in, all carrying their Holy Bible Fellowship leather folios.

Having served as associate pastor at Holy Bible for fifteen years, Richard Newland had risen to the position of senior associate and therefore outranked Harry Borkin and William Josephs. Both Harry and William had come to Holy Bible less than five years ago; both were in their early forties, clean cut. Harry Borkin constantly battled his portly build. His outgoing personality ideally suited him for membership associate. William Josephs was the youngest of the three associates, a winsome man, athletic, buzzed haircut. He worked with the youth. Richard, older and more seasoned than his two counterparts, set himself apart, as usual with his impeccable manner of dress.

Matthew sat back in his desk chair and briefed them on his meeting with Howard and Kenneth.

"Richard, start calling the pastors you think might get involved." He looked at his calendar. "Ask all of them to meet here on Wednesday morning. I'd like to hold the press conference on Thursday afternoon. And those who are on board with this—maybe we can persuade them to preach about it this Sunday. That way we're a united front. Everyone who's going to hear it will hear it at the same time."

Richard Newland made a note in his folio. "I'll get right on it." As usual his reader glasses sat on the tip of his nose, his white hair flawless.

"Harry, think of how we can approach the entire congregation—maybe an email blast. Something like that."

The stout man nodded as he made notes. "Not a problem."

"William, work on a plan for the youth as well as the Academy. Something to reinforce what God expects of Christians. Especially in the Bible classes in the middle and upper schools before exams begin. I don't want to call attention to this," he said, tapping the newspaper. "But I want them to hear what is right and good and Christian in the eyes of God and, of course, what the Bible says. Also, what the Academy's core values stipulate. We can't control what they hear and read outside of school, but we will while they're on this campus."

"I'll get right on it," William Josephs said.

"I'll make out some sort of time line and email it to you." Matthew made more notes. "And I've got some phone calls to make, a letter to write and a sermon to prepare. That'll be the easy part," he said with assurance as he continued writing. "If we can't stop this thing, we can at least make ourselves heard."

As the three associates left, Matthew picked up the phone. "Gwen, get me the mayor."

He turned in his chair to his computer and opened a new document page. "Dear Editor: I have read the first article in your series about homosexuality and the so-called Gay Pride gathering in latter June of homosexuals from across North Carolina in Elmsborough. As a minister this concerns me greatly. People who choose to follow the homosexual lifestyle are in flagrant violation of God's law which is clearly stated in the Bible as a sin and '… an abomination.' (Leviticus 18:22). God has shown them his wrath for their behavior by creating AIDS—"

The telephone buzzed. He picked up the receiver.

"Reverend Winslow," Gwen said. "The mayor's secretary is putting your call through to him now. Line four."

"Thanks." He pressed the button and heard one ring before Mayor Anthony Borelli answered.

"Good morning, Reverend Winslow." The voice was warm.

"Good morning, Mr. Mayor. Thank you for taking my call."

"Of course, Reverend. Always glad to hear from you."

"Very kind of you. I'm sure you're busy so I'll get right to the point. I'm calling about the gathering of homosexuals next month in the downtown area, especially the permit for a parade." He picked up the paper and read. "To celebrate gay pride, the morning paper says. That just seems a bit extreme in an open public place. To have an influx of homosexuals from all over North Carolina. Downtown is so vibrant. Families with young children go to the park just a few blocks from Governmental Plaza."

"Well, Reverend, the committee for this event applied for a permit and have followed all the necessary regulations. They're not breaking the law. The city council decided unanimously to allow it. It's not a protest or a march. They have assured me, the police and the city council that this will be a peaceful and even educational event for Elmsborough."

"Educational? Could you explain that?"

Mayor Borelli spoke calmly. "It's an opportunity for the straight community to see what the gay community is like. It's about co-existing peacefully and respectfully. The city council thought it was a good idea for citizens to experience the diversity."

"Well, I'm sure that you realize if the majority of citizens disagree with you and the council, come election time you may wish you had taken a different stand."

"That's always the chance any elected official takes."

Matthew remembered what Kenneth Ward had said about name recognition with the public. "I would welcome the opportunity to dissuade the council. When is their next meeting and how do I get on the agenda?"

"Second Monday in June. You'll have to submit a request in writing a week ahead of time to my office," the mayor said. "That's the policy."

"Very well. I'll have it in by the end of the week."

"I'll look forward to getting it."

"Thank you for your time, Mr. Mayor."

"Not at all, Reverend Winslow. Always a pleasure."

Matthew hung up the phone. Perfect opportunity, he thought. What God intended. First the letter. Then the press confer— If he mentioned at the press conference that he would be speaking to the city council, the media would show up to cover it. Name recognition. The Coalition would really be pleased. He turned back to his letter to the editor and read what he had written. "I believe that our city council has shown poor judgment in allowing homosexuals from all over North Carolina to take over a public place, so near the park where families with young children play, where citizens enjoy the fountains and listen to music. I call on people of all religions and faiths to contact the representative for your district. Write letters. Be heard. Otherwise, this will be a sad day for our city. Reverend Matthew Winslow." As required he listed his contact information.

He pasted the letter in an email and clicked "Send," then leaned back in his chair. He would have all three of the associate pastors send a letter also. One a day. Yes, inundate them. And an email to the entire congregation to write in. If they could get the ministers from other churches to do the same, something would have to change. Maybe they could even stop this whole event. That would impress Kenneth Ward and the Coalition—he, Reverend Matthew Winslow, had led the fight and halted this Gay Pride sideshow. A good move, he thought.

He pictured himself, preaching in the spotlight on the stage of the modern worship center, opened Bible raised high in his left hand. Televised nationally. He might even be interviewed on a national news show. Asked his opinion. He looked at the portraits across the room. Then they would be proud of me, he assured himself. Proud indeed. Suddenly, he remembered the night before. The deciding question of the competition. His wrong answer. He was going to study his verses and reread the Bible. He would never be wrong on another quote.

Miriam leisurely pushed her cart down the canned vegetable aisle in the grocery store. She stopped and took two cans of green peas off the shelf, moved on and picked up three cans of sweet potatoes. She loved the combination of the two. They would go well with the roasted chicken she was planning for dinner. And she needed another bottle of salad dressing. Balsamic vinaigrette was what Matthew preferred. She rolled her cart on to the next aisle—pasta, soup. Deciding that she didn't need anything there, she started to move on to the next one. Halfway down she saw two men, young, late-twenties, hovering over a grocery list. Both wore shorts, t-shirts, flip-flops. One was clean-shaven while the other had not shaved in a few days. They appeared unsure about something to buy or some ingredient. What drew her attention was how close they were standing to each other. She started to continue to the next aisle, but for some odd reason—maybe curiosity—she turned her cart in their direction. As she got closer, she could see that their arms were actually touching. They sounded so normal.

"I think this one's healthier."

"Are you sure?"

The unshaven one didn't answer at first but looked up at Miriam. "Excuse me, ma'am," he said politely. "Could you tell us what to look for in a cooking oil? I mean, as far as what makes one healthier than another." He held up two bottles.

Miriam hesitated. Something told her not to respond, but another part of her asked what harm would there be.

"I always judge by the amount of saturated fat. The less saturated, the better."

The other man read the nutrition label on a bottle of olive oil. "This has only one gram of saturated," he said. "So Canola for cooking and olive for salads."

"And none of this," said the one who hadn't shaved, holding another type.

"Right," Miriam said.

"Thank you so much for educating us."

She smiled slightly. "You're welcome."

She looked behind the men and saw her neighbor, Eloise Gardner, approaching. The expression on the older lady's face signified definite disapproval.

"Hello, Miriam."

"Eloise."

Eloise Gardner attended Holy Bible Fellowship and lived down the street from the Winslows. Nathaniel cut her grass in the summer. "How are you?"

"Doing well. And you?"

"Fine. Thanks." Eloise watched the two men continue down the aisle even though she was still talking to Miriam. When they were out of hearing distance, she lowered her voice. "What did those two men say to you?"

"Just asking which cooking oil is healthier."

Eloise shook her head and moved closer. "I just can't believe it. Some of the things you see out in public. While ago I saw them standing very unnaturally close to each other at the salad bar, laughing, then one of them put his arm around the other one. And that series in the newspaper is very disturbing. Is the Reverend going to respond in some way?"

"I think he's planning to. He's upset by it."

"Lee was, too. We didn't know what to think. It's all so blatant," she said, then added, "and un-Christian." She shook her head in dismay and sighed heavily. "Well, anyway. I am so proud of Nathaniel for winning last night. It was just wonderful. But I'm not the least bit surprised. He is such a wonderful young man and so grown up. You must be so proud. And of Sarah Elizabeth, too, of course," she gushed without taking a breath. "And please tell that wonderful husband of yours that he preached a wonderful sermon Sunday. As always."

"Oh, thank you, Eloise. I'll do that." Miriam smiled more about her neighbor's use of *wonderful*—her favorite adjective. "Did you have a good Mother's Day?"

"Yes, wonderful" she said, smiling brightly. "Lee and the kids and grand kids took me out to lunch, gave me some flowers, did all the cleaning and straightening of the house on Saturday. It was wonderful. How about you?"

"We went out to lunch at Proximity."

"Oh," Eloise said with widening eyes. "How elegant."

"Yes, it was very nice. And they gave me a book. It made me feel very special."

"That's because you are. Your whole family is special. Those two wonderful children would make any mother proud."

Miriam smiled broadly and thanked her.

"This whole city is a better place because of Reverend Winslow and Holy Bible Fellowship all through the years."

"It is amazing how people are so drawn to it," Miriam said.

"Well, it's all due to your husband's wonderful leadership. And now Nathaniel is following right along for the next generation. It makes me feel so much better knowing that after seeing this sort of thing." She turned her gaze down the aisle indicating the two men.

After a few more pleasantries, they both moved along to finish their shopping, Miriam savoring Eloise's comment about Sarah Elizabeth and Nathaniel.

Miriam paid for her groceries and went out to her car where she saw the two men again as they drove away. She put her bags in the car and got in. As she exited the parking lot, she could not help but wonder how Matthew would have reacted to them speaking to her. She thought it best not to tell him. She knew what the Bible said— about it being wrong and a sin. When she stopped for a red light, the image of the two men still lingered. Why couldn't she stop thinking about them? Standing close together. They must live together, too. Suddenly, the driver in the car behind her blew the horn to let her know the light had changed.

"Hey Nate."

Nathaniel turned from storing his books in his school locker to see Mike Caviness approaching him. "Hey, Mike. How's it goin'?"

"Good, man. You?"

"Not bad."

"Is, uh, Sarah here today?"

"Yeah, she headed straight for homeroom from the parking lot. She said to tell you if I saw you."

"Oh, okay." Mike hesitated. "Is, uh, she okay, I mean, feeling okay?"

"Yeah, she's probably ninety percent."

Mike looked around at the hall clock. "Maybe I can catch her before homeroom starts." He trotted off. "Thanks. Later."

"Later." Nathaniel smiled after Mike had moved on.

"Hi, Nate."

Nathaniel turned to see Jason. His smile quickly disappeared. He looked around before he spoke. "Why'd you do it?" he asked, his voice lowered. "I know you knew the answer to that verse last night. Was I supposed to give the wrong answer, too? And keep it going?"

Jason moved to lean his shoulder against the adjacent locker. "No, I was just kidding about that. I don't know. I guess I just got nervous."

Nathaniel stared at him, shaking his head. "I don't believe that."

Jason glanced down the hall, avoiding Nathaniel's eyes. "Because I—" He stopped, then turned to face him. "You deserve it more than I do."

Nathaniel shook his head. "No, I don't. That's crazy."

"It's okay. Don't worry about it." He shrugged.

Again, Nathaniel stared at him, but this time said nothing. Memories of them in the locker room showers, the dreams and the two of them studying together on Jason's bed flashed through his mind.

Jason tried to reassure him. "Really. No big deal."

"Aren't you still going to Freedom?"

Jason switched his book bag from one shoulder to the other but didn't look directly at Nathaniel. "Where else would I go?" he asked.

"What did your father say?" Nathaniel asked.

Jason shook his head. "Nothing much. He muttered, 'Nice try.'" He shrugged.

"Sorry." Nathaniel took one more book and notebook from his locker and put them in his book bag.

"No problem. If he wasn't pissed about that, he'd find something else. Listen," he began, sounding a little nervous, "you want to come over tomorrow night and call out those chem formulas before the big test Wednesday?"

Nathaniel felt his stomach flop in a funny way. He pushed his locker door closed and swung his book bag onto his shoulder. "Uh, sure, I guess so."

Jason smiled, still nervous. "You can never know too much with old Mr. Turkey," he said in a low voice, referring to heavy-set Mr. Cheshire whose nickname was derived from the wattle that hung from his chin.

Nathaniel smiled, still feeling hesitant. "What time?"

"Seven?" Jason asked.

Nathaniel nodded. "Sounds good." He started down the hallway.

Jason went in the other direction. "See ya in chem."

"Okay." He walked toward his homeroom. Why had he agreed? He didn't need the help and neither did Jason. He was just as smart. Yet, there was a part of him that wanted to go. Nothing would happen, he told himself.

He checked the clock in the hall. He had time to go by Martha's homeroom and say hi. He changed direction and rounded the corner and saw her just before she went into the classroom.

"Hey," he said, brushing up against her after checking to be sure that no teachers were close by.

"Hi. I was wondering where you were." Martha was dressed in the traditional school uniform. Her deep reddish-brown hair was tied back with a ribbon that complemented her complexion and clothes.

"Sarah Liz was moving a little slow this morning. Sorry."

"That's okay. I'm glad to see you."

"Me, too. Not enough time to say more than just hey, so 'hey.'"

Martha laughed. "You're so funny."

He nudged her hand and she responded by hooking her finger with his. They both watched for teachers. "Well, I try."

Just then the warning bell sounded.

"Better go." He spoke softly and squeezed her finger with his. "See you at lunch."

"Okay. Save me a seat." Her voice was intimate as she returned his squeeze.

"Will do." He turned and began walking quickly as the hallway cleared of students. He was okay. Martha was so pretty and nice. How could he not be okay? She was the perfect girl for him. Both going to the same college followed by a few years of divinity school for him. Then they would come back here and he would be an associate pastor. They would have children. Life would be ideal for all the Winslows.

He walked into his homeroom class just as Mrs. Knight was about to close the door.

"Good morning, Nathaniel. Congratulations."

"Thank you, Mrs. Knight."

"How many other churches are willing to speak out?" Matthew asked from behind his desk. Across from him were the three associates.

"So far I've talked with five who definitely want to do something," responded Richard Newland. "Roy Graham at Holy Christian, Glenn Ferndale at Fellowship, Calvin Morgan at Tabernacle Baptist, Lloyd Hill at Faith and Kirk Hayes at Holy Light have all said they would be at the meeting on Wednesday morning. Scott Jarrett said no and so did Robert Abernathy. I'm not surprised though."

"That's still excellent," Matthew said, nodding his approval. "Hopefully, those other five will want to be at the press conference."

"I've still got calls out for three others."

"I'd like all of you to write emails to the editor over the course of the next two weeks—before the next city council meeting. We'll ask these other ministers to write also. Also urge some members in your respective committees to take action."

"William, what about the Academy? Any ideas?" Matthew asked.

"With the end of school next week and final exams it won't be feasible to do anything long-term," Josephs said. "But we're going to take a look at targeting all the summer youth programs. In the meantime, Harry and I were working on a church-wide email with scripture, et cetera ."

Matthew squinted his eyes as he nodded approval. "That's good. I just had an idea. A large city-wide rally—not a protest but a service of some kind—at the old baseball stadium. All the ministers could take a brief part. Right before the homosexuals have their parade. Then we would stand along the parade route in one long line with signs. True solidarity. Lots of press coverage, too."

"A marvelous idea," Harry said.

"We can't just sit back and do nothing public," Richard added.

Harry nodded. "I agree."

Matthew leaned forward with his elbows on his desk and looked at the three ministers thoughtfully. "I'm truly blessed to have you three as associates. Thank you all."

"You're the one to be thanked for taking the initiative," Harry Borkin said.

Matthew felt proud but waved away the compliment.

The baseball team spoke an "Amen" together when Coach Stansbury finished his prayer standing at home plate.

"Okay, gentlemen, rally round." He held out his stout arm with his palm down. All the players came in close and created a mound of hands on top of their coach's.

With all the arms and the bodies in such close proximity, it was impossible not to be touching. Nathaniel thought he recognized Jason Daniels' arm next to his and his hand on top on his. He glanced to his right and saw enough of Jason's face to know it was him. Just then he felt Jason's hand on his shoulder.

"Who's going to win on Saturday?" Coach Stansbury yelled.

"Disciples."

"How are we going to play?"

Nathaniel felt a shift behind him and now Jason's chest was against his back.

"Clean."

"Who can't lose no matter what the score is?"

"Disciples."

"One. Two. Three."

"Goooo Disciples."

The pile of hands went down and rose up high with the final cheer. And with it, Jason squeezed Nathaniel's shoulder.

"Okay, guys. Hit the showers."

When the group spread apart, Nathaniel didn't look at Jason, but began talking to Joe Blackmon and others around him as they walked to the gym and locker room.

While he undressed, Nathaniel joined in the chatter with his teammates, but the shower was foremost in his mind. Maybe Jason wouldn't be across from him. If he was, he would close the shower curtain like always. No more lingering extra seconds. Following the locker room rule, he put the towel around his waist and reached underneath to pull down his jockstrap and cup. As he turned to go to the showers, Jason was just ahead of him.

"Good practice, Nate," he said as he kept walking all the way to the last two shower stalls, one on the left and one on the right, directly across from each other.

Nathaniel had to follow since all the others were taken. "Yeah, you, too. Nice shagging those fly balls."

"Got lucky." Jason said as he stopped at the last one on the right and turned to face Nathaniel. "Just hope I'm that lucky on Saturday."

Nathaniel saw that the same thing was happening today that had happened last week. He would have to take the one directly across from Jason. "You will and you better," he said, forcing a laugh.

As they both stepped into their respective showers and pulled the curtains closed, Nathaniel could feel his stomach flutter. He knew he should pull the curtain completely closed and drape the towel over the curtain rod. No temptation. None whatsoever.

Instead, he removed his towel, pulled the curtain open just enough to reach out with his towel and hang it up. As he did, Jason was doing the same. For a moment they took quick, furtive glimpses of each other. Jason closed his curtain only slightly but stood to the side of the shower so that he could still see Nathaniel. Nathaniel did the same. Only a slit of space. He kept glancing across as he turned under the water and saw Jason's lean, muscular body. The cascading water flattened his thick crotch hair and the hair on his legs and chest, making it appear even darker. Several times he could see Jason watching him. Then, he realized that he was getting an erection. He couldn't do that. He just couldn't. He pulled the curtain closed completely and turned the water to cold. Stop it, he demanded of himself. Don't do this. Don't. Think of something else. Think of school. Homework. Mowing the grass. Martha.

Finally, he finished showering in cool water. His erection had diminished somewhat. He reached out for his towel, dried off quickly and left Jason still in his own shower, the curtain pulled completely closed. Even though he bantered with his teammates, Nathaniel quickly dressed and left the locker room with some of his friends without seeing Jason again. He wanted to get home in time to text or email or even call Martha before dinner.

"How was practice today?" Matthew asked Nathaniel at the dinner table. Miriam and Sarah Elizabeth were quickly clearing the dining room table for family spiritual time.

"Really good. Coach Stansbury said we're looking ready. The team's all hyped up." Nathaniel placed his elbows on the table and crossed his arms. "I think we're all really looking forward to playing them."

Matthew smiled. "I can't wait. I know it'll be a great game. Rivalry is good when it's kept in perspective."

"We're all just looking to play well and hard," Nathaniel added.

Matthew nodded. "Good. Good to hear."

Miriam and Sarah Elizabeth came in and sat down in their usual places. The only object on the table was Matthew's Bible. He sat up straighter than he had been, reached out his hands to Sarah Elizabeth on his right and Nathaniel on his left. Each of them held their mother's hand who sat at the opposite end of the table.

"Let's pray. Oh, Father, God, we come to you tonight with a very serious topic to discuss. Guide us in our thinking and our words as we attempt to serve you and stand up for the righteous living that we know you demand from us. Purify the hearts and minds of those who are sinning against you. Help us to help them as we keep you foremost in our thoughts and lives. Amen."

They released each others' hands. Matthew opened his Bible and pulled at the red ribbon which marked the passage he wanted to read but then closed it. "Tonight we're going to discuss Leviticus 18:22. And I'm going to ask our Bible scholar to quote it for us."

Nathaniel steeled himself against any emotion or sign of acknowledgement. His heart began beating faster as a knot appeared in his stomach. Instantly, he thought about Jason and the way they had looked at each other in the shower. Had somebody seen them? Had his mother found something on the sheets or his underwear? Please, God, don't let this be about him.

"'You shall not lie with a male as with a woman; it is an abomination.'"

"Correct. You're probably wondering why that particular passage." Matthew looked around the table. "Well, a series of articles began running in today's newspaper. It seems a group of homosexuals is planning a rally and parade in connection with some kind of celebration in many places—cities—all around the country. These people are truly not of God."

Nathaniel's hands were becoming sweaty. Should he take them off the table? That didn't seem natural. Suddenly, he didn't know what was natural to him. Any minute he expected his father to accuse him.

"To celebrate such sin and iniquity so blatantly and publicly is wrong. And as a minister of God's word I feel led to do something about it. You're going to be hearing more about all this and I want you to be strong in your faith and commitment to God. We must pray for these sinners that they renounce the demon that has entered their hearts and minds and ask Jesus for forgiveness."

Nathaniel looked down. He felt warm all over. Please don't let it show, he prayed. I'll never do the shower thing again. I swear.

"It is a terrible, terrible thing to live like these people are choosing to live. I am just so glad that we all, especially the two of you," he pointed to Nathaniel and Sarah Elizabeth, "are in an environment where you're protected from all this." He paused and sighed. "There are even groups in the public school systems that condone this behavior. So, I thank God that my grandfather and father were led by the Almighty to create Holy Bible Fellowship and Academy." He stopped and looked directly at Nathaniel.

Nathaniel clamped his teeth together without realizing it.

"Which you will someday continue to lead—that will be a refuge from this kind of sinful choice. So tonight—"

Please make Dad stop talking, Nathaniel thought as he shifted slightly in his chair.

"—I and the other three ministers are using our special family spiritual time to talk with our families about this. We're going to send out a letter to the congregation to do the same in each household. When you hear about this at school, I want you to do your part not to ridicule, not to sink to using any common names or listening to anyone who does. This is a serious evil in the world. If these people won't give up their sinful ways, then we must pray for them, that they will open up their hearts to Jesus and let him come into their lives and give up this awful, awful sin. As you might imagine, I'll be preaching about this on Sunday."

Nathaniel fought with all of his might not to look any different than he usually did. Maybe he didn't know. Maybe nobody knew anything. Nobody had seen anything. Maybe.

"So I'm going to end with this. If either of you has any questions, Sarah Elizabeth, you talk with your mother. Nathaniel, if you have anything to ask, you talk with me. Okay?" he asked.

"Yes, Dad," Nathaniel said quickly.

"Okay, Dad," Sarah Elizabeth said meekly.

"Well, then, let's pray." He held out his hands as they all joined again.

"Oh, Lord, thank you for this clarity, this openness, this honesty. We pray that those who have strayed from you will see their error and their sin and will renounce the demon that is in them and choose you. Keep us safe in this house and in our lives. May we be examples of your word and the way you would have us live. Amen."

They released hands.

"Okay," Matthew said somewhat jovially. "Homework," he looked at Nathaniel, "is waiting." He looked at Sarah Elizabeth. "And also for you after you help your mother in the kitchen. And I've got a sermon to prepare."

They all stood and went to their respective assignments. Nathaniel went upstairs to his room and closed the door. Immediately, he sat down at his computer and began an email. His fingers were still sweaty and now jittery as he typed.

"Jason...Sorry but I won't be able to come over to your house tomorrow night. I have to do something for my Dad....Nate."

He reread what he had written. Then memories of the shower and his dreams began plaguing him. He wasn't one of those. Maybe Jason was. But he was not. He just wasn't. All these thoughts were going to change. Someday. They had to. He read the email again, his finger hovering, ready to press "Send."

If he wasn't one of those people, then why should he have to worry about going to Jason's house? If anything happened, he would just simply say he didn't want to, that he wasn't that way, that Jason should get help, that maybe his Dad could help him. Maybe go to that place where Steve Baker went last year to get help. That would be what Jesus would want him to do—help another person to change. As he remembered that Steve had run away, he gritted his teeth.

He read the email again. No, this was different. This was a good thing that was happening. Maybe. An opportunity to help Jason—if that's what he needed. He moved the mouse to delete the email, thought for only a moment and clicked on it. As he did a wave of uneasiness wafted through him. He would be confident. He *was* confident. Confident that he could take care of any situation. He reached for his chemistry book and opened it to study.

That night after the family prayer circle in the hallway, he put a towel underneath him when he went to bed. Just in case.

CHAPTER THREE

Tuesday—May 12

"I spoke with Fred Haskins yesterday about setting up a meeting with the Bible faculty—the middle and high schools, that is," William Josephs said. He sat in Matthew's office with Richard and Harry. "He suggested having the department chairmen meet over the summer to come up with some concrete tenets on homosexuality and implement them in the fall. We can also address this to some extent in Sunday school, summer Bible study and the youth gatherings through the summer."

Matthew nodded and turned to Richard Newland. "Is the meeting with the other ministers still on for tomorrow?"

"Oh, yes," Richard answered. "I've added two more to the list since yesterday. It's set for ten in the conference room."

"I saw your letter in the paper today," Harry Borkin said.

"Thank you. I was surprised since I only sent it in yesterday, but then I read the theme for today's article." He picked up the paper and read aloud the heading as he stood up and walked to the other side of his desk and leaned against it. "'Welcoming Gays in the Church.'" He shook his head. "Tragic. But when I consider some of the so-called ministers they interviewed, it doesn't surprise me." He looked at the paper again to search for a quote. "Pastor Ben Thornton of Trinity Baptist says he doesn't see any conflict with God's word and homosexuality. Says he would even marry people of the same sex." Matthew put the paper on his desk. "I just can't believe it," he said. "No wonder that church lost its affiliation with the national and state organizations. He's a real renegade," he scowled.

"Doesn't he also support abortion?" William asked.

"Yes, he's the one," Matthew answered. "I wish the paper had called me."

"We've all written letters to the paper," Harry said.

"Wonderful. We just have to do what God is leading us to do." Matthew turned to Richard. "How's the letter to the congregation coming along?"

"Almost done. Just putting on some finishing touches. It will arrive in the homes on Monday after your sermon. I think that's the best strategy. Same thing we did with the abortion issue."

Matthew stood and returned behind his desk. The three associates closed their Holy Bible leather folders and rose to leave.

"Okay. If any of you get any ideas or solutions, let's talk," Matthew said. "It's important to maintain communication. Again, good work, gentlemen. The Lord is pleased, I'm sure."

Miriam drove into the gas station. She swiped her credit card at the pump. An unusual series of beeps on the small screen rendered the message, "Pump Fuel. Pay Inside." Miriam assumed some malfunction. She took the nozzle from the pump, filled her car with gas and went inside. The attendant was waiting for her.

"Sorry about the inconvenience, ma'am. The pumps aren't reading the credit cards today for some reason," he said politely, holding out his hand for her card.

"Oh, that's fine." While he processed the purchase, she glanced down at a stack of the morning papers on the counter. Matthew had taken the paper with him again today. She read the headline, "Welcoming Gays in the Church."

"Here you are," the attendant interrupted her thought.

Miriam took the receipt and turned to leave, but hesitated. "Uh, excuse me, how much are the newspapers?" she asked.

"Fifty cents."

Standing at the door, a battle in her mind ensued. She knew Matthew wouldn't approve of her taking it home because the children might see it. Buying it just to read one article and then throw it away was surely a waste of money, maybe even a sin.

"Something else?" the attendant asked. He was perhaps of Middle Eastern heritage but had no accent. His complexion was dark and his hair black as coal; his smile and voice kind. Staring at him, something told her to do this forbidden thing.

"Yes, I'd like a newspaper, please." She reached into her purse for change and handed it to the man.

Miriam hurried out of the station to her car, her heart racing. Driving down the street, her conflict grew. Why read about this issue? Matthew was handling it. There was no need for her to be bothered with it. Her children were normal. But the word "normal" jumped out at her. "Nathaniel and Sara Elizabeth are well-adjusted," she restated aloud, avoiding the pitfall of "normal." Nevertheless, she wanted to read it. More importantly, she would have to dispose of it somewhere. Not in the trash at home.

Stopped at a traffic light, she noticed a small strip shopping center in the next block, its parking lot fairly empty. She should just drive in and find a public trash can and throw it away. It was just a waste of her time to read something that didn't impact her. When the light changed, she drove halfway down the block and nervously turned in. However, instead of driving up to a trash receptacle, she parked away from the buildings and other cars. Gripping the steering wheel tightly, she prayed aloud, "Oh, God, please forgive me if this is bad, especially for going behind Matthew's back." She shifted into park and picked up the newspaper from the seat beside her. "And please don't let anyone from church see me here."

She unfolded the newspaper. The article began with interviews with actual gay people and how they felt about God and how they thought God felt about them. Jim, whom the paper identified as a student at Loflin Community College, felt abandoned by his pastor and church. "I don't have a problem with God and I think God accepts me just as I am." Bob, a waiter, said he would never set foot in a church again. Stefan, a musician and actor, said he was not mad at God, just at the narrow-mindedness of the church. "I think God wants me to be proud of who I am. After all, He made me." Miriam took particular notice of what Reverend Ben Thornton was quoted as saying, "I see no conflict between homosexuality and God's word and teaching. I would marry two people of the same gender." Matthew must not have read that part before he left home, she thought, for he most certainly would have said something about it. In his opinion, Ben Thornton and all of Trinity Baptist were already an abomination. Still, Miriam had to wonder about— So much to consider, understand. She looked at the final sentence. Tomorrow's installment—parents.

She lowered the paper as more thoughts streamed through her mind. What must mothers think about their gay children? And the fathers? Do they feel it's their fault? What do they say to each other? Where do they begin to— To what? she wondered. She replayed in her mind the things that Matthew had told the children. An abomination. Sinners. Choosing to live as they did. A demon entering their hearts and minds. Again, she recalled the two young men in the grocery store. They seemed so average. Even "normal."

Then, she remembered something. Matthew had not read the article that morning. He had read something on the editorial page but didn't comment. She had seen the page as she poured his coffee. Quickly she turned to the back of the section and looked at the half dozen letters and saw his. His words sounded so much like him. It would have been recognizable even if it had no name with it, but, of course, it did.

Just then a car horn sounded on the street and reminded Miriam where she was. She quickly folded the newspaper, started the car and drove up to one of the store fronts. She stepped out and dropped the paper into a trash can. She told herself she would have to get a paper tomorrow. Somehow. Even if it meant buying it at a gas station or convenience store or anywhere that no one from church was likely to see her.

Driving home, she remembered vividly the exchange Matthew had had with her sister Carolyn on this topic. Carolyn had never been afraid to wade into a discussion on a subject she felt strongly about which was always fodder for Matthew's criticism. "It bothers me that your sister doesn't know her place," he had told Miriam on the way home. "And her liberal views are very out of line. She needs to put the Lord first in her life. Jim, too. We'll pray for them."

Miriam sighed. Carolyn wouldn't be concerned about anyone seeing her read anything in a newspaper.

After school in the locker room, Nathaniel pulled his towel tightly around his waist then leaned over to reach underneath to take off his sweaty jockstrap and cup. The afternoon practice had been especially hot and dusty.

"See you later on?"

The voice startled him because he recognized it. Jason had walked up behind him on his way to the shower. Nathaniel tossed the dirty strap and cup into his locker. He told himself to take control of his emotions. He could not let this happen anymore. He didn't want it to. He was not like that.

"Sure. Did you say seven?" He made sure his tone was friendly, just as he would talk to anyone else on the team.

"Yeah, sounds good," Jason answered.

They walked to the showers. Other team members talked and joked. Nathaniel joined in. Be just one of the guys, he told himself. You're not any different. Still, he watched as Jason went to the last shower, walked in and closed the curtain without looking back. The one opposite was available, but so was another several stalls away. For a split second Nathaniel thought he would shower across from Jason as he'd done the day before. Just to prove to himself that he was normal. Instead, he chose the one that wasn't nearby. He didn't have to prove anything, he told himself. Nothing. He took this stall because it was more practical.

He showered quickly, telling himself the whole time that he had not done anything wrong. That he wasn't different. He wasn't like— like the guys his father talked about last night.

When he stepped out of the shower, he started to look in Jason's direction but stopped himself. It didn't matter. He didn't need or want to look. The clock in the locker room showed it was nearly 5:30. He had to hurry. Sarah Elizabeth would be waiting for him at the car. He chatted with his teammates, dressing quickly. Jason was still in the wet area when he left the locker room.

Sarah Elizabeth turned cautiously toward the library desk to see if Miss O'Malley was still watching them. "I don't know anybody who's—" She lowered her whisper to an even softer level. She checked to be sure no one was close by. "—gay," she finished. "I mean, don't you think it would be obvious?"

Mike Caviness hesitated, glancing down, then around before he leaned closer to her across the table. "Some of the guys think that Keith acts kinda weird."

"Keith Smith?" Sarah Elizabeth slowly shook her head. "I don't think so."

"I don't either, but he doesn't hang out with anyone, girls or guys. His mom's always picking him up and bringing him places."

"I know, but I just think he's shy."

"He sure hates P. E." Mike looked around again. "Some of the guys give him a really hard time. You know, Jerry and Phil and Wayne."

"Ugh, I can't stand those bullies." A look of disgust crossed her face. "They're so immature and stupid."

"I know. I try to talk to Keith, but he just doesn't have much to say to anybody except the teachers."

"That's sweet of you. You're a good guy." She smiled coyly.

Mike grinned, enjoying the moment and at the same time feigning embarrassment. "Gosh, Sarah Elizabeth, I try to do everything my mama and daddy tell me."

Sarah Elizabeth almost laughed out loud but covered her mouth just in time to squelch the noise. "You're so funny.'"

"No, no. I'm not one of those kind," Mike said with his eyebrows raised in seriousness.

This time she did laugh out loud as his humor caught her off guard.

"The library will close in ten minutes," Miss O'Malley announced, eyeing them from the checkout desk.

"Uh oh, I've got to meet Nathaniel in the parking lot in five minutes." She quickly gathered her books and notebooks and Mike did the same.

Strolling down the hallway from the library, Mike brushed his arm against hers every few steps.

"I can't stand the way, Miss O'Malley stares at us," she said, looking over her shoulder before she spoke.

"I know. I'm surprised she let us even sit at the same table," Mike responded. "We weren't doing anything wrong." He shrugged.

"I was studying," Sarah Elizabeth said, then giggled. "Do you think she saw us talking?"

"If she didn't, she probably imagined it. Just for her own fantasy."

Sarah gasped as she laughed. "That's terrible."

"Sad but true."

They reached the stairwell and started down. When they got to the landing halfway, Mike took her hand.

"Your hand's sweaty," she said softly with a laugh, faking disgust but without letting go.

"That's the effect you have on me. I get nervous when I'm around you. In a good way," he said, half teasing and half serious as he smiled.

Sarah Elizabeth gave him a look of hesitant disbelief. "Really?"

"Really." He looked both up and down the stairwell, then at her. He leaned closer. She offered no resistance. The kiss was quick.

She pulled back. "We better be careful. If somebody saw us, my father would lock me in my room for life and throw away the key."

Mike backed away. "I'd find you and break you out of prison," he teased.

She laughed. "My hero." They continued down the stairs and outside. "Uh-oh, there's Nathaniel," she said, walking faster.

Nathaniel was waiting in his car, looking around. Before Sarah Elizabeth and Mike ever got to the car, he started it.

"Bye. See you tomorrow," she said, getting in.

"I'll text you tonight." Mike leaned down to the window as he closed the door. "Hi, Nate. How's it going?"

"Hey, Mike. Good. You doing okay?"

Mike nodded. "Great." He grinned at Sarah Elizabeth.

"Later," Nathaniel said as he put the car in gear and started off.

They drove without speaking. Sarah Elizabeth was thinking about Mike kissing her. It wasn't the first time. And she hoped it wouldn't be the last. She had felt a slight roughness on his chin from the few individual whiskers that grew to visible length every few days.

As Nathaniel turned a corner, she noticed there was dampness on the steering wheel where his hand had been. She remembered that the night before his hand had been damp, cold even, when she had held it during family prayer in the hallway. That had never happened. Mike's words came back to her. He got nervous. She started to say something, but the intense look on her brother's face said he didn't want to be bothered.

After dinner as Nathaniel drove to Jason's house, he reassured himself more than once that there was nothing to worry about. He knew who he was. He was sure of himself—totally. He and Martha were becoming more serious. There was no doubt about that either. Nothing had happened in the showers. Nothing. There was no proof. There was no need of proof. If Jason ever made up any lies, it would be his word against Nathaniel's.

As he drove up to the curb and turned off the ignition, he saw Jason's and his mother's cars in the driveway. Maybe his dad was away on one of his business trips. He hoped so. He was always intense.

Nathaniel took a deep breath, slid on his flip-flops and got out of his car. He thought maybe he should tuck his t-shirt inside his shorts but decided not to. He walked up the driveway and sidewalk to the front porch. Before he could ring the bell, Jason opened the door.

"Hey. Come on in." He, too, was wearing shorts and a t-shirt—out, not tucked in his shorts—and his feet were bare.

"Hi, thanks." Nathaniel stepped inside, fighting the nervousness that threatened to expose itself.

"Hello, Nathaniel." Jason's mother, Claire Daniels spoke from the den off the foyer.

"Hi, Mrs. Daniels. How are you?"

"Fine. How's everyone at your house?"

"We're all fine. Thanks."

"Tell your mother hello for me. I don't ever get a chance to talk to her at church."

"Sure, I'll do that."

"Okay, you guys study hard. Make us all proud." She smiled as she turned back to the newspaper.

Nathaniel wondered if she'd read the articles about the gay event his father had mentioned. And had Jason read it? He had no intention of asking him. He didn't care.

"Come on up," Jason said, leading the way to his room upstairs. Once inside he closed the door.

As Nathaniel had seen on many other visits when they studied, papers, notebooks and books sat in disarray on his desk. His basketball, soccer ball, baseball glove and bat and tennis racket shared a corner and a shelf under the window. Posters of Roger Federer and David Wright were taped to the wall.

"Too bad you couldn't play tennis and baseball," Nathaniel said, noticing the poster of Federer.

"Yeah, had to choose," Jason said, shoving his hands in his pockets and shrugging. "I get to play some, just not for school."

"Maybe next year at Freedom," Nathaniel offered.

Jason hesitated. "Yeah, maybe."

Nathaniel saw his sketch pad open on his desk and walked over to it. "Is that— Oh, no, that's Mrs. Medlin," he said, laughing at the caricature. "The huge glasses and little wart or whatever it is on her jaw—they're exactly right," he said, examining it with a grin. "And that chain for her glasses."

"Ol' Eagle Eye Medlin," Jason said modestly.

"It's perfect."

They stood in awkward silence for a moment before Jason picked up his chemistry book from his desk and sat down on the bed. "I hope I know these things. I've been looking at them for three days and they just aren't sticking with me. Or maybe it's because this is the last regular chemistry test I'll ever have to take."

"Yeah, well, there're some tricky parts for me, too."

Jason slid back and flopped across the head of his bed. "Mr. Turkey said this was going to be the hardest chapter." He propped his head on his hand with his book in front of him as he lay on his side. "Do you want to go first?"

Nathaniel kicked off his flip flops and lay across the foot of the bed. "Okay, I'll try, but you may have to give me some hints."

"Doubt it."

They began the coaching. From the outset Nathaniel struggled with retrieving the information from his brain. He fought to keep from looking at Jason's legs and the unusually thick dark hair that covered them. To solve the problem he closed his eyes. Even so, Jason had to prompt him on formulas that Nathaniel had easily remembered the night before on his own.

"Okay, my turn," Jason said when they had finished going through the list the first time. He handed his book to Nathaniel and lay flat on his back, his eyes staring at the ceiling.

As Nathaniel called out the formulas he could not resist the urge to glance at Jason's muscular legs again. As he did, he felt himself getting aroused. He crossed his legs and pushed his book lower.

When Jason finished his turn, they switched back. Nathaniel remained on his side but closed his eyes. This time he was able to remember more than he had on his first attempt.

They switched several more times. Finally they decided they would each have one last round of practice. Jason was last. Just as he lay back flat on the bed ready for the first formula, he sat up halfway.

"It's hot in here." With that he reached down and pulled up his t-shirt and took it off. When he lay back down, not only did he clasp his hands behind this head, he had moved closer to Nathaniel.

Nathaniel said nothing about the temperature or his being so close; neither was he able to prevent his eyes from roving over Jason's solid torso. The trail of dark hair that appeared from underneath his shorts up to his navel. The thick patch of black hair in his armpits. The hair that spread across his defined pecs, the deep brown nipples raised to a point.

Nathaniel's arousal pushed against the confines of his shorts and made his nervousness more pronounced. Perspiration oozed from his underarms. His mind whirred with confusion and fear. He couldn't hear his own voice or Jason's. Was he giving the right answers? He shifted his legs again to conceal his erection. Was anything going to— No, nothing was going to happen. Then, it seemed, Jason's review was complete.

"I think we know these blasted things, don't you?" Jason asked softly. The tone of his voice and his countenance held more than a simple inquiry about chemistry.

Nathaniel met his eyes but didn't answer. He forced himself to look away but didn't move. For what seemed like an eternity to Nathaniel, neither of them spoke, but he could tell Jason was still staring at him. Then, Jason took his hand from behind his head and extended it toward Nathaniel's chest, which was heaving with thundering heart beats. Nathaniel watched as his teammate's hand came closer. He wanted to move, to get up and walk out, but something inside him would not allow it. Jason put the back of his fingers against Nathaniel's chest and for a second did not move them. But then they were moving toward his left pec, then stroking his soft rigid nipple. Nathaniel's breath quickened, his mind paralyzed. He could not speak or lift his hand to counter the move, the rock-hard arousal between his legs a frightening barometer of all that was happening. He pressed his legs together tighter. He had to hide it. Jason rolled onto his side toward Nathaniel, their bare legs touching. He reached up and touched the side of Nathaniel's face with the palm of his hand. His thumb slowly stroked his cheek. Nathaniel wanted to touch him, to stroke the hair on his chest, to— Suddenly, his father's voice from the night before and words from the Bible burst into his consciousness. Sinner. Demon. Abomination.

"I've got to go," Nathaniel said and without knowing how he had done it, he was off the bed, picking up his book, sliding on his flip-flops and walking toward Jason's bedroom door. He pulled his t-shirt down as far as he could and held his book in front of him as naturally as possible, knowing Jason could tell he had a hard-on.

"Nate, don't leave."

But it was too late. Nathaniel had already opened the door and was horrified as he nearly ran into Claire Daniels just outside the door.

"Oh, Nathaniel, are you boys finished already? I had some iced tea for you." She held up the two glasses.

Nathaniel's chest felt as if it would explode, his face hotter than fire. She hadn't seen or heard anything. She couldn't have. They hadn't been talking and the door had been closed. He now used both hands to hold his chemistry book in front of him. "Oh, Mrs. Daniels. Uh, yes, ma'am, we're finished studying. Just now. Uh, this minute."

"Ready to make a hundred tomorrow?" she asked in a cheerful voice.

"Uh, yes, uh, ma'am." His entire being was in a state of panic. "For sure." He tried to smile. He had to hide this—this whatever it was.

"Oh, hi, Mom." Jason now stood behind Nathaniel in the doorway. "We'll do you proud."

Nathaniel glanced back, relieved to see that Jason had put on his t-shirt.

She smiled. "Never a doubt in my mind." She held up the teas glasses, again. "Will you stay long enough to drink some tea?"

"Oh, uh, no thanks." He edged passed her toward the stairs, being careful to hide the bulge in his pants. "No, I, uh, need to get home. Other homework for tomorrow."

"Okay, well, tell your parents hello." She handed one of the glasses to Jason, then started toward the opposite end of the hallway with the other one.

"I will."

Nathaniel bolted down the stairs. He could tell Jason was following him but didn't say anything or acknowledge him in any way. He opened the front door and went out.

"Nate, hold up," he said in a whisper.

Nathaniel didn't stop but turned around, still holding his book in front of him, and walked backward a few steps down the driveway.

His mind was still reeling as he looked at Jason. He wanted to tell him to stay away from him. To leave him alone. To never speak to him again. That if he ever said anything about tonight he would call him a liar. But something inside him wouldn't allow those words to come out of his mouth. The expression on Jason's face—doubt, fear, hurt? He couldn't be sure. Everything was happening so fast. Spinning. Nathaniel kept walking backward.

"See ya." He turned back around and walked toward his car. As he drove away he didn't look back at Jason, but in his periphery he saw him watching him from the front lawn.

Nathaniel gripped the steering wheel until his knuckles whitened. His heart still pounding. His mind reliving Jason touching him.

He was so confused. What if his father—if anybody, but especially his father—knew or found out, they would— What would they do? This was a sin. His father's words haunted him as they relentlessly echoed in his mind. Demon. Abomination. Choice. But he wasn't choosing this. If he wasn't choosing it, then what was wrong with him? Why didn't he make Jason stop sooner? Why didn't he get out of there when Jason first started looking at him like he did? What if he couldn't have stopped himself from touching Jason? But then the thought interrupted him. He did stop himself. He didn't touch Jason. Not once. Never even reached in his direction. So he didn't do anything wrong. He hadn't committed a sin. He wasn't one of *those*. Still, he labored within his mind. Thoughts whirred. He had gotten a hard-on. Why? he screamed at himself. He didn't know why. And what about those dreams of him and Jason? Dreams didn't mean anything. They were stupid. Then the Bible verse charged through his mind, attacking like an army. Leviticus 18:22. "You shall not lie with a male as with a woman; it is an abomination."

Nathaniel turned up the radio—some unidentifiable pop or rock-n-roll. But nothing would drown out the thoughts that were clawing at him. He had to shut off his mind. Call Martha. No. She was in that French Club meeting. He had to go somewhere. Not home.

Not now. Not yet. He glanced at the car clock. Still time before his parents expected him to be home. And it was an acceptable place to go. He had enough money for about sixty pitches.

Several blocks later he turned onto a main thoroughfare toward the other side of town. Within less than ten minutes he pulled up in front of the Trainer's Baseball Academy and Batting Cages. He put on a pair of tennis shoes that were in the back of his car. With his bat, he went inside, bought some tokens and headed for the first available empty cage. The coin clanged into the box. He took his stance and waited for the mechanical arm to hurl the first ball. He connected, but it would have been foul. The second he hit into the floor. The third a pop up. The fourth a line drive to the third baseman. On and on he swung. As hard as he could. Teeth clenched. Finally, he connected solidly which made him muster even more power in an effort to annihilate each ball that sped toward him. With the first twenty pitches completed, he put in a second token. Ball after ball. Swing after swing. His rhythm perfect. Now each ball soared to what would have been the outfield, the fence or over it. Sweat glistened on his arms, legs and face. His t-shirt became damp. He dropped in the third token and continued hammering the round objects flung toward him. Each hit solid. Again and again. Finally, the light on the machine turned off. No more pitches. No more tokens.

Nathaniel breathed hard. He turned toward the gate to the cage and stopped, gripped by a thought. Stepping out would be like stepping into another cage. A bigger cage. A permanent cage. A cage with no escape. His mind still held him prisoner. On Jason's bed. The two of them touching. Helpless, he looked at his watch. He had to get home. He had other homework to do before the family prayer circle.

As he drove he called Martha on his cell. He didn't care if the French meeting was still going on. It shouldn't be. Not now. After a few rings, she answered.

"Hey," her voice was cheery.

"Hey," he said, feeling nervous and relieved at the same time. "Is the meeting over?"

"Yeah. Did you and Jason finish studying?"

That she even knew he had spent time alone with Jason made him anxious. "Yeah, we're ready for the test. Who all's with you?" He wanted her to say that she was alone, but he could hear the voices of other girls in the car.

"Colleen, Jill and Rachel. Are you at home?" Martha asked.

"No. On my way." He wanted to see her, to be with her, but not with the other girls around. "Where are you guys? Could I meet you and finish driving you home?"

"Oh." He could hear disappointment in her voice. "We're sitting in front of my house and my mom is out in the yard talking with the neighbor. She already told me I had to be in early tonight for some dumb reason."

"Okay. Well, I'll text you later."

"Promise?"

"You bet."

Nathaniel finished the drive home without turning on his CD player. Nothing could protect him from his confusion and fear. The barrage was constant. But talking with Martha felt almost normal. That helped some. Go home and study and stop thinking about it.

As he walked into the kitchen, his mother waved to him as she continued talking on the phone. His father was in his nightly haunt— his study. Sarah Elizabeth was in her room. Upstairs in his room he closed the door. Kicking off his tennis shoes, he sat down at his desk. He opened his chemistry book and began reviewing. However, even the most elementary of words on the pages were only symbols in black ink. Words and concepts understandable an hour ago were like a foreign language now. He propped his elbows on his desk and held his head between his palms. He had just closed his eyes when the door opened preceded by only two quick knocks. Nathaniel jumped as if caught doing something he shouldn't.

"Ready for your test tomorrow?" Matthew said.

Nathaniel felt his stomach knot up. "Yeah, I mean, yes, sir." He leaned back and crossed his arms over his chest, trying to act nonchalant.

"I have no doubt." Matthew came in and closed the door but did not sit down. He put his hands in the pockets of his pants. "I just wanted to check in."

Nathaniel uncrossed his arms and put his elbows on the arms of his desk chair. Please let this be about school, he said to himself, or the team or the game this Saturday.

"About our talk last night around the dinner table. Those people who are not normal. Homosexuals."

Nathaniel froze. Was this about Jason? His mother couldn't have heard or seen them. Did Jason say something to her?

"I just wanted to alert you to, well, if you ever see anyone at school, not that I think there are any of them at our school, but if you ever suspect anyone, I want you to tell me immediately so we can deal with it. Take whatever steps are necessary."

Nathaniel felt a trickle of sweat roll down his side from his armpit. He wanted to ask a lot of questions. What would happen to such a person? How would they know for sure? Did he or the teachers already suspect someone?

"I don't think we have any. Nobody at our school acts that way. Those people are so obvious that I think we'd know. It would be hard to miss."

Some relief washed over Nathaniel. "That's true."

Matthew took his hands from his pocket and reached for the doorknob, then stopped. "That's a very special young lady," he said, pointing to Martha's picture on the shelf next to his desk.

Nathaniel glanced over at it. "Yes, sir, she is."

"She's also lucky." He raised his eyebrows, indicating him.

Nathaniel forced a smile. "No, I'm the lucky one."

"All right. I'll let you get back to studying." He looked at his watch. "Prayer time in about an hour."

"Okay." He watched as his father closed the door behind him. The footsteps, especially the squeak in the fourth step from the top, told him his father had gone downstairs. *Those people are so obvious.* His father's words echoed. He wasn't like that and neither was Jason. But Jason was responsible for Jason. He knew there was nothing obvious about him. So he must not be like those other people. Still, he was confused. His messy dreams. His arousal while looking at Jason's body. The touch of his fingers on his cheek. Nathaniel realized he was getting hard. He reached down and pressed against it. "Stop it," he whispered through gritted teeth. "Don't do this." However, the more pressure he exerted with his hand, the more determined his erection. He squeezed his eyes shut as he pressed more. He knew the feeling would be pleasant. And it was. But it was wrong. Genesis 38:9-10 said so— about Onan not wanting to take his brother's place. "So when he went into his brother's wife he spilled the semen on the ground, lest he should give offspring to his brother. And what he did was displeasing in the sight of the Lord, and he slew him also." It was one of the required verses that everybody in the middle and upper schools had to know.

With reluctant stubbornness he pulled his hand away and fought to concentrate on chemistry, but staring at the pages accomplished nothing. He had to do well on this test. The school year was almost over. He had to hang on. Next year would be different—away at college, away from all these memories. And when he wasn't studying, he would focus on Martha. Out of nowhere, his promise to her shot into his mind. He picked up his phone and began texting.

hey wuzup
After a moment. *not much thought you forgot me*
not in million years busy studying test will be hard
means you get a 99 not 100
ha i wish
i know you mr A+ 4ever.
stop
true got to go mom on warpath see ya tomorrow
sweet dreams
u2

Nathaniel gazed at her picture on the shelf and imagined the two of them in his car. Holding her hand. Taking her in his arms and kissing her passionately. Her hand on his cheek. The same way Jason had touched him. Yet, there was no excitement, no arousal, no erection to press down. He clenched his fists. What was wrong with him? Why was he so messed up? He stared at the page in his chemistry book. Nothing. A wall. He tried to read the words, but his thoughts were racing. Nothing connected.

At 9:45 his father knocked on his and Sarah Elizabeth's doors, opening them just enough to announce that it was time for prayer circle.

Nathaniel took a deep breath and exhaled. He could do this. He could go out, pray and get back into his room, and be calm the whole time. He opened the door and went into the softly lit hallway and stood with the rest of his family. His mother seemed to be watching him closely or was he just imagining it? He forced himself to smile at her as he took hers and Sarah Elizabeth's hands.

"Let us pray," Matthew said.

Instead of listening to his father, Nathaniel tried to think of something to pray for in case his father called on him first.

"And now, Lord, please listen to the prayers of this family. Nathaniel."

Nathaniel shifted his feet. "Lord, please be with all the students at school as this year comes to a close—in our exams and tests, in our friendships as we graduate and leave for college or jobs." He stopped, then added. "As we strive to serve you."

He felt so relieved that he did not listen to his mother's or sister's prayers. All he wanted to do was return to his room.

After his father announced the final Amen, he shook hands with his father and hugged Sarah Elizabeth. When he hugged his mother, she held on a bit longer than usual.

"Night, sweetheart," she whispered, rubbing his back.

"Night, Mom." He smiled at her as she let go. Still, she looked at him directly, longer than usual. Why was she doing that?

A few moments later, with the door closed, he heaved a sigh. But the monumental obstacle in his mind held him in an unrelenting lock—inside. Inside where there was no chance to escape. He sat at his desk for a few minutes, trying to study. But it was useless. He got up and turned down the sheet on his bed and went into the bathroom for a towel. He spread it crossways, halfway between the foot and head. Lying in the dark, he remembered backing away from Jason in the front yard, toward his car, escaping. The look on Jason's face. What was it? Hurt? Rejection? Then, it hit him. He didn't remember him saying it at the time. But he must have. He was certain he did. Now he remembered it vividly.

"Please don't go."

Nathaniel wrestled with the three words as they resounded in his head. Over and over like torture. He rolled onto his side and silently recited Psalm Twenty-Three.

Lying in bed Sarah Elizabeth thought about Mike—bumping her arm that afternoon. And the kiss. So special and still was. She smiled thinking of it. And his wet hand and her making him nervous. Then she remembered. Nathaniel's hand was cold and clammy tonight. Why would he be nervous? All he had done was go over to Jason's to study. Then, a moment of excitement struck her. What if he had met Martha instead? "Oh, my gosh," she whispered with a smile. "Good for him."

CHAPTER FOUR

WEDNESDAY—MAY 13

Matthew sat at the head of the oval shaped mahogany conference table. Three of the walls were of rich paneling. The one behind him was a replica of the background on the stage in the worship center—golden drapes, "Holy Bible Fellowship" arcing over a modern bronze sculpture of an open Bible. Plush Berber carpeted the floor. Pitchers of water and glasses were spread down the center of the table. Flanked by his three associates—Newland, Borkin and Josephs—he counted nine other area ministers. Twelve in all plus himself, he thought, noting the irony. Dressed in suits and ties, each minister had his own note pad and pen, although note-taking essentials had been placed around the table—everything with the Holy Bible Fellowship logo. All leaned back in the executive leather chairs, keenly listening as Matthew began.

"I'm so very glad to see so many of you here today. I think this is truly a sign that God wants us to take action." He clasped his hands in front of him on the table. "Let us open this very important gathering with prayer." All the men bowed their heads. "Dear God Almighty, creator of man and earth, thank you for this assembly which represents your faithful servants here and in their respective houses of worship. We pray, God, that you would guide us as we seek the best way to further your holy teaching set forth in your scripture in the face of this affront to your word that is slated to take place in our city. Show us, we pray, how to bring about reform and repentance of the sins of these people seeking to force their sinful ways upon us. Grant us courage and strength to do your holy will. In your precious son's name, Jesus Christ, Amen."

A chorus of "Amen" filled the room.

Matthew drew in a deep breath. "Well, gentlemen, I thought we'd begin by telling you what we here at Holy Bible Fellowship are planning to do in our own church and academy. Then, I'd like to hear your ideas." He gestured toward Richard. "I'd like to ask Richard Newland, our senior associate minister to enumerate briefly."

Richard Newland opened his leather Holy Bible folio and perched his reader glasses on the end of his nose. "Strategies to serve as a response to the gathering and parade of homosexuals in downtown Elmsborough." He looked up over his glasses. "Send out a letter to the congregation announcing our stance, strongly urging each family to discuss this issue. We'll include Bible verses to drive home the point, ways to teach the younger children, warning them of strangers. Put together a curriculum for church school and youth programs over the summer." As he continued reading some of the ministers jotted down notes. Others nodded in agreement. "Finally, Matthew will preach this Sunday about this. We hope you'll do the same." He sat back and removed his glasses, putting the end of one temple in his mouth.

"Thank you, Richard," Matthew said. "Comments?"

"Matthew," Kirk Hayes of St. Timothy's spoke up. "What about a prayer vigil at some point during that weekend, either at one particular church or in all of our churches, at the same time with a notice in the newspaper that this is available to anyone who wishes to attend?"

"Excellent idea," Matthew responded along with several vocal approvals around the table. "I would say that we do it the Friday night before the parade. It would be more effective if we all met in one church, but I think the number would be too great to fit into any one of our churches."

"What about demonstrating along the parade route?" said George Mabe of Holy Gathering. "Silently. No engaging of conversation whatsoever. Just simple non-threatening signs about repenting and forgiveness."

"I had wondered about that myself," Matthew responded. "I think it would be tremendous to get several hundred people as a show of support for the churches and that we're not taking this matter lightly. I'd love to be able to announce that in the press conference." Conversations sprang up around the room. "How many would support that?" He raised his hand and looked around the table. Every minister had his hand up. "That's excellent. Then it's a go. I urge each of you to talk to your congregations this Sunday. Even if you don't preach about it specifically, try to work it into your sermon. Read scripture, especially Leviticus, if you can. We'll get the permit from the city. Harry, will you see to that?"

"Absolutely," Harry Borkin said, noting the mandate in his leather folio.

The discussion and exchange of ideas continued for another forty-five minutes.

Before he adjourned the group Matthew had one final statement. "We'll call the television stations and newspapers for a news conference tomorrow. Here. I think it would be very impressive if all of you could be present for that. It would show solidarity. How many of you can be here, say two o'clock?" Every minister raised his hand. "That's wonderful. I truly feel that we have done the Lord's work here today and that he is pleased."

"Amen," came the collective response. The ministers rose and began shaking hands, some grouping for further discussion.

Matthew spoke to each of them, thanking them for their participation. They would defeat this movement by the homosexuals in Elmsborough, North Carolina.

* * *

Miriam turned in at the Woodfield Haven driveway, a rest home—as Matthew referred to it—for people with Alzheimer's. As she drove down the shady lane to the visitors' parking lot adjacent to the modern three-story building, she remembered Matthew's question—the same question he asked every Wednesday morning. "Are you going to see mother today? Please tell her hello for me." His schedule was just too hectic, he always said. He would try to find time. Soon, he always added. But he rarely went—once every two or three months or on special occasions but then for only a scant ten or fifteen minutes. And honestly, Miriam couldn't blame him.

After his father died, for no apparent reason, Ruth began to swear whenever Matthew visited. Not *at* him, but simply saying vulgar words. At first she only did it occasionally, but then it was constant. But only in front of Matthew. Even when he prayed with her, Ruth cursed the whole time—until he left. Miriam had attempted to console him early on, but he dismissed her sympathy and ordered her never to discuss it with him or especially anyone else.

As she approached the entrance, the automatic sliding glass doors opened. At the desk the stout, middle-aged security guard, whose name plate merely said McDuffie, greeted her warmly.

"Good morning, Mrs. Winslow. It must be Wednesday." His smile matched his sparkling brown eyes. His shock of red hair was heavily speckled with gray.

Miriam returned his amiability. "Yes, it is Mr. McDuffie. How are you?" She slowed but continued moving toward the elevator.

"Very well, ma'am. Have a nice visit."

"Thank you."

On the third floor Miriam peered around the door to room 304. It was typical for Woodfield—a twin bed to one side and a sitting area on the opposite. A private bath was by the door. "Good morning, Ruth," she said gently before walking slowly inside.

Ruth Winslow sat where she did everyday—on her floral print loveseat—staring blankly at the television, the volume scarcely loud enough to be heard across the room. She wore a deep blue high-neck, long-sleeved dress which set off her fluffy snow white hair.

"Hello," she said, smiling. "Do I know you?"

Miriam smiled, accustomed to the question which she asked every Wednesday. "I'm Miriam," she said simply. She had learned quickly not to give unnecessary information that would confuse her. "You look so pretty today. I love your blue dress." She sat down beside her.

"My mother said I could go to the fair this weekend."

"How exciting. That will be such fun." She reached into a bag. "I brought you some of that hand lotion that you like so much. Would you like for me to put some on your hands?"

"When are we going home?"

"I'm not sure. Maybe later." Miriam made small talk as she opened the bottle of lotion and gently bathed the elderly hands. They were warm and soft, but the skin was wrinkled and her fingers rigid and gnarled from arthritis. "I was thinking we could go to the sunroom and sing some hymns. Would you like that?" She closed the lotion bottle and stood up.

Ruth looked at her blankly. "Mother said she would buy me a doll."

Miriam helped her stand and waited until she secured her balance. Then she took her arm and the two strolled at a snail's pace down the hallway. "That's very sweet. Will you give your doll a name?"

Ruth's only response was a blank stare.

They passed several other patients sitting in chairs along the wall who stared blankly at them or who said things she didn't know how to respond to. The nursing staff spoke kindly, recognizing Miriam from her weekly visits and genuine regard for her mother-in-law.

In the sunroom Miriam scooted the piano bench down, allowing Ruth to sit beside her. She took a hymnal from her bag.

"How about this one?" she said, opening to *Dear Lord and Father of Mankind.* She began playing and singing the first verse.

Immediately, Ruth joined in, singing all four verses without looking at the hymnal. Next, Miriam selected *Be Still, My Soul.* Again, Ruth sang all the verses from memory, her soprano voice mostly on pitch though a bit raspy in the higher range, a testimony to years of singing in the choir at Holy Bible Fellowship. Miriam sang the alto line, producing pleasing harmony.

On and on they sang—*It Is Well With My Soul, What a Friend We Have In Jesus.* Sometimes, Miriam just played, but no matter which hymn she chose, Ruth knew every word or just repeated the first verse. As happened every week, several other patients slowly migrated into the room and joined in, just listened or nodded their heads in time to the music. After almost an hour a nurse came to the door—another usual occurrence.

"I'm so sorry to interrupt," she said gently, "but it's time for lunch."

Miriam walked Ruth to the dining area and sat with her while she ate, helping when needed. Afterwards, she walked her back to her room and her television programs and hugged her goodbye. Riding down in the elevator, she thought, Next week, if the weather wasn't too hot, she would take Ruth outside for a walk and sit by the small lake behind the building. And, she smiled, maybe she would bring her a doll.

As she left the elevator she had to walk around an older gentleman holding an older lady's hand. She wondered which one was the resident.

"Have a nice afternoon," McDuffie said, smiling as she walked through the lobby.

"Thank you. You, too." The idea came to her when she saw the newspaper laying on the desk, folded, the pages crooked as if it had been read. Would it be too forward of her to ask? Would anyone know? She stopped walking and took a deep breath. "Is that your newspaper?" she asked, trying not to sound timid but without success.

McDuffie looked down. "Yes, would you like to have it?"

"Oh, no. I—" she stammered.

"I'm done with it." He picked it up and held it out to her. "I'm just going to throw it in the trash."

"Well, if you're sure. Thank you. Thank you so much."

As she walked to the car, she labored to convince herself that Matthew would never find out. It was better than spending money on it and then throwing it away.

On the way home she pulled into a small shopping area and read that day's installment of the series. She all but lapped the words from the page. "For years psychiatrists thought that homosexuality was the result of overly influential and protective mothering. Too much maternal closeness with sons was thought to be the reason for feminine behavior in boys or what was considered unnatural or abnormal interests for boys. Girls, on the other hand, who had too much paternal closeness were thought to have more likelihood of turning out to be lesbian. For some time researchers have attempted to identify a genetic marker for homosexuality, but to date no discoveries have been announced. 'Homosexuality isn't caused by anything or anyone just as heterosexuality isn't caused by anything or anyone,' responded one gay man. 'It's not a disease. A person is who he or she is. You're born that way. It's the way God makes you. Why do people have to analyze this ad nauseam? The real issue is treating all people equally and fairly.'"

Miriam read to the end of the article, folded the paper and sat staring at nothing. In her mind she replayed an endless reel of scenes with Nathaniel—the times she played with him when he was a toddler, how he ran to her with his little arms outstretched, wanting to hug and kiss her and her never once denying him. Their bond had always been special. He had been such a loving child. And he still was. She relished the moments when they were alone and could laugh or even share things, knowing that each was safe with the other. Their relationship was special but not overly affectionate. Not like the article was talking about. As he had gotten older there had been less of those private moments, but their bond was still intact. She sensed it, and not just because she wanted it to be so. It was there. Just like those few minutes they had together every morning after Matthew left and before Sarah Elizabeth came downstairs. Special time. But not unnatural. She had not been overly protective or influential like the article had said. So why should she be concerned about his—all of this talk about such private matters? He was a good boy. An athlete. A scholar. And he was very much interested in Martha. A sweet girl. Both so devout. The perfect couple. Everyone remarked to her about them, and what a great preacher Nathaniel was going to be. Just like his father. And Sarah Elizabeth. She was not like these women in the newspaper. She and Matthew certainly had not been that close. She was very feminine. And very much taken with Mike Caviness. She was young and would be dating soon. But she knew in her heart that her daughter was just as normal as her brother.

And whatever was bothering Nathaniel—the way he was at breakfast today, not having much to say, just eating and leaving—that was probably just a mood thing. Not unusual, she tried to convince herself.

Miriam closed her eyes. "Please, God. Look after them." She took a deep breath and reached down to the keys in the ignition. It wasn't until she was already out of the parking lot and into the street that she realized she hadn't thrown away the newspaper. A wave of worry passed through her. She glanced at the clock on the dashboard. Matthew said he was having lunch out. She could put the newspaper deep in the kitchen trash where no one would see it.

Still, from the minute she turned onto their street, she searched the driveway for her husband's car. As she pulled in and touched the garage door remote, relief washed over her when she saw both spaces were empty. She parked and quickly went inside. The garbage can under the sink was almost three-fourths full. Digging through the plastic wraps, Styrofoam containers, wadded paper towels and other trash, she created a pocket, then rolled the newspaper into a tight wand and placed it in the middle of the contents. She covered it up with other trash and washed her hands. When she finished drying them, she spread the paper towel over the contents in the trash can. She closed the cabinet door and sighed with relief. Still, a complete feeling of assurance would not come until that particular trash bag was in the city garbage truck and away from their house.

Going through the family room on her way upstairs, she stopped for a moment to admire the collection of pictures of Nathaniel and Sarah Elizabeth. Each one was from a particular event in each of their lives—Nathaniel in his junior varsity basketball uniform, the varsity baseball team, the varsity basketball team, and a photo of him winning the Bible Scholar Competition as a senior would go right there, she thought. And Sarah Elizabeth at the girls' auxiliary, in the school play, her piano recital last year. They were good children, Miriam told her herself. Her pride produced a smile. She wanted them to be happy. She wanted to protect them from the ugliness of the world. She nudged one of Nathaniel's pictures to make it level. But that was up to God, not her, and not even up to Matthew—although she would never say that aloud.

Nathaniel rushed down the noisy hallway, trying not to bump into people but still speaking to his friends as he went. He had asked Martha to meet him at the top of the stairs so he could walk her to class.

"But your class is at the other end of the building," she had said that morning before homeroom. "Won't you be late?"

"Not if I'm fast," he had said, making himself smile. "Don't you want me to walk with you?" Martha had grinned and rolled her brown eyes, her auburn hair bobbing as they walked. "You know I do. That's a dumb question."

"Well, a guy likes to be sure," he teased.

"You can be sure."

When they met at the stairs, they had to walk fast.

"If you're late, I'll feel guilty," she said as they rushed without even taking time to say hello.

He dodged a group lingering by some lockers. "It won't be your fault."

Finally, they arrived at the door to her math class. Nathaniel started to lean against the door frame and talk. "Don't you dare stop. Go. I don't want you to get into trouble." She pushed him gently with a shooing motion.

"Okay. See you at lunch," he said as he rushed off. "Save me a seat," he called over his shoulder with a wave.

"Good luck on the test," she said.

Nathaniel looked back, smiled and gave a thumbs up.

When she disappeared into the classroom, Nathaniel began walking as fast as he could. With the hall almost empty he knew there wasn't much time, but it was against the rules to run. He was dreading this. Advanced Chemistry. The big test. And seeing Jason. Memories from the night before still swam through his mind. Jason's seat was not near his. Less chance of conversation. He was going to avoid him as much as he could. But as he got closer to the classroom, tension mounted throughout his body.

Rounding the last corner, he saw Jason starting into the chemistry room. The knot already in his stomach, the one that began the night before lying on Jason's bed, tightened. He panicked even more when he saw Jason had stopped to wait for him.

"I guess we're both cutting it close," he said as Nathaniel got to the door.

"I was walking Martha to her class," Nathaniel said dryly and brushed by him. Going to his place, he traded comments with his friends who joked about his almost being tardy.

"Had to make sure Martha was safe and sound in her class," he teased back with a purposeful grin. A twinge of some unknown emotion passed through him. Something inside felt vengeful, a desire to hurt. He glanced at Jason who was about to sit down three seats in front of him. He was smiling but not genuinely, as if he were masking a hurt. Nathaniel knew in that moment that his words had struck home and he regretted it. As the bell sounded, he put his books away and sat down.

The test was long and tedious. Elements that he should know—had in fact known, just the day before—blurred in his mind. All of it made him recall the night before. Jason without his shirt. His shorts riding well below his navel. The hair on his chest. Nathaniel squeezed his eyes closed. He had to concentrate. Focus. Read the questions. Put everything else out of your mind, he ordered himself.

But his internal battle was unrelenting. Normally, he was one of the first to finish, to turn in his test, and spend the remainder of the hour studying another subject or beginning the assignment Mr. Cheshire always had on the board. But not today. When the bell rang to end the class, he was scurrying to complete the final question. His classmates were leaving as he handed in his paper and collected his books.

"How was it?" Mr. Cheshire asked, looking over the top of his glasses.

"Little tougher than I thought." Nathaniel tried to sound upbeat. He knew his father would be inquiring. "I studied more for this one than any other test, I think."

"I'm sure you'll get your usual A."

"Thanks, Mr. Cheshire. I hope so." He slung his book bag over his shoulder. "See you tomorrow."

As he exited the classroom, Jason was leaning against a locker by the door.

"How'd you do?"

Surprise and fear shot through Nathaniel. He wanted to say nothing and walk away. "I have to meet Martha. I can't talk—I don't want to talk." He wanted to say more. He wanted to tell him to leave him alone. Stay away from him. But even as the words formed in his mind, something would not allow them to have a voice. That same unnamed feeling told him not to inflict hurt.

In the school cafeteria he spotted her sitting at a table with a group of their friends. Some of the guys from the team were there. Nathaniel sat in the chair that Martha was saving for him.

"How was the test?" she asked.

He looked at her without speaking. For an instant, it seemed that all the chatter and clanging in the large room ceased. Everyone froze in place except Martha who sat looking at him, smiling sincerely, caring for him, wanting to be with him. Suddenly, a feeling came over him. It was as if he could not touch her, even though he was sitting only inches away. She reached over and touched his forearm.

"Are you okay?" she almost whispered.

Nathaniel blinked his eyes. He had to get a grip on himself. He forced a smile. "I'm fine. That test just kinda blew my mind. It was hard. I don't think I did too good—well."

Martha still looked concerned. "I doubt that. I've heard you say that before." She looked around to be sure a faculty monitor was not nearby. Seeing no one, she gently squeezed his arm. "Are you sure you're okay?"

"Yeah, I'm fine. Sure." Even though she was touching his arm, he still felt as if she was miles away. He looked to be sure no teachers were watching and then touched her hand. Still, something was missing. Something was different. He rubbed the back of her hand with his thumb. "I'm just hungry, I guess." He leaned forward to stand up. "I'll be right back." He lowered his voice just for her to hear. "Don't go anywhere." He winked.

Martha smiled. "I'll be here."

He watched her over his shoulder. The confusion was agonizing. Whatever was going on—he could handle it. It would get better. Last night had just thrown him. Something he hadn't expected. He would be okay. As he stood in line, he looked back at Martha. She was laughing with Katie but also keeping a worried eye on him.

* * *

Matthew turned onto Century Avenue and drove until he came to the entrance to the academy. He waved to the security agent inside the small guardhouse and passed the signs directing traffic to the various buildings on the sprawling campus—the lower school, the middle school, the upper school, the gymnasium, tennis courts, the athletic fields. He checked his watch. Baseball practice would finish in another twenty or thirty minutes. Perfect.

He took note of the grounds people tending the shrubs and lawn, making sure no one was standing idle. At the baseball field he parked near the main entrance, checked his hair in the rearview mirror, put on his sunglasses and got out of the car. He strode through the gate, passed windows for concessions and climbed to the third row of the bleachers . Down on the field Coach Stansbury saw him and waved. Matthew half-heartedly returned the greeting, then surveyed the players and quickly spotted Nathaniel.

He watched as Stansbury took them through a grounder, scoop and throw drill, Nathaniel doing the drill perfectly. A natural. In basketball, too, and of course the classroom. Remarkable, he thought. His father is the most important man in the church and academy, but it hadn't affected Nathaniel's popularity. He instinctively knew how to fit in with his peers, able to laugh and joke with them.

As he watched his son, memories of his own time in the academy drifted through his mind. He hadn't been as gifted as Nathaniel in sports, never chosen first for teams in phys ed, never played basketball or baseball. And, while he always got good grades, he had to work for them, not always getting perfect hundreds on tests but many times low A's. "You can do better than this," his father, Reverend Jacob Winslow, said whenever he missed getting the hundred. "I expect it and so does God. To be the leader of this church you have to be the best. I want you to be the top man in your class." But in his senior year he had only managed to be named salutatorian and came in fifth in the Bible Scholar competition. He knew his father had been deeply disappointed. Yet here he was today—head of the church, a perfect family and a son to follow in his footsteps.

And Nathaniel would inherit it all. Martha Davies—what a wonderful Christian girl for Nathaniel to be seeing on a regular basis, a perfect match for him to marry and create a family, become a minister and one day take over this glorious institution, just as he had done. One day. One day the sign in front would read, "Reverend Nathaniel Winslow, Pastor." That would be a proud day, he thought. For himself. And his father and grandfather.

Matthew drew in a deep breath and watched as another section of the team moved into position for batting practice. Each took his turn with the outfielders in their respective positions. The infield players practiced hard, long throws on the sidelines. Nathaniel gave a quick nod to his father from near the backstop fence as he took several practice swings.

Coach Stansbury walked over to the fence as he always did when Matthew appeared at a practice. His stout frame hovered over his noticeably thin legs, a testimony to his eating habits. His gray hair outnumbered the dark. His skin deeply tanned.

"Afternoon, Reverend," he said from inside the fence, removing neither his baseball cap nor his aviator sunglasses.

"Hello, Ralph." He didn't move from his seat on the bleachers. "How're we looking for the big game Saturday?"

"Oh, we've got a great chance. Everybody's healthy and fired up to play."

"That's great. St. Paul's lost last week, didn't they?"

"Right. That was their only one though for the season. Nathaniel's looking good," he said. "All the seniors really want to win this one since it's their last game."

You're trying to change the subject, Matthew thought. But I'm not going to let you get by that easily. "What's your record this season?"

Coach Stansbury didn't hesitate. "We're three and eight," he said, then waited for Matthew to respond.

"Well, let's hope it'll be four and eight on Saturday."

"We'll do our best. Guess I'd better get back out there. Thanks for stopping by, Reverend."

"Yes, of course." You better hope it's four wins, he thought, watching the coach waddle away. It will be your last game at this school if it isn't.

Matthew waited until Nathaniel's turn to bat. He watched him hit several balls near the left outfield fence but he also fouled off several and hit grounders for others—all unusual for him.

When practice ended and Coach Stansbury sent the team to the locker room, Nathaniel trotted over to the fence. Matthew got up and came down to join him.

"Hey, Dad."

"Hey, son. Nice hitting today but you seemed to miss some, too. Everything okay?"

"Oh, just excited about the game, I guess," he said, shifting his feet.

"Well, we all want you all to do some damage on Saturday. To win this final game."

"We're ready to win, too. Everybody's really concentrating."

"Concentration's important." He nodded looked away then back. "All the players seem to really like Coach Stansbury. I mean, he's a good coach, isn't he?"

Nathaniel nodded with enthusiasm. "He's really good. It's not his fault we haven't won any more games than we have."

Matthew smiled. "Well, let's just hope this one on Saturday will be a win."

"We're going to try."

"That's good. That's good. Okay, I need to go over to the office. See you at home for dinner."

"Okay." He began walking backwards. "See you."

Matthew watched his son run effortlessly toward the gymnasium. How blessed he was to have such a child. His miracle child. God was definitely watching out for him. When he saw Stansbury walking off the field, he remembered Kenneth Ward's words.

* * *

81

"And, Lord, we ask that you will keep us safe and healthy so that we might play our best and represent the true spirit of sport," Coach Stansbury prayed. "We ask in Jesus' blessed name. Amen."

The team stood in the center of the locker room as they echoed, "Amen."

"Okay, guys," the coach yelled, holding out his hand, palm down.

The entire team crowded into a tight circle around the coach, sweaty body smells still radiating. Nathaniel made sure he was nowhere near Jason. As team captain, when he put his hand on top of the coach's, he was glad that Jason's was somewhere higher up.

"Who's the best?" Nathaniel shouted.

"We are!" came the loud cry with a pump of the pile of hands.

"Who's going to win on Saturday?" he asked even louder.

"Disciples!"

The pile of hands pumped once more, but this time ended with arms raised and fists punching the air overhead with determination.

"Okay, great practice, guys," Coach Stansbury said, holding up his hand for one last announcement. "Get showered up. Go home, eat healthy, get your assignments done, pray and get to bed early." He clapped his hands. "Let's go."

Chatter, laughter and slamming metal locker doors echoed throughout the room. Nathaniel nervously joined in the camaraderie but also focused on how to avoid showering near Jason. Once stripped of everything but his jockstrap and cup, he wrapped his towel around his waist, then reached underneath and took them off. He walked to the shower area forcing himself to laugh and joke with others but gratefully no sign of Jason. He stepped into an empty shower stall, pulled the curtain half closed and removed his towel. Just as he reached out to hang it on the hook outside, Jason was walking passed and stopped. For a split second they looked at each other, not scanning each others' body, but directly eye to eye. Nathaniel's entire insides tensed, but also a rush of excitement surged through him. A silent dialogue struggling to be heard. When someone pulled open a nearby shower curtain, Jason walked on. At the same time

Nathaniel closed his shower curtain all the way and turned the water on. It had lasted only seconds. Had someone noticed them staring? His heart pounded with fear and at the same time last night roared into his mind. Hairy legs, chest, navel. He changed the water to cold to keep from getting an erection. He was not going to let this happen.

He turned to the soap dispenser and began washing his body and hair. When he reached out for his towel a few minutes later, Jason had already left his shower, and was talking with Mark Jones and Billy French, as they walked to the locker room. Everything seemed normal. Relieved, Nathaniel dried off in the privacy of his shower and went to his locker. Joe Blackmon was three lockers away.

"Nice hittin' today, Nate," he said, pulling on his t-shirt.

Nathaniel looked away. "Thanks, but not as good as it needs to be," he said seriously. He pulled up his boxer shorts, his towel still around him. He turned to face Joe and at the same time could not help but steal a glance at his muscular legs.

"You're just saving the good stuff for Saturday," Joe said, raising his hand for a high five.

Nathaniel slapped his hand but did not smile. "Hope so."

"You are." Joe turned to leave. "Catch you tomorrow."

"You bet."

Nathaniel finished dressing. As he was walking toward the exit of the locker room, so was Andrew Perryman.

"Yo, Nate. We gonna win Saturday," he said light-heartedly.

Nathaniel forced a smile. "You know it." Just as he spoke, he glimpsed Jason at the far end of the room combing his hair in front of the mirror. Jason turned. The two looked at each other for a split second, ignoring everyone else. It was Andrew who broke the miniscule silence.

"Jase, later guy." Andrew pointed his index finger at him.

"See ya," Jason responded.

"See ya," Nathaniel muttered, turning away from him before he could speak.

* * *

Upstairs in his room Nathaniel texted Martha.

r u ok she asked.

Yes why

dont know seem different a good different

Nathaniel smiled. *glad you like*

definitely Like the attention

test bad today game on Saturday lots going on

still #1 in class 4sure

dont know chemistry may be end of me

funny get real

got to go family prayer time

tomorrow

cant wait—

Nathaniel stopped before sending. A wave of excitement over something that was wrong yet acceptable, something not allowed at the school or church, but was considered normal—all of it made him feel bold. *—to hold your hand.*

Later as he lay in bed, he combated his thoughts. What if he failed that test? What was he going to tell his father if he found out? Would Mr. Cheshire tell his father? What excuse could he make? What was Mr. Cheshire going to think of him? What would he tell the others in the class when they asked him what he made? He rolled over. Maybe he could think of something clever. And the game this Saturday. Martha. What would he tell her? What if he had another dream about— The memory of Jason lying shirtless beside him popped into his mind. He stopped and rolled back to the other side. Jason looking directly at him today in the shower. No. He wasn't going to think about that—about him. He wasn't. He rolled onto his back and forced himself to fantasize about Martha— holding her hand and kissing her.

CHAPTER FIVE

THURSDAY—MAY 14

Matthew entered the empty hospital elevator and stood in front of the panel of buttons. As he pressed number four and moved to the side, two African-American nurses stepped in. As the elevator began its ascent, he put his Bible under his arm and took out a small bottle of Purell from his pants pocket. He squeezed until a small pool of the clear gel dribbled into his palm and at the same time made a squishing noise. Almost empty. The faint odor of alcohol wafted around him. He snapped the lid shut, pocketed the bottle and fastidiously rubbed his hands together until the gel dissipated.

He took his Bible from underneath his arm and at the same time looked closely at the mirror plate on the wall with all of the elevator's buttons. Examining himself unobtrusively, he searched for the gray hair on his right temple he'd found that morning. Just how noticeable was it? There it was. Every day another one or two invaded appearing as bold as a billboard in his otherwise dark hair. At least it wasn't falling out. Frank could touch it up. He wanted to be sure that he looked good on television this afternoon.

He checked to be sure that his plastic nametag pinned to his lapel was on straight. He and the other ministers always wore them as good advertising when they visited in the hospitals. He consulted his list and notes inside his worn Bible. One more stop—Estelle Caviness, eighty-two-years old, had been in the hospital for nearly a week with pneumonia. Good thing pneumonia wasn't contagious.

When the bell signaled the upcoming stop, Matthew shifted his stance and looked at the mirror for a final hasty centering tug on his necktie and exited behind the two nurses.

Making his way down the hall, he politely skirted around hospital carts and patients with walkers. He spoke a grand and kind "hello" to most everyone but kept moving briskly so he wouldn't have to engage in conversation. He had no time for chatting.

As he neared Mrs. Caviness's door, he saw two men standing outside the room across the hall. As one cried quietly the other one held him—immediately catching Matthew's attention. The door to the room next to them was closed but had special instructions in large print taped to it. Matthew made no effort to read the notice but continued to watch the two until he arrived at Mrs. Caviness's door.

"Knock, knock, Miss Estelle," he said, softly tapping on the door when he saw that she was awake. "And how are we feeling today?"

The elderly lady turned her head slowly toward the voice. Wisps of white hair splayed out from her head onto the pillow. She struggled to lift her bony hand to greet him. "Reverend Winslow." The plastic tube of oxygen around her ears and over sunken cheeks ended in her nostrils. "So good to see you," she finally managed a decibel above a whisper. A small humidifier on the bedside table emitted a ghostly mist.

Matthew limply took her hand. "I do believe you're looking more chipper today than last week." He knew he would have to do most of the talking. "A lot more color in your cheeks for certain." He tried to sound convincing.

Miss Estelle smiled. "I believe I do feel better. I'm breathing some—" She paused to inhale. "Somewhat easier today," she finished.

"Well, that's just wonderful news. The Lord is truly watching over you."

"I hope so." She gave a polite chuckle which provoked a coughing spell.

Matthew released her hand and stepped back slowly, away from potential germs, and watched helplessly while the elderly woman struggled to clear her air passage. Finally, her coughing subsided.

"I'm so sorry." She swabbed her mouth with a tissue.

"Not to worry. Is there anything I can do for you?"

With her other hand she pointed to the plastic water pitcher and cup on the bedside table. "Could you pour me some water?"

"Of course. I'd be glad to." He walked around the bed, poured some water and held it for her. As the elderly lady drew the water through the flexible straw, Matthew noticed that a doctor had joined the two men outside the room across the hall. He tried to listen to their conversation, but Miss Estelle interrupted.

"Thank you so much, Reverend." Her head relaxed into the pillow.

"You're so very welcome." Matthew placed the cup back beside the pitcher. "Is there anything else you need?"

"No, I think not." Again, she dabbed at her mouth. "I'm afraid I'm a little drowsy still this morning. It must be—" She stopped and took a deep breath. "It must be the medication."

"That's quite all right. You don't need to apologize for anything. Would you like for me to quote some scripture and say a prayer for you?"

"Oh, would you?"

"I'd be happy to." He thought about sitting down but decided it would be better to keep his distance. She would probably fall asleep in a few minutes. He moved to the end of the bed. "This is one of my favorite Psalms," he said. Miss Estelle closed her eyes. 'I will lift up mine eyes unto—'"

"No!"

Matthew looked out into the hallway but continued reciting. The doctor had obviously given them bad news. The young man who had been crying now sobbed. When his friend held him, again, he put his face against his shoulder and wept softly.

Miss Estelle did not stir or open her eyes. Sleeping, he thought. For a moment, he turned his attention to the hallway while he began praying without closing his eyes.

"Heavenly Father, God, bless this dear, dear lady, your servant. If it be your will, heal her to vibrant life. Keep her free of pain and suffering. Strengthen her in body, in her mind and in her spirit. Forgive her sins. Bless her doctors—"

In the hall the doctor shook hands with the less emotional of the men and went into the room. The two walked away.

"Bless her doctors and nurses," Matthew continued. "Guide them as they tend to her. Bring Miss Estelle back to our midst. In the name of Jesus, Your Blessed Son and Savior of us all. Amen."

He quickly but gently patted Miss Estelle's hand and quietly walked out. As he made his way toward the elevator, he held his Bible under his arm and reached into his left pocket for the small bottle of Purell. He squeezed out the last dollop, dropped the container into a hallway trashcan and bathed his hands.

When he reached the elevator the two young men were there waiting, one still with his arm around the more tearful. The down arrow lit, Matthew waited to the side. The elevator arrived with four occupants. No one exited. The three stepped in and silently faced the front.

After the doors closed, the one cried softly. His companion put his hand on the back of his neck and pulled him against his body. He stroked the back of his head and neck. Matthew watched without speaking. Finally, the bell rang and the elevator slowed to a stop.

When the doors opened, the two walked out, the stronger one with his arm still around the other's shoulder. Matthew followed them through the hospital lobby, out the automatic-opening double doors and toward the parking garage.

He felt God would want him to do his duty as a Christian. "Excuse me," he said just as they neared the drive into the garage.

The two young men stopped and turned.

"Do you realize you're breaking God's law? Two men. It's not right." He held up his Bible.

The more emotional of the two clutched the other one's arm. "Let's go, Jerry. It's not worth it."

"God wants you to repent of your sins so that you can enter the Kingdom of Heaven," Matthew said calmly.

"You go on to the car," Jerry, the stronger one, said, pointing his remote control at the entrance to the garage. Inside the parking deck a dull beep sounded.

"Jerry, no. Please."

Jerry was calm. "It's fine. Everything's fine." His voice conveyed no harshness or excitement. "Go," he said gently. "I'll just be a minute."

Reluctantly, the emotional young man turned and walked to the car as Jerry watched. When his friend had closed the car door, he turned back to Matthew.

"Satan has triumphed over you," Matthew said. "All you have to do is repent and God will forgive you."

Jerry approached Matthew smiling.

"Jesus died for your sins."

Jerry squinted at Matthew's nametag still on his suit coat. "'Reverend Matthew Winslow—Holy Bible Fellowship,'" he read aloud. "Oh, yes, I read your letter in the newspaper just this week." He held out his hand in a friendly manner, looking directly at him. "My name is Jerry."

Matthew met his eyes but hesitated for a moment before taking the offered hand and shaking it. He quickly decided he would not be outdone by one of these people.

"I would be more than happy to listen to your confession of sin."

"You seem to be opposed to the gay and lesbian population in general and the Gay Pride celebration in particular. That AIDS is God's wrath." Jerry's voice remained natural and calm. Still shaking Matthew's hand, he now grasped it firmly with his left hand at the same time. "I must tell you that I just do not agree with you. You see, that man in the car is my partner and I love him more than, than life itself," he said, tightening his grip on Matthew's hand.

Matthew thought of pulling his hand away but decided he would not let this person get the better of him. It was more important to show him he wasn't afraid. "Confess your sin and God will forgive you."

"Our relationship is not a sin. If there's a sinner around here, it's you and your self-righteousness."

Matthew looked him directly in the eye and returned the firm grip with his own.

"Oh, I'm glad to see you aren't afraid to touch me, Reverend. Just like Jesus wasn't afraid to touch the lepers. We've just been visiting our friend who's dying of AIDS. So since you're so holy, I'm sure God will protect you like he protected Jesus."

Matthew smiled defiantly to mask the bolt of fear that shot through him. "If you don't repent, you'll go to hell for all eternity."

"Listen to me, Reverend," Jerry said, releasing Matthew's hand. He lowered his voice but his tone was now firmly commanding as was his index finger which he pointed directly in Matthew's face. "If you ever see me or any of my friends at this hospital again, you keep your fucking holier-than-thou preaching and judgments to yourself." He turned and walked toward his car.

"Dear God, lead this man to Your truth. Help him to see that his way is wrong," Matthew called out.

"Better wash that hand, Reverend," Jerry called over his shoulder.

Matthew continued toward his Lexus, his right hand isolated. "Lord, let him know Your loving forgiveness." When he reached the car, he put his Bible under his right arm and reached across awkwardly with his left hand to retrieve his keys from his right front pocket. "Show all whom he knows Thy way also. The way to salvation." After some struggle he was able to get his keys and unlock the car door. Once inside he immediately locked the doors, watching in the rearview mirror as the two men drove away. He opened the console with his left hand and took out a large bottle of Purell. He flipped the cap open and poured a generous amount into his right palm. "Forgive them, Father. In Your Holy Name, Amen," he said, vigorously rubbing the gel over every crevice of his right hand.

When Frank Winston, Matthew's barber of fifteen years, handed him a mirror, Matthew meticulously searched his right temple for any gray strands. Next the left temple. Then the front view and the back, using the handheld and large wall mirror behind the barber's chair. All the gray was hidden.

"Great job, Frank," he said, "as usual."

"Thanks, Reverend. Glad to be of service." Frank was an older, quiet man. He and the other four barbers wore a soft blue cotton shirt with "Elm Blvd. Barbershop" stitched in dark blue where a breast pocket would be. His own hair was thin but perfectly combed. His barber's chair sat in a separate cubicle toward the back to allow privacy for men whose hair needed coloring or who removed their hairpieces for trims of their real sprigs.

Frank removed the cloth cover from around Matthew's neck, sweeping it away so that the loose hair fell on the floor.

Getting up from the chair, he reached for his billfold and took out a twenty and a ten for the cut and color touch up and three ones for a ten per cent tip, the same as a tithe, he had reasoned for years. "Same time next week?"

"Got you down," Frank said, taking the bills. "Have a good week. Tell Nathaniel I said good luck in his game on Saturday."

"I'll do that," Matthew said. He walked out of the cubicle into the area where the other barbers were working. "You fellows have a good day, now," he said to no one in particular.

The other barbers and some of the clients chimed in with farewells as Matthew strolled out of the shop and got into his car. Now those men respected him, he thought to himself. Unlike that homosexual at the hospital. He pulled down the vanity mirror to check his hair one more time. As he drove across town, he reached into the console and again took out the Purell for another cleansing.

"Lord, God, forgive those tortured souls back there at the hospital," he said out loud. "Bring them to their senses. Let them know you." He sighed as he slowed at a red light. "Amen."

While driving to the church, he continued thinking about the confrontation. Those men— He had encountered that kind before, but none had ever forcefully grasped his hand and held it so that he couldn't get away. He would be more wary in the future—especially of shaking hands. He wasn't afraid of them. He would always stand up against that kind, but he would be more careful about touching.

He made a left onto Century Avenue, now four-lanes with a center turn lane. Because of the magnitude of the church and accompanying buildings they had petitioned the city to widen the road, bringing opposition from the home owners who lost parts of their front yards to public domain. But the church had won. His church. Pride coursed through him as he approached the main entrance with the contemporary sign of steel and stone. "Holy Bible Fellowship." Below that, Reverend Matthew Winslow, Pastor." On the next line, "Founded by Reverend Benjamin Winslow." Then underneath, "The Word of God Made Manifest." Finally, "Sunday Services 9 and 11 a. m." A digital screen flashed alternating announcements and short Bible verses. As he approached the massive church, he thought about how miraculously it had all come about and where it was going. Nationally televised. God was, indeed, a bountiful God.

At two minutes before two o'clock just inside the doors of the main sanctuary, Matthew was joined by the twelve ministers from the meeting the day before. Checking his watch, he stepped back from the group. "Well, gentlemen of God, it's time. Let's have a word of prayer." The other ministers bowed their heads. "Holy Father, we come here this afternoon to continue to do your work, to speak for you against the evil that is growing in our city among your people. Guide us in our actions as we seek to lead the way of righteousness. In your name we pray." The collective "Amen" echoed through the high modern ceiling of the vestibule. "Well, let's go." Matthew opened the very large steel and stained glass door and walked out onto the front steps of the church.

"Good afternoon. Thank you all for coming on such short notice," he said to the half dozen reporters who stood back from the steps. He stepped up to the portable lectern with the church's name prominently displayed on it. Three microphones had been placed in front of it. Technicians with video cameras began filming. The reporters stood ready to take notes.

"I and the twelve clergymen here with me today have met to discuss a grave issue that is growing in our community. We feel that the issue is detrimental to the people of Elmsborough and as clergymen, men of God and professors of God's Holy word," he said, holding up his Bible, "it is our duty to speak out. I refer, of course, to the Gay Pride celebration, parade and other events that are scheduled to take place on June 27 in the downtown area. As believers in the word of God, we cannot sit idly by as our city government grants these people and organizations the right to publicly assemble in an effort to gain attention and encourage others to join their ranks. The Bible clearly states that homosexuality is a sin against God and, to us as men of God and leaders in our various churches, it is unthinkable that such activity is being condoned by Mayor Borelli and the city council. We call upon all citizens to join us in prayer for the correction of this misguided decision and publicly protest these events. We will silently and peacefully be present along the parade route if the parade is allowed to be held and we will hold prayer vigils in our respective houses of worship the evening before so that all citizens, regardless of their church or religious affiliations, may sign petitions against any future gatherings and pray for these sinners. I will also address the city council at its next meeting in early June. Reverend Newland, associate pastor here at Holy Bible Fellowship, will now hand out a list of the churches speaking out against the event and other information about our activities. While he's doing that, I'll take questions."

"Reverend Winslow, have you talked with Mayor Borelli about this?" one reporter asked.

"Yes. Mayor Borelli told me that these people are not breaking the law and that they are within their rights to assemble. If extra police will be on duty that, of course, means the city will be spending more of the taxpayers' money than is necessary. Voting in November is another way citizens can show their disapproval for how the city council and the mayor are handling this."

"Have you talked directly with the organizers of Pride weekend?" another reporter asked.

"No, I have not."

"Why not?"

Matthew nervously shifted his feet. "I didn't feel that I could convince them otherwise, but I have been praying for them, that they would see the error of their ways and return to obeying God's word."

"Would you be willing to hold a debate with the organizers?" the same reporter asked.

"This is not a debatable issue. This way of life is clearly a sin against God. There is no middle ground. No gray area. It is wrong and those who engage in this kind of behavior are not acceptable in the eyes of God. It is an abomination. That is clearly stated in Leviticus 18:22." Again he held up his Bible.

"And what about AIDS, Reverend?" asked a third reporter.

"This has been said now for the last thirty years. AIDS is clearly God's wrath on homosexuals for their sinful behavior."

"And what about heterosexuals who have contracted HIV?" the same reporter pushed.

Matthew shifted his stance a bit nervously. "The fault lies with those whose behavior goes against God's law."

The half dozen reporters and camera men were silent.

"Are there any more questions?" he asked, trying not to show his disdain for the questions asked and what seemed to be a complacent attitude of the reporters. "This then concludes the press conference. Thank you all very much for being here."

Some of the television reporters spoke to their videographers about doing a follow up trailer to the conference, reporting on the list that they had been given. Matthew and the other ministers went back inside.

"I hope you would all agree that went fairly well," he said to them once the doors were closed.

"Excellent, Matthew."

Everyone gathered around him.

"Very well, indeed."

"You're a good soldier for the Lord, Matthew."

"Thank you for your courage."

Matthew acknowledged their adulation as he shook hands with each minister. Later, in his office, he called Miriam.

"I want to delay dinner until six-thirty. I want us all to watch the news at six."

"Is something special happening?" Miriam asked.

"Yes, we had a press conference today. I want to see if they cut out anything. So plan on dinner later. Tell the children when they come home. They can start their homework."

"All right. Will you be home at the usual time?"

"Yes. Nothing else will change."

At precisely six o'clock all four of the Winslows were seated in the den. Matthew was in the imposing and expensive Swedish recliner. Miriam sat in her usual place, a chair intended to be a companion to the Swedish but matched only in color. Nathaniel and Sara Elizabeth sat on opposite ends of the sofa. The television was tuned to the local station. The press conference was not the lead story, but it was mentioned before the first commercial as an upcoming news item. When it had not appeared before the second advertising break, Matthew shifted impatiently in his chair.

"I hope they're not going to wait until the very end to air it," he said with frustration.

Miriam tried to think of something reassuring to say. Sarah Elizabeth wanted to be in her room doing other things but did not dare give any indication. Nathaniel kept reassuring himself that he had done nothing wrong. This didn't apply to him. This was an issue that his father was bringing up. And by the time he was a minister in the church—well, it wouldn't matter then. He and Martha would be married and have children, leading healthy respectable lives. And his grade on a chemistry test would be history. Even if he hadn't done well, he was going to make up the difference on the exam next week.

The commercial ended and the scene returned to the newscast. Behind the anchor's head was a cross and the phrase, "Gay Pride Not Welcomed."

"Here it is," Matthew said, pointing the remote to turn up the volume.

The camera panned the exterior of the sanctuary, the sign in front and the group of ministers exiting the building to meet reporters on the front steps. The whole time the reporter narrated the reason for the press conference. Next Matthew spoke. From his armchair he listened for possible edits, but nothing was omitted. Even the reporters' questions and his answers were included. When the video of the press conference ended, the anchor said that they had contacted the chairman of the committee for the upcoming Pride event for his comments. When the video clip began, Matthew leaned forward in his chair.

"I'm very sorry that Reverend Winslow and the other ministers are so fearful of gay people. I also regret that they choose to represent God as narrow-minded and unloving. We welcome peaceful protestors along the parade route. We welcome everyone to come to the event and the exhibits. It's a wonderful chance to get to know gay, lesbian, bi-sexual and transgender people and see that we're just regular folks. Unlike these churches of God, we don't discriminate. We welcome all."

When the video ended, the anchorman went to the weather reporter.

"Well, I guess we know where the television station stands on this issue," he said, sitting back. "You would think they would have the courtesy to let me know that they were planning to talk to those people. This world has become a frightening place. Let's pray." He leaned forward again with his elbows on his knees. Nathaniel did the same. "Holy Father, we pray for these misguided people who have strayed from you and your love. Help them to see the error of their ways and the hurt that they are inflicting on their families and the world in general. Keep us strong in the face of this adversity. Grant us strength and peace as we go forward spreading your word and your love to all the world. In Jesus name. Amen."

As usual, they were all silent, waiting for Matthew's direction. "Well, I suggest that we put this out of our minds for now and enjoy the delicious dinner that's waiting for us."

Miriam and Sarah Elizabeth quickly brought the bowls of food into the dining room table, filled the glasses with iced tea and took their seats. Matthew rested his elbows on the table, his hands clasped together underneath his chin.

"Lord, we thank you for this bounty that you have provided for us. Bless this food so that we might be nourished to go out and spread your gospel to the world; that our bodies might be strong to compete; that our minds might be pure; that our bodies may be healed. Keep us safe. In your Most Blessed Name. Amen."

Nathaniel, Sarah Elizabeth and Miriam echoed, "Amen" and put their napkins in their laps.

"Miriam, this roast looks wonderful," Matthew said as he began carving the first serving of beef.

"Thank you, dear. It was a good price. On sale," she added.

"Even better," he said, sawing a second slice. It was part of the ritual at each meal. Matthew carved or sliced the meat, placing a portion on each plate.

"Not too much for me, Daddy," Sarah Elizabeth said shyly, then added, "please." She stared directly in front of her, not wishing to make eye contact with anyone.

Matthew stopped slicing and took half of the meat from her plate and placed it on Nathaniel's.

Miriam glanced guardedly at her daughter as she passed the plate to Sarah Elizabeth. When everyone had a plate, the bowls of vegetables were passed. Sarah Elizabeth took small portions.

"Practice tomorrow as usual?" Matthew asked Nathaniel, passing a bowl of potatoes.

"Batting practice and some drills. Not a heavy one."

Matthew began cutting his beef. "Good idea."

"Coach says we're playing well as a team," Nathaniel added.

Matthew chewed and swallowed. "And a good word for that would be?" he quizzed.

Nathaniel thought for only a moment. "Cohesive?" he responded, looking at his father for approval.

"Yes, that's the word. Very good. Never be afraid to use good vocabulary."

"Yes, sir."

Matthew took a bite of peas as conversation temporarily ceased. "Classes going well?"

Nathaniel nodded as he ate without looking up. "Fine." He hoped his father wouldn't remember the chemistry test.

"And the Advanced Chemistry test? When? Yesterday?"

"Hard—I mean, difficult."

"I'm sure you did well, as usual."

Nathaniel continued staring at his food as he ate.

Attention to eating brought on another brief pause. The only sounds were the sounds of gentle, infrequent tapping of silverware against dinnerware.

"Sarah Elizabeth, how are you progressing in French?" Matthew asked without looking at her.

The fifteen-year-old stopped eating. "I got a B minus on the last test," she said with hesitant pride. The subject was difficult for her. She didn't have her brother's academic talent.

"Very good, dear," Miriam said sincerely.

Matthew put his fork down and drank some tea. He lightly dabbed his mouth with his napkin and nodded at the same time. "True. That is an improvement," he said. "But do you think you could have done better?"

Sarah Elizabeth stared at her plate and pushed some peas with her fork. She struggled to compose her answer so as not to elicit more comments from her father. Presenting an excuse, she had learned, never worked. "I should have studied the irregular verbs more."

"And why didn't you study them?" He looked at her. His tone was soft but with unmistakable authority.

"I was sure that I knew them, but when I got the test, they all got mixed up in my head."

"They all got mixed up or *you* mixed them up?"

Sarah Elizabeth wanted to sigh but knew that would be disrespectful. "I don't know, Daddy. I just couldn't remember them when it was time for the test."

"Well, then, before exams, Miriam, maybe you should quiz her on the material. Just for an extra boost."

Miriam looked sympathetically at her daughter. "Of course. We'll work on it. With a little help, you'll end the year with a solid B." She smiled encouragement at Sarah Elizabeth.

"Nothing wrong with a solid A either," Matthew rebutted. "Right, Nathaniel?"

Nathaniel felt sorry for his sister. He didn't want to betray her, but he knew that his father expected him to agree with him. "I think you'll do great, sis."

"Mediocrity is not an option," Matthew injected, pointing with his fork at no one in particular. "Always strive for your best.

Always. Both of you. Now, Miriam, how was your day?" Matthew asked, stabbing a morsel of roast with his fork.

"We had a communion committee meeting this morning," she said, glancing at Sarah Elizabeth as she spoke. "We set up the roster for baking bread and buying everything, preparing. It's all taken care of for the summer months. It went smoothly."

"Excellent. That's good to hear." He chewed the beef, savoring the flavor. "Delicious roast, dear."

Miriam smiled. "Thank you, Matthew." She stole another glance at Sarah Elizabeth.

They continued eating with Matthew directing the topics of conversation.

An hour later Matthew was in his study. when the phone rang.

"Is this Reverend Winslow?"

"Yes. Who's this?"

"I just want you to know that if anybody is going to hell for the way they live their life, it's going to be you. The way you sit in judgment of other people is despicable. What makes you so much holier than anybody else?" The person hung up.

Matthew put down the phone. He thought about calling the police, but the caller made no threats. Still, he made a note of the date and time of the call. Next he logged onto his email address at the church and found dozens of messages. He began opening them.

"Reverend, thank you for being so strong and a loving pastor."

"Matthew, great press conference. I support you all the way."

"Reverend Winslow, I saw you on TV tonight. You spoke so eloquently about such a difficult topic."

He read for nearly fifteen minutes before coming to the last one. He counted them. Fifty-seven to one phone call. He wished he had time to answer them all. He'd do that generally in his sermon on Sunday. He sat back in his leather executive chair. It would not have mattered if the numbers were reversed. He was doing God's work and for that he felt very good.

"Are you feeling better?" Miriam asked as she rinsed a glass and handed it to Sarah Elizabeth.

"I'm fine now, Mom."

"Good." She put a glass in the dishwasher. "Let's work on your French every night between now and your exam next week. Then maybe it won't seem so overwhelming."

"Sure. Okay," she said as she took a plate and put it in the dish-washer.

They finished loading the dishwasher and other straightening without talking. When it was all done, Miriam closed the kitchen door and hugged her daughter.

"Your father only wants the best for you and for you to do your best," she whispered.

Sarah Elizabeth said nothing for a moment as she stood slump-shouldered. "I try, Mom. I really do try," she said softly with a sigh of defeat, willing back any tears.

Miriam released the embrace but still held her daughter by the shoulders. "I know you do, sweetheart. And when you do, you don't need to feel bad. Okay?"

Sarah Elizabeth looked down. "Okay."

"Now, do you want me to call any French words out to you now or later?"

"We got some new vocabulary today. Let me study it a while and then later?" she asked.

"Whenever you want."

"Thanks, Mom." Her mother hugged her again before she went upstairs.

* * *

Nathaniel sat at his desk, staring at his open history book. He was trying to read, but the words meant nothing. His mind was spinning—first, him and Jason on his bed, then the chemistry test. Why was this happening to him? He felt like the world was caving in on him. He rested his elbows on his desk and buried his face in his hands. He wanted to run away, scream. What if his father found out about any of this?

Suddenly, his computer signaled a new email. He clicked the icon. From Jason. For a moment he froze. He told himself to simply delete it. Not even open it. Pretend he never saw it. But something else inside him—something deeply hidden and desperate—told him to read it. He clicked on it.

"hey nate...just want to say about the other night...well, I'm sorry... please don't hate me...jas"

Nathaniel stared at the screen. He read it, again. And again. Over and over. He wanted to delete it, but he couldn't. He just kept on reading it. "...please don't hate me...." The words stung.

He rested his fingers on the keyboard, ready to type. What could he say? He stared at the screen. There was only one thing he could say.

"jas...sorry...i'm not like that...nate"

The thought shot through his mind to add "...please don't hate me...." But he couldn't bring himself to say it.

Suddenly, images burst into his mind—Jason lying on his bed, shirtless, his hairy, muscular legs, his navel— Nathaniel realized he was getting hard. He squeezed his eyes closed. What was wrong with him?

He reached across his desk and picked up his Bible and opened it to Psalm 23 and read it over and over, then closed his eyes and repeated it again in a soft whisper. After the third repetition he reached over to his keyboard and pressed "Send."

* * *

102

Miriam lay perfectly still on her back as Matthew kissed her. Unbuttoning her nightgown he fondled her left breast and tonight her nipple. Pulling up her nightgown, exposing her, he lay on top of her and entered her and began thrusting. Miriam remained still, her arms merely resting over his shoulders. With complete lack of emotion she waited while he plunged into her again and again. Finally and gratefully, he finished and withdrew.

"Thank you, God, for this Holy Act and for my husband," she whispered.

As always he patted her hand and rolled onto his side away from her. Miriam sat up and pulled her nightgown down to her ankles. Taking the edge of the sheet she covered herself as she lay back down with her back to Matthew. She knew he would want to have sex tonight after his big appearance on the news, his letter to the editor and leading the other churches in this campaign. To be sure, he was pleased with himself, she thought.

With as little motion as she could she reached down and gathered her nightgown between her legs to dry herself. She hoped for sleep. However, she couldn't help but worry about Nathaniel. Again that morning he had been distant at breakfast, even coming downstairs after Sarah Elizabeth. So unlike him. Something was troubling him. She could feel it.

CHAPTER SIX

FRIDAY—MAY 15

Miriam listened for Matthew's car to back out of the driveway. She then tuned her ears to the stairs and heard Nathaniel's heavy descending steps, as usual before Sarah Elizabeth.

"Hi, sweetie," she said as he gave her a briefer than usual hug.

"Hey, Mom." He went to the refrigerator and poured a glass of juice.

"Eggs? Oatmeal? Both?"

Nathaniel hesitated. "I'm not all that hungry. Maybe just some toast." He drank several gulps of juice.

Miriam looked at him. Third morning in a row, she thought. So unlike him. He was always hungry. "That's not going to be enough to get you through the morning, is it?"

He half smiled. "Okay. Oatmeal."

She went to the stove and spooned out a bowl full as he sat down at the table. She had to at least ask. "Everything okay?" She sprinkled on brown sugar and raisins.

Nathaniel didn't answer right away. "Sure. Fine." He stared at the juice glass. "Had an Advanced Chemistry test Wednesday." He drank more juice. "It was really hard. I don't think I did so well on it."

This was the first time Miriam had ever heard him say anything about a test being difficult or not doing well. "Have you told your father?"

"No."

Miriam wished she hadn't asked the question because his answer was immediate, definite and even. Automatic, she supposed. As was his tone.

She placed the oatmeal in front of him and at the same time rested her hand on his shoulder for a moment, then sat down at the table opposite him.

"I've just got my mind on the game tomorrow. It's a big one," he said, then added, "an important one."

"I know. I'm looking forward to it." She watched him eat, but the entire time he kept his eyes on the oatmeal. "Maybe you did better than you think on the test. I'd wait until you get it back before worrying about it."

Nathaniel blew on a spoonful of the hot cereal. "I guess. We'll see," he agreed, but he didn't sound convinced. He took several more bites, focusing solely on his breakfast.

Something was wrong. "I guess Martha'll be at the game tomorrow?" she asked, thinking that was the problem. A spat, maybe?

He nodded as he drank some milk and continued eating. "Oh, for sure." Just then they heard Sarah Elizabeth coming down the stairs. Miriam reached over and put her hand on his arm. "I love you," she said softly. She stood up and kissed the top of his head. "And if," she began uncertain if should say this, "well, I'm here." She halted. "If you need a sounding board."

He took in another spoonful of oatmeal, still not looking at her. "Thanks, Mom." Then, hesitated, too. "I love you, too," he said, just as his sister came into the kitchen.

While Nathaniel finished his oatmeal and Sarah Elizabeth ate a small amount to please her mother, the conversation centered around the fact that her math teacher, Mrs. Grayson, was pregnant and would not be returning the following year to teach. "She is a great teacher," she said between bites. "I wanted her next year. She teaches juniors, too, and we all want to be in her class again."

Miriam listened but kept a watchful eye on her son who had little to say. As always, from the kitchen window she watched them drive off. "God, please watch over him." Then she realized what she had said. "Them," she whispered. "I meant 'them.'"

In his office at the church Matthew scrolled through the additional emails he had received since the ones he'd read the night before. Several names he did not recognize. When he opened them, most were from supportive people but not members of his church. A few judged him. He shook his head in frustration. How could they be so wrong?

After the last one he cleared the screen and opened a new Word document. He typed in the title: "An Abomination to God." Then the text for the day: "Leviticus 18:22. If a man lies with a male as with a woman both of them have committed an abomination." He nodded. This was going to be one of those sermons where he would need very few notes. Just topics. First off, talk about what's going on in the rest of the country and, for that matter, in the world—other countries sanctioning same sex marriages. The horrific homosexual pornography on the internet. Might as well include all pornography, he thought as he typed. AIDS—the epidemic that those people have brought to the world and have spread to normal people. Yes, he thought to himself. Build it up to the world level and then bring all of it right back here to Elmsborough, North Carolina. He thought of the two men at the hospital. AIDS is here, too. They even have the nerve to ask for donations to help pay for caring for those with the disease. He read the list of topics, again. Yes, this would be a very easy sermon.

He wrote a quick email to the secretary with his title and the scripture for the bulletin and the digital sign out front. He picked up the newspaper. Finally, that idiotic series was done. He turned to the editorial page and the letters from readers. He saw several from other pastors, all supporting him. "Well written," he muttered to himself. He made a mental note to email them his appreciation. There were three from people whom he did not know. Maybe this would be a chance to grow membership. That was another important reason for him to have taken the lead in this. Then he read the letters from the two who opposed his view. "Liberals. Misguided liberals. God, forgive them," he prayed. That was all right. Let them send in all the disagreements that they wanted to. He knew that God approved of what he was doing. That was all he needed to know. It was the right thing. It was written in God's holy word.

Yes, the time was right for broadcasting the Sunday service and reaching an even broader audience. He would get that off the ground and running well before Nathaniel took over as the lead pastor. And with the way technology was advancing, that should not be a problem whatsoever.

Matthew leaned back in his executive leather chair. Yes, this epidemic was here, and he was sorry about it, but it was happening at just the right time.

After leaving Martha at her class, Nathaniel rushed without running down the hall to chemistry class. He scarcely got inside the door when the bell sounded. He went to his desk, greeting his friends with high fives and fist bumps but without much enthusiasm. His stomach was knotted knowing that he would have to face Mr. Cheshire at some point and today would probably be the day. It all depended on whether or not he had graded the tests yet, and with exams next week, he most likely had.

As Nathaniel sat down and looked to the front of the room, he saw Mr. Cheshire beginning to return the tests. The tension in his stomach grew. Nathaniel kept his eyes down, avoiding his teacher's. When he put his test on his desk and moved on, Nathaniel wanted to evaporate. He could see through the folded paper that there were a lot of red marks. He put his hand over it so no one else could see the spillage of red ink. He unfolded his paper with as much secrecy as he could without being obvious. When he saw his grade, his heart fell. The fifty-one in red at the top of the page glared at him like a death sentence. Mr. Cheshire's note below wrenched his insides even more. "Please see me after class."

Nathaniel listened intently as Mr. Cheshire went over the test. He understood every single answer—now. He paid close attention as he reviewed for the exam, because he wanted his teacher to see his earnest attempt to excel, to make up for this—this disaster.

After class Nathaniel took his time packing up his books. Thankfully the room had cleared quickly. He walked up the aisle to Mr. Cheshire who was standing behind his desk. He crossed his arms over his sizeable stomach.

"Nathaniel," he began, "I was very surprised at your test. That's quite a drop from your usual A. Did you forget about the test?"

Shaking his head slowly, Nathaniel wanted to avoid eye contact, but his father had told him never to do that. "No, sir. I studied. I guess I should be ashamed to admit that. But I did. I suppose I've just got tomorrow's game on my mind."

"That's understandable, but sports has never interfered with your studies before, has it?"

Nathaniel forced himself not to look down. "No, sir." He had to think of something logical to say. "I guess it's part of being a senior. Last year. Last baseball game with my friends. We're all so close. It's going to be hard to leave." He hoped that he was convincing.

Mr. Cheshire's expression did not change. "I did some averaging. This grade has brought your average down to a B for this grading period. A good exam grade will salvage that for the year. I'd hate to see that perfect A average dip."

"It won't, I promise, Mr. Cheshire. And thank you for talking with me."

"Okay. If I can help you, let me know."

"Thanks."

Once Nathaniel was out the door he rushed down the hall toward the cafeteria. He would make an A on the final exam. He knew it. Mainly because he knew that he wasn't going to study with Jason, he thought to himself as he entered the cafeteria and looked for Martha and their friends in their usual place. Winding his way through the tables, he put on a broad smile for everyone. No need to tell anyone anything. His grades were private. He just hoped that Mr. Cheshire wouldn't cross paths with his father and tell him. Please, God, don't let that happen.

That afternoon at baseball practice Nathaniel could tell that Jason kept looking his way, as if he was trying to catch his eye, trying to speak to him but needing some kind of recognition or sign that it was okay to do so. Nathaniel purposely ignored him. He felt awkward. He didn't like having to be on guard. Maybe he should just tell him he wasn't going to commit any sin with him. He wasn't going to report him either. Although if his father found out that he knew someone like that in school and he didn't report it— He had to stop thinking about it. He would avoid being alone with Jason. And when they were with others, he'd be civil but not encouraging.

Practice was easy, just drills, easy cardio and batting. "Stay loose," Coach Stansbury said. Afterwards, he told the team to get a good night's sleep.

"Everyone in bed by ten," he ordered them as they sat in the locker room. "If anyone can beat this team tomorrow, it's you guys. But you've got to come out ready and believe in yourselves. You have all the skills. Every single one of you. Keep your wits about you. You'll be fine." The team was silent. He nodded. "Okay, let's pray." All of them bowed their heads. "Father, thank you for healthy minds and bodies, for the opportunity and ability to play ball and be athletic. Thank you for keeping us all in shape for this competition. Always help us, no matter the outcome tomorrow, to remember what's important in life—your son, Christ Jesus. Amen."

"Amen" chorused the team.

"Okay, showers. Go home. To bed early," coach said as he exited the locker room.

Nathaniel went directly to his locker and engaged Andrew Perryman in conversation just in case Jason came over to him. He took a quick shower, dressed and walked out the door without ever seeing Jason. Probably still in the shower at the far end. Maybe even waiting for him. He pushed open the gym door and started for the parking lot where he saw that Sarah Elizabeth was already sitting in his car, waiting for him.

"Nate."

Jason's voice caught him off guard. He turned and saw him still dressed in his practice uniform. He was sitting on a bench changing his shoes. He had left without taking a shower. "How'd you do on the chem test?" He finished tying his shoe, stood up and heaved his gym bag onto his shoulder.

Nathaniel did not even consider telling him the truth. He knew it was wrong to lie, but the truth in this case would be far worse. "I got a B." His tone was flat. He turned and continued walking toward his car.

"So did I." Jason started walking with him. "Look," he began after being sure no one was nearby. "I'm sorry, uh, about the other night. At my house."

Nathaniel stopped but didn't turn toward him. He just stared toward the parking lot. He wanted to be mad. He wanted to draw back and punch him in his face—hard, as hard as he could possibly drive his fist. Break his nose or give him a black eye. It didn't matter. Anything. Just hit him and maybe all this—this whatever it was—would go away.

"I didn't mean to cross the line," Jason finished. "I hope, I mean, I don't want to lose you—" He stopped. "I don't want to lose you as a friend." He hesitated. "It won't happen, again."

When he did turn and look at him, Nathaniel knew that hitting him wasn't possible. Yet, frustration coiled inside of him. Somewhere inside of him, he heard himself saying that it was okay, not to worry. He wanted to say those words, but he knew he shouldn't.

"I think, uh, maybe from now on, for exams, I need to study, uh, on my own." He heard himself stammer. He was doing the right thing. He knew it. There was no doubt in his mind. The Bible, his father, God—the answer was all around him. Even though he had stumbled over his words, he felt stronger for having said it. He was certain. Still he wanted to leave, to be away from him. He wasn't afraid, but he needed to get away. He started walking toward his car. Jason walked along with him.

"Okay. Sure. No problem."

Nathaniel tried to discern if he sounded hurt. A clue.

"But, if you change your mind," he began. He said it slower than usual. The rest of his sentence was softer, secretive, something just between the two of them. "—and I hope you will," he paused before finishing, "you know how to find me." He started veering off toward his car. "See you tomorrow."

Nathaniel responded simply and blandly, desperate to hide any feeling. "Tomorrow." He walked toward his own car while Jason's words— *And I hope you will*—echoed in his mind. He got in and drove without speaking to his sister, those five words reverberating in his mind.

"What's wrong with you?" he finally heard her ask. She'd been staring at him.

Nathaniel realized his silence. "Huh? Nothing."

She eyed him even more deliberately. "Uh, not buying it."

Irritated, Nathaniel fought his desire to tell her to mind her own business. But it wasn't her fault. He glanced over at her. For an instant, he thought of entrusting her with his confusion. But it evaporated as soon as it appeared. What was he thinking? There was nothing to share. Nothing.

"Sorry. I'm just thinking about the game tomorrow." Hopefully, she would believe him.

Sarah Elizabeth's silence made him fear that she sensed something. That was all he needed right now—for her to think something was wrong and tell Mom, or worse, Dad.

"You know," he said as jovially as he could. "The big game. Tomorrow. Our school. Baseball." He reached over and gave her playful nudge on the arm.

"Yeah, right. Stop it."

"Senior Day. Last game. Got to win. Cheering fans. Cheering sisters."

"We're not Catholics," she said.

He grinned. "Very funny." Then added, "For a sophomore. Very clever. I think you should tell that one at dinner tonight."

Sarah Elizabeth looked at him with a sarcastic sneer, then turned to look out the window.

"Tell Mom I'm going to the batting cages," he said as he drove into the driveway. "I'll be back in plenty of time for dinner."

Sarah Elizabeth got out of the car. "Okay, but you better not be late."

"Promise." He forced a smile and carefully backed out once she closed the door. Nathaniel gripped the steering wheel, the muscles in his forearm flexing rigid. *And I hope you will.* He tried to ignore the sound of Jason's voice, but it was there, like a battering ram in his head, relentless. He had to keep from thinking about him. He had to focus on Martha. He had to focus on anything else.

He looked at his watch. Ten minutes from the cages. He would need fifteen to get back home with rush hour traffic. Fifteen for batting. He just hoped that there wasn't a crowd.

The sign for the batting cages was visible from the far end of the block. Nathaniel surveyed the number of cars. Only seven. He hoped he wouldn't have to rotate with anyone, but that would be better than waiting. He parked, grabbed his bat from the back of his Cherokee and went inside. The man at the counter took his money and gave him four tokens. The sound of metal bats against baseballs and softballs rang in the hallway that led to the large, high-ceiling room. Once inside he saw that one hitter was just exiting a cage with a machine that threw at the speed he wanted. No one else was nearby.

Nathaniel entered the cage. After a few practice swings and arm and shoulder stretches, he dropped in the first token and took his stance in the batter's box. Even before the balls were flung from the machine, he had them in his sight, just as he would with a live pitcher. Over and over he swung at the balls. Some were line drives. Others were fly balls. A few he was sure were over the fence. A couple were pop ups. All, however, went into the netting that surrounded the cages before dropping with dull thuds onto the planks and rolling back toward the collection gutters. He finished the first twenty balls and, not wanting to break his rhythm, put in a token for the second round. Again, the machine hurled twenty balls toward him. The third token. Twenty more. Fourth token. A total of eighty. Almost robot like. Mechanical for almost thirty minutes. Anything to keep him from thinking.

When the red light went out after the final set of balls, Nathaniel realized how hard he was breathing. His t-shirt was soaked. As he turned to exit the cage, he noticed that several people seemed to be watching him. He ducked his head at the gate and walked through the tunnel to the lobby and drove home, Jason's words still haunting him.

"And, God, we thank you for bringing these children through another week of school," Matthew prayed with the family that night in the upstairs hallway. "For the gift of education, especially such a fine Christian education, surrounded by your spirit every minute in every classroom."

Miriam felt the cool dampness of Nathaniel's hand. She half opened her eyes and looked at him. Did he have a fever? He seemed fine. He ate well at dinner. Still, he wasn't the same. Something was different.

She closed her eyes and gently rubbed the back of his hand with her thumb. She felt him return the gesture. Maybe he was honestly feeling pressure about the game tomorrow. But he had never seemed nervous about games before. He had more confidence than that. She was afraid it might be the chemistry test and he knew how disappointed Matthew would be if he hadn't done well. More likely that was the issue. But he had never struggled in any subject. Maybe sometime tomorrow morning she would have a chance to talk with him.

"And, God, grant us all the courage of our convictions—to speak out when something is against you, to try and right the wrong that is so clearly before us in your holy word."

Sarah Elizabeth also noticed that her brother's hand was cold and wet. The idea swept quickly through her mind that he and Martha were getting friendlier than was allowed, like she and Mike or, like she wished she and Mike would be. No, that wasn't it. She was sure. Nathaniel had said it was the game. She would just endure the clammy hand for now. It wouldn't last long. At least she was over her period for this month.

"Miriam," Matthew said.

"Dear Father, thank you for this family. Guide us all to do our best, to be loving and caring to everyone."

"Nathaniel."

"Holy Father, thank you for good health and for family, for keeping us safe. Watch over all students as we begin exams next week."

"Sarah Elizabeth."

"Dear God, thank you for family, for school, for friends. Help us all to get along better and make the world a better place."

"Father, hear these prayers. Keep us safe through this and all nights, Holy God. Bring us together in the glorious day of tomorrow, rested, strong, ready to do your will as you have given us in your holy word. Amen."

The other three Winslows repeated the "Amen" and began telling each other good night. Miriam hugged Nathaniel an extra long time and whispered that she loved him.

In their bedroom she wanted to ask Matthew if he had noticed anything but didn't want him to question Nathaniel.

"I think Nathaniel must be a little nervous about the game."

"Why would you say that?" he asked.

"Well, he just seems a little preoccupied the last day or two. It's nothing, I'm sure."

Matthew stopped and faced her. He spoke with a distinct edge of exasperation. "Miriam, Nathaniel is eighteen. He's going to college in three months. He's not your little boy anymore. He's a man. He's not going to cling to your skirt forever. You have to accept that. 'When I was a child, I spoke like a child, I thought like a child, I reasoned like a child; when I became a man, I gave up childish ways.' I Corinthians 13:11. This is God's way, Miriam. So there's no need for you to say anything to him about his preoccupation, as you put it." He turned and walked into his closet to undress.

Miriam accepted her dismissal as she was expected to do. She finished folding the comforter, hung it on the rack and stacked the shams on the chest next to it. She went into the bathroom and began getting ready for bed. She knew she would have difficulty sleeping.

Wearing his sleeping boxers and a t-shirt, Nathaniel sat on the side of his bed holding his Bible, trying to decide what to read. After only a moment he placed the book on the night stand and recited Psalm 23. When he finished he closed his eyes. "I will fear no evil," he whispered to himself. "Please, God, take this demon out of me. Make me pure. Take all abomination out of me. Wash those thoughts from my mind." He squeezed his fists tightly, his nails digging into his soft palms. He opened his eyes and lay down. He reached over and turned off the lamp. In the darkness all he could see was Jason's bare chest. *And I hope you will* echoed in the background.

Nathaniel turned on the lamp, got out up and went into his bathroom. From the closet he retrieved a towel and spread it across the bottom sheet on the middle of his bed. He lay down again. All of the events of the last two days ricocheted in his mind like a pinball machine. He turned onto his side, trying to fall asleep, but nothing. His mind was too wracked. Jason. The grade on his chemistry test. Martha. Martha was his only hope—other than God. He closed his eyes and prayed some more.

CHAPTER SEVEN

SATURDAY—MAY 16

Nathaniel sat with his mother and sister at the kitchen table, waiting on Matthew. Sarah Elizabeth was talking about who she was going to sit with at the game. Nathaniel only pretended to listen, with no thought of teasing his sister. When they heard Matthew coming down the stairs, Sarah Elizabeth stopped talking.

"Good morning, all," Matthew said cheerfully as he entered the kitchen and eyed the usual Saturday morning special breakfast of pancakes and bacon.

Miriam got up to pour his coffee. "Good morning, Matthew."

"Morning, Dad."

"Hi, Dad," Nathaniel said.

Matthew sat down and put his napkin in his lap. "Ready for today?" he asked Nathaniel, placing his elbows on the table. "Sleep well?"

"Yes, sir," Nathaniel said, knowing in his heart that he was lying. He'd scarcely slept more than four hours.

"Sleep is very key," Matthew said as Miriam sat back down. "Let's bless our breakfast. Holy God, bless this meal and this family.

Guide us today through our every moment, keeping us safe and knowing how to follow your will found in the holy scriptures. May the baseball game this afternoon be a fun time for all. Help Nathaniel to play his best in this his last game." A renewed wave of tightness wafted through Nathaniel. "Show us all the way to be your servants. Amen."

"Amen," they all repeated.

"What time do you have to be at the field?" Matthew asked, passing the platter of pancakes and bacon.

"Noon," Nathaniel answered, trying to sound confident as well as calm. Even though he had no appetite, he took four pancakes and three strips of bacon. "Coach wants us to have a leisurely warm-up." He poured syrup on his pancakes and passed it to Sara Elizabeth.

"Yes, indeed. It is a great day and will be even greater when we beat Saint Paul's this afternoon." Everyone continued eating while he offered comments between bites. "Since they beat us in basketball, it would feel good to take them down today." He picked up a strip of bacon and bit off one fourth of it. "And a great way to end the school year."

Nathaniel finished his meal but did not request more as he usually did on a game day. "May I be excused?"

"What? Just four pancakes?" Matthew asked with surprise.

"I don't want to get too full," he answered, ready to rise from his chair. "We're having some food a few hours before the game since it's not until four."

"Okay. Okay, go rest up." Matthew waved him off lightly.

Nathaniel put his dishes in the sink. When he leaned down to kiss his mother on his way out of the kitchen, she patted his hand on her shoulder. He hoped she wasn't worrying about him, that he had been masking his emotions well enough for her not to notice.

Upstairs he texted *Good morning* to Martha but got no reply. He tried to occupy his mind with studying but found himself only staring at the pages in his books. Every few minutes he looked at the clock next to his bed. Time was dragging by. He picked up his notebook of Bible verses and began reading the ones he had learned when his father started him on this practice at age six. The child-like printing took over his mind more than the scriptures. He remembered the Sunday afternoons of copying them and reciting them to his father before going outside to play. Twelve years ago. It seemed so long. He was happy then. School was fun. Church was fun. Then there were no problems. Now he was eighteen. An adult. A man. Three months from being in college, then divinity school and finally an associate pastor. And someday he would be the head of it all. Like his father. In charge. Why couldn't he be in charge now? In charge of his haunting, unsolvable problems. He looked up from the notebook and his gaze went toward his bathroom. The door was open. There on the floor was the towel from last night. The one that he had put across the bottom sheet. Soiled by his "spilled seed." With no barrier to stop it, his dream replayed in his mind. Jason on the bed, him touching his—

Nathaniel slammed shut the notebook and tossed it aside. He dropped to the floor and began doing pushups, counting softly aloud. As he neared sixty his pace slowed. At seventy-five sweat was beginning to bead on his forehead. At ninety he was forcing himself. His arms strained with each press back up to the starting position. Finally, at the one hundred mark, he lowered himself on his elbows so that his body was just inches from the floor. He held it as long as he could, his abs burning, until finally he dropped flat on the carpet and rolled onto his back, his chest heaving for oxygen.

When his breathing slowed, he turned and looked at the clock. Still, too much time to kill. He closed his eyes and sighed. He felt like an animal being preyed upon by some unknown monster, a monster that he could not see but most assuredly could feel, as if claws and talons clutched his throat. Nathaniel fisted his hands as he thought of Jason. *And I hope you will.*

Suddenly, he lurched from his prone position, drew his feet close to his butt, his knees toward the ceiling and began doing ab crunches. Short, quick. Just raising his shoulder blades off the floor, his finger tips touching his head behind his ears. He was not going to get caught like some helpless little boy being bullied by a bigger kid. He would fight it. He counted thirty and began spitting out short bursts of air with each crunch as his stomach muscles began to burn. At sixty-five he looked at the clock and wished he had noted the exact second he had begun. Must have been about a minute. That would be one a second. He had done that before. I can do this, he told himself. I can do anything—his father's words rang out in his head. I won't give in to Satan, he told himself. At one hundred-ten he glanced at the clock. Two minutes. He should be at one hundred twenty. He was losing. He sped up his pace. Some spittle came out with some of his bursts of air. Now his lungs were burning along with his abs. At one hundred fifty the clock registered three minutes. He had fallen even further behind. He tried to pick up the pace but knew he wouldn't make it. Besides, he needed to save his strength for the game. At two hundred he stopped. He didn't look at the clock. He didn't care about the pace. He cared about the game. "God, please let us win," he whispered between sucking air into his exhausted lungs. "Please." He closed his eyes and silently prayed, "Please don't punish me."

Matthew shaded his eyes against the warm May sunshine. From the edge of the home team dugout he watched as the players took their final warm ups and stretches on the field. He particularly eyed Nathaniel. What a legacy he was creating for the family at Holy Bible Fellowship and Academy. His son. He was so proud and thankful that his firstborn had been a boy. A smart, athletic, good-looking boy. He was definitely a lucky father. Thank you, God, he said silently, for this great gift.

"Afternoon, Reverend."

Matthew turned and saw Bill Young, the technical manager for the athletic department, coming toward him with a wireless microphone in his hand.

"Hello, Bill." They shook hands. "Can I use this to cheer the team on during the game?" he asked jovially as he took the microphone.

"If the opposing fans will let you," he said with a laugh. "We should be ready to go any time now. Have you seen the minister from Saint Paul's?"

"I just had a call from him. Should be here any minute."

Bill nodded and walked off to tend to other duties. As he did, the music teacher directed the school choir onto the field in preparation to sing the national anthem.

Just then Garret Hastings from the opposing school joined Matthew on the field.

"Matthew, so sorry to be late. Traffic backed up because of a fender bender," he said. He extended his hand.

"Not a problem. Good to see you." He turned as the lead umpire called his name and signaled they were ready to begin. "See. Right on time." He laughed as they walked toward home plate. Matthew turned on the microphone.

"Good afternoon to you all," his voice echoed through the speakers. "What a glorious day the Lord has given us for this game." The crowd applauded. "And what a glorious opportunity to come together in healthy competition in the name of our savior. Even though there are two teams competing here today, we are all on the same team. God's team." A muffled, imperfect unison of "Amen" came from the people. Matthew decided to say what all should have said. "Praise God." A more structured repetition of the two words wafted over the field. "I want to welcome my friend and fellow follower of Christ, Reverend Garret Hastings from Saint Paul's who will lead us in prayer." He handed the microphone to the other minister who was greeted with polite applause.

Garret Hastings was a younger man with a moustache that Matthew did not approve of. However, the few times he'd heard

121

him pray and preach, he found his message to be worthwhile and effective. "Please stand and pray with me. Father God, thank you for these two schools where your truth can be heard daily. Thank you for healthy bodies and minds and souls of the members of these teams and coaching staffs. Let us all enjoy this outing and leave here reveling in your greatness which has made all of this possible in the first place. In Jesus name we pray. Amen."

Again, "Amen" echoed audibly across the field. Then the music teacher raised her hands and the thirty voices sang the national anthem as everyone turned and faced the American and the Christian flags just behind center field fence. When it was over, Matthew shook hands with Garret Hastings and both ministers strode toward their seats as the Disciples took the field. The Holy Bible side of the small stadium erupted in applause and cheering.

Matthew took his seat with his three associate pastors—Richard Newland, Harry Borkin and Williams Josephs. Miriam and the other three wives sat together in a group behind them.

Richard Newland turned toward Matthew so that no one else could hear what he was about to say amid the crowd noise. "Garret didn't seem all that prepared, did he?"

"I noticed that, too," Matthew responded as he applauded. "I hope those rumors aren't true."

Richard nodded in agreement.

"Did you contact him about the meeting last Wednesday?"

"Yes," said Newland. "He declined."

Matthew said nothing but a look of mild disgust came across his face as he turned his attention to the game.

Nathaniel trotted to his spot around third base. He did a few vertical jumps to get the blood going, touched his toes for a full hamstring stretch, then pulled each foot to his butt to stretch his quads. The first batter for Saint Paul's walked toward the plate, stretching and taking simple practice swings. When Bill Young announced his name, the visitors in the small stadium stood and cheered.

Nathaniel readied himself. His eyes riveted on the batter. The first two pitches were balls. The batter swung at the third and hit a weak grounder to the short stop who scooped it up and threw to first in time for the out. The second batter swung at the first pitch and hit a short fly directly to Billy French at second. The third batter hit a one hopper to Nathaniel who threw easily to first for the out. A spurt of confidence coursed through him. As he jogged to the dugout, he glanced toward his father who was standing and applauding him. Then he saw Martha seated directly behind the dugout. She was smiling and watching him. He was going to be fine. He was normal, he told himself.

The first three of the Holy Bible batters made contact with the ball, but none made it to first base. In the second inning the Saint Paul's players all flied out. In the bottom of the second Nathaniel was first to bat. On the third pitch he managed to loop the ball over the third baseman for a single. The Disciples roared. However, the next three batters failed to advance him.

The game grew more exciting in the third inning when the number one player for Saint Paul's hit a solo homerun over the leftfield fence. Their fans went wild.

Both teams played intensely. The batters' swings were full tilt. The throws to get runners out were hard but not always on the mark, resulting in errors that saved the runner but not changing the score. The single run advantage lasted through the fourth, fifth and sixth innings.

In the top of the seventh and final inning, the team from Saint Paul's sent the top of their batting order to the plate. The first two got on base with singles. The third batter popped a high foul ball near the third base line which Nathaniel caught. On the first pitch the cleanup player hit a solid ball between the right and center fielders. The ball rolled all the way to the fence and died in the dirt. Jason got to it first. Andrew Perryman at first base was observing the runners. Seeing that the first two were going to score, he yelled to Jason to throw for third. Jason released the ball with all of his might. The batter stumbled as he turned second but was still trying to get to third. Jason's throw was dead on target to Nathaniel who was in perfect position to receive it and make the tag. The runner was out. Even so, the score was now three to nothing. The next batter hit a grounder to Billy French at second who threw him out at first. The Disciples had one last chance to change the outcome of this final game of the season.

"Okay, guys," Coach Stansbury said in the dugout. "You can do this. You're just as, no, you're more capable than they are. Eye on the ball. Just get hits. Don't need to hit homeruns. Just good solid hits. Now, let's do it." He put out his hand and they all stacked a hand on top of his and shouted, "Go, Disciples."

Nathaniel felt the closeness of his teammates' bodies. The sweaty smell. The dirt. He felt a hand on his shoulder. When the team separated, he saw that it was Jason.

"Go get 'em, Nate," he said reassuringly. He looked at Jason. For a split second, there was a knowing, a special connection between the two of them. Something no one else could see. Nathaniel felt it in his gut and immediately dismissed it. No. He wasn't like that. Then the rest of the team joined in as Nathaniel picked up his bat. "Come on, Nate....Swing for empty spots in the field...Show us how it's done....Let's go...."

The home crowd had begun cheering, urging the Disciples on in this last effort. Bill Young announced a new pitcher for Saint Paul's which brought a roar of support from them. Then the volume from the Disciples rose as Nathaniel stepped out of the dugout and walked toward home plate. He had played sports all his life. The noise didn't bother him, but other things were playing around in his mind. He told himself to focus. Watch the ball, Coach had said. He took a few practice swings and stepped to the plate. The cheering lessened but never stopped. He tapped his bat on the plate and took his stance. With his bat hovering over his right shoulder, he riveted his eyes on the pitcher who was glaring past him at the catcher. The windup. This was a new pitcher, likely not to be in the groove and too nervous to throw something too perfect. The delivery. Nathaniel liked the look of it. They wouldn't expect him to hit the first pitch, but this was right where he wanted it. He pulled his bat back just inches and swung, only to touch the hot humid air. Saint Paul's fans roared approval. The Disciples dismay turned in an instant to support for the next swing. The dance continued. Nathaniel readied himself. Touched plate. Took his stance. Stared. Windup. Throw. This one, too, looked to be heading for his favorite spot. He swung just at the precise moment but heard only the dull thud of the ball in the catcher's mitt. Again the crowd's reaction was an even mixture.

"O and two, batter," the umpire reminded.

Nathaniel took his stance and eyed the pitcher as he wound up. The ball seemed to leave the pitcher's hand in an odd way. Maybe it was a trick. Maybe a mistake—a mis-throw. It looked to be perfectly hittable. Nathaniel swung and, this time, the resulting sound was the solid ping of the metal bat against the baseball, sending it over the third baseman's head and down the left field line. The crowd roared, but Nathaniel didn't hear anything except his own breathing and his cleats digging into the dirt as he ran for first base. Coach Rudisill, the first base coach, was waving him on to second. As he turned and ran even harder, he saw that the left fielder was throwing the ball toward second. Nathaniel slid into the base in plenty of time.

The Holy Bible Fellowship crowd continued to show their approval. Nathaniel stood up and brushed the dust from his pants and hands as he caught his breath. He stepped on the bag, then moved toward third as Ted Wilson came to the plate. Got to keep the pitcher on his toes. Worry him. He took another step away from safety, then leaned forward with his arms dangling freely in front of his knees, watching the pitcher. Ted swung at the second pitch and popped it up directly to the second baseman for the out. Nathaniel tagged up again. The Saint Paul fans were on their feet screaming.

As Jason Daniels came to bat, Nathaniel tagged up, then moved a few steps away from second base, again leaning forward, arms hanging. Jason pulled his pant legs up to allow for his wide batting stance. In an instant, the image of him lying on his bed nearly naked flashed through Nathaniel's mind. The dark line of hair on his lower abs—

The ping of the ball hitting the bat jolted him back to the game. He saw the ball bounce just to the right of the pitcher's mound. A grounder, he told himself. He turned and began sprinting for third. He was only a few strides from the base when he saw the ball coming into the third baseman's glove. Instantly, he knew he should not have run. Trapped, he tried to reverse but lost his footing. The third baseman threw to the short stop who tagged him out. Now the lead runner was all the way over on first.

Naturally, the Saint Paul's fans cheered. Their team was one out away from a win. Nathaniel stood up but didn't bother to dust off his pants. He trotted across the infield to the dugout with his eyes riveted on the ground. The Holy Bible Fellowship fans politely applauded his effort, but he knew what he had done. He had made a crucial mistake. When he went into the dugout, he sat down. All of the team said, "Nice try, Nate" or "Don't worry about it," something to make him feel better. But he knew that he had probably blown their only chance. He leaned forward and buried his face in a towel.

After a few pitches Phillip Randolph hit the ball deep into left field. Nathaniel came to the dugout fence with all the others. Jason made it all the way to third, Phillip on second. Nathaniel's insides soured. If he hadn't made the error, if he hadn't run from second on Jason's hit, he would have scored and scored easily. As it was now, the Disciples had runners on second and third. Mark Jones came to bat. Please, God, let him get a good hit. But on the first pitch he popped the ball into right field for the final out. The game was over. Holy Bible had been shut out.

Matthew and the other ministers all stood and applauded the Disciples.

"I guess we'll be looking into hiring a new coach," William Josephs leaned over and said confidentially.

"Definitely," Matthew responded. "I'll plan on meeting with Fred Haskins after graduation. We can't have this kind of season another year."

"What was it? Three and eight?" Richard Newland asked.

"After today it's three and nine," Williams replied, raising his eyebrows.

"Definitely time to look around," Richard said.

Matthew battled his son's assessment of Coach Stansbury and Kenneth Ward's advice. The man had a family. Children. He would find another job, he reassured himself. Something in his area would open up.

"I'll do a confidential search to see who's out there," Harry Borkin said.

Matthew nodded as he called to Miriam and Sarah Elizabeth that it was time to leave.

As the Saint Paul's players jumped and high-fived each other in celebration, the Disciples lined up and waited for the traditional, obligatory handshake. Walking to the locker room with his teammates afterward, Nathaniel heard Jason's voice.

"Sorry I didn't get a better hit," he said to no one in particular.

Nathaniel didn't bother to turn. He knew it was his way of consoling him. Instead, he kept walking without turning around or speaking to anyone. The mood in the locker room was somber. Coach Stansbury came in and called the team together.

"You played a good game, guys." His voice was even, but neither his tone nor body language revealed defeat or disappointment. "The score doesn't mean they are better than you. On any given day, we could have gotten the breaks they did and the outcome would've been reversed. Don't beat yourselves up. Life's bigger than a baseball game." He got down on one knee. "Let's pray," he said and without waiting too long began. "Father God, we didn't score more runs than the other team. Help us to know we're still winners in your eyes and that your eyes are the eyes that count the most. Lift the disappointment from the shoulders of these players. Keep them proud, strong and able as they end this school year. In your name we pray. Amen."

The team muttered an unenthusiastic "Amen."

He stood up. "It's been a pleasure coaching you guys. You're a great team. See you at the banquet next Saturday. Good luck with exams. Now, hit the showers and leave your uniforms with Steve." He pointed to the team manager.

The team members moved slowly to their lockers. No one wanted to leave. No one wanted to face the students and parents who would be waiting outside. No one wanted to see the other team celebrating as their bus left the parking lot.

Nathaniel undressed and went to the shower. He didn't look around to avoid Jason. He went into the stall and pulled the curtain closed completely. He stood under the cool cascading water with his eyes closed. Over and over he saw himself leading from second base and then breaking to run, only to feel the tag of the short stop's glove on his arm. And each replay bore into him deeper than the time before. At one point he remembered Coach Stansbury's consoling words. However, he knew they did not apply to him. Everybody else paid attention to what was going on. They weren't thinking about how another guy on the team looked when he was lying next to him on a bed half-naked.

Outside in front of the gym, parents, students and other supporters from Holy Bible stood waiting to cheer the team as they exited, clearly dejected by the loss. Nathaniel saw Martha who greeted him with a broad smile and a quick, appropriate hug. But nowhere did he see his father. Without him, he knew it would be useless to look for his mother and Sarah Elizabeth. In that moment the weight of losing and his impact of his error compounded.

Nathaniel lay in bed that night, his blunder in the game replaying nonstop. He appreciated what Coach Stansbury had said, trying to bolster the team's spirit. No one really blamed anyone, least of all him. Every guy at some point in the locker room had told him he'd played a good game. But he knew the truth and he had cost his team the game.

He rolled over onto his other side, feeling the soft roughness of the towel underneath him. At the school party that night, he'd forced himself to smile some, trying to get into the spirit. Even though he was sure a lot of his friends were not happy with his error, nobody said anything about it or treated him any differently. He was still popular with everyone—athletes and non-athletes. He remembered what Martha had said about the game. That it didn't matter. She knew they were all disappointed, but God gave us disappointments now and then to see what we'd do with them, she told him. Nathaniel tried to let her words sink in, but the turmoil in his mind would not slow down long enough for reason to be heard. The only larger memory was his father's absence after the game, and worse, his not mentioning it when he got home, not even during prayer time.

He rolled over again and sighed out loud. No dreams, God, he thought. Not tonight. Please. Not tonight.

CHAPTER EIGHT

SUNDAY—MAY 17

"My hope is built on nothing less than Jesus' blood and righteousness; I dare not trust the sweetest frame, but wholly lean on Jesus' name...."

Nathaniel shifted his stance as he followed the words to the hymn on one of the giant screens. While Martha, standing on his right, sang the familiar hymn with her ringing soprano voice, he tried to concentrate on the words to the hymn. Seeing the topic of his father's sermon in the bulletin had unnerved him—"An Abomination to God." And to make matters worse he had spotted Jason sitting with his parents about fifteen rows up on the right hand side. He told himself he wasn't going to look at him. There was no reason to. He had to—*wanted* to devote all of his attention to Martha and, of course, his father's sermon.

"On Christ, the solid rock, I stand; all other ground is sinking sand. All other ground is sinking sand."

From the corner of her eye Miriam looked to her left past Martha to Nathaniel. She still ached for him—his last baseball game of high school a defeat. She had thought that the school party last night honoring the team would have boosted his spirits, but it obviously hadn't. She had cooked him his favorite breakfast, trying to cheer him up. He looked tired. She hoped that this wasn't going to weigh too heavily on him for too long. Final exams were coming up, but she knew that he would do just fine, as always. She looked back at verse two and to her right at Sarah Elizabeth who was obviously smiling at Mike Caviness sitting with his parents a few rows up on the left side.

"When darkness veils his lovely face...."

Matthew surveyed the congregation. The sanctuary appeared full. The ushers were scurrying around setting up folding seats for late arrivals. The capacity was 5000. They had come to hear him speak about this terrible thing that was invading Elmsborough and how God was on their side. And he was going to tell them.

"His oath, his covenant, his blood...."

Matthew sang out with his solid baritone voice. He looked at the three associates—seated on either side of him—each with his own role in the service. This was the place to be. He eyed the spots around the sanctuary where the television cameras might be placed in addition to the closed circuit ones. Not much to change. They would easily fit without too much distraction. He wished that they were here today. This was one of his more important sermons. This one was meant to be heard by more than just the people in this sanctuary. This one was meant for the world.

"On Christ, the solid rock, I stand; all other ground is sinking sand..." The music director conducted the organist, pianist, the instrumental ensemble and the choir to slow the tempo of the final phrase, and emphasize each note. "All other ground is sinking sand. Amen."

William Josephs came to the pulpit as the congregation sat down.

"The scripture for today is from the book of Leviticus, chapter eighteen." Reverend Josephs cleared his throat and began reading. "'And the Lord said to Moses....'"

Nathaniel commanded himself to breathe normally and look directly at Reverend Josephs. He could feel his body reacting to this.

His armpits dampened. Just get through this, he commanded himself. He could do it. He had to. He had done nothing wrong. Still, the words stung him. Nakedness. Wickedness. Then that part—a man lying with another man as with a woman. Abomination. Defile. Vomit out. Vomit out.

"This is the law of God," Reverend Josephs said finally and sat down.

As Matthew stood and walked up to the pulpit, the general lights on the congregation, the choir and the remainder of the stage dimmed slowly, leaving only him in the center of a pool of pure white light with no shadows cast. His face filled the giant screens on both sides of the stage.

He looked silently around the congregation, his eyes narrowed, steeled by determination. The sanctuary was thick with silence. He placed his hands on both sides of the pulpit and leaned forward. "'You shall not lie with a male as with a woman,'" his voice poured out with unmistakable firmness, "'it is an abomination.'" He continued to stare out at the people before him though they appeared only as shadowy bumps in the dimness. He straightened up, tall and authoritative. "'An abomination,'" he said deliberately. He paused yet again, for exaggerated emphasis. "I could easily end this sermon right now with just those words. For those words are enough. Those words leave no room or need for argument, no room or need for debate. They are the words of God and they are clear." He stopped and dramatically paused, slowly raising his pointed index finger for emphasis. "And God is clear. Unequivocally clear." He slowly lowered his hand. "As I'm sure you've either read in the newspaper or heard on television, in just over a month homosexual men and women will gather for what they call Gay Pride right here in downtown Elmsborough. They will march through our streets for all to see. They will have speakers delivering their message. They will have information booths. The mayor told me over the phone that this will be an educational opportunity for the community to learn how to get along with these people."

He stopped and looked out and shook his head. "To get along with these people." He paused again. "Our mayor wants us to learn to get along with people who are sinners and who flaunt that fact by celebrating what they call their 'Pride.' My fellow Christians, I have to tell you that I have a problem with that." He held up his Bible, high over his head. "And this is why. You heard Reverend Josephs just moments ago tell you why we should all have a problem with that." He held his Bible out. "These people take pride in sinning and they want to, according to the mayor, they want to educate us about their sinning. Well, maybe the mayor wants that kind of education for himself and his family and his children, maybe the city council wants that kind of education, but we don't because we believe in the Holy Word of God."

Many expressed "Amen" or applauded lightly in the cavernous worship hall.

Nathaniel felt warm. He wasn't going to take part in any rally downtown. This didn't affect him. Why should he have to worry about it? He shifted nervously and when he did, his upper arm brushed against Martha's. She responded by subtly pushing back with her arm. He smiled, welcoming the contact. He glanced across the sanctuary at Jason, hoping that he saw their exchange. But he wasn't looking. He was staring downward, downward at nothing.

"Unfortunately, their propaganda is everywhere, especially on the internet—an endless array of horrific homosexual pornography. Whatever happened to Christian values? What about the home and the young? I beg you to safeguard your children, especially the younger ones, so that they don't accidentally stumble on to something."

As Miriam listened to her husband, something inside of her became more and more unsettled. The memory of talking with those two men in the grocery store jumped up in her mind. They seemed so nice, so normal. Yet she knew she could never question Matthew. But, then, he was right. Of course. What he was saying was in the Bible. There was no denying it. She inwardly sighed and silently prayed that this Pride event would pass without too much fanfare and that things would get back to normal.

"And now there is a disease as a result of their sin. Yes, I'm talking about AIDS. Auto-Immune Deficiency Syndrome—meaning the body cannot fight off this virus. Meaning it's intended to take the life of its victim. Even with all the research for a cure, those people are still dying. We don't have to wonder if this is the wrath of God. His Holy Word says that man lying with man as a woman is an abomination. What a mess this sin has caused in our world. This 'gay' mess, this 'gay pride.'" Matthew shook his head in complete disbelief. "It is offensive to the English language. It is offensive to the human race." He paused again before leaning into the pulpit. "It is offensive to God."

The last three sentences struck Nathaniel. They came at him like wild pitches, one ball then the next, hurled directly at him. Again, he shifted in his seat as if trying to dodge his father's stinging words. Martha turned and smiled at him when he again brushed her arm.

"And while they continue to flaunt their lifestyle, they are not ashamed to ask for money, donations, to pay for the care of those who have their disease. That is also an abomination and it would seem to me an abomination to contribute to that cause, a cause which goes directly against God's Holy Word." Again, he held his Bible high into the air. "But God would also have us pray for these misguided ones. We must hate the sin and we must pray for the sinner."

Even though Nathaniel kept his eyes on his father, he began to pray in earnest for himself. He promised God that he was going to change. He would no longer keep those—those thoughts in his head. Whenever they happened he would change them, just like changing to a different track on a CD. Since baseball was over he would no longer be tempted to look at Jason and there would be no need to study with him. He was going to make all A's this final semester. Advanced Chemistry included. He was sure this was God's way of giving him a second chance. A chance to rededicate himself to serve God for the rest of his life. A chance to purify himself. God forgives. So he was asking God to forgive all the evil that had infected his mind. Yes, that was it. All this was like an infection. And now that he knew, that he had seen clearly, he could ask God to heal him. Maybe this was a test. Since he was going to Freedom Bible University in a few months with the intention of becoming a minister, maybe this was a test to see if he was ready to serve God and to lead others to God. His father was absolutely right. This was a sickness. An evil sickness. And with God's help he was going to heal himself, rid himself of this. God was too powerful not to lead him to overcome these feelings. He had given them to him as a test and now it was time to flush them away.

Martha crossed her legs and the movement brought Nathaniel out of his prayerful state. He turned and looked at her. She was pretty and he cared for her. Almost as much as he did for his family. That must mean that he was on his way to falling in love with her. Truly in love. And that love would grow and she would love him. When she met his glance, he smiled at her. He wanted to reach over and hold her hand but knew that wasn't allowed.

Nathaniel slowly took a deep breath and exhaled. Yes, he told himself. Everything was going to be just fine. God was in charge.

"And now, I invite you all to come forward as a promise to God. We're going to do this today and next Sunday as well. A promise to God to uphold his word and to show him and all others on the last weekend in June that we will not sit idly by and allow these evildoers to trample upon his word. Everyone who is a high school graduate and older, will stand along the parade route and show the city officials that you are against what they are condoning. That you are standing up for God and for what he has said in this almighty book. That you are praying for these people to repent of their sin. That you will be a Servant of God." He held out his Bible high with his left hand. His right arm he held out to welcome the congregants to make their way to the altar. The choir began softly singing "Just As

I Am." "The ushers will guide you so that the ministers at the altar or prayer leaders along the sides can lay hands on each and every one of you here today. I bid you come in the name of the Risen Lord."

The members who were ordained prayer leaders took their places all around the immense arena-style sanctuary as the congregation spilled into the aisles to receive their blessing.

Nathaniel looked at Martha, then at his mother. He leaned forward, ready to stand, as if there was no doubt that he—that they all—should go down to the altar to be blessed. This was his private renewal. A renewal between him and God. And now God was providing this laying on of hands. This blessing. All of them stood and moved into the aisle, then toward the altar.

Matthew had stopped speaking but stood and watched as his congregants slowly but steadily moved toward the front and other locations around the mammoth sanctuary. When he saw Nathaniel, Miriam and Sarah Elizabeth, and Martha, he came down to meet them at the altar and gave a special blessing to his wife and daughter while Martha received her blessing from Reverend Newland. First Matthew placed a hand on Miriam and Sarah Elizabeth at the same time and spoke to them together. Afterwards, he put a hand on each of Nathaniel's shoulders and pulled him close.

"God, guide this young servant. Make him strong and wise and courageous. Keep him safe. Teach him to be a leader so that one day he will bless others as I am blessing him today. Let his life be an example to those who would choose evil, those who would fall prey to lust and sin of the flesh." Matthew squeezed his shoulders and then patted them. "Amen."

As they took their seats Nathaniel looked across the sanctuary at Jason who was looking back at him. Quickly he jerked his eyes downward and focused on the back of the pew in front of him. He moved his arm so that it brushed against Martha's. He looked up at the people gathering around the altar, praying with the other ministers and the prayer leaders. They were right. Now he knew the truth about himself, about the test God had been giving him.

He bowed his head. God, thank you for healing me, for making me see that I am normal, for taking those thoughts away and replacing them with normal thoughts, the ones I'm supposed to have, the ones everyone else has. Everyone else except maybe Jason. He thought for a moment. He would pray for him. Pray that he could be rid of the evil inside of him, too. And God, help Jason to be normal, too. Take away this— He searched his mind. Take away this abomination from him. Make him see that he can be healed.

Just then the choir sang the final verse of "Just As I Am," but the organist continued to play softly. When the last person turned and walked up the aisle and the prayer leaders returned to their seats, Matthew stepped back into the pulpit, closed his eyes and raised his right hand.

"Father, God, we are committed to serve you. We have received your blessing. Make us better witnesses to you and your son. Make us strong in our faith, strong enough to offer healing to those in need of it. Amen."

Nathaniel had opened his eyes for just a moment and joined the congregants as everyone held up both of their arms, some swaying them from side to side, while his father prayed. He glanced at Jason, who was also looking at him. Again. Nathaniel closed his eyes but not before he noticeably leaned closer to Martha. He had to be subtle so he didn't know if Jason could see what he had done, but he hoped he did.

At the end of the prayer, the organist, pianist and brass ensemble immediately began playing a brief introduction to "Onward, Christian Soldiers." The congregation stood for the final hymn. Many raised their arms in praise to the Almighty as they sang.

"Lord, we thank you for this beautiful day in May. Flowers and blooms, green leaves on the trees, green grass—signs of your glory and majesty are everywhere. We thank you for our church, our congregation and for the direction you have given us to tackle this problem in our community. We thank you for that guidance and the strength you provide in us to carry it out. Thank you for this family, this nutritious meal so lovingly prepared. Bless Nathaniel and Sarah Elizabeth during this upcoming week of exams. Guide them as they prepare to do their very best and ultimately serve you. In your blessed son's name, Amen."

All of the Winslow family repeated the same, "Amen."

"Miriam, once again, this pork looks delicious," Matthew said as he sliced the meat on the platter. "And look, so tender."

"Yes, Sarah Elizabeth is responsible for that and the sauce. She cooked it in the slow cooker," Miriam said. "And it was on sale—two for one." She began passing around bowls of vegetables and rice.

"Well, very nice, Sarah Elizabeth." He passed a plate with generous portion to Nathaniel. "It's important for young ladies to know how to cook." He handed another plate to her. "I can't wait to taste this."

"Thanks, Dad. It wasn't very hard."

"Difficult," Matthew corrected without looking at her. "Better word."

Sarah Elizabeth forced a smile and looked down.

"Wow, this is good, sis," Nathaniel added as he chewed.

Miriam smiled at Sarah Elizabeth. "It is delicious," she complimented her daughter.

"Thank you all," Sarah Elizabeth said and nothing more.

"Well," Matthew began as he ate. "My sermon certainly must have touched a nerve with our congregation."

Nathaniel immediately felt tension in his body, but then decided there was no reason to feel any way but relaxed. He drank some iced tea and continued eating and listening.

"I received nothing but compliments from everyone who spoke to me." He gestured with his fork. "It just proves what I've said all along. People are just not willing to have this kind of thing in their midst without speaking out." He put his fork down and buttered a roll, then stabbed another bite of pork and put it in his mouth. "But enough about that. It's not a good topic to discuss over a delicious meal like this." Matthew chewed for a moment. "As is our custom prior to exams—just a reminder to everyone—that the rest of today and tomorrow afternoon and evening as well as every afternoon and evening on exam days are for solitary studying, prayer and reflection. No phoning, texting, emailing." Again, he pointed with his fork back and forth at Miriam and Sarah Elizabeth. "The only exception is tutoring with French."

Miriam tilted her head and smiled at her daughter. "I think a very good grade is definitely going to happen with French," she said with confidence.

"Thanks, Mom." Sarah Elizabeth forced yet another smile at her mother.

Matthew helped himself to another portion of pork from the platter. "Just delicious and so tender. Don't even need a knife to cut it."

As he did every Sunday afternoon, Matthew secluded himself in his study and read emails from congregants who complimented him on his sermon. Today's batch was the most he'd received in quite some time. From Lee Gardner, their neighbor down the street, "...just what we needed to hear...." From someone named Ronnie Lowe, "...so glad you're not afraid to call this as you see it...." From Shelia Chapman, "...we'll be there for the parade with signs...." On and on. Must be nearly a hundred, he thought proudly. And not a single person who didn't support what he was doing. And from the associate ministers—Richard Newland, "...should have preached to the whole city...." From Harry Borkin, "...most powerful sermon I've ever heard you or anybody preach...." From Williams Josephs, "...with people like you, Matthew, there's hope...." From Howard Carr,

"...Just ecstatic over your sermon today. Kenneth was right. We *are* fortunate to have you....."

Yes, he told himself, he was lighting a fire under this issue and not letting up. The community was going to know that The Reverend Matthew Winslow was a force to be reckoned with, especially those people on the city council and the mayor, not to mention the newspaper. Holy Bible Fellowship alone could be represented by at least 1500 demonstrators, maybe even 2000. This was going to generate plenty of publicity. This movement—Servants of God—was going to speak out for the purity of God's written word. The church would surely get more members and, therefore, more money. If all of this came off the way he planned, Kenneth Ward and the Coalition would definitely support televising Sunday services. He knew the three associates and Howard Carr and the Board of Trustees were in favor.

He looked at the large photograph of the front of the Holy Bible Fellowship with the sign in front with his name on it. Yes, life was good. And he knew his father and grandfather were smiling down on him.

Miriam had sent Sarah Elizabeth on to her room to begin studying, relieving her of her kitchen duties. She sensed that her daughter would rather have helped than study, but she made no protest.

Turning on the dishwasher, Miriam went into the family room and sat down alone—as was her custom on Sunday afternoons. Today, however, she was surprised to see that the entire newspaper was on the coffee table. Matthew always took the editorial and sections containing the news with him to his study, leaving the homemaking, fashion and cooking sections in the den. But today, for some reason, he had not taken any of it. Miriam had not been able to get away and buy yesterday's paper because of the game and the family being together all day. It was still in Matthew's study.

The last of the series on homosexuality was on Wednesday, but letters to the editor still appeared on Friday which she had read sitting in her car at the strip mall. The newspaper on the table seemed like something forbidden, not to be touched, certainly not to be caught reading what she wanted to read.

She listened for the sound of any movement in the house. Maybe she was being silly, she told herself. Still, she remembered how adamant he'd been about the family not reading the series or anything related. She looked toward the door, listening. Total silence. Quickly, she sat on the sofa and thumbed through the sections, found the editorials, slipped it out and turned to the letters on the last inside page. She scanned the headline blurbs of each letter. Five letters. She read each one quickly at the same time listening for anyone to come into the room.

"...Judgment is for God, not we mortals. That's in the Bible, too...."

"...I think it's great that our city officials are so broadminded and open to diversity...." "...My son is gay and I fully support him and his partner of twelve years. I couldn't ask for a better son-in-law. They love each other as much as my husband and I do. The real sins here are discrimination and bigotry, just to name two...." Miriam read the name—Maxine Shelton. A mother who bravely embraced her son and his "partner," Miriam thought as she glanced over the letter again. "...support...twelve years...." Two men loving each other. Were those two men in the grocery store "partners"? Did they love each other? Love, she thought.

She moved to the next one.

"...It's purely disgusting and revolting that people carry on like that...."

"...Those people should not be allowed to flaunt their life in our faces...."

One praised Reverend Matthew Winslow "...for his courage to speak out on behalf of all Christians." The letter was signed Alfred Mabe. She didn't recognize the name. He could be a member of the church. She had no idea.

Miriam closed the section and slipped it back inside the rest of the newspaper. Again, her exchange with the two men in the grocery store came to mind. She wondered if they would be at the event downtown. Would they march in the parade? Would they see her standing along the side of the street in protest? She thought of the irony. But why was she so drawn to read these letters and the series? Why was the word "love" foremost in her thoughts?

Sarah Elizabeth stood in her bathroom, the door closed, with a thick towel over her head, trying to muffle her voice.

"I can hardly hear you," Mike said.

"I'm not supposed to be on the phone," she whispered. "And I was just calling to tell you that. My father is making me study for exams," she said, then quickly added, "Nathaniel, too. It's like being in a prison until Thursday. We have to come straight home from school everyday."

"I'll see you before classes. And I can meet you and walk you to Nate's car," Mike said.

"Oh, sure. That'd be great. I just didn't want you to wonder why I wasn't answering the phone if you called. I meant to tell you yesterday at the game."

"Yeah, I'm glad you did. I would have thought you were dumping me."

"Not hardly," she said, feeling giddy.

"So, if you're not supposed to be doing this, we'd better hang up," Mike said. "I don't want you to get in trouble, or worse, get grounded."

"Me either."

"See you tomorrow."

"Okay," she whispered. "Bye."

She turned off her cell phone, took the towel from over her head and lightly fluffed her blond hair. She leaned closer to the mirror.

"Please, don't let that be a zit." She pressed and probed her chin with her fingernail and sighed. At least her period was over for another three or so weeks. "If Dad would only let me go on the pill." She sighed with exasperation. She opened her bathroom door, turned off the light and sat down to study. French verbs, she thought. What a pain.

Sarah Elizabeth studied diligently but decided that she could take what she labeled "Mike time" during the study lockdown, texting him once in the afternoon and again in the evening. But only briefly. She feared getting caught and losing privileges—not the way she wanted to begin her summer. And she especially didn't want her father to take away her cell phone for a month or longer. She thought of it as being disobedient, but certainly not breaking the commandment about honoring your father and mother.

"only 5 min," she nimbly texted Mike that night, "is ok, a break"

She had to spend extra time on French, asking her mother to quiz her on vocabulary, spelling, verb tenses, irregular verbs and idioms. I'm going to hold on to the B minus, she told herself. Maybe then Dad won't lecture me or put me down as much.

Nathaniel read Martha's instant message. IM-ing her was against his father's rules, but somehow it seemed a lesser wrong. Anyway, he was feeling somewhat emboldened after church—now that he had figured out his life and what was going on. He could protest at the parade because he knew it was wrong. Hate the sin, love and pray for the sinner. And what he had gone through was a phase, a test and he had hit a home run. He even felt like being bolder with Martha.

"cant wait to c u tomorrow," he typed.

"me2"

"meet u @ your locker & walk you 2 homeroom"

"next Sunday, well be graduates"

"think we can call ourselves college students now"

"really?"

"why not? we wont be in high school anymore"

"Ooo...like the way u think mister"

Nathaniel laughed, then thought about his role as a man and someday a husband. A little scary, he thought. But he'd get used to it.

"better go dont want to get caught"

"me2 need to study"

"cu tomorrow."

"K."

He thought for a moment. Should he write "Love ya"? That might be a little much, but it felt good to entertain the possibility.

"hugs," he typed.

"U2."

When would he tell Martha for the first time that he loved her? In college? On the quad there at Freedom? That would be pretty cool. He imagined them sitting in his Jeep Cherokee one night. Maybe in the fall. Cool crisp night. Harvest moon. The leaves all beautiful and crunchy underfoot. It occurred to him—maybe it was time for them to be a little more intimate. Not go all the way or even close to it. But more kissing, longer kisses, maybe even some open mouth kissing. Who knows? Maybe some touching. He smiled to himself. It would be okay. They were graduating. Done with high school. Going to college. They would save themselves until they got married—most assuredly. But maybe it was time for things to move to the next level. Maybe it was up to him to make that happen. It was what a guy was supposed to do. Take charge. And sometime soon—maybe this summer or next year when they got to Freedom— he would tell her he loved her.

And maybe during exams a five minute break with a few texts exchanges was acceptable. But only once at night after prayer time and before going to bed. Maybe that would cause him to dream about her. Not a bad plan, he thought with a smile. And he would spend extra time on chemistry. He had to make up for that fifty-one. He would review the questions on that test and know everything in that chapter. If his final average was on the border between an A and a B, he hoped Mr. Cheshire wouldn't penalize him because of just one test grade, especially if he did well on the exam. He would pour over his notes, labs and textbook everyday. I'll be ready for this exam on Thursday, he assured himself. I'm going to knock "Mr. Turkey" right off his feet.

That thought brought to mind Jason and his drawing of their teacher. Chinless Mr. Cheshire a.k.a. "Mr. Turkey."

It's okay, Nathaniel encouraged himself. Just think of Martha—holding her hand, kissing her. After Lynnette's party on Friday night, maybe he would be bolder, more intimate with her, be a little more in charge but also respectful. It didn't matter that Jason was going to Freedom, also. Sure, they would probably see each other once in a while. But Freedom was large. There were several dorms for freshmen guys, spread out over a large stretch of the campus. But none of that mattered. Not now. He and Martha were going to be closer, starting Friday. No more thoughts about Jason. No more messy dreams. Done. He was okay. Thank you, God, he thought. Thank you.

Later, when he went to bed, he considered not spreading the towel over the sheet. But what if he messed up the sheet and his mother saw it? Not worth it. Smoothing the towel out, he vowed that his new perspective was going to change that, too.

CHAPTER NINE

MONDAY—MAY 18

As she did every morning from her vantage point at the kitchen window, Miriam watched her children back out of the garage and drive down the street until they turned out of sight at the corner of Ferris Avenue. One more week, she thought. The final week of school. She began rinsing the dishes and putting them in the dishwasher. A busy week—exams, senior awards banquet, graduation. Then another school year would be over. Sarah Elizabeth would officially be a junior and Nathaniel would be going to college. Time seemed to be racing by—hours went by like minutes, days like hours. She wanted life to slow down. She wanted her children to grow up, but at the same time it was going to be so difficult to release them to the world. The thought of the house eventually being empty stunned her. Just her and Matthew. But that meant less cleaning and washing. She stopped. But that was two years away, she tried to convince herself, when Sarah Elizabeth left for college. First, there was the excitement of Nathaniel's graduation. She closed the dishwasher door and dried her hands. He had seemed happier today, and especially after church yesterday. Whatever was bothering him—the chemistry test—she wondered if he ever discussed it with Matthew. Then again, maybe losing the baseball game— She supposed it didn't matter now. He was in better spirits and that was all that mattered. His maturity was probably responsible for him putting it all in perspective. Resilient. That was Nathaniel. After all it was just a game—although she would never say that to him or Matthew.

She thought of him leaving for college—in three short months—and how much she would miss him. These mornings together for a few minutes, just the two of them. But he was ready. He'd proven that over and over. He would be fine on his own. The question was—would she be able to deal with him not being at home? But he would be back. After college and divinity school. Here at Holy Bible where she would hear him preach occasionally until Matthew retired. Suddenly, a shiver coursed through her. Retirement. "Miriam Winslow," she said aloud. "That is a long way off." One step at a time, she told herself, wiping off the kitchen table and then the countertops. Graduation. That would be huge. She already knew she would cry.

Graduation, she thought. She wished she had invited Carolyn, Jim and the children. No, Matthew would frown on their coming. Most likely suggest reasons why it would be impractical. Still, deep down she missed her sister.

She sighed and took a pad and pen from a drawer and sat at the kitchen table to make a grocery list. As she wrote she remembered that it was one week ago today that she saw those two men—asking her about cooking oil. She wondered if she would see them again today. And Eloise. "Wonderful" Eloise Gardner. She smiled as she continued writing. Energy snacks for the children to take to school this week.

The wind from the open window caused Sarah Elizabeth to use her index finger to push her hair behind her ear several times as she read her library book. After several attempts she simply held her hand against the side of her head to control her flapping hair.

"Did you have to read this for English?" she asked Nathaniel. She held up *The Robe*.

He glanced at the title. "Oh, yes. Required," he said.

Sarah Elizabeth returned to reading, as if that were the end of their exchange.

"Tough read?" Nathaniel asked.

She looked up. "Not so much. It's just that Mrs. Baxter asks such picky questions. It's like you have to know every detail. I don't think even Lloyd C. Douglas could make a hundred on her test." She rolled her eyes to punctuate her sarcasm.

"She's giving a test on the last day of classes?" Nathaniel asked.

"Just on the last part," she said. "Wants to keep us on our toes 'til the last minute, I guess." She started to return to the reading but instead turned to her brother. "You seem pretty happy today—for a Monday."

Nathaniel didn't answer right away. Martha said the same thing yesterday afternoon. He knew what it was all about, but he wasn't saying anything. It was between him and God. "I don't know. Last Monday of school. No more tests, just exams. Graduation. College. I'm just really hyped up on everything, I guess." He paused for a moment. "You don't exactly seem down in the dumps yourself lately."

"I'm excited about the party this Saturday. Mike asked me to go." She beamed.

"First big party. A sophomore going to a junior party. Big doins."

"Don't make fun," she defended.

"I'm not. I think it's great. Mike's a nice guy."

Sarah Elizabeth smiled as she held her book against her chest. "Yeah, I know."

Nathaniel rolled his eyes. After a few seconds of silence he spoke in a more serious tone. "Listen, if I wasn't so nice last week—well, I'm sorry. It was the game—" He thought of mentioning the test, but decided not to. He had only told his mother. "—and, well, stuff. So I'm sorry." He reached over and lightly pulled several strands of her hair. "You know I love ya," he said with a fake, overstated tone.

"Yeah, whatever," she said, pushing his hand away. "I love you, too."

"But Mrs. Baxter's not going to put that on your test. Read," he commanded, pointing at her book.

Sarah Elizabeth smiled and continued focusing on her book.

Nathaniel looked at his sister from the corner of his eye. He was glad that she had noticed his change. That meant it was true—all that he had figured out during church, about this being a test for him. But he was even happier today. Last night he had dreamed about Martha. It was the first one he could remember ever having about her. He was going to tell her. But maybe he'd wait until a special time. It wasn't one of those messy dreams like he'd had about Jason. It was about him and Martha going to the senior party at Lynnette Burch's house on Friday night after the awards banquet. This had to be a sign that his test was over. That he wasn't going to have those thoughts anymore. Maybe now he wouldn't need to sleep with a towel underneath him and worry about his mother seeing the mess he—

"There goes Keith Smith with his mother." Sarah Elizabeth had looked up as she turned the page and saw the car passing them. "Do you know him?" she asked.

"No, why?"

"Mike says some of the kids think he's gay, but I told him I think he's just shy."

Nathaniel tensed but said nothing.

"Do you think anybody at school's gay?" she asked.

"Don't know. Never thought about it." He tried to sound matter-of-fact. Still, his stomach knotted. "Never heard of Keith whatever-his-name-is. He's not going to be on your test. Read."

Sarah Elizabeth pretended to be annoyed but returned to her book.

Nathaniel told himself to relax. There was no reason to get uptight about being asked a question like that, he tried to convince himself. It was reasonable for her to ask. She wasn't asking about him, he thought. He took a quiet, deep breath. He was okay. Everything was okay.

He turned into the student parking lot. This was going to be a good week. Even with exams. Even with the chemistry test that he'd failed. He would still get an A for the year. He was looking forward to the banquet, the party and graduation at church on Saturday night. After that he would be a college man. A big weekend. And then— There would be that demonstration that his father talked about yesterday. A shiver coursed through him. The gay pride event. That was okay. He could think about it. It wasn't for another month. He and Martha were adults. They could go like everyone else in his church and demonstrate along the parade route. Like everyone else there, they would be examples of the good Christians his father had talked about.

He parked the car in his assigned place and turned off the ignition.

"Okay, after school—" he started.

"I know. I know. Come straight to the car. We've got to go home and study," she finished.

"Too smart," he said. "Now make a hundred on that quiz."

"Yeah, right," she smirked.

Pressing the remote to lock the car, he smiled. All was well with him, he told himself. Well with him and everyone he knew. And, more importantly, he was well with God.

As Matthew eased out of Estelle Caviness' room, he saw that the room across the hall—the one where that homosexual had been a week ago—was empty. AIDS and death both crossed his mind at the same moment. Pushing the down button for the elevator, he decided it wasn't his concern. If the man had not sinned, he wouldn't have become infected. And that one at the entrance to the parking deck—he could still recall his grip. The gay plague. You reap what you sow, he thought, dismissing the incident.

The elevator bell rang as the door opened. As he stepped in he ignored the two interns who were talking in private tones. He put his Bible underneath his arm and went through his ritual of cleansing his hands with his ever-present bottle of Purell. As the elevator slowed to a stop he smoothed his collar and made sure his hair still lay the way he intended.

Driving to the church he continued thinking of the emails he had received yesterday from his congregants and associates. Then, several phone calls last night—all praising him for his stand. And the one, he'd said his name was Al Lowe, urged him to submit his sermon as a editorial in the newspaper. "Not just a letter," this Al Lowe had said. "A whole article." The more Matthew thought about it, the more he agreed. He'd seen those guest editorials. They were always in the Sunday paper. More people would read it. And almost always a picture accompanied the article. Maybe one of him with the front of the sanctuary in the background. Next Sunday. It would have to be in next Sunday's edition, so that more people would read about the demonstration along the parade route. More publicity. Just the kind of thing the Coalition would approve of.

Thinking about the Coalition triggered a reminder. He needed to talk with Fred Haskins, the principal, about when and how to fire Ralph Stansbury. They had to have a better showing in athletics if they were going to continue to get funding from the Coalition, he thought. Kenneth Ward hadn't said so, but he knew it was expected. He also knew it was necessary for an overall, well-rounded program—to attract better students—or Kenneth as referred to them, "God's future army."

He turned down Century Avenue and almost immediately caught sight of Holy Bible Fellowship's modern, towering steeple three blocks away. He slowed as he drove by the sign bearing his name and his grandfather's. Pride swept over him every time he saw it. He pictured his grandfather. He would have to be proud, he thought. How could he not be?

He turned into the staff parking lot. As he slid out of the leather seat and strode to the church administration building, he felt the warmth of the late May sun. A lot going on this week, he thought. But God has ordained it all and will see us through.

"All right, now, class, there's one last reminder for the exam. I will be expecting you to give me feedback on Dr. Polder's short stories that we read this semester." Alice Medlin glanced down at her list of reminders to her senior English class as she stood to the side of her lectern. "It would be a good idea to go over your notes on the literary merit and content from the Biblical perspective." She raised her eyebrows and looked over the top of her glasses. "And, yes, that's a hint."

Her announcement brought some groaning. Nathaniel's reaction was different. He still had Jason's notes and book with underlined parts at home. He'd had to borrow them because he'd been at Freedom three weeks ago to tour the School of Divinity when Mrs. Medlin had discussed the book. He glanced at Jason, two rows over and up one seat. Jason met his eyes. Nathaniel nodded his obligation and began devising his strategy. The exam was tomorrow, so he couldn't wait and bring it to school to give him. He'd have to take it to his house. Why had he forgotten to do that when he went over there to study for the chem test? Instantly, he knew the answer—all part of the test. Just like the shower, the glances, the dreams, being at Jason's house. But that was over. No need to worry about that anymore. Simply take Sarah Elizabeth home, tell his mother what he needed to do, take the stupid book and notes to Jason's house and leave. Not even go inside, he told himself. Ten minutes. That's it. He took a deep breath and slowly let it out and tried to keep his attention on Mrs. Medlin.

When the bell rang, Jason waited for him at the door. Before he could speak, Nathaniel took charge. He had to be in control here.

"I forgot I still had your book and notes," he said, walking out the door, not even looking at Jason. "I'll go home right after school and bring them over to you." He stopped out in the hall and turned to him. "You going to be home?"

Jason nodded. "Yeah," he said. His voice was quiet. Defeated. He said nothing more as he avoided looking at Nathaniel.

Nathaniel saw the hurt on his face. But he couldn't let this get to him. He wasn't like—like Jason. Still, something inside would not allow him to be cold.

"I'm sorry," he said without the abruptness that he had put in his voice. Suddenly, he wanted to say more but he couldn't. "I'll be there right after I go home and get them."

"Okay." Jason turned and walked in the opposite direction.

Throughout the remainder of the day, Nathaniel replayed what he'd said to Jason. He had been harsh. He'd meant to be. He knew. But he also knew he did not want to hurt this person who'd been his teammate, friend. But he just wasn't *that* way.

At home after school he explained to his mother the errand to Jason's house.

"Okay, he doesn't live that far away. Don't stay."

"Promise."

Upstairs he quickly changed to t-shirt, shorts and flip-flops. It was a hot afternoon. It didn't matter how he was dressed. He wasn't going inside. He found the book and notes and rushed to his car. There and back, he told himself. That's it.

Jason's car was in the driveway. Nathaniel went to the door and rang the bell. Don't go inside. Suddenly, Jason opened the door and began walking back from the door.

"Yes, ma'am." He was on the phone. He motioned for Nathaniel to come in and covered the phone with his hand. "I'm taking a message for my mom," he said softly, turning to go into the kitchen.

Nathaniel hesitated. Jason was dressed in shorts and loose tank top. He battled the memories that were flooding his mind. He could go inside. He was in charge of himself. Nothing was going to happen. He wouldn't let it. He stood in the foyer, waiting, hearing Jason talk on the phone.

"Phone's been ringing off the hook ever since I walked in," Jason said, coming in. "Sorry. I think my mom must've turned her cell phone off." He crossed his arms over his chest. "She's directing this woman's daughter's wedding Sunday afternoon and she's freaking out."

Nathaniel nodded. Awkwardness consumed the room. He could see a sprig of black hair peering out from Jason's armpit. He looked away. Fight it, he thought. "Here's your book and notes." He held them out. "Sorry I forgot about them last week."

"No problem. I didn't need them until now anyway." Jason took the book and papers, looking down at them. "I've still got your Sports Illustrated DVD you loaned me. The one about the history of the World Series. It's in my room. I'll get—"

Just then, the house phone rang. Exasperation covered Jason's face. "I've gotta answer this. It's probably something about that wedding," he said, walking backward toward the kitchen door. "If you want to, go on up and get it. It's on my desk." He disappeared into the kitchen.

Nathaniel hesitated. He'd forgotten about the DVD. He thought about just leaving it, but Sarah Elizabeth had given it to him for his birthday and it had autographs of a lot of famous players. Got to get home to study. Dad's orders. Maybe this was God's way of helping him get away while Jason was on the phone.

He quickly went up to Jason's room. The bed was rumpled, more so than last week. Don't look at it. The DVD lay on Jason's desk just where he'd said it was. He picked it up and at the same time saw his large sketchpad also on the desk.

In the distance he could hear Jason still talking on the phone. He wondered if Jason had done anymore drawings of teachers. He hesitated. He would just glance at them for a few seconds. With his index finger, he flipped open the cover. His mind went blank when he saw the first drawing. Himself. Just his face with light stubble. Serious but so life-like. He turned to the next page. The same but a different angle. The next. Another angle. Another page. Himself and Jason, from the shoulders up, looking down, their two foreheads almost touching. The next page. Similar, different angle, but looking into each other's eyes, both unshaven. Another. Similar, different angle, Jason's hand on his cheek, like last week on the bed. The next one. Himself with no shirt. Another page. Himself nude. He turned to the next. Himself and Jason nude, Jason's hand on his chest. The next. Similar, his hand on Jason's chest, his fingers like a comb in the hair. Another. The two of them on the bed, holding each other. Kissing. Bodies pressed together. He stared at the drawing, examining every detail—the body hair, the lips, the closeness—spellbound, his erection signaling that he knew he should and wanted to hate this, this torturous beauty, so vile and evil, yet he was riveted.

Without turning toward the door, he realized Jason was standing there, but he said nothing, only continued staring at the sketch. His heart pounded. Jason gently closed the door and slowly walked to him. Still Nathaniel stared at the drawing, motionless. Don't let this happen, he heard inside his head, but something else—something bigger rendered him powerless. Powerless when Jason put his hands on his shoulders, his warm breath on the back of his neck. Powerless when Jason slipped his arms around his waist and pressed his body against his. Powerless when he pressed back and Jason slowly put his hand under his t-shirt and moved his hand over his abdomen, then up to his chest and stroked his nipples. Powerless when he closed his eyes and brushed his hands over Jason's arms, feeling the hair. Unable to keep his arms at his side when Jason pulled his t-shirt up, took it off, kissed his bare shoulder, then gently turned him around and, leaning down, kissed first one nipple, then swabbed his face across his chest to the other one, the rough stubble of his beard like velvet. Jason leaned up, the two looking at each other. Nathaniel felt he was dreaming as Jason reached up and touched his cheek. He turned his head to it and kissed his palm. As Jason pulled his tank top over his head, Nathaniel touched the thick patches of hair in the pits of his arms. They moved forward to kiss, Nathaniel putting his arms around him, pressing their bare chests together, sensual electricity coursing through him. A rawness engulfed him—passionate, uncontrollable, insatiable—clamoring to escape, to be free, like a suffocating insect trapped inside a jar, its lid tightly sealed, clamped shut, now opened.

Nathaniel moved his mouth over Jason's rough cheek, then down to his neck and shoulder. He bathed his face in the hair on his chest, his tongue lapping his nipples. And in the same moment he began unbuttoning his shorts.

Nathaniel lay perfectly still on the bed, staring at the ceiling, his arms to his side. The only sound he could hear was the thundering of his heart. No longer in passion but with a different, inescapable range of emotions. In his head a litany which he was powerless to silence began bombarding him—memorized scriptures, his notebook filled with lines, Bible class at school, but most of all his father's voice. Condemned. Sinner. A man shall not lie with another man. It is an abomination to God. Burn in—

"That was—" Jason began as he rolled onto his side and put his hand on Nathaniel's chest and crossed his leg over his.

"I've got to go," Nathaniel interrupted, bolting upright off the bed, picking up his clothes off the floor. He pulled on his boxers, his shorts and t-shirt, all without looking at Jason.

"Nate, don't leave. Please." He got up and went to him.

"I'm supposed to be home studying." He slid his feet into his flip-flops, ignoring Jason's arm around him. Just then the house telephone rang. "You'd better answer that. Might be important."

"You're all that's important to me." He tried to hold him, but Nathaniel pulled away.

"I can't," he began without looking at him. "I can't do this. I'm not—I'm not like you. I can't be like you." He turned and hurried from the room, down the stairs and out the front door. As he walked across the lawn to his car, Mrs. Daniels was driving up. She called to him, but he only waved and forced a smile.

As he drove home the siege in his mind continued. He had sinned in the worse way. How could this have happened? He wasn't one of—one of those people. He gripped the steering wheel like a vise. But he had done this terrible act with another male. Why couldn't he stop himself? Why was he so powerless? Had Jason left his sketch pad there on purpose? To tempt him? The DVD. Had he planned all of it? But there was the phone call. He couldn't make that happen. But why didn't he wait and let Jason get the DVD? He beat the steering wheel with his fist. He was a sinner. He had done it. He had sinned against God in the worse way. He thought of his father's sermon and all the plans he was making for that rally. What would his father do to him if he ever found out? He could never tell him. He pummeled the steering wheel. Why was this happening to him? How could he ever be a minister when God hated him? How could he ever stand in front of a congregation and preach if he was an abomination to God?

When he turned down his street, his gut tightened. He had to hide this. His mother could read every expression on his face. She always knew when something was wrong with him. Just like' last week. He took several deep breaths. He had to get through this—getting into the house to his room, dinner, prayer time, then breakfast tomorrow morning. He stopped his Jeep in his place on the side of the driveway. Pray, he told himself. No good. God didn't want to listen to him. Not now. Not ever again.

He hoped his mother wouldn't be in the kitchen, that he could get to his room without seeing her, but better to give her an explanation now for being late than at dinner in front of his father.

"Hi, Mom," he said, forcing cheer into his tone and avoiding her eyes. "Sorry I'm late."

She looked at the clock. "Thought you were coming right back," she said, checking a roast in the oven.

Nathaniel noted the lack of accusation in her tone. Please, Mom, believe what I'm about to tell you. "We studied the book, the same one I took back to him. Mrs. Medlin told us she's including it on the exam tomorrow." He opened the refrigerator and pretended to be looking for something to eat. Anything, he told himself, not to have to look at her.

"Okay. Well, I'm sure your father would be okay with that since you were studying."

He closed the refrigerator door and forced himself to look at her. She looked up from basting the roast to smile at him. "Yeah, I think he'd be okay with it."

"Want something to eat?" She closed the oven door.

Nathaniel moved to the door. Get upstairs. "Uh, no. Thanks. I'm fine 'til dinner."

"Okay."

He took the steps two at a time and closed the door. A deep, desperate breath. He sat down at his desk. All he could think of was what he had just experienced. Touching Jason's body. Kissing him. The closeness. He began to sense the excitement all over, again. He closed his eyes tight like fists and pressed his hands against the pressure happening between his legs. Slowly, wetness seeped from his eyes and spilled down cheeks. Why had he— Who was he? What had made him want—

Confusion ran rampant through his mind. He had to think of something else. Anything. He flipped open his laptop. Emails. One from Martha. He stared at the line. Friday night after the party at Lynette's house. When he took Martha home. Just the two of them. In his car. He would prove it then. Not have sex, but at least do enough—kissing and touching—to get excited. Excited the way he had—just a while ago. And he would get excited. He knew it. He would. He had to.

He wiped the tears from his face and clicked on Martha's email.

"Hey...I'm sure you're studying very diligently. NOT!!! Probably got your ear buds in. Anyway, just wanted to say hi and let you know I'm thinking of you. Miss you honey bunches. (smiley face) Or miss you bunches, honey. I like that one better. Hugs. Marth"

Nathaniel hit reply.

"Hey back to you..."

He stopped. He was going to say more than he had been. He was going to get more serious. He had to. And he wanted to. He did.

"No ear buds, no music, just thinkin of you. Be so glad when exams are over. Really lookin forward to the party after the banquet on Friday. I want that to be a special night for us...but any time that I'm with you is special. VERY SPECIAL. Study lots. Look for another email from me later tonight. Big hug to you. Nathaniel"

Without hesitation he clicked on "send." He closed his laptop but immediately what had just happened played over and over. He opened his English book and tried to study, but he had no control over his mind as it raged against him, pummeling him, telling him how evil he was. A demon. A monster. Again and again, he tried to convince himself that he wasn't one of those people. He wasn't. Still the memories were branded into his mind. He wanted to be sick, to vomit out his sin. He took a shower, crying as he stood under the cascading water, his arms wrapped across his chest. He would never be clean.

As he went downstairs for dinner, Nathaniel ordered himself to act normal. Nobody knew anything. And they wouldn't if he could just act normal. Still the word itself suggested betrayal. He could act normal until Friday night. He had to keep thinking about Friday night and Martha.

He sat at his place, forced himself to smile, met everyone's eye as much as he dared. The remainder of the time he riveted his eyes on his plate.

"So which exams do you all have tomorrow?" Matthew asked as they ate. "Nathaniel?"

He swallowed. "English and history." He drank some tea.

"Don't you read Polder's stories in senior English?"

"Yes, Dad."

"I always liked the one about the fellow learning to pray. What was his name?"

Nathaniel felt the knot in his stomach tighten. He churned his brain.

"Surely you remember," Matthew said.

Nathaniel searched his mind. He supposedly had just studied this with Jason less than two hours ago. "Oscar Gooden." He almost added, *I think*, but caught himself.

"Oh, yes, that was his name. Love that story. A great sermon could come out of that." He took a bite of roast. "And your exams?" he asked, looking only briefly at Sarah Elizabeth.

Nathaniel heard his sister say math and French, then his mother added something about helping her. However, his own dilemma hammered in his head. She knew that was the book he was returning to Jason. He had lied to her about them studying and being late. He looked everywhere except at her. Maybe she didn't remember it. Still he could not look at her. She would know.

He asked to forfeit dessert and return to studying—something he knew his father would admire but might possibly alert his mother. Still, he had to get away, be alone. In his room he sat down at his desk with his English book still open to the same page as when he'd returned from Jason's. For hours he sat as the voices in his head droned like bees in a hive—sinner, abomination, hatred. Then, suddenly, from out of nowhere, the other words he'd heard but never used—faggot, queer, homo—assaulted him without mercy. He pressed his hands against the sides of his head. What could he do? Nobody to talk to. Nowhere to turn. He wanted to pray, but it was too late for that now.

Time seemed to drag by, yet suddenly it was prayer time in the hallway. Quickly he decided what he would say when his father called on him. The whole time standing in the circle he heard nothing his father said. He only listened for his name.

"Nathaniel."

"Father, give strength and wisdom to everyone to do well on exams, that we may move on to the next stage of our lives." He felt his mother rub her thumb against his hand as she held it. When his father said Amen, he hugged his sister and shook hands with his father. When he hugged his mother, she held him an extra few seconds. She knows something is wrong, he told himself. He had to look at her. He had to show her he was okay.

"Night, Mom," he said.

Miriam looked directly at him for several seconds before she spoke. "Night, honey," she almost whispered.

Get into the room and close the door, he ordered himself.

Miriam lay on her side, facing away from Matthew, her mind centered on her son.

Something was wrong. It couldn't be his grades and chemistry. It just couldn't. He was too good of a student to be in academic trouble. Had he and Martha broken up? That couldn't be it, either. They had been so close yesterday at church. So lovey-dovey in their own quiet, respectful way. No, it was something else. He had said something tonight in his prayer about moving on to the next stage of life. Was he worried about going away to school? Sad, maybe? That didn't make sense. Not with half of his class going to Freedom.

She took a silent deep breath as Matthew stirred next to her. Instinctively, she closed her eyes as if she were sleeping.

CHAPTER TEN

TUESDAY, WEDNESDAY, THURSDAY
MAY 19, 20, 21

Nathaniel waited in his room listening for Sarah Elizabeth to go downstairs to breakfast. He wanted to spend as little time as he could with his mother. He had already lied to her. He didn't want to, again. She would hate him if she ever found out. Even though she'd never said anything about—about those people—like his father had, she would hate him. She would have to. She would never disagree with his father. Never.

Just then, he heard Sarah Elizabeth. He waited only a minute. He didn't want his mother coming up to his room to see if he was sick. With his book bag, he went downstairs.

"Where have you been?" It was Sarah Elizabeth who spoke first as she sat at the kitchen table eating a piece of toast and drinking juice.

"Up late studying," he replied. He put his back pack on the floor near the back door, then poured himself a glass of orange juice. "And early morning last minute cramming. Morning, Mom," he said all at once as he put the pitcher into the refrigerator. He noticed she didn't respond immediately like she usually did.

"Morning, sweetheart."

She was smiling but also looking at him longer, in an odd way. She couldn't possibly know, he told himself. Just be yourself.

She placed a plate of eggs, toast and bacon at his setting on the table.

"Oh, thanks, Mom." He sat down and began eating. He had hoped to skip breakfast, but that would arouse her suspicions. He had to get through this.

Nathaniel kept glancing at his sister, grateful that she was studying her French notes. That meant silence, one that didn't feel so awkward. From the corner of his eye he could see his mother leaning against the counter, drinking her coffee. Please don't let her sit down next to me. I can't look at her. He ate faster than he ever had, almost gobbling most of his food, enough, he thought, not to raise questions.

"Ready?" he asked his sister, standing up while he continued chewing. He hoisted his back pack onto his shoulder.

Sarah Elizabeth heaved a deep, laborious sigh. "As I'll ever be," she said, picking up her plate and juice glass and putting them in the sink.

While she turned to kiss her mother, Nathaniel realized he had left his plate and glass on the table. Quickly he carried them to the sink and kissed his mother. "Bye, Mom."

"Energy bars," she said, pointing to the counter by the door.

When they had gone, Miriam sat down at the table. Not one time since he started first grade, she thought, had Nathaniel ever forgotten to put his dishes in the sink. Not once.

"Thank you for my text message this morning," Martha said privately as they stood outside her classroom before the first exam. She leaned against the wall and smiled up at him. "You've never done that."

"That's because you're special," he said softly, smiling. He meant it. He reached down and brushed his hand against hers as he looked around for any teachers who might be in the hall.

"Well, it was sweet." She pressed the back of her hand against his.

He lowered his voice. "Want to go out on Thursday night? Maybe a movie or just dessert?" he asked. He'd thought about this during the night when he wasn't able to sleep. A prelude to Friday night.

"Oh," she said, frowning. "I can't. Marilee has invited some of us to an all-girls party at her house Thursday. I wish I hadn't already told her I'd come."

A mix of let down and reprieve coursed through him. "That's okay. Just so long as you have me down on your calendar for Friday night and Saturday."

"Absolutely. Those two days have been on there for months," she said with a smile.

The warning bell rang.

"Go," Martha said, moving away from the wall and toward her class.

"I'm just two classes down the hall," he said. He had to keep her from becoming suspicious. "You trying to get rid of me?" That was clever. He wanted her to think he was that and more.

"No." She playfully poked his arm and continued shifting toward the door. "I'll see you after."

"Yes, you will." He pointed to the wall. "Right here."

Martha giggled and went inside her class. When she was out of sight, Nathaniel's smile instantly disappeared. As he walked into his class, he saw Jason and immediately looked away. He took his seat, talking to others nearby. Act normal, he told himself. You are normal. You just proved it with your girlfriend. Your *steady* girl-friend. There's nothing to worry about, he thought, half-listening to Mrs. Medlin as she gave instructions about the exam. At the same time he glanced over at Jason. He looked at his mouth, his cheek, his neck as memories flooded his mind. Stop it! He looked down at his desk. Don't do that! he ordered. Just then, Mrs. Medlin began passing out the exam pages. He turned and looked at Jason, again. Jason was glancing at him. Nathaniel looked away. He couldn't—he wouldn't let this get to him. He wouldn't. He was—

"Nathaniel, are you okay?"

He looked up at Mrs. Medlin as he felt his face become warm. His chest pounded. Everyone was looking at him.

"Yes, ma'am." She put an exam on his desk and kept moving.

Nathaniel looked down at his test. Jason was probably staring at him. He forced himself not to look at anyone. Did they know? Could they look at him and tell what he was hiding? Had someone found out and started rumors? He had to get control of himself. You've got an exam to take. Put everything else out of your mind.

He surveyed several pages, glancing over the questions. He recognized most of it. At least he thought he did. As he began writing what he knew, facts that he'd once known now eluded him, disappearing out of his mind. As he worked he skipped the things he didn't know right away and came back to them. Over and over, turning back and forth to random pages. Short answers. Short essays. Polder's stories. His father's favorite character Oscar Gooden about him learning to— To what? To have faith? To believe in God? Why couldn't he think? They had talked about it just last night. Think, he ordered himself. He poured over the pages. Erasing answers here and there and writing new ones. Guessing at others. Suddenly, the bell rang. Everyone was leaving. He still had a lot of blanks. Too many. His average would plummet. His father would know. It would show on his report card. He'd demand an explanation.

"Nathaniel, was it that bad?" Mrs. Medlin was standing next to him, the room empty of students.

What was he going to say? "Uh, no, ma'am." She would know something was wrong when she graded it. "I guess I just wasn't expecting some of the questions." He had to get out of there. He stood up and picked up his book bag.

"Well, I'm sure you did fine. You always do and I'm sure I won't be disappointed this time either." She took his exam. "It's been a pleasure having you in class this year. Good luck at Freedom Bible next year."

College. Him at Freedom Bible University. "Yes, thank you. I've enjoyed this class a lot." He edged his way up the aisle. "You're a great teacher."

"Thank you, but it's having conscientious students like you that make my job easier." She smiled. "Well, I'll see you at the banquet Friday night."

"Yes, ma'am." He walked toward the door. He saw Martha standing just outside in the hallway.

"How was it?" she asked.

He looked at her. Why did everybody have to know everything about him? "Piece of cake," he said. He had to hide it. He *would* hide it. "Let's go get something to drink." They walked to the commons area for lemonade provided by the parents.

He shared his energy bar with her while she talked about her exam, but all the while his mind spun like a turbine, spewing doubt and fear throughout his being like an insidious cancer. How could all this be happening to him? What was he going to do?

His next exam was history. As he sat down, he reminded himself that he hadn't studied for this one either. All he had done was stare at the same two pages of his English book all night and then slept scarcely more than an hour or two. He was going to do better on this one. Mrs. Rudisill gave very easy tests. He would be all right in here. An A with no problem. Jason wasn't in here. Nothing to remind him— Except he was there again yesterday afternoon. In Jason's room. The sketch pad and—

Mrs. Rudisill put the test on his desk. He had to concentrate. He had to forget all that. Forget about yesterday.

He took a deep breath and began. Page after page he supplied answers. He answered most with absolute certainty. Skipped a few, but not many. Still he felt he should have known them. But all the while his mind tossed as thoughts ricocheted like a pinball machine. Yesterday. The drawings of him and Jason together.

The test over, Nathaniel met Martha. The whole time he forced himself to act normal. That was going to be his only thought from now on. Believing he was normal.

Luckily Martha made no comment about him acting odd. Now another afternoon, dinner and prayer time. More pressure to be normal. He could do this. He *was* doing it. Just hang on 'til Friday night and Martha, he told himself. Friday and this will all be settled.

Whenever he was at home for the next two days, Nathaniel plotted his every move. He had to avoid his family as much as possible. The best and only excuse was studying. Secluded, he thought. Stay away from everyone. He was careful to plan his answers to questions that his mother or father might ask. Especially, if his mother asked about what might be wrong, was he feeling okay. *I just want to do well on exams*, he planned to say. *I want you and Dad to be proud of me.* Then they would say all these wonderful things about him. Things that they wouldn't say if they knew what he had done.

At school he spent every minute he could with Martha—before and after every exam. In the afternoons and evenings, he disobeyed his father and texted her several times. With each communication he tried to feel bolder, more assured that Friday night he would prove who he really was.

After each exam, he worried that he had done poorly. Not an A, or even a B. Especially in English. Each time, however, that he tried to concentrate on his exams, his thoughts drove him back to Monday afternoon and Jason's room, the two of them naked in bed. For a moment, a scene would replay—but only briefly before he would shut it down. Then, the sketches appeared, plaguing him. Why? Why the sketches? They had trapped him there in Jason's room. Even if he hadn't "planted" them there for him to see. More and more they floated through his mind. And each night as he lay in bed, fighting his father's condemnation as well as the Bible's, memories of their friendship began to drift into the diatribe and for a moment—so brief a moment—he felt a reprieve. More than just friends—close friends, buddies, trading eye-rolling looks when Mr. Turkey or some other teacher tried to be hip, the unspoken bond about their fathers, pairing up in baseball practice for drills, Bible buddies, studying together, sharing, so much sharing. And Jason's ultimate—throwing the Bible Scholar competition. All comforts—comforts that now he had to deny.

On Thursday he sat in chemistry class taking his last exam. He had tried to study for this one more than any of the others. He had to bolster his average after failing that last test.

He had come in just as the bell rang, again because he was with Martha—a fact he mentioned aloud so that Jason would hear. Jason sat two seats in front of him. Still, he ignored him when he passed by him. However, during the exam, he glanced up once in a while and saw his broad shoulders and thick dark hair down to the collar of his button-down. And they were there in his room, on the bed. And then for some reason, some very strange reason, another memory—a drawing Jason had done of Coach Stansbury and his enormous pot-belly, hanging over his belt, his shirt not long enough to reach the top of his pants and his having to reach around the abdominal mass (as they secretly labeled it) as well as under it to scratch his crotch. Nathaniel smiled to himself, then realized he couldn't do that. Not anymore.

Having answered all the questions he could, he turned in his exam just before the class ended. He was sure he had been able to get at least a B on it. Maybe more.

"Your attention, please, for the following announcement." It was Reverend Haskins, the principal. "I doubt that there's any need to remind you to pick up your yearbooks in the gym immediately after the bell. They will be distributed by homerooms." He paused. "Please pray with me. Father God, we thank you for another success-ful academic year here at Holy Bible Academy. We ask your loving guidance over the seniors who will be graduating as they go forward in their lives. We also ask that all students, faculty and staff have a safe and pleasant summer vacation, that we all may grow in your love and faith. We ask in Jesus name. Amen. Have a wonderful, careful summer."

"Hey Jase, Nate," Andrew Perryman called as they walked up the aisle after the bell rang. "Tryin' to get enough for a game at the ball field this afternoon about two. You guys in? We can sign yearbooks before."

Jason had turned and glanced at Nathaniel who immediately turned away.

"Can't," Jason said. "Got to help my Mom with a party she's catering tonight. I'll have to do signing at Lynnette's tomorrow night."

"Nate?" Andrew asked.

"Sure, I'll be there." When he turned, Jason had already walked out.

"Hey," Andrew said quietly to Nathaniel, "did you two have a fallin' out?"

Nathaniel fought to act natural. "No, why?"

Andrew looked at him. "I don't know. You act like you're mad at each other."

"Exams." A thought popped into his head. "And pressure from home." He looked at Andrew. "You know. Fathers."

"Gotcha."

Nathaniel hoped Andrew had bought his story. It wasn't a lie. Everyone knew about Jason's father's expectations as well as his own.

Receiving their yearbooks right after the last day of exams seemed like the perfect reward for enduring the three days of tests. Many sat down in the gym floor and began swapping signatures, Nathaniel and Martha among them. After an hour, however, Reverend Haskins announced that it was time to close the gym.

At home Nathaniel looked over the book page by page. When he got to Jason's profile, he read his favorite scripture—something all students were required to submit. "For God did not give us a spirit of timidity but a spirit of power and love and self-control. Second

Timothy 1:7." Nathaniel couldn't believe it. The same verse that he had missed at the competition. Now everyone would know that he missed it on purpose. Would they think that Jason wanted him to win? That he had handed him a four-year scholarship? Then they'd ask why? Especially Mr. Daniels—if he saw it. He ran his fingers through his short hair. Maybe nobody would read it or remember the verse from the competition. Anyway, Jason's the one who would have to answer for it, not him. But, he hoped nobody would notice, particularly, Jason's father.

Most of the team showed up at the ball field. After taking some time to sign annuals, they took turns hitting and fielding. With enough players they organized a game. Even though Jason wasn't there, Nathaniel had a hard time concentrating, bobbling easy grounders, misjudging pop flies and even striking out. The only hits he got were singles. By five, the game ended. As he drove home, he wondered what the other guys thought of his playing so poorly. What would they think of him if they knew about—knew about what he and Jason—? Stop it. He grasped the wheel as if trying to choke the life out of it. "I'm not," he declared through clenched jaws. At home he showered and stayed in his room until dinner, texting Martha.

"How's your graduation speech coming along?" Matthew asked at dinner after blessing the food. "I assumed you've finished it?"

Nathaniel winced inside. "Mostly. I still have a little polishing to do."

"Reasonable." He put a slice of roasted chicken on a plate and passed it. "I'm sure it's fine, but work on it tonight and in the morning if you need to and email it to me by lunchtime." He added some peas to his plate and passed them. "And on Saturday we'll work on your delivery."

"Sure, Dad. Thanks." Nathaniel drank some of his iced tea as the knot in his stomach tightened. He hadn't looked at the speech in over a week.

After dinner he pulled up it on his laptop. As he read through it, each sentence was like a punch in his gut as his world closed in on him even more than it already had. How could he talk about the importance of following the word of the Bible, of living a Christ-like life when he had done what he'd done? And what he was planning to do tomorrow night with Martha—taking it to the next level? How could he stand up and preach this when he had sinned, when he'd done exactly what the Bible said not to do? This entire speech was one gigantic lie. He was a liar. The future leader of Holy Bible Fellowship was a bold-face liar and a hypocrite. How would he ever be able to put this behind him? No matter what happened tomorrow night with Martha? He wished he didn't have to do this speech. What if his grades were so bad that he wasn't the first in his class? What if he got a phone call tomorrow and Reverend Haskins told him his grades had dropped him to second or third or worse? How would he ever face his father? A sickening feeling spread through him. Even if he had to give the speech, he knew his grades weren't the best. Not anymore. Not after that chemistry test and his English exam. And the awards banquet— He buried his face in his hands. How had all this happened?

He had to finish the speech. His father was expecting to read it tomorrow. He stared at the computer screen for several minutes before the idea came to him. It was the least he could do. He returned to the beginning and read through it. Every sentence where he urged his classmates using "we" or "let us" he changed to "you." He read the last sentence after transforming it. "I challenge you to go forth from Holy Bible Academy and lead an exemplary life, a life so that others will look up to you, as a leader for God and for his son Jesus Christ, so that God will welcome you into his kingdom and say, 'Well, done, my good and faithful servant.'"

Nathaniel clicked "Save" and closed his laptop.

CHAPTER ELEVEN

FRIDAY—MAY 22

Nathaniel lay motionless in his bed, listening to the sounds from downstairs. He was waiting until his mother left for her meeting at the church before he got out of bed. He had mentioned the night before that he might sleep late—his first morning free of exams. However, like all the other nights since Monday, he had slept only a few hours. And each morning since Monday he had orchestrated a hasty departure from the house to avoid his mother's scrutiny. When she said she had an early morning meeting at the church, he seized the opportunity to elude her once more.

Finally, he heard the garage door rumbling open, followed by her car starting. He eased out of bed and watched through the blinds to be sure she had gone. She would probably be gone for two hours, but he wasn't going to take any chances. He would leave in an hour. With Sarah Elizabeth spending the day with some girl friends at someone's house, he was alone.

He pulled the protective towel from his bed and stored it in the bathroom. He quickly made his bed, put on some shorts, and went downstairs. In the kitchen his mother had left a note on the table. "See you at lunch? Love, Mom" His heart twisted as the gut wrenching thoughts of five days ago pummeled his mind. He gripped the back of the chair until his knuckles whitened. But he was going to fix that tonight. His date with Martha. After the class party at Lynnette's. He was going to prove to himself and to God that he was not— He tightened his hold on the chair then suddenly let go, refusing to even finish his own sentence in silence. He turned to the refrigerator and yanked open the door, got the pitcher of juice, poured a large glass and drank it. He was going to get everything done and get out of here.

Even though he wasn't hungry, he managed to eat a banana while he rinsed his glass out and put it in the dishwasher. Back in his room, he read through his speech on his computer. Crummy, he thought. Somebody else should be giving this. Not me. His memories plagued him. Disgusted and loathsome, he attached it to an email and sent it to his father. No message, just "Graduation speech" in the subject line.

He clicked on email inbox. One from Martha.

"Off to do all sorts of girl things 2day—I won't bore u with details. Soooo looking forward 2 2night. Our night! Can't wait. See u at 6, right? Luv ya, Marth"

Nathaniel stared at the two words—"our night" with an exclamation mark. His stomach churned. Why couldn't he be excited like she was? Whether she meant she was excited about the banquet and party or their being together, he should feel something—something other than having to prove who he really was. He clicked on reply.

"Off to do all sorts of things today, too. Guy things. No details, really boring. Can't wait til 2night, 2. Yes, I'll pick u up at 6. Nate" He stopped and riveted his eyes on the ending to Martha's message. "Luv ya." He did love her. He knew it. He clicked his pointer to the space before his name and added, "Luv ya more." He looked at it for only a moment before pressing send.

He showered and dressed. Downstairs he responded to his mother's note. "Mom, Gone to get a haircut and some other errands." He started to write that he was meeting some guys for lunch, but that would be a lie. "Won't be here for lunch, eating out, but will be back in time to cut Mrs. Gardner's grass and ours." He paused and looked at her note. He hesitated. Don't hate me, he thought. "Love, Nathaniel."

The large room adjacent to the grand ballroom in the Marriott Hotel buzzed with nervous excitement as one hundred nineteen seniors waited to be officially announced and ushered one at a time into the banquet hall. Mingling in slow, deliberate, robot-like steps in their formal wear they paid no attention to the ornate draperies and sconces.

Nathaniel tried to hide his tension and uneasiness as he stood with Martha, Lynnette Burch, Billy French and several other couples. He already knew he was the valedictorian and would win other awards tonight. The whole time he wondered what his teachers were saying about his exam results. He brushed the back of his hand against Martha's. She nudged back and smiled up at him.

"So, Nate," Billy said, "got your speech ready for tomorrow night?"

Nathaniel forced a smile. "Yeah, but don't worry, I'm not telling any of your secrets."

The group laughed, including Billy. "I have no secrets. My life is an open book." He held out his arms to gesture his innocence. "Nate on the other hand—"

Nathaniel laughed with them but felt a twist in his stomach. At that same moment he saw Jason standing behind Billy. Their eyes locked for several seconds. Just then, he felt Martha's hand on his arm.

"Well?" she asked.

Nathaniel looked at her blankly. His mind raced, trying to catch up to what had been said. What had his missed? He quickly replayed the words "cry" and "mushy" that were faintly echoing in his mind.

"Don't worry," he said. "I'll leave you guys rolling in the aisles."

Just then, the junior marshals and Mrs. Tate, the senior sponsor, came in and told them to line up in alphabetical order. As he glanced at Jason, Nathaniel quickly squeezed Martha's hand as they moved to their respective places in line. He knew that because of their last names she and Jason would be sitting at the same table. It didn't matter. Jason wouldn't say anything about—about what had happened. At least he hoped he wouldn't do something that underhanded. "See you later," he said.

She smiled and whispered. "Good luck."

Nathaniel was the last one in the line. God, please get me through this. Please don't let Dad be humiliated by what I did. My grades. Forgive me for what I've done and for what I need to do tonight. Please. If I'm supposed to say anything to Jason, then give me the words and the opportunity. He took several breaths and tried to convince himself that he felt better. That he was at peace. That God would see him through. Still, his insides squirmed and fought to know what was right.

When he finally heard his name, Nathaniel entered the room and followed the marshal. As he strode down the wide aisle, his classmates were all standing at their chairs, their parents seated next to them. The applause was huge, louder than for any other student. He tried to ignore it. He didn't deserve it. He tried to focus on the room. He saw that the front of the grand ballroom was adorned with the American and Christian flags on either side of a fifteen-foot banner which declared the class theme—"Into The World For God." As the marshal guided him to his table directly in front of the podium on the dais, he saw his father and mother, a vacant seat between them, waiting for him. As he got closer he could see that the centerpiece on each table elaborately arrayed a graduation cap complete with tassel, a diploma tied with a ribbon and an open Bible. The decorations matched the school colors—gold and brown. Ornate programs and place cards were at each place setting. Each table was set for nine people—three seniors and their parents. Already standing at the table were Ted Wilson with his mother and father, a bank president, and Gwen Warren with her mother and father, the chief executive officer of a mega-insurance corporation.

When Nathaniel had arrived at his seat between his parents, Reverend Haskins announced, "Ladies and gentlemen, the class of 2009." With those words the parents applauded and rose to stand alongside the seniors.

Matthew immediately grasped Nathaniel's hand. "You've accomplished so many great things, son. Congratulations." Finally, he released his hand and resumed applauding.

"Thanks, Dad." He turned to his mother and hugged her.

She kissed him on the cheek. "I'm such a lucky mother to have you for a son," she whispered in his ear. "I love you, Nathaniel."

"I love you, too, Mom," he whispered back. "But I'm the lucky one." He felt her arms become tighter around him. When he looked at her, she had tears in her eyes. Oh, God, don't ever let her find out.

After several minutes the applause diminished and everyone sat down. "Ladies and gentlemen, it is my honor to call on the senior minister of Holy Bible Fellowship, Reverend Matthew Winslow, to offer a blessing for this banquet and ceremony," the principal said.

Matthew left the table and walked to the podium. "Friends, let us pray. Holy Father, God, we thank you for another successful school term, for the growth both intellectual and spiritual of all the students at Holy Bible Academy. We thank you especially for this senior class which is so ready to go out into the world in your name and spread your gospel, to be a light to others, to show the way to others both near and far. Thank you for this sumptuous banquet, those who prepared it, those who are in charge of all the details. Bless us all as we go forward with your truth as our sword and your word as our shield. In Jesus' holy name. Amen."

As he returned to his table, the hall swarmed with salad carrying waiters. As his father initiated conversation which he would dominate throughout the meal, Nathaniel saw that Martha was three tables away. As he took his first bite of salad, he knew he should pay close attention to what his father and the others were talking about. He was sure he would be expected to comment.

"So, George and Ken," Matthew said to two other fathers, "these three are all headed to Freedom Bible University next year. I'm sure you all are as pleased as I am."

"Couldn't be more pleased, Reverend," George Wilson said.

"We should all be proud," Ken Warren responded as he winked at his daughter.

"Oh, I couldn't agree more," Matthew said. "They're going to make a great school even greater. And these two'll help out the baseball team, too." He pointed to Nathaniel and Ted with a nod. Pleased with his insight he stabbed around in his salad with his fork. "And Gwen, I know you'll be an important part of the student body, too. What do you plan to major in?"

"Christian education and English, Reverend Winslow," she said politely. "I'd like to be a teacher."

"A double major and a teacher. Very commendable. Perhaps you'll come back here to teach at Holy Bible. We'll be looking for your application."

"Oh, yes, I'd like that."

"And Ted, have you thought about going to law school after college?" Matthew asked. "Freedom has some courses you can take as an undergraduate to give you a sampling."

As his father held forth, Nathaniel kept watching Martha's table but never saw her talking to Jason.

As the applause was dying down from the previous award, Reverend Haskins consulted his program—the final award to be announced.

During the evening Nathaniel had been called to the podium three times to accept trophies—best male student-athlete, a faculty academic choice; best all-round male, a student choice; best disciple award, designated by the principal. With each award he felt more uneasy.

His grades had dropped. He knew he hadn't scored well on his exams. And all because of last Monday. He didn't deserve any of this and his teachers knew that. If his classmates ever—

"And now for the last award of the 2008-2009 academic year," Reverend Haskins announced. "And that is the trophy for the winner of the Bible Scholar Competition, the most important and coveted award at Holy Bible Academy. And with it comes a full four-year scholarship to Freedom Bible University. We already know who the winner is. But I'll remind you again that Nathaniel Winslow is the first senior to have won the contest every year since he was in the first grade. Nobody has ever done that in the history of the school. Nathaniel, please come forward."

As he stood, the room broke into applause, then standing applause which continued after he arrived at the podium. Reverend Haskins joined in. When the clapping diminished, the people sat back down and the principal stepped to the microphone. "Nathaniel, as you know, it's tradition that I ask you one unofficial question before turning over the trophy. Even if you don't know the answer, but I'm sure you will, you still get the trophy. So here it is: In what book and chapter does the Prayer of Jabez appear?"

Nathaniel had known this would happen. His Bible teacher, Reverend Sessoms, had made a point of it on the last day of class. Even if he hadn't, Nathaniel had written a term paper on the Prayer of Jabez a few months before. It was a fail-safe question. "First Chronicles, chapter 4, verse ten."

Reverend Haskins looked at the audience. "It is certainly no surprise to anyone here that that is correct." He handed the trophy to Nathaniel. "Congratulations, Nathaniel."

Again, applause filled the room as Nathaniel made his way back to the table. Matthew stood and greeted him with a hearty handshake, clasping his other hand over Nathaniel's. "That's wonderful, son," he said, pulling him closer so he could be heard over the applause. He gestured toward all the trophies on the table. "All of this is wonderful."

"Thanks, Dad." Nathaniel set the trophy on the table with the other three and sat down as Miriam leaned over and hugged him. "I'm so proud of you."

"Thanks, Mom."

Matthew was called to the podium to end the program with a prayer. While his father was making his way, Nathaniel looked over at Martha who was wearing a huge smile, aimed at him. He smiled back. Just over her shoulder he saw Jason, also looking at him, calmly smiling. He had his hand on his plaque that he received for his Highest Achievement in Art award.

"Let us pray," Matthew said. "God, Father of us all, we thank you for these young men and women, for your guidance through the last twelve years of schooling, molding them into decent, upstanding Christians who will go forward as their motto says, 'Into The World For God.' Continue to guide them through their future studies so that they can become citizens who will fight the wrongs and sins of this world. Thank you for blessing them and their families. In the name of your most precious son, Jesus. Amen."

Reverend Haskins came to the podium as Matthew returned to his seat. "Let us stand and sing all four verses of the school hymn."

The band director had the student band play a brief introduction. Then, the banquet hall was filled with music. "Onward, Christian soldiers, marching as to war, with the cross of Jesus going on before. Christ, the royal Master, leads against the foe; forward into battle, see his banners go! Onward, Christian soldiers, marching as to war, with the cross of Jesus going on before...."

Without the need for the words the parents and students sang heartily all four verses. When they finished, another round of brief applause rose through the room as the band played exit music. The students and parents immediately began milling about congratulating each other.

Instantly Nathaniel was surrounded by fellow students, especially guys with whom he'd played sports, all shaking his hand. Many adults came up complimenting him.

Martha made her way through the crowd and eventually to Nathaniel's side. "I'm so proud of you," she said, giving him a light and very brief, permissible hug. Her smile and tone said that everything was fine. Apparently Jason had said nothing. For only a moment he felt a sense of relief, but the heaping adulation gnawed at him. He didn't deserve all this. He had to pretend to be excited and respond as he knew his father expected him to.

After Martha, others came up to congratulate him while she stood nearby. Then he felt a hand on his shoulder. He turned and saw Jason, extending his hand.

"Congratulations on all the hardware. That's terrific."

For what seemed like minutes Nathaniel was frozen. The surprise of Jason being so close, so unexpected, caught him off guard. He was here right beside him, looking so directly at him, so unafraid in front of all these people. In his silence, Nathaniel felt locked, attached to Jason as he stared into his eyes. This was the first time they had talked since last Monday. And Jason was acting normal, just as he always had—smiling, friendly, all of it seemingly real and honest—as if nothing out of the ordinary had ever happened between them. As if they were the best of friends.

"Thanks," Nathaniel said as naturally as he could. He shook Jason's hand.

"You deserve it," he said.

As Nathaniel loosened his grip on Jason's hand, he felt Jason continue to hold firmly but without saying anything, just staring at him. Finally, he let go. The lingering glance sent a ripple of fear through Nathaniel. More than a dozen other students plus adults, including his parents, were standing there. Had anyone noticed? Was Jason trying to hold his hand? He turned to someone else who was patting him on the back and congratulating him. When he turned back Jason was still there.

"You going to Lynnette's?" Jason asked.

Nathaniel took an extra moment to calculate his answer. "Yes, Martha and I are going."

"I'll see you there then," Jason said. He turned away as someone patted him on the back to congratulate him.

Nathaniel didn't respond but continued to talk to other classmates and their parents, forcing himself to go through the motion of smiling, shaking hands and hugging. But all the while his mind was whirring. The exchange with Jason pressured him.

As he drove Martha home, he silently told himself that he was fine. He was here with his girlfriend, a good Christian girl. And they would probably be married after college. He reached over and took her hand as they drove.

"I'll be back in twenty minutes," he told her as she opened the front door to her house.

"I'll be ready," she said, beaming with excitement.

Nathaniel drove home to change clothes. He came in the front door, carrying his trophies, plaques and scholarship letter, and went upstairs. As he reached the stop step, his father came down the hall.

"Need some help there?" Matthew asked. He was dressed in casual clothes.

"No, thanks, Dad. I've got them."

Matthew followed him into the room and closed the door. "You did me proud tonight, son. I just couldn't be more pleased with what you've accomplished. And tomorrow night's graduation— Well, I'm so looking forward to that. And your speech is perfect. You're on your way now."

"Thanks, Dad. I couldn't have done it without you," he said, then added, "and God." After the words were out of his mouth, he realized he should have added his mother to the list. He put the trophies and plaques on his desk.

Matthew waved a hand. "God, yes, for sure." He put his hands in his pockets. "I hope you took note of the conversation tonight between myself and George Wilson and Ken Warren. They're important men. As a minister you'll have to learn to play the political game with people who have influence and money. That's something we can work on when you come back for summer internship and as an associate."

Nathaniel took off his tuxedo jacket. "Okay, Dad." He also nodded, trying to appear normal but more importantly enthusiastic.

"But don't worry about that tonight. Have fun over at the Burches. Remember, home by midnight." He turned and opened the door.

"I won't be late," he said. He began to take off his tie.

"Oh, by the way," he said, stopping and turning back. "Carl Daniels, Jason's father, and I talked tonight."

Nathaniel froze. He stood staring at his father, scarcely breathing. His throat instantly felt like cotton.

"I told him I might be able to get Jason some financial aid to Freedom. There are some people recruiting incoming freshman for the new law school. I think Jason might make a fine attorney, don't you?"

Nathaniel fought to get words to come out of his mouth to answer his father before he suspected anything was wrong. He inhaled as normally as he could. "Sure." No need to say more. Just breathe, he told himself.

"His father was certainly interested." Matthew stepped to the threshold. "I thought it would be a nice gesture since he lost the Bible Scholar Competition. Don't say anything to Jason about it. His father's pretty excited. Said he'd talk to Jason."

Nathaniel nodded. "I won't mention it."

"Okay, have fun." Matthew closed the door.

Nathaniel sat down on his bed, closed his eyes and took several deep breaths. He would be fine. Nobody knows anything, he tried to convince himself. Just him and Jason. This was a most important night. After tonight he would never feel this panicky again. He was going to prove that to himself in a matter of hours. He changed into shorts and a polo shirt. He had to hurry. He had told Martha twenty minutes.

When he opened the door into the hallway, Sarah Elizabeth was standing just outside.

"Quite a haul, Mr. Senior-Everything," she said, looking into his room at the trophies.

He stepped back for her to see. "Thanks, sis."

"At least you're modest." She hesitated a moment. "I was going to tell you this tomorrow night, but I might as well do it now." She pointed to the trophies. "Just another trophy for you." She waited. "I couldn't ask for a better brother. I'm really proud to be your sister." She smiled sheepishly, stood on her tiptoes and kissed him on the cheek.

He put his arms around her but wondered how tightly. He was so confused by everything. Maybe after tonight—no, for sure, after tonight, his mind would be clearer. "And I couldn't ask for a better sister. I'm proud of you, too."

She gave him a squeeze and then took a step back. "But I'm not giving you your graduation present until you've actually graduated." She turned toward her own room. "Have fun at the party," she said, then added in a teasing, sing-songy tone, "You and Martha."

Nathaniel smiled until she had closed her door. I hope you won't ever change your mind, he thought. When he came down the stairs, Miriam was waiting for him, smiling. A wave of guilt wafted over him for avoiding her so much during the week.

"You look nice, as always," she said softly. "I know you're in a hurry, but I want to tell you again how very proud I am of you. I just—" She paused.

Nathaniel waited. "Just what, Mom?"

She looked down, then back up at him. She took his hands. "Have fun tonight." She thought for only an instant. "No. Have a *great* time." She dropped his hands and hugged him.

Nathaniel held her tightly for several moments. "I will, Mom. But I'll be home on time." He kissed her on the cheek, then moved backward toward the front door.

Miriam's genuine smile had not faded. "I know you will."

He didn't know what made him say it. He hadn't plan to. He hadn't told her all week. Where did the words come from? So spontaneously. They just tumbled out of his mouth. "I love you, Mom."

She beamed. "I love you, too." As he opened the door and left she waved to him, then turned and walked into the kitchen.

Outside, Nathaniel jogged across the lawn to his Cherokee. As he neared the driver's door, he saw a figure, a person move from behind it toward him. At first, even in the dimness of the streetlight, he wasn't able to see who it was. Then, when he did, for a split second his heart rushed, beating faster.

"What are you doing here?" he asked. He hadn't planned on this.

"Waiting for you," Jason said. He had changed clothes, wearing shorts and a t-shirt.

"Why?" He reached for the door handle. "Aren't you going to Lynnette's?"

"I don't know. I haven't decided yet."

"I've got to pick up—"

"I want to talk to you. No. I *have* to talk to you. You've been ignoring me since—" He hesitated, then took a deep breath. "Since last Monday afternoon." The only sound was the chirping of crickets. "Please, Nate."

Nathaniel remembered his bargain with God—talking with Jason, what to say. Now here it was. He had to be strong, not afraid. He would take care of this. He would stay calm and speak his truth. The truth of God. "Get in," he said. Jason went around to the other side of the car. This was it, Nathaniel told himself. If this was his time to give his testimony to Jason, that's what he would do. Convince him that this was wrong. A chance for him to change.

Jason handed him a DVD case. "Here's your DVD. *The Sports Illustrated*. World Series. You left it last Monday."

Nathaniel took the DVD and reached around, putting it on the back seat but said nothing.

"All I wanted to say was that I'm sorry if I rushed you or pushed you too fast. If you're not ready—"

Nathaniel shook his head but did not look at him. "It's not about me being ready. It's about— I'm not that way. It's not who I am. And I don't think you are either." He kept his eyes focused in front of him, toward the garage. "I've done a lot of praying about—about last Monday. I think it was a test from God. A test to see if I was strong enough to resist temptation. And I—"

"You don't believe that. You can't believe that. You know it's not true. What about all those times in the shower at school when we looked at each other? Not to mention Monday afternoon. What was that about?"

Nathaniel looked out the side window of the car to avoid facing him. "That was part of the test. A mistake. I'm going to be—"

"That's bullshit and you know it."

Nathaniel didn't acknowledge the profanity. "I'm going to be a minister. I'll have a lot of tests from God. This was just one of them." He thought about what to say next. "You can change, too. You don't have to be—to be like that. You can be normal. Like I am."

Jason looked at him. "They said you'd say that."

Fear shot through every fiber of Nathaniel's being. He turned to face him. His eyes wide with terror. "They? Who have you been talking to? Who have you told about me?"

Jason saw his wildness and dread. "I didn't tell anybody your name," he said calmly. "It's a group I've been going to. My parents don't even know about it—obviously. A kind of support group. There's this counselor. He's great. I wish you'd come and talk to—"

Nathaniel turned away and gripped the steering wheel as if he feared being swept away. "I told you I'm not—not that way. I—"

"You can't even say it, can you? You can't even say the word 'gay.' If you're not gay, then why can't you say it? It's just a simple word. One syllable."

Nathaniel ignored him. "You've got your whole future before you. At Freedom. You don't want to go through your life like this."

Jason's voice depicted resolve and determination. "I'm not going to Freedom."

Nathaniel looked at him. "What are you talking about?"

"I want to study what I want to. I want to draw, create, be free. Not memorize my way through school." There was excitement in his voice. "I've got a job this summer. In August I'm going to Loflin Community College and take classes in art and design. Maybe transfer to State in a year or two. Advertising. Graphic design. Architecture. I don't know yet."

"Your father's not going to let you do that."

"My father's not going to rule my life anymore. I'm going to be who I am, not what he wants me to be. He told me tonight he wants me to think about going to the new law school at Freedom." His voice was filled with sarcasm and disbelief. "I mean, how asinine." He turned to Nathaniel. "You can do that, too," he said genuinely. "Be who you are."

Nathaniel closed his eyes. What should he say? Help me, God, he thought. He looked at Jason. "You can get help. There are places you can go to get this abomination out of you. You can be normal. God wants you to be normal." He turned his body halfway toward Jason. "He doesn't want you to sin. If you keep on, you'll go to hell. But you've got to repent and admit it." He stopped. Jason hadn't interrupted him. Maybe he was getting through.

"Yeah, one of those places. Like they sent Steve Baker to. And what did he do? Ran away."

"That was different. He was different."

"That's right. He was different. But that didn't make him wrong. It didn't make him bad or a sinner."

Nathaniel looked away.

Jason shook his head. "I was so hoping."

Nathaniel could hear the calm in his voice—quiet, sincere emotion. He watched as Jason slowly reached over and put his hand on his bare leg and lightly stroked it. Nathaniel didn't pull away for a moment as exciting electricity shot through his body. Then he forced himself to move his leg.

"Just another test?" Jason asked softly.

Again, Nathaniel looked out the side window, his guts churning.

"I won't bother you again. If you change your mind, you know how to find me." He put his hand on the door handle but waited before opening it. "I—" He stopped, hesitating. "I want you to know that I love you," he whispered. He opened the door and got out of the car.

The three words paralyzed Nathaniel. The sound of his car driving away wrenched his heart. No, he ordered as thoughts poured through his mind. He wasn't that way. God had protected him. No one knew about last Monday. And if Jason had ever told anybody, he would deny it. *I love you* echoed through his mind. He was safe. God was with him. *If God is for you, who can be against you?* Romans 8:31. No harm can come to him. *I love—*

Just then his cell phone rang, jolting him from his thoughts. He reached into the side pocket of his cargo shorts. His heart was still racing. Martha. Thank you, God. "Hi, there. I'm on my way," he said, starting his car. He had to sound normal, as if everything was okay.

"Oh, no, I wasn't checking up on you. Honest. I just wanted to remind you to be sure to bring your annual."

He backed down the driveway. "Oh, yeah. It's here in the back seat." Calm down, he told himself.

"Oh, well, I should have known that you'd have thought of that ahead of time."

"Well, I appreciate that and I appreciate the reminder anyway. As a matter of fact, I appreciate you totally." He did appreciate her.

"Well, aren't you sweet?" she said softly with coziness. "Thank you. I appreciate you, too. So very much."

Nathaniel heard her words. This was what he needed to hear, he told himself—Martha's voice. "I more than appreciate you." He couldn't believe he'd said that. But why not? He was safe. Now. "I'll see you in a few minutes."

"Okay," she said, again softly. "I'll be waiting."

He put his phone back in his pocket. God had intervened to help him. Martha's call had come at just the right time. Talking with

Jason had been another part of the test. And he had passed. And Martha calling was proof of that. Yes, everything was just fine. And whenever the words, *I love you,* tried to break into his thoughts, he would force himself to think of something else. Martha. Yes, *I love you* would make him think of her.

He drove as quickly as he dared. The girl that he liked. The girl that he wanted to be with. The only person he wanted to be with. He knew that the day would come when he would tell her that he loved her, that they would get married and have a family. That she would follow him and be there to support him as he continued his father's and grandfather's ministry. All of that should be enough to prove that he was normal. That all these—these thoughts and even the wet dreams—were just part of the test God had given him. He had pulled away from Jason's hand on his leg. He hadn't said anything about loving Jason. The thought never entered his mind. That was just too— What was it? Not normal. An abomination. His father was right and so was the Bible.

Minutes later at Martha's house he rang the doorbell. She opened the door with her mother standing in the hallway talking on the phone. She waved to Nathaniel and he waved back. She put her hand over the receiver and whispered, "Have fun. Remember, midnight."

"We remember," Martha whispered. Then, in the same whisper she jokingly whispered to Nathaniel, "I'm ready."

"Okay," he whispered, playing along.

Mrs. Davies pointed toward the door for them to leave as she shook her head at their making fun of her. Nathaniel grazed Martha's arm as they went out the door. She grazed back.

"I thought the banquet was awesome," she said as he started the car, put it in gear and drove away.

"Yeah, it was great. The whole thing was pretty amazing. It gets better every year." Stay calm. Be normal.

"And you with all those awards. You're so awesome."

The compliment made him tighten inside. Scenes of Monday afternoon. Jason's hand on his leg. *I love—*

"You're the awesome one," he said in a quiet voice, his gut wrenched with torment. He put his hand on the console next to hers. He wanted to be bold. He needed to be. Tonight more than ever. He needed to be a man, a Christian man. But he needed to break the rules, just this once. He reached over and took her hand, interlocking his fingers with hers. Martha looked at him, then down at their hands. She smiled and moved her hand so that the angle was not as awkward. She had put on some kind of soft fragrance. It was nice but not—not as exciting like Jason's scent had been. He gripped the steering wheel tighter. Stop it.

They rode the rest of the way to Lynnette's house in silence. He wished he could feel the same excitement— He *would* feel the same excitement. Later tonight. After the party. He knew he would.

Just as he slowed to park, Nathaniel squeezed her hand and let go. As they walked toward the house, he looked around for Jason's car. He didn't see it. Maybe he wasn't coming. That was unlikely. This was the senior event. Everyone was invited.

Several times during the party as Nathaniel and Martha signed yearbooks they glanced at each other across the room and smiled. A secret smile. A secret between them, just them.

Eventually, Nathaniel saw Jason. He was alone but quickly began passing his yearbook to people to sign. Maybe he would avoid him. He hoped Jason would see him and Martha as they smiled at each other, not to be vindictive, but to understand—to understand that he didn't want to be with him. That he was not like him. He continued signing and talking with his friends, acting just like he always had. He wasn't going to let Jason spoil the party for him. He would depend on God. God would show him the way.

"Can I be next?"

Nathaniel sat cross-legged on the floor of the screened back porch amid eight or nine other seniors. He had just signed Andrea Smithson's annual and was handing it to her in exchange for his when he heard the request coming from behind and above him.

He recognized Jason's voice immediately. A cold shutter coursed through him. God, please protect me, he prayed.

"Sure," he said evenly but did not look up at him. He offered his annual as Jason sat down on the floor beside him, bumping his own bare knee against Nathaniel's, the thick hair tickling. Nathaniel moved his knee so they would not be touching. Jason did not react.

Nathaniel opened his book and found a small space. He had to write something simple and short. No cryptic messages. Nothing at all personal. Yet, he didn't want it to be so brief that anyone else who saw it might think something was wrong. "Best of luck with college and beyond," Nathaniel wrote trying to hide his paramount fear. "You're a great baseball player and student. I know you'll go far in life." He wanted to wish him luck with all of the tests that God was bringing his way but knew that he couldn't write that. "God bless you. Nate."

He closed the book and was about to hand it to Jason, but Jason was still writing. Shear horror moved through him. He would have to read it before handing it to anyone else. What if Jason was writing something about—about what had happened between them? He wouldn't write what he had told him in the car, would he? That—that he loved him? Nathaniel could feel his armpits getting wet. He started talking to others around him. Pretending to ignore Jason but making sure that he kept him in his periphery. That he could get his annual before it went to anyone else.

Just then someone said something that made everyone laugh. Nathaniel hadn't heard it but laughed anyway.

"Okay. Done," Jason said. They exchanged books. "Thanks, Nate."

"No problem."

Jason then exchanged his with someone else and began writing.

Nathaniel stood up, holding on to his annual. "I think I'll get something to eat," he said to the group. Then added, "And find Martha." Just for assurance, clarification, to emphasize his stance, he thought. Jason did not look up.

He started for the kitchen but was hoping to go down a short hallway to the bathroom. He could go in and read it. Instead, Martha caught him.

"Hey. Come in here." She took his arm and gently pulled him into the den where Jerry Hines was showing everyone his new laptop that his parents had given him for graduation. Nathaniel forced himself to appear interested but all the while clutching his yearbook. "He's using the built-in web cam to record everyone saying something. Then he's going to send it to all of us. Isn't that a neat idea?"

"Go on, Nate. You're next. You and Martha say something," Jerry said as others cleared the way for them to hold the laptop and view themselves on the screen.

Martha giggled and sat closer to him. "Okay, you go first."

"Me?" Nathaniel said. "Okay. Um…it's, uh, been a great however many years we've all been in school together, but the last four of high school have been awesome." Cheers and whistles went up around him. "I'm just looking forward to Freedom Bible U, uh," he paused, trying think of more to say. He wanted to end this because Jason had just walked into the room and was watching. "Where Martha and I are going together. It'll be another great four years. Right?" He turned to her. "Your turn."

Martha giggled, again. "Well, uh, yes. It has been great here with all of you for so long and the next four years will be great, too. And who knows after that? Whatever God decides." She looked at Nathaniel and smiled. He returned it as everyone in the room agreed with applause, whistles and a few "Amens."

When Nathaniel looked back, Jason had left the room and he didn't see him anymore from that point on. When he was finally alone in the bathroom, he read what Jason had written. "Nate, I guess I won't see much of you after graduation. I regret that. You're a special guy and your friendship has meant the world to me. I wish you every happiness. 'Always, Jase.'"

Too personal, he thought. Not what a guy should write to a guy. And why did he write 'Always, Jase' like that with quotes? He wanted to tear the page out of the book. Maybe he would when he got home. Just cut it out so no one could tell. What if his father saw it? At the same time, he was relieved he hadn't written what he'd told him sitting in the car. The three words ran through his mind, again. Stop it, he ordered himself. He flushed the toilet and ran some water so anyone waiting outside the door wouldn't suspect anything.

Around eleven-thirty Mr. And Mrs. Burch and the other chaperones began urging everyone to leave and drive carefully.

"That was a great idea that Jerry had," Martha said as they drove. "I can't wait to see the finished version. I'll probably watch it a million times."

"Yeah, me, too," Nathaniel said, stroking his thumb against hers as they held hands.

She held his hand tighter. Her voice cozy. "I'm glad we did ours together."

Nathaniel felt an uneasiness. He could see she was snuggling back against the seat. Why was he so nervous? They had kissed before. But never with so much privacy that he was planning on. Dark and deserted.

She said very little else, but Nathaniel sensed as she rubbed her thumb over his that she was giving him a sign. Maybe permission. If she wasn't, then she wouldn't appear so—so what? Ready? As he processed all this, he wanted to feel excited. Physically. It was almost their curfew. He had to decide what he was going to do. It was a special night. After Jason earlier— He had to prove to himself.

He slowed the car and pulled to the curb several blocks from Martha's house. She didn't say anything. There were no houses nearby. No streetlights. He released her hand and turned the car off.

"I thought maybe we— I mean, would it be okay with you if we stopped here for some private time?" he asked, holding her hand, again. His voice was shaking, his heart pounding. He tried to tell himself it was the same kind of feeling he'd had on Monday.

Martha did not hesitate. "Very okay," she said softly, turning toward him and putting her other hand on top of his.

Nathaniel tried to grin, to show he was pleased that she accepted his invitation. Instead, his countenance didn't change. He released her hand put his arm around her shoulder and gently pulled her to him, both of them leaning across the console. He pressed his lips against hers and felt her hand on the back of his neck. He concentrated on the softness of her cheek. She slid her hand from the back of his neck to his cheek. He felt her lips kneading his and he followed her lead. He waited for something more from himself, some spark, some urge to do more, to touch more. He had to do something. He needed proof. But what? Maybe bring his hand from her back closer to her side, near her breast. That wouldn't be right. That didn't matter. He had to know. Slowly, he brought his hand around. He felt Martha leaning closer and at the same time maneuvering her body to make her breast more accessible. The possibility was there. He kept moving. This wasn't right. He shouldn't be doing this. He didn't want to do this. They weren't married. Still, she was not stopping him. He moved his hand until he was finally cupping her breast. Martha's breathing became more rapid as she pressed her mouth tighter against his. He felt her lips parting. He opened his. Her tongue touched his lips. He knew he should gently squeeze her breast, massage it, stroke it. He was supposed to do something. He was supposed to— Supposed to what? Why was he having so much trouble? What was happening? Why couldn't he want this? Martha was wanting this. He had to want it. He did, too. Maybe he hadn't done enough, gone far enough. Maybe the next step would make him feel something, make him want something.

He heard her moan as they continued kissing, the tips of their tongues lightly touching. With uncertainty Nathaniel stroked her breast. She sighed, making his anxiety heightened. Was she giving him permission? He reached down and put his hand under her shirt, touching her bare waist, then up her side and to her bra. Without pulling away, Martha put her arm behind her back, under her shirt and unhooked it. The looseness allowed him to put his hand underneath it. The soft mushy flesh. Her nipple, supple and pointy. Why wasn't he enjoying this? Why was this—

Suddenly, the memory of last Monday plunged into his mind like a knife. In Jason's room. The two of them on the bed, naked together, entangled, insatiably wanting—

Martha sat back and began to lift up her shirt over her head.

Nothing was happening inside him. No erection. No desire. No unforgettable sensation coursing through him, wanting more. Not like last Monday. He took his hand away and turned in his seat, looking straight ahead. His mind hollow.

"Don't," he whispered. He looked down, unable to look at her.

Martha stopped, frozen, and sat back. Her voice was soft but her tone was apprehensive. "What's wrong?"

He felt so utterly vulnerable, exposed, as if she had just found out, as if she had walked in on him and Jason and knew everything— every last detail, every feeling, every thought, every messy dream—

"Nathaniel, what?"

He could hear emotion in her voice. He just shook his head.

"Did I do something? Did—"

"No," he said calmly. "You didn't do anything wrong." He started to tell her that he was the one who'd done something wrong. Him, the future minister. Him, the Bible Scholar. Him, with the student-athlete award, the best all-round male trophy, the best disciple plaque. Him, the queer, the faggot, the homo. He was the one. He was the failure. The sinner.

He had to say something—an excuse to assure her this was not her fault. "I'm just not feeling good. Maybe something from the banquet or the punch at the party."

"Are you sure?"

"Yes," he said.

Martha put her arms behind her back and fastened her bra, then reached over and put her hand on his arm.

"It's my stomach."

He said nothing more but simply started the car and drove Martha home. He did not reach for her hand. When they got to her house, he got out, met her on the other side of the car and walked to the front door, his hands in his pockets, silent.

At the front door, Martha turned. "Are you sure I didn't—"

"Absolutely sure." He spoke softly. "It's me." Saying those two words aloud, he realized that was the first time he had expressed any real honesty.

"Please call me tomorrow and let me know how you're feeling."

He nodded. No smile. Simply blank. "I'm sorry," he said.

She shook her head. "Just be better." She reached out for him.

"I will." He hugged her briefly, then turned and went to his car.

He drove away without thinking where he was going. Not home. Because now everything was different. He saw it all. He saw now that he could never tell Martha or any girl that he loved her. Not that way. Not in a romantic way. Not cherished, like in marriage vows. No. He knew now that he could love only one way. The wrong way. The condemned way. Condemned by God, the Bible and his father. Even though the litany of denunciations in his head continued, there was nothing to fight. Not anymore. No undoing who he was. No undoing his love for Jason. No erasing or even easing the shame. Everyone would know.

Driving toward the highway, he thought about praying the Lord's prayer but decided he didn't deserve to say the words. The same with the Twenty-Third Psalm. A sinner didn't have the right. And he was a sinner. And God hated him.

CHAPTER TWELVE

SATURDAY—MAY 23

The alarm clock buzzed loud and piercing. Matthew jolted awake and turned it off. As usual he did not press the snooze bar. When it was time to get up, it was time to get up. He didn't even look at it. It was seven a. m. The time he got up every Saturday. He wanted the house to himself, totally quiet while he reviewed his sermon for the next day, the only interruption being Miriam bringing him coffee before the family had breakfast together.

He swung his legs out of bed and went into the bathroom where he shaved, showered and brushed his teeth. He dressed in casual clothes and opened the bedroom door into the hall. As he turned to go downstairs, he noticed that Nathaniel's door was half open, precisely as it had been when he, Miriam and Sarah Elizabeth had prayed before going to bed. It wasn't like Nathaniel to get up this early on a Saturday. Matthew looked inside. When he saw his tuxedo spread neatly across the still made up bed and the bathroom dark, all thoughts about his sermon and day's agenda evaporated. He went downstairs into the kitchen and looked outside. No Jeep Cherokee. He looked around the kitchen for a note. Nothing.

He picked up the house phone and dialed his son's cell. The ringing seemed endless. Finally, he got his voice mail.

"Nathaniel," he said with unmistakable concern and authority. "This is your father. Call me immediately." He hung up. Should he call the Davies? If Martha hadn't come home, they would have called last night. If he called them, they would wonder why he waited until this morning to find out where his son was. What if they hadn't realized she wasn't home—as he hadn't? But if she was home now— What if others in the church found out? Say he was a bad parent? His mind ran rampant. He had to do something. He went from the kitchen through the dining room into the foyer.

Miriam was coming down the stairs, tying her robe. "There's a car in front of the house with two men in it." She discerned the perplexed look on Matthew's face. "What's wrong?"

Matthew ignored her question as he looked out the window by the front door. Two males were emerging from a plain sedan parked in front of the house. Neat, clean cut, fit. Both with blank faces. One carried what looked like a manila envelope. "Did you hear Nathaniel come home last night?" he asked.

"No." Alarm was evident in her voice. "Isn't he here?"

"No," he said simply, not looking at her as he stood by the door. "Is his car here?"

"No."

"Did you call his cell phone?"

"Of course, I called it," he snapped. "And there's no note any-where, either." "Call the Davies and see if Martha knows anything."

"No, I'm not going to do that. It's too early. I don't want anyone to know that I didn't know he didn't come home."

Miriam had a desperate urge to take up for her son, to demand something be done, but she held back, kept it in check as she was expected to do.

The doorbell jarred the room. "Go upstairs and get dressed," Matthew ordered sternly.

Miriam hesitated. She wanted to know where her son was. But Matthew's eyes pierced any resolve she might muster.

He stood with his hand on the door knob and watched as she ascended the steps. When he saw her disappear down the hallway and heard their bedroom door close, he opened the front door as the doorbell sounded a second time.

The two men were dressed in sport coats and knit shirts, open at the collar. Both with wallet like folders—one half in their outer breast pocket, the other half hanging out revealing a badge. One who stood back and to the side was younger, and had dark hair with a part near the middle of his head. The other was taller, crew cut peppered with gray, a solid build. He quickly emerged as the spokesman.

"Yes?" Matthew said.

"Sir, I'm sorry to bother you so early. I'm Detective Gary Sparks. This is Detective Bill Montgomery. We're with the sheriff's department. Is this the home of Nathaniel Harris Winslow?"

Matthew answered quickly. "Yes. I'm Reverend Matthew Winslow. I'm his father."

"May we come in, please?"

"Where's Nathaniel? What's wrong?"

"Reverend Winslow, I think it would be better if we could talk inside."

Matthew's heart raced as he stepped back and ushered the detectives into the foyer and then into his study. He glanced up the stairway to be sure that neither Miriam nor Sarah Elizabeth was out in the hallway. He closed the door. All three men remained standing.

"What is this about? Where is Nathaniel?" he asked immediately. He stood next to his desk.

"Sir, I'm sorry to tell you that—that your son died last night shortly after midnight."

An unfathomable hollowness opened inside Matthew. His entire body weakened. He pushed it back. Suppressed it. He put his hand on the desk to steady himself. "That's impossible." He forced a nervous, disbelieving smile. "He's graduating tonight from high school. Holy Bible Academy. An A student. Top of his class. He's going to college next year. Full scholarship. You've made a terrible mistake." He shook his head, still smiling almost laughing nervously one instant, then serious the next, denying any possibility that something so horrendous could happen to him or to Nathaniel. He started for the door to usher them out.

Detective Sparks took a photograph from a manila envelope and held it out for Matthew to look at. "I'm sorry to have to show you this, Reverend. Is this your son?"

Matthew refused to touch the photo as if doing so would lend credence to what this detective was saying. For several moments he looked only at the detective's brown eyes, not the photograph, refusing to confirm any possibility, refusing to believe that his life could be so disrupted. Finally, he turned his eyes downward to the empty, pale, young face, the neck striped with dark bruises.

Matthew's smile of denial faded as he stared at the photograph. This wasn't happening to him, to his family, to his son. He sat down limply on the sofa, leaned his elbows on his knees and buried his face in his hands.

"Reverend," Sparks asked after a few respectful moments, very softly as he returned the photo to the envelope. "Is this your son?"

Matthew could not bring himself to speak. This simply was not happening to him. Not him. He had the perfect family. He had worked so hard to make everything perfect. Nathaniel going to college, then Divinity School, then becoming an associate at Holy Bible, eventually the senior pastor. Preaching on national television. What did this mean? How could he be dead? His son. How? What? He felt his tears on his palms. He sniffed back his emotion.

"Reverend?" the detective asked sympathetically.

Matthew merely nodded his head. After a moment he wiped away the wetness with his hands. When he spoke, his voice was scarcely a whisper. "Who did this to him? Who would do such a thing to my son?" he asked, looking up at Sparks.

The two detectives looked at each other. Sparks kept his voice soft and concerned. "We don't suspect anyone else was involved."

Matthew was incredulous. Instantly, his demeanor changed. "What are you saying?"

The detective took a deep breath and spoke with compassion. "All the preliminary evidence points to the fact that Nathaniel took his own life, Reverend Winslow."

"No." Matthew stood up. "No." The smile of denial appeared again and was gone just as quickly. "That's not possible. Nathaniel would never do such a thing. That's a sin and he knows it." He was vehemently shaking his head and wagging his finger as he moved across the room and turned back to the two men. "No, you're wrong. I don't care what the evidence is. No, no, no." He stared at Detective Sparks. "There's nothing you can say that will ever convince me of any such thing. He loves God too much. He is a Christian. A fine, upstanding Christian boy—young man. He has everything going for him. No, sir. God would not let this happen."

Detective Sparks didn't stop Matthew from pouring out his anger.

"Just what evidence do you have?" he asked, his tone exuding defiance, his only weapon.

Detective Sparks took a small notebook from inside his coat pocket. "It occurred out on Ratchford Road, just about a mile off of rural Highway Seven, not far from the Interstate. A farmer found your son's Jeep and—and your son's body—" He stopped and looked at Matthew with sympathy. "I'm sorry, Reverend—your son's body hanging from a tree limb. He used a bungee cord. An identical cord was found in the Jeep which was next to the tree." He paused again. "The farmer called 911. When we arrived at the scene we found that the bungee cord was wrapped around his neck several times. That's why there is so much bruising. We believe that's the sole cause of death." He paused for a moment. "As for anyone else being involved—there's just no evidence. There were no other tire tracks in the grass. Your son was wearing shorts. His knees, legs, arms and hands all had minor scrapes consistent with coming in contact with the bark as he climbed the tree."

As the detective spoke, Matthew's demeanor softened, the color in his face drained. He stared at Sparks for a several moments as the silence in the room seemed to echo. "You said you believe that—that this is the cause—the bungee cord. You're not sure?"

"We can never say for sure until the medical examiner gives us a final report," Sparks said with compassion. "With cases like this an autopsy is mandated by state law."

"So it could be drugs. I mean, somebody could have drugged him and—and—done this. I've been quite outspoken about homosexuals. In the newspaper and on television. Maybe some of them did something. Lured him or ganged up on him."

The detective looked down. "Reverend, we saw nothing that gave us reason to suspect that."

Matthew turned and walked toward the window.

"There is one other thing, Reverend Winslow," Sparks said.

Matthew turned and looked at him but did not speak.

"Is that your cell phone?" He pointed with his notepad to a phone on the credenza behind Matthew's desk.

"Yes," Matthew answered with suspicion. "Why?"

Detective Montgomery moved around the desk and unplugged the phone from its recharging cord.

"I know this will be very difficult for you, Reverend. Please know I respect completely the shock you're going through, but the law dictates that we have to take your phone because your son's phone shows that he placed a call to you around twelve-thirty a. m. Did you receive a call from him?"

"No, it's been down here recharging since before eleven last night."

"Since he left no written note, he may have left a voicemail which could give us some valuable information—something that's not at the scene. A reason. Another person, as you suggested."

Watching as Montgomery put the phone in a plastic bag, Matthew frantically rubbed his forehead. "Can I at least check to see if he left a message?"

"I'm sorry, Reverend. That's not within the parameter of the law and handling of evidence."

"I know the mayor and some very powerful lawyers," he said, growing furious. "You can't just come in here and take that."

"I'm sorry, Reverend," Detective Sparks said. "As I said it's considered evidence." Before Matthew could respond, he added, "I have a search warrant signed by a judge." He took a folded piece of paper from his coat pocket and handed it to him. "When we've listened to the voicemail, if there is one, and analyzed it, we'll return the phone to you."

"When exactly?"

"In a few days."

"A few days!" Matthew unfolded the paper and merely glanced at it before leaning on his desk, his stiffened arms supporting him, the search warrant crumpled in his hand. He stood silent for several minutes, staring at the photograph on his desk of his family, his eyes riveted solely on Nathaniel. Had he called him? The thought of his son calling for help…. That he was in some kind of danger and had called in vain….

Sparks again showed his respect and sympathy in his tone. "Just one last question, please Reverend. Had your son been depressed or been behaving in any way out of the ordinary?"

Matthew continued staring at the photograph. He shook his head. "No. Last night he received four or five awards at a school banquet." He spoke as if he were reliving memories from years ago. "He went to a class party with Martha Davies, his girlfriend. He was supposed to be home by midnight, his curfew. He's never late."

Sparks wrote in his notebook.

Matthew detached himself from his memories as he returned to the present. He dropped the rumpled warrant on his desk and faced the detectives. He felt emotion threatening, again. "Is there anything else?"

"No, sir. Not now. Here's my card if you have any questions." Sparks handed him a business card and took a slightly deeper breath than usual. "We'll call you when the medical examiner releases the body. And again, Reverend Winslow, you have our deepest sympathy." He waited for a moment while Matthew stared at the card, silent, motionless as a statue. When he didn't speak, the detective made a suggestion. "Reverend, is there someone else here? Someone who could be with you now?"

Matthew looked at him. "My wife and daughter. Yes, I'll have to tell them."

"Very well. We'll see ourselves out."

Matthew didn't listen for the front door to shut as he sat down on the sofa. He looked down. His hands were trembling. He clasped them together as the one word embedded itself in his mind. Suicide. No. A sin. Not Nathaniel. He couldn't believe it. He *would* not believe it. No matter what some detectives said. They don't know him. They don't know Nathaniel. Someone did this horrible thing to his son. Someone would pay. The message on the phone would give them reason enough. They'd have to investigate and find out—

"Matthew?" Miriam stood in the doorway, apprehension consumed her.

He stood up, staring at her, as if in a trance, completely void of reality.

"Matthew?" she said with more force as she came into the room and stood in front of him. "Who were those men?"

He closed his eyes for a brief moment, took a deep breath, then looked at her. He slowly walked to the door and closed it. "Is Sarah Elizabeth still asleep?" he asked.

"Yes," she said simply, staring at him, waiting for him to speak.

Matthew almost ignored her, gazing off, contemplating, planning. He had to be very careful. He had to be sure that Miriam would stay composed, strong. Yes, that was it. Strong. But first he had to be the strong one. He gripped one hand with the other. He had to hold everything and everyone together. He was the head of the house. He could do this. He had to. He was supposed to. He was the leader of this family *and* the church. Strong like his father and grandfather. He had to act as they would act.

"Matthew," she said, fighting to control the urgency in her voice. "Where—what's happened? Where is Nathaniel?"

He had to think. Suicide. He could not allow that to become public, especially since it would be proven false in the investigation. He had to keep everything under control.

He led her to the sofa and sat down with her, taking both of her hands in his. "Those men—those men are detectives with the sheriff's department," he began. "They said that Nathaniel was— A farmer found him. Out in the county." He looked into her eyes—blue, deep blue, surrounded by white. Then a memory floated into his mind. The first time he saw her in the hospital holding Nathaniel just minutes after he'd been born, then again later after she had breast fed him for the first time and he was sleeping in her arms—

"Matthew," Miriam said with more force than she'd ever dared in all of their years of marriage.

Still he stared at her, turmoil now pushing into his mind, prodding him. Control. Maintain control. Prepare yourself. Prepare her. He had to prepare Miriam to be strong.

"A farmer found him? Doing what?" Tears edged to her eyelashes.

Matthew took a deep breath and at the same time took her hand, feeling the cool dampness in her palm. "I want you to be strong, Miriam." He fought the shaking in his voice and his hands. "You must be strong. This is terrible. It isn't going to be easy for any of us. I am tortured by this, but God will see us through." His own eyes filled.

Miriam began shaking her head, small movements at first then larger, more determined ones. "No," she said. She clenched his hands.

"He's gone." Matthew held her so that she could not pull away. "Nathaniel is dead, Miriam."

Miriam gasped as her eyes widened in disbelief. "No," she said again but louder. She pulled her hands away from his and covered her mouth. Her face blanched with shock and horror. Tears began cascading down her cheeks as she stared at him. Her breathing was labored and panicked.

Matthew wanted to hold her, put his arms around her, but Miriam sat slumped into her own cell of grief, numb and unreachable. His mind raced.

"The detectives said that—they haven't finished with the investigation. They don't know yet, not for sure." He leaned closer, grasping for control of himself and her. "We're not going to believe it. Not ever. No matter what they find."

"Believe what?" she asked distantly.

He reached out and pulled her hands down, firmly holding them.

"They said it appeared he had hanged himself from a tree using a bungee cord in his car," Matthew blurted. "But I don't believe it. Nathaniel would never commit such a sin. Never." He gripped her hands tightly, more to hide the shaking of his own.

Miriam's eyes widened in horror. She riveted her gaze on Matthew. She spoke softly, shaking her head saying a mere single word again and again. "No." She continued shaking her head, her voice still scarcely audible, dampness covering her cheeks.

"Miriam, shh, listen to me," Matthew said with soothing patience. "You must listen to me."

Miriam stared at him void of comprehension. "He can't be— be—." The final word needed unimaginable effort to escape from her mouth, and with it came more tears.

"You must get a hold on yourself. You must control yourself. You have to be strong. I'm relying on you. God is relying on you. When the truth comes out, then we can know that our son never committed this sin. Those detectives are simply wrong." He squeezed her hands and shook them gently. "Can you do that, Miriam? Can you do what God is asking you to do in this most difficult time? Can you be his servant? Can you?" His voice was desperate, pleading.

Teardrops hung on her jaw and fell onto her blouse.

"Can you do this for God and for me, for Nathaniel and for Sarah Elizabeth?" Matthew shook her hands for emphasis with each name. "Can you?" He leaned closer, pleading. "Will you?" he whispered. "Remember the scripture: 'Yea, though I walk through the valley of the shadow of death, I will fear no evil. For thou art with me.'" He gave her hands another tug. "Will you do this?"

Miriam simply stared at her husband and finally nodded.

"Right now I want you to go upstairs and tell Sarah Elizabeth while I see to matters concerning the church." Still gripping her hands, they stood up together. "Come along. God will get us through this. But no matter what, we have to be strong. We are the first family in our church. People look up to us, expect us to be an example of strength."

Miriam looked at him, dazed.

"After I call Richard, I'll be upstairs and we'll pray. I'll take care of everything."

He led her to the door and, finally releasing her hands, ushered her out. "I'll be up in just a minute," he said, trying to reassure her. "You must be strong, Miriam." Slowly, he closed the door, leaving her in the foyer.

He sat down at his desk. How could this be happening? Oh, God, no. What should he do now? He fought his emotions, the fear of being overwhelmed by this catastrophe. The fear of falling apart. The fear of failing. The church. What will they think if this turns out to be true? No, it wouldn't. Not Nathaniel. He wouldn't do such a thing. Why would he? Yes, why would he sin against his own father and his Father in Heaven? No. It simply was not true. That would be his stance. His stance with his family, the church and anyone else. That's what his father would do. He had to be careful how he handled this. He gathered his thoughts. The police report would be forthcoming but certainly not public. Hopefully.

Still, he knew he could not hide it. Trying to cover it up now would only lead to problems later. But he could deny it. He knew his son. The police did not.

What should he do now? The church, yes. He would call Richard Newland and ask him to call Harry and William. As for graduation, that would have to be postponed until later in the week. Perhaps next Saturday. He breathed, almost gasping for a moment. He reached for the phone and saw his hands still trembling. He folded his arms across his chest, his hands fisted. He felt tears on his face. Stop it. God, help me. He wiped his eyes. He could do this. He forced his hand around the receiver and dialed.

"Hello, Richard," he began solemnly. Control, he ordered himself. "I'm sorry to call so early, but we have just received tragic news." As he thought about what he had to say, he fought the emotions building deep within him. He took a deep breath. Help me, God, he silently pleaded. He grasped the receiver with both hands to stop their shaking. "Nathaniel—Nathaniel is dead...an accident...No, the police don't have any details yet...We're all in shock...Thank you...Devastated...Yes...About graduation, I would like to postpone that until after the funeral, perhaps next Saturday...Yes, would you handle that?...Thank you so much. I hate to drop all of this in your lap, but I'm just—we're all just shattered, but we'll be strong...Yes, God will see us through...Yes, thank you. I'll tell them. I'll be in touch when...Yes, I will. That's so thoughtful of you. Thank you. Goodbye."

He concealed his face in his hands. He had not lied. It was an accident. The truth would come out. There was an answer for all of this. The photo the detective had shown him suddenly shot into his mind. The bruises. The blank sleeping face. Shouldn't he go see him? Where was he? The morgue. Where was that? He didn't know where his son was? Again, streaks of tears ran down his cheeks.

* * *

Miriam stood at the bottom of the stairs, her hands trembling, tears trickling down her cheeks. Her mind at once racing and immobile, vacant, void. She wanted to crumble, fall down in her disbelief. She wanted to scream. She wanted to cry torrents of tears. She wanted to be held and comforted. She wanted to know what had happened to her son. She wanted—wanted to demand of God or someone, whoever— *She wanted her son.* But the sound, the reminder of Matthew's words overruled her. Her thoughts. Her feelings. Be strong. She had to be strong for Sarah Elizabeth. That much seeped into her mind. That much was acceptable. Sarah Elizabeth will be—what? she thought. Through her tears, she looked up the staircase toward the second story landing. She had to tell her daughter that her brother was— She could not even think the word. She closed her eyes. Think of your daughter, she commanded herself. She would have to tell her to be strong. That was what Matthew expected from her. From both of them.

Somehow Miriam found herself—unknowing of how—nevertheless, found herself moving up the stairs. One step after another. Uncertain that her feet touched the steps. Numb, yet upright and moving, she arrived in the upper story hallway and stared at Nathaniel's door, partially open. Like a barrier, a wall, a curtain, something held her back. Maybe this was a dream. Maybe he was in there, just as he should be at this hour on a Saturday morning. She wiped the wetness from her cheeks with the back of her hands and eased the door open. His room, as usual, neat. Tuxedo on the bed. No clothes strewn around on the floor. His desk orderly. All the trophies and plaques on it. His bed made. From the doorway she could see that the bathroom was clean as well. She folded her arms tightly around her abdomen. Oh, how she wanted to fall apart. Sit on his bed and hug his pillow. Touch his school backpack, run her hands over his clothes hanging in his closet. To feel his presence at his desk, at his computer. Anything to be near him again. Oh, God, please don't let him have suffered. And where was he? Where was he now? She would have to see him. She would. She didn't care what Matthew said.

Not about this. She tightened her arms around her. But she couldn't do this. Not now. Now she had to think of Sarah Elizabeth. Matthew would be up here any minute and she wanted to tell her daughter. She wanted to be alone with her when her world caved in on her. Before Matthew came in.

Miriam backed out of the room slowly, almost with reverence, pulling the door closed. She turned and took the several steps to her other child's room. She stared at the door for a moment. What would she say? How could she tell her? Which words would hurt the least? She knocked lightly, then turned the knob and eased the door open. In the dim early morning light she could see the soft, stuffed animals on her bookshelves. Her precious child sleeping so peacefully. Her other child. Now, her only child. The thought welled up inside her. She squeezed her fists forcing it back. Strong.

She quietly closed the door and slowly moved toward the bed, futilely drying her eyes. When she sat on the edge, Sarah Elizabeth stirred, then woke up, her eyes scarcely open.

"Mom?" she mumbled more than spoke. She looked at the clock beside her bed.

Miriam forced a half smile but did not speak as more tears broke free. She brushed Sarah Elizabeth's blond, rumpled hair back from her face. Her lack of response awakened her daughter even more.

"Mom, what's wrong?"

Miriam took her hand. "We got some bad news this morning, honey. Just now. This morning." She fought to keep her voice from breaking.

Sarah Elizabeth sat up, facing her mother, fully awake, alarmed. "What's happened?"

"It's—it's Nathaniel." She paused. "There's been an accident."

Sara Elizabeth swung her feet around to sit beside her mother. "Is he okay? What kind of accident?"

Miriam put her arm around her. "He's—he's—" She squeezed her eyes shut tightly. Then opened them. Strong, she ordered herself. "Gone." Her voice was a mere whisper.

Shock covered Sarah Elizabeth's face, her eyes wide. "You mean he's— What do you mean 'gone'?"

Miriam could not say the word. She stared at her child, then tried to pull her close, but Sarah Elizabeth would have none of it. "Do you mean he's—he's dead?"

Miriam could only nod her head.

Sarah Elizabeth pulled back, staring at her mother as tears spilled down her face. "I don't believe you."

As Miriam reached for her, Sarah Elizabeth screamed. Miriam fought off the resistance and grabbed her arms. The younger of the two continued to fight but only for a moment. Defeated, she collapsed into her mother's comforting embrace.

Just then Matthew abruptly opened the door. He came over and sat beside his daughter, but Sarah Elizabeth did not let go of her mother. Matthew put his hand on her back.

He tried to sound soothing. "I know this is difficult, but it is our responsibility to be strong. It is what the church expects of us and what God has ordained. I am certain that Nathaniel is in heaven with his Maker. While we are sad, we also must rejoice that God has taken him to His eternal home. I know that Nathaniel has committed no sin. He was my son and would never go against God. Now, I want us to kneel right here and pray." He knelt next to the bed.

Miriam did not release her daughter but gently coaxed her to the floor, all the while keeping her head against her shoulder as they both continued to cry softly.

"Let's hold hands," Matthew said softly, holding out his hands to them.

Miriam gently pulled one of Sarah Elizabeth's clutching hands free. Matthew took it.

"Oh, God, this is a sad day for us. Our dearest, precious son and brother has gone to be with you. We miss him more than we can imagine. He brought such joy to us. He was one of your most faithful disciples while he was here. He did no wrong but was always loyal to you and the Holy Spirit, putting you first, Lord, above all else.

211

I ask that you take Nathaniel into your arms. Bless him. Let his life be a shining example to those of us here on earth of how to live a Christian life. Comfort all of us in this time and let us remember that, as Nathaniel showed us so beautifully every minute of his life, we are your servants. Amen."

When he said "Amen" both mother and daughter released Matthew's hands and resumed holding each other as they remained on the floor leaning against the bed.

Matthew stood up. "I've spoken with Richard. We think it best that the church make this announcement since we are all so devastated and in no mood to answer questions," he said, speaking softly.

Miriam heard him but gave no acknowledgement. She continued to allow herself to cry softly, taking comfort in giving comfort. But her emptiness felt bottomless. How could she ever, ever deal with this loss? She pulled Sarah Elizabeth even closer. She did not hear the door close as Matthew left the room.

Miriam did not know how long they sat crying almost inaudibly. As the whispered sobs lessened, she could hear Sarah Elizabeth's doing the same.

"What did Daddy mean when he said Nathaniel hadn't sinned?" she asked.

Miriam stroked her daughter's hair, her head still on her shoulder. "The police, I mean, sheriff detectives came and talked to your father. Alone. They seem to think it was—" She stopped. How could she say this?

Sarah Elizabeth sat up and looked at her mother. "Mom, what?" Again alarm rose in her voice.

Miriam fought for calm. "They think— They think he—did this—to himself." She couldn't say the word.

Sarah Elizabeth pushed her hair from her face. Horror again covered her face. "You mean—he killed—"

Miriam took a deep breath as she pulled her daughter to her. "Yes."

"Why?" she pleaded.

"I don't know."

Sarah Elizabeth searched her mind. "I thought something— He was different this week. He didn't talk much driving to school or coming home, at least not after Monday."

Miriam held her daughter to her. "I don't know. I don't know." She closed her eyes. "We have to trust in God." She slowly rocked Sarah Elizabeth and at the same time with her hand smoothed her hair. "Just trust in God," she whispered. But she felt as if those words had come from someone other than herself, that she was saying something which wasn't true for her.

Miriam didn't know how long they sat on the floor next to the bed. Time had no meaning or reason for her. Not now. She looked at the clock next to Sara Elizabeth's bed. Nearly eight-thirty. "You should take a shower and dress. People will probably be coming over and we need to get ready." She hugged her daughter more tightly. "I know this isn't going to be easy for us, but we can get through it. We have to. For Nathaniel." She felt Sarah Elizabeth's arms tighten around her, not wanting to let go, not wanting to be left alone, not knowing what to do. And Miriam understood, holding her for several more minutes. Having her arms around her second born, she felt as if she were holding herself in some odd, obscure manner. They had to hold on to each other. Grieving demanded it.

Eventually, they released each other and stood up and embraced again. Miriam first wiped her daughter's eyes, then her own. She helped her pick out something to wear, laying a blouse and skirt on the bed. "I'll be back after you shower, okay?"

She stroked her hair as Sarah Elizabeth nodded. After watching her go into her bathroom, Miriam went into the hallway. She looked back at Nathaniel's room. Even as Matthew's words to be strong echoed in her head, she told herself to look away.

She stepped toward the top of the stairway and listened. Matthew was on the phone in his study. The door closed. She hesitated and processed. She had to call her sister, Carolyn in Raleigh. They hadn't talked in so long. She wanted her and Jim to come. But not today.

Matthew wouldn't want them here. And Carolyn knew that already. Maybe just let her know what's happened for now. She could call again later with details.

She turned down the hall and went into the bedroom, dabbing at her wet eyes and trying to compose herself. She unhooked the recharging plug, found her sister in the list of contacts and pressed "Send." As the phone rang, Matthew's words once again ran through her mind. Strong, she heard.

"Hello." It was Mike, Carolyn's son, who was just one year younger than Nathaniel.

"Hi, Mike. It's Aunt Miriam." She struggled to get the words out. "Is your—"

"Oh, wow, hey, how's it going?" he asked, cheerful as always.

She squeezed her eyes closed. "Is your mom there?"

"Sure. Hang on."

She could tell they were in the kitchen. Breakfast. She heard Mike tell his mother who was calling. On her way to the phone Carolyn told her daughter Elaine to watch the pancakes on the stove.

"Mir? What a wonderful surprise," she said.

Miriam could not speak. At the mere sound of her sister's voice, tears again streamed down her face. She fought to control herself, to be strong as Matthew had said. "Nathaniel." All she could say was his name as she fought for composure.

Carolyn's alarm was evident in her voice. "What about Nathaniel?"

Miriam took a deep breath. Strong, she commanded herself. Somehow, the words came. About the men from the sheriff's office, the apparent suicide. She heard her gasp.

"Oh, my God, Mir."

They both cried softly.

"I can be there is two hours. Jim can take care of the kids."

Her words—wanting to be with her, to help her, to be her strength, to comfort her—rushed into Miriam. She grasped them and held them as if they could save her life. Save her from drowning.

Then she added, "Unless my being there would cause too much of a problem."

Miriam almost held her breath. Carolyn had always understood. Since their marriage she hadn't always held back her opinion and differences about Matthew and his church.

She knew what she had to say, what Matthew would expect. "No, don't," she said, wiping her eyes. "There will be so many people here from the church. We won't be able to talk. I'll call you later today or tonight when I know more about—about everything. Arrangements and all that."

She could hear Carolyn crying softly. "Whatever you need, I'll be there. Whatever you need, whenever you need it."

Miriam put her arm across her waist. Strong, she told herself. "Thank you."

Carolyn did not respond for a moment. When she did, it was a whisper amid tears. "I love you."

Again, the words gripped Miriam, like arms pulling her to safety. "I love you, too, and I—"

Just then the bedroom door opened. Matthew stopped, looking at her, his disapproval readily apparent.

Immediately, Miriam's stomach tightened. "Okay," she said, wiping her eyes. "I'll keep you posted." Abrupt. She hated herself. The words had come out, automatically, before she could stop them.

"I'll have my cell phone with me all the time," Carolyn said. "Call me no matter when—day or night." She paused. "I'll be thinking of you every minute."

She fought not to weep. "Okay. We'll talk later. Promise." She hung up her phone.

Matthew stood silently, staring at her.

"Carolyn," she said simply. "I had to call her." She put the phone down and dabbed at her eyes.

His look of sternness changed. "Of course you did," he said. "Is she coming?"

"No. I thought it better to wait and—" She hesitated, unsure. "Wait until we know more, I suppose." She didn't really know what she meant.

"Probably wise." He came into the room, closing the door. "I've talked with the ministerial staff. They'll be coming over soon to discuss what announcement to make at church and what to do about graduation." He paused. "A committee will most likely come over here to take care of food so that you and I can receive visitors. And Sarah Elizabeth, too, of course. I'm sure her friends will be dropping by. So could you straighten up the kitchen just a bit? Make as much counter space as you can." He put his hand on the door knob to leave. "I've already contacted Crossly's Funeral Home," he said, not turning to look at her. "I can't do anything about a day and time until I hear from the sheriff's detective. I'll take care of—of everything." His voice was unmistakably authoritative. "For now we will tell people that arrangements are incomplete." Again, he opened the door to leave but stopped. "I think you should put on something different. A dress. And help Sarah Elizabeth pick out something appropriate." He was gone into the hallway.

Miriam sat immobile, listening to his footsteps as he again retreated downstairs to his study and closed the door. As if automatically, she thought about the tasks before her. The kitchen. She could put the toaster and the crock pot in the pantry. And the coffee maker because they will probably bring a coffee urn from the church and cups and—

She stopped. For the first time, the image swept into her mind, colliding with her grief and her attempts of strength—Nathaniel hanging from a bungee cord on a tree limb. She buried her face in her hands as tears streamed from her eyes. Oh, God, no. She wanted to fall back on the bed and sob. To disintegrate in her sorrow, but the sudden, loud ringing of the house phone startled her to the point of jerking upright. As always when Matthew was at home, she waited for him to answer. As always he picked up by the second ring. The intrusion nudged her to proceed as she had been instructed. She checked her cell phone battery status. Completely charged. Good for all day. For when Carolyn called her. Or she called Carolyn. She switched the ringer to vibrating mode.

From her closet she chose a navy blue skirt and a long-sleeve polished cotton blouse, light gray. From her jewelry box she took her small gold cross on a delicate chain that she always wore on Sundays. She draped it over her fingers as her emotions once again begged to rise up. Nathaniel had given it to her on her last birthday, just two months ago. As the memory of that morning began to focus in her mind, Miriam shifted to the reality of the moment and put the gold chain around her neck, guiding the clasp to fasten. She put her cell phone and handkerchief into the scarcely noticeable skirt pocket.

Out in the hallway she again listened at Sarah Elizabeth's door. The shower was off. She lightly tapped on the door. Her daughter's meek response gave her permission to come in. In the dim morning light she sat on her bed wearing her thick white terrycloth robe, her wet, blond hair lightly brushing the robe's high collar. She was holding a framed photograph of her and Nathaniel taken at a youth rally. They were singing karaoke, all smiles, arms around each others' shoulders, heads together, holding their mikes.

Miriam went to her and held her, stroking her moist hair, fighting her own emotions as she tried to console. She didn't know why she had said it. The words just seemed to speak themselves. "You and I can and will get through this," she whispered.

She felt Sarah Elizabeth lean against her even more, hugging her fiercely.

Throughout the day she kept a constant grip on her phone in her pocket.

"Matthew, this is just such a shock," Harry Borkin said. All the associate ministers, dressed in khakis and polos, sat in his study at home.

"Delores and I—well, of course, all of us," he signaled the other three, "want to do anything to help."

"Thank you, Harry. That means so much."

"Yes," echoed William Josephs. "Pam will be over with the others to help with visitors dropping by. We all support you and Miriam and Sarah Elizabeth."

"Absolutely," said Richard. "We've already arranged for the Bereavement Committee to come in before lunchtime to help out."

"That's so kind of all of you," Matthew said, sitting behind his desk. "This is a true church family." His mind wanted to get to his agenda, stay on track. That would help him get through this. Hold him together. "Graduation. What about it?"

As senior associate, Richard Newland took the lead. "I've already talked with Fred Haskins. Next Saturday afternoon. That would accommodate people being off from work, rather than a weekday or night."

"Yes, good idea," Harry said.

"I think we should go ahead and send out an email to all the students, faculty, staff and congregation," Richard said. "Folks will want to know and be praying for you and your family."

"Probably the best approach," Matthew said.

Richard shifted nervously on the sofa. "Should we say an accident, I mean, car accident? I'm assuming no one else was with him in the car?"

"No, no one." Matthew leaned back. Now was the time. He had to do this. "I need to let you know what the sheriff detectives told me. But first, I want you to know that I don't believe them. I won't believe it. Not for one minute. And, if necessary, I intend to get legal representation to fight it." The three associates sat in rapt attention. Matthew took a deep breath. "They said that it appears that he—Nathaniel—took—" He stopped and looked down as his emotions threatened. God, let this be the right thing to do, he thought. "That he took his own life."

William Josephs responded spontaneously. "Oh, no." He put his hand over his mouth.

"It's only something they suspect," Matthew defended quickly. "They're not sure, by any means. But you all know Nathaniel. He is as solid a Christian as any of us. Going to be one of us after college and Divinity School. He would never commit—never do such a thing. No. Something is just not right here. And I'll get to the bottom of it if it takes the rest of my life." He jabbed his index finger on the top of his desk to punctuate his last several words. He watched them all closely, trying to gauge their reactions. "I've thought it out. Especially if the detectives insist on there being no one else involved, I want to start my own investigation immediately. For now, I'm asking you to dispel any rumors that you encounter."

"That goes without saying," Richard said. He wrote in his leather folio.

"Of course, Nathaniel would do no such thing," Harry stated flatly. "That's ridiculous."

"That's what I told them, but they have to investigate." He sat forward at his desk. "I just don't want Nathaniel's good name tarnished." His voice broke for a moment as his emotions tried to take over. He made his hands into fists. His father would be strong, not cry.

"Of course not. Absolutely not. Not possible," the three associates said, speaking at the same time.

He took a deep breath. "I've called Crossley's Funeral Home. The detectives are supposed to let me know when the—" He stopped. It was difficult to get this out. "When the medical examiner has released—is done with his report. We can't make any arrangements until then. I hope it won't be too long. The people at Crossley's seemed to think it could even be later today." He breathed deeply. "If that's the case, I'd like to have the funeral on Monday and the visitation tomorrow night." He took a deep breath.

"I know the folks at Crossley's," Richard said. "They're good people. They've always been good to work with. We'll handle things at the church. Don't you give it a second thought."

"I think your plans are excellent, Matthew," Harry said. "If any of us can do anything, please don't hesitate."

"Thank you, Harry. Thank all of you." He clasped his hands on the desk and looked down. "It means so much that you all would understand my strong feelings about this and support me. I do want to grieve and will grieve, but not until this is resolved."

Detectives Gary Sparks and Bill Montgomery pulled up in front of the suburban home, noting the well manicured lawn and shrubbery. "That's probably him," Montgomery said of the teenager washing a car in the driveway.

Sparks looked at the young man, then at the picture in Nathaniel's yearbook. "Yeah, that's him." He closed the book and put it on the dashboard. "Let's go ruin someone else's world with our news."

Montgomery sighed. "That little Davies girl was really upset."

Sparks shook his head. "Yeah, and something tells me this kid is going to be even more torn up." The two men exited the car and walked up the drive, their badges visible in their breast pockets.

Sparks introduced himself and Montgomery. "Are you Jason Daniels?"

"Yes, sir." Jason looked bewildered.

Just then, Carl Daniels came out of the house. "Can I help you?"

Sparks made the introductions a second time. "Are you Jason's father?"

"Yes, Carl Daniels."

"We need to speak with your son."

"Not without me being present you won't," he said bluntly, putting his hands on his hips.

Sparks turned to Jason. "Are you eighteen yet, son?"

"Yes, sir."

"Then it's up to you," Sparks said.

Jason looked at his father. The return stare left no uncertainty. "It's okay."

Sparks nodded. "Could we sit on the porch?" He nodded toward the breezeway between the garage and the house.

Carl Daniels turned and led the three to the covered walkway where they all sat down.

Sparks asked Jason about the party and the time he got home and did he talk with Nathaniel Winslow at the party? At the mention of Nathaniel's name, Jason showed obvious concern.

"I talked to him some."

"Did you see him before or after the party?"

"Not after. I went to his house to give him his DVD just before he left to pick up Martha. Martha Davies. To go to the party."

Sparks opened a manila envelope and removed the Sports Illustrated DVD which was inside a plastic bag. "Is this the DVD?"

"Yes." Jason shifted nervously on the chair. "Has something happened to Nate?"

Sparks ignored the question. "And the note and drawing inside the DVD case. Did you draw the picture and write the note?"

Jason looked at Sparks, then out toward the street.

"I don't mean to intrude on your private life, but I need to ask you if you intended it as a joke?" His voice was calm and sympathetic, almost caring.

Jason now met Sparks' eyes and stared at him, not in defiance but with unmistakable confidence. "I meant exactly what I wrote." He didn't hesitate. "And the drawing was something that—it was us." Words began to tumble out with courage. "Last Monday. Just once, but it was real. Very real." His confession now flowed as he glared at his father. "It was the most real of anything or anyone that's ever been in my life." He looked back at Sparks. "Now, please tell me," he pleaded. "Has something happened to him?"

Sparks returned the DVD to the envelope. "I'm very, very sorry to have to give you this news, Jason, but Nathaniel—" He waited. "It appears that Nathaniel took his life last night."

Horror covered Jason's face. "Wha—" He shook his head. "No, no that, that can't, can't be true."

"A farmer found him in the country." Sparks' voice was gentle.

Jason slowly shook his head as tears began streaming from his eyes. Suddenly, he screamed, "NO," and buried his face in his hands, sobbing uncontrollably.

Carl Daniels registered complete astonishment as he watched his son's reaction. Claire Daniels heard him and rushed from the house to the porch.

Sparks and Montgomery sat quietly as his parents—without question mystified by his unusual reaction— tried with little success to console their son.

"Jason, what's going on?" Carl Daniels asked. "What's this all about? Detective?"

Sparks watched Jason, unreachable by either of his parents. "Mr. Daniels, I think your son has lost a very good friend. A best friend. Maybe this is the first time he's ever experienced a shock like this. And it's difficult." He reached into his coat pocket and took out a business card. He reached over and put his hand on Jason's shoulder. "Jason, just in case you need more information."

Through his grief Jason looked up and took the card and nodded his appreciation.

Sparks apologized to the Daniels for disrupting their morning and he and Montgomery left the porch and walked toward the driveway to their car.

"Jason, what is going on?" Carl Daniels demanded loudly without sympathy. "What was he talking about—the DVD and a drawing and a note? And intruding on your personal life?"

Montgomery shook his head. "That kid's in for a rough day," he said quietly.

"No. It's going to last longer than that," Sparks replied.

For Miriam the day had been a blur—an endless array of church members, muffled chatter, familiar faces, grief-stricken friends, especially faculty and students from the Academy. But now the house was quiet and empty of strangers. The bereavement committee had cleaned and straightened every downstairs room. Nevertheless, several folding chairs and the stand from the funeral home holding the registration book stuck out like infected blisters, blemishing the otherwise normal, perfect skin that enfolded Matthew Winslow's household.

Miriam stood in the foyer, listening. She could hear Matthew talking on the phone in his study. He'd said he needed some time to himself. Sarah Elizabeth was upstairs in her room, talking on the phone with her friends even though so many had come to the house during the day.

She went into the kitchen, closing the door. Taking her cell phone from her pocket, she realized that she had clutched it most of the day. Carolyn's words had sustained her since this morning— wanting to be here, willing to do whatever she needed, but most of all, telling her that she loved her. Even as she sat down at the kitchen table, she still wanted to sob, to unleash her sorrow. But she wouldn't. Not now. Not yet. She had to think of Sarah Elizabeth.

She called her sister's number. Carolyn answered after only one ring.

"Mir?" she said softly. "Hey."

Miriam felt relief just hearing her voice. "Hi."

"Rough day?"

"Oh, I don't know." For the first time, she thought about how to describe what the day had been like, and more importantly, how she felt. "I'm too numb to know."

"I'm sure. How is Sarah Elizabeth?"

"We're both dazed. In shock, still. Right now I'm just trying to put one foot in front of the other whenever I'm told to. The sheriff's detectives called late this morning and said that the medical examiner had released—" She couldn't bring herself to say "the body." Not about her son. "—had finished," she said. "Matthew has scheduled the service for Monday at eleven. Visitation will be tomorrow evening."

She sighed and rested her elbows on the table. "I'm just so confused. We're all just confused. We don't know why. Matthew's convinced that something sinister happened, some other person's involved, that Nathaniel wouldn't do this. That maybe somehow he was drugged or something. He's planning to talk to the detectives in depth next week. Maybe we'll know more then."

"Mir, I'm so sorry. I cannot begin to imagine how you must feel."

"I loved him so much." Tears trickled down her cheeks.

"Of course, you did. He was so very special," Carolyn said softly. "Your joy and soul. Both your kids are."

Miriam tried to compose herself. "Thank you for being there for me."

"Oh, honey. Always."

"I know we've drifted—"

"No. Don't even go there. I'm always going to be there for you."

Emotion again caught hold of Miriam.

"Listen, as soon as we hang up, I'm going to call and make reservations at a hotel. Jim has already made arrangements at work for a few days. The kids are out of school. We'll leave tomorrow morning and be there by afternoon. Don't worry about us or try to watch out for us."

Her words again swept over her, holding her. "Thank you. I'll be so glad to see you."

They chatted a few more minutes. When she hung up, she felt somewhat better, relieved, if only a small bit. Carolyn had asked about her. She had cared. And she had answered truthfully.

At Matthew's beckoning, Miriam and Sarah Elizabeth gathered with him in the upstairs hallway for evening prayer. Miriam felt the emptiness in her heart as she was forced to confront the cold, hard fact that their circle now would be three rather than four. Her grasp of Sarah Elizabeth's hand was almost rigid and her daughter's grip equally fierce.

"Dear God," Matthew intoned solemnly, "this has been a trying day. We thank you for the support of our church and friends. They have all been a blessing, and for this we praise your most holy name."

Miriam tried to concentrate. She knew she would be asked to pray. What would she say? She fought the emptiness that threatened to spill out but then thought of Sarah Elizabeth. She had to be there for her. Suddenly, she realized that Matthew had hesitated. Something he'd never done, not during prayer. She opened her eyes to look at him. She saw no emotion. Then, he continued.

"Keep us all pure, Father. Free from sin, free from hurting others, free from feeling the hurt that others might try to inflict." He stopped, again. "Watch over your servant, Nathaniel."

He must be tired, weary of all the day's events and people. They all were.

"Miriam," Matthew interrupted her thoughts.

She took a deep breath. "Father, watch over Nathaniel. Keep all of us strong." She squeezed Sarah Elizabeth's hand.

"Sarah Elizabeth."

Sarah Elizabeth sniffed back her tears. "Make me strong for Nathaniel," she said.

"Father, hear our prayers, your servants. Bless us to do the work of your kingdom. Amen."

As they dropped their hands Matthew hugged his daughter. "Good night," he said. "Try to sleep."

She turned and hugged her mother. "Will you sit with me a while?" she asked.

Her request somewhat surprised Miriam, nevertheless she welcomed it. "Of course." She kissed the top of her head.

In the privacy of her room, Sarah Elizabeth sat on the edge of her bed. "I don't think I'm going to be able to sleep." She began crying softly.

Miriam sat beside her and pulled her to her, stroking her hair. "I know."

"No, it's something else." She sat back. "Please don't get mad at me, but I have to ask you something."

Miriam shook her head. "Promise."

Sarah Elizabeth looked down. "Do you think Nathaniel is—" She stopped and closed her eyes. "Mike told me about something that happened this morning. Billy French and Andrew Perryman went over to Jason's house—Jason Daniels—because they had found out about Nathaniel and when they tried to call Jason, he didn't answer. So they went over there and when they got there, Jason was in front of the house and Mr. Daniels was bringing out his things—clothes, books, I don't know what else. All of his belongings. Just throwing everything out in the yard. They said Mr. Daniels was mad. Crazy mad. They said some of his drawings were blowing around on the yard and that they were of Jason and Nathaniel. Together. Without clothes on."

Miriam stared into nothingness as puzzle pieces in her memory began to surface and align themselves.

"Mom, do you think Nathaniel—do you think he was gay?" she asked softly.

Miriam looked at her daughter and took a deep breath. "What about Martha? He was dating Martha." She knew the question applied as much to herself as it did to Sarah Elizabeth.

"I know. I thought about that, but he was acting different, odd, not like himself, this whole past week. And last week, too. Rushing to be with her more than he ever had."

Miriam pulled her daughter to her. "Well, you know that things get turned around, exaggerated when people are upset. Let's try not to think about this right now—"

"But maybe that's why he—" She didn't finished. She didn't need to.

Miriam stroked her hair in silence for a moment. "Let's just try to get some sleep tonight. We have a lot going on the next few days.

We can deal with this later. Right now I think we need to keep Nathaniel and our memory of him foremost in our thoughts." She kissed the top of her head. "Okay?"

Sarah Elizabeth nodded. "Do you think Daddy knows about this?"

Miriam closed her eyes. "I don't know."

She waited while Sarah Elizabeth went into her bathroom and changed for bed. When she came back, they sat on the bed without talking, Miriam with arm around her daughter, stroking her hair, rocking ever so gently. Eventually, Sarah Elizabeth slipped beneath the covers and Miriam leaned down and kissed her on the forehead.

"I love you, Mom," she whispered.

Miriam looked at her beautiful child. "I love you, too, sweetheart."

They hugged once again before Miriam eased out of the room. She quietly entered her own bedroom, grateful to see that Matthew was already in bed, lying on his side, facing away from her side. In the bathroom as she undressed, the pieces of the puzzle continued to shift in her head. Matthew had scarcely mentioned Nathaniel in his prayer. He had talked so much about being pure and free from sin and being hurt by others. He's heard what happened to Jason Daniels, she thought. Was that why he wanted to have the funeral so quickly? Get it over with. She closed her eyes and leaned on the vanity. No, that couldn't be. He couldn't—he *wouldn't* be so uncaring.

CHAPTER THIRTEEN

MONDAY—MAY 25

Miriam sat on the front pew at Holy Bible Fellowship, holding Sarah Elizabeth's hand. It was a mutual, unspoken act. They had simply reached out to each other. Matthew sat on their daughter's other side, poised and strong, his hands folded in his lap. He had walked between them at the start of the service coming down the aisle, a hand on each of their elbows, as if he were steering them. Carolyn and Jim and their children sat behind them.

Miriam fought to keep her eyes on the various speakers as they came to the pulpit—Fred Haskins, Coach Stansbury, William Josephs, the youth minister, and now Richard Newland who was giving the main eulogy. Even though she appeared to be earnestly paying attention, riveting her eyes on each speaker, she wasn't. She was avoiding looking at the casket which was only ten feet in front of her. She was afraid that if she looked at it she might fall apart and that was what Matthew had warned both her and Sarah Elizabeth against. Again and again, like a mantra, he intoned his wishes. "You must be strong," he had told them before they went out to get into the limousine that drove them to the church. "People will be watching us, expecting us all to be faithful, to put matters in God's hands, to believe in Him, that He will take away our sorrow."

Matthew had taken charge—selecting the casket, making arrangements with Crossley's Funeral Home, the plot at the cemetery and, of course, the church's role. He had selected the day and time, and asked Fred Haskins to oversee asking students from the baseball team to serve as pallbearers. He had even made suggestions about what she and Sarah Elizabeth should wear. "Nothing ornate. Simple, modest, dark, preferably black, a suit or dress. Either would be appropriate," he told them on Sunday. "I'll wear a black suit."

Miriam knew her husband needed to appear in charge and in control, both of the situation and his emotions. He never wanted to appear weak, not to anyone, not ever. Still, she had seen a difference in him since Saturday—fidgety, on edge, constantly moving, not sleeping. Even now in the service, he was crossing and uncrossing his legs more than usual but still in a controlled and deliberate manner. Word had gotten out. That Nathaniel had taken his life. That was something he couldn't control, but she suspected he had tried. Of course she hadn't asked, but she was certain that was why he wanted to have the funeral so quickly. And she couldn't forget what Sarah Elizabeth had told her about Jason Daniels.

Miriam heard Richard now speak Nathaniel's name. Listening to him for only a moment, she wondered what he knew of Nathaniel. For that matter, who here in this sanctuary really knew her son and what were they thinking?

She had noticed the way people had acted and looked at her last night during the visitation—sympathetic but distant, almost mechanical. Even Eloise Gardner didn't say "wonderful" in regard to Nathaniel. Just that she was sorry. Sarah Elizabeth had said that her friends had seemed remote, not as caring as she was expecting. Even Mike Caviness had only spoken to her briefly, then left.

"It's because Nathaniel—the way he died, isn't it?" Sarah Elizabeth had asked her after family prayer on Sunday night. They sat on the bed, her mother holding her "And what Jason said about Nathaniel?"

Miriam had no answers. She felt lost herself, swimming in an emptiness, yet she was feeling pulled but toward what? Where? She didn't know. And today, when they entered the sanctuary, she was surprised that it was so empty, the floor only half full, no one in the upper seats. She closed her eyes briefly as she felt her stomach knot up. It doesn't matter, she told herself. The only thing that mattered was honoring her son. Honoring his memory.

She was so glad that Carolyn and Jim and their children had arrived. They hadn't seen each other in nearly a year and a half. Feeling her arms around her, hugging her—it had taken away some of the sting. Even now, with Carolyn sitting in the pew behind her, a few feet away, she could feel their sisterly kinship. It hadn't gone away. And Carolyn had not been deterred by Matthew's abrupt departure from the house soon after they arrived yesterday. "A meeting at the church," he'd explained. "With the associates. To plan the service."

Richard Newland finished speaking and sat down. The lights dimmed slightly as an organ fanfare rang out and the choir stood and began singing an anthem. The giant screens came to life with a montage of photographs of Nathaniel, most from school. Miriam felt Sarah Elizabeth's hand tighten on her own. She looked over and saw the tears in her eyes as she fought to contain them. She released her hand and put her arm around her daughter, pulling her to her, placing her head on her shoulder. Miriam did not look at Matthew. She didn't know if he was looking at her or not. It didn't matter. She could imagine his disapproval.

The montage had been brief, obviously so, and ended with Nathaniel's senior class picture from the yearbook. Miriam fought her own tears as she stared at the enormous photo. Richard Newland again spoke, briefly this time, probably a benediction, but she didn't hear it. A man from Crossley's signaled the pallbearers to escort the casket up the aisle, then directed Matthew, Miriam and Sarah Elizabeth to follow.

As they slowly walked out, Miriam again noted that the church was not filled like she had thought it would be. People were working, perhaps. Probably another reason Matthew had chosen this time.

She did not look at anyone directly, but kept her gaze forward and slightly upward, and that was why she saw him. Up high, in the very last row where no lights had been turned on, in near total darkness, scarcely a shadow, sitting on the floor. She wondered who it was. By then, they had reached the exit into the main vestibule and Sarah Elizabeth reached for her hand.

The family limousine followed the hearse. Matthew sat looking out the side window, Sarah Elizabeth close to Miriam. No one spoke until they drove into the cemetery gates and wound through the narrow lanes.

"Remember to be strong. God will see us through this," Matthew said quietly as the driver stopped the car.

Miriam heard the words but felt numb to them. She reached over and took Sarah Elizabeth's hand and gently squeezed it.

The casket sat over the grave, a carpet of fake grass spread around it. They sat in cushioned folding chairs. Only Richard Newland spoke, but Miriam, again, heard none of what he said. For the first time she stared at the container as if she was trying to see inside. To see her son. One last time.

The memory of yesterday afternoon, before the visitation began at the funeral home, haunted her now more than it had all night long, lying in bed, sleepless. Matthew had said that the casket should remain closed to the public, but that the family would go privately, alone to the view the body. The three of them had walked into the silent room. Approaching the lone casket, half of it open, Miriam could not fathom what was happening. It was a dream. It had to be. As she stood only a few feet away, she saw Nathaniel's body resting on the satin cloth, so peaceful in his blue suit. Sarah Elizabeth had clutched her, almost desperately. Miriam held her as she battled her own helplessness. It was him. Really him. Not a nightmare. She wanted to lean over and embrace him, wake him up, heal him, make him whole. But the bitter truth damned her hope. His life was over. Her son. Her baby boy. Gone. Oh, God, how had this happened? Why had it happened? She remembered him hugging her on Friday night, just before he left for the party. He seemed so happy, but he couldn't have been. Oh, Nathaniel, what torment have you endured? Why couldn't you tell me? Whatever it was, why didn't you come to me?

Now sitting there in the cemetery beside his casket with all the finality of this ritual, she felt moisture dripping from her face onto her hand in her lap. Another drop. Then another. Silent. She didn't try to stop them. She didn't reach up and dry her eyes. She let the tears fall. From a nearby tree, perhaps, or flowers from another grave, a butterfly drifted by and, for a moment lit on a nearby tree limb, its wings slowly waving as if for balance. A monarch, she thought. At that moment Sarah Elizabeth gripped her hand more tightly. She had seen it, too, Miriam thought. Then, a light breeze nudged the golden orange and black creature to take flight. Miriam followed it as it flew higher and away. She returned her gaze to the casket, her tears still falling, but somehow softer, more peaceful than before.

"I have to go out for a while," Matthew said softly to Miriam alone in the upstairs hallway.

Miriam looked at him bewildered. They had just buried their son a mere three hours ago and many people had come to the house for lunch after they returned from the cemetery, some even sitting outside while eating. Although many had left, a good number still remained. And he was leaving? "But there are people here from chur—"

He raised his hand to halt her. "It can't be helped. If anyone asks, just explain to them that it's an urgent matter concerning the church.

I'll be back in an hour or so. I'm sure you can handle things for that long." He held her upper arms very gently. "You must be strong. This is your expected role as my wife."

Miriam took a deep breath and nodded but did not meet his eyes. "I'll slip out through the kitchen."

Matthew found a parking place near the local governmental complex. Once inside, he followed Detective Sparks' directions and found his office without a problem. He shook hands but offered little in the way of pleasantries, taking a seat opposite the detective's desk. He saw his cell phone as well as Nathaniel's and his keys laying on top of a file folder on the desk along with a DVD and The Holy Bible Academy yearbook.

"You said you've concluded your investigation and have the doctor's report?"

"Yes, sir."

"Are those mine?" Matthew asked, nodding toward the phones and keys.

"Yes, sir, but I must ask you to sign this release." Sparks slid a paper to the edge of his desk. Matthew glanced over the document and signed it, then pocketed the phones and keys along with his copy of the receipt but left the DVD and yearbook.

"Reverend Winslow, in addition to the physical evidence that we found at the scene—the evidence I told you about on Saturday—"

Matthew's voice was curt. "I already know what you said. My son is dead. I want to hear what the medical examiner thinks happened. How the accident happened." He rested his arms on the armrests, clasped his hands together and stared at Sparks.

Without registering any impatience, Sparks picked up a folder and opened it.

"As I told you there were abrasions, small cuts and bruises on Nathaniel's arms and legs that are consistent with climbing the tree.

There was a scrape on the side of his head that we believe he received from the limb where the bungee cord was attached. The break in his neck and the bruises on his neck indicate that he must have tied the cord to his neck and rolled off the limb. Death was most likely instantaneous due to the weight of his body and the sudden trauma to his neck."

Matthew shifted in his chair. He forced himself not to visualize what he was hearing. Somebody else had made this happen. Nathaniel was the victim of some lunatic.

"The forensic investigators found small traces of your son's blood on several parts of the tree, particularly the limb the cord was tied to. Again, scrapes from climbing." Sparks paused.

Matthew did not—would not believe this. This was not possible. "And you don't think that he was forced to do this? Somebody holding a gun on him? Threatening him in some way? Some drug-crazed person wanting money? A teen from one of the public schools? Maybe they forced him to take drugs or drugged him when he didn't know it?" He spoke with authority. He had to because this detective knew nothing of Nathaniel and he obviously didn't care to know.

"No, sir. There were no traces of drugs or alcohol. He did have some cake and a coke about an hour before his death. We assume this was from the party he went to."

"Maybe somebody there put something in his drink."

"No, Reverend. There was no trace of anything mind altering in his system, but there's further evidence."

"What evidence?" He maintained eye contact with the detective.

"Do you charge your cell phone every night?"

Matthew's expression was complete confusion. "Yes, but what—"

"Always in your office?"

"Yes."

"So you wouldn't hear it if it rang?"

"Not if I was upstairs." His irritation was growing.

"Did your son know that?"

"My whole family knows. We all charge our phones every night. It's a house rule."

Sparks' voice remained kind. "If Nathaniel was in danger, then why didn't he call your home number around midnight if he knew your cell was in your office and you were in bed?"

Matthew stared at the detective incredulous. He searched for words, excuses, reasons, but his mind blanked. "If he was in danger, he might have forgotten that. He wouldn't stop to think—"

"The voice mail he left for you on your cell phone doesn't show any sign of danger," Sparks said softly.

Matthew hesitated. "So he did leave a message?"

"Yes sir, but even though he doesn't appear to be in danger, what he says coincides with why we think he took his life."

"Oh. Why you *think* he did this," Matthew said, not hiding his indignation. "So you don't know for sure?"

Sparks ignored the question but closed the folder and dropped it on his desk. "We talked with a few of his friends. Martha Davies and Jason Daniels."

"I've heard the lies that Daniels boy has been spreading."

"And that his father threw him out?" Sparks asked evenly.

Matthew nodded. "Yes. Regrettable, but I'm sure Carl Daniels did what he thought God was leading him to do."

Detective Sparks looked away, then back. When he spoke, he did so with authority. "Okay, Reverend, here it is. Jason Daniels saw your son before the party on Friday and returned his DVD to him." He nodded toward the DVD on his desk. "Inside the case, he put a picture that he had drawn of the two of them. An intimate drawing. He signed it, 'I love you, Nate. Always, Jase.' We found it in your son's car. Jason confessed that they had—they had been intimate. The voice mail that he left you confirms that."

Matthew's face had reddened. He leaned forward, his expression and his voice on the brink of threatening, his index finger raised for emphasis. "You be very careful what you say, sir." He paused, glaring at Sparks through narrowed eyes. "Are you saying," he spoke evenly, "are you saying that my son—are you calling him a—" He stopped, his voice and face exuding contempt and loathing.

Sparks spoke with a composure that conveyed he was not intimidated. "We have concluded, based on the evidence, that your son was having difficulty dealing with his sexuality. Whether he was gay or just confused, we don't know. We do believe that whatever it was led him to take his life. Those are the facts in evidence, and those facts are enough to say that no further investigation on our part is called for. The district attorney's office concurs. Therefore, the case is closed."

Matthew glared at the detective. His stare, however, was no match for that of the seasoned officer's. He fought the rage that wanted to erupt. "This is not over. I'll talk to the district attorney myself and you can rest assured that I'll mention the sloppy job you have done on this."

Sparks looked down for a moment, then back up at Matthew. When he spoke, it was with compassion. "Before you do that, sir, I'd suggest that you listen to the voice mail on your cell phone."

Matthew stared at Sparks as he fought the sinking feeling that was trying to pull him down, this defeat that was looming over him. Emptiness began to pour into him. He'd never known this feeling. What was it? What was happening to him? He had to remain in control, in command of this situation. He could not falter. As lead minister he had to be strong—for his church, for his family. He was in charge. He stood up.

"Nathaniel could never be a—one of those people," he said with evenness. "He's going—" He stopped for an instant. "He was going to be a minister. Become the head of Holy Bible Fellowship and Academy. Like I have, and his grandfather and great-grandfather. He plays sports and is a gifted student." He stopped, again. "Was a gifted student. Well-liked by everyone, teachers, students. A girl friend, Martha Davies. Those kind don't have girl friends, now do they?" He looked at Sparks' desk, then back at the detective. "If there's nothing else?"

"No, sir, nothing else." He stood up. "Your son's car is in the city parking lot just down the street at the corner of Lindsay. If you'll give them that receipt, they'll release it."

Matthew moved toward the office door.

"Reverend," Sparks said, "I'm truly sorry for your loss."

Matthew looked at him but made no acknowledgement as he opened the door.

"Reverend?" Sparks called.

Matthew turned. The detective was holding up the DVD and yearbook for him to take. He scarcely took notice of them before walking out.

In the hallway Matthew put on his sunglasses and made his way outside to his own car. He retrieved the folder he had brought from home off the front seat and walked down the street to the parking lot. He gave the attendant the receipt and the keys and waited while the car was brought to the entrance. He signed yet another release form and took his copy. Looking at the boxy shape of the red Jeep Cherokee, he suddenly remembered the day he had bought it for Nathaniel. "It's great, Dad." He couldn't contain his excitement as a huge smile broke across his face. It was the kind of car he'd always wanted. "Thanks so much. I love it." "You deserve it, son. I know you'll take care of it and be responsible." "Yes, sir, I—"

"Something wrong?"

The attendant's interruption startled Matthew. He looked at the man with his scruffy, unshaven face but made no reply as he got into the car and drove away.

He had to be strong. This would all be over and life would be back to the way it was. The allegations that the detective had made—ridiculous, he thought.

He drove to the opposite side of town to a place he thought he remembered. As he went down Fontain Avenue he saw it. He drove into the lot and parked near what appeared to be the office. A man whose paunch rendered him incapable of seeing any of his lower extremities waddled out. His face a deep bronze, his jet black hair plastered straight back from his receding hairline, the buttons on his white short-sleeved shirt strained against the protrusion underneath. His pencil-thin moustache was perfectly shaped. Large tattoos covered both forearms.

"Help you, buddy?"

"I want to sell this car. It's paid for. I have the title with me."

Miriam sat alone with her elbows on the kitchen table. She put her face in her hands and massaged its entire surface. Carolyn, Jim and their children had just left. A few minutes before ten, according to the clock on the microwave. The day, the last three days, had been clouded, out of focus, and yet the only way she had managed to move had been to focus. Target one minute, one step, one thought at a time. Then wait for the next one. Saturday seemed like a life-time ago when she first heard about Nathaniel and, in some moments, it felt like five minutes ago. She had to think what day of the week it was. Monday. The funeral had taken place this morning. She crossed her arms on top of the table and peered down at her suit. She hadn't even changed clothes. She could at least do that. Maybe something more comfortable. Matthew would soon be calling for prayer time.

She turned off the light and walked through the back hallway toward the stairs. In the foyer she saw that the door to Matthew's study was slightly ajar. She could hear him talking on the phone.

"Yes, the detective told me there was no evidence...Well, I think the rumors are just that—rumors. The Daniels boy...right, I wouldn't trust him—I don't trust any of those people. I think he was just fixated on Nathaniel...I feel sorry for Carl Daniels and I think he did the right thing...Yes, I know. I suppose we should have had a private funeral, just family. I wish I had thought of that. It would have saved the church members from being conflicted...Thank you, Kenneth. Thank you for your vote of confidence. It means a lot...."

Miriam closed her eyes and breathed. She felt something tugging inside her, a gentle urge to go to Sarah Elizabeth. Nothing to be alarmed about. Simply go to her. And love her.

After hanging up the phone, Matthew heaved a sigh of relief. At the same time he covered his face with his hands and pressed against his closed eyes. He realized there was moisture on his forehead and wiped it away. He hadn't told a lie. There *was* no evidence—nothing concrete. He didn't care what that detective said or thought. Without proof— Well, it was over. Kenneth concurred. He clasped his hands together on his desk. There didn't need to be any further discussion about any of this. Eventually, people would forget. Certainly, he would grieve. They would all grieve. Everyone would grieve. It would be hard. But he had handled it the way his father would have. He was sure of that.

He looked down at his clasped hands. His knuckles had whitened from his vice-like grip.

CHAPTER FOURTEEN

TUESDAY—MAY 26

Miriam sat in the waiting area, her purse in her lap, her hands folded over it. Her shoulders sagged, unaware of the people who entered the room and those who moved through the maze of desks behind the counter. She did not perceive the ringing telephones, the voices of the workers, the opening and closing of doors. Only when she was spoken to did she enter the present moment.

"Excuse me, the secretary said you wanted to see me."

Miriam looked up at the tall, solidly built, man. Even though he appeared rugged, she prayed that he would be humane. But it didn't matter. She had to do this. Slowly, she stood up. "Were you the detective in charge of my—" She halted, struggling for strength. "In charge of investigating Nathaniel Winslow's death?"

"Yes, ma'am. May I ask your—" He stopped when he realized.

Miriam looked directly into his eyes. "I'm his mother." Her eyes threatened to brim with tears. "Mrs. Matth—Miriam Winslow."

Sparks nodded his understanding. "Mrs. Winslow, yes. I guess we've never met. I'm Detective Gary Sparks. Please know that I am so very sorry for your loss."

His voice had softened, his concern evident. She had seen and heard. Maybe her prayer had been answered. "Thank you," she managed. "May we speak privately?"

"Yes, of course." He gestured toward his office down the hallway. "This way." Once inside, Sparks closed the door. As he moved to his desk chair, he invited Miriam to sit down.

"How may I help you?" His voice was gentle, sympathetic.

Miriam looked down, her grief evident, and took a deep breath. "After you came to our house last Saturday and talked with my husband, he told me that Nathaniel had—" She stopped to force the word to form and come out of her mouth. "Had died—" She halted, again. "That it was suicide. Then, one of his friends said that Nathaniel was, uh—" She sighed deeply, still staring at her hands, her purse in her lap. "He said that Nathaniel was a homosexual, was gay." She looked away. "I asked my husband this morning to tell me what he knows, what he's learned from you, what you've told him about—" She waited for a moment, closed her eyes to gather herself. "What you concluded from your investigation, but, uh, he says I shouldn't be concerned about it." She inhaled with intensity and held it. When she spoke, her words came only through great effort, struggling to be heard. "But I am concerned. I am his mother." She raised her eyes to meet Sparks'. "I want to know what happened." She took another breath. "I want to know the truth." Her eyes had become teary, but she kept them in contact with his, fearful yet determined.

Sparks met her gaze and for a moment did not respond. He looked down, then back at Miriam. "Mrs. Winslow, are you sure?"

Miriam closed her eyes, searching for strength and courage, but she could only nod.

Sparks' voice was filled with compassion as he described the scene where Nathaniel had died, the medical examiner's findings and the DVD with Jason's drawing inside. Miriam inwardly flinched, aching for the suffering that Nathaniel had endured, the anguish he had lived with, the secret that had torn him apart, that had shamed him, made him feel unloved.

"My partner and I, the captain of detectives and the district attorney's office all agreed that there was no foul play involved in your son's death, especially after we heard the voicemail he left on your husband's cell phone. There was no need for further investigation and the case could be closed."

Miriam's attention deepened. "Voicemail?" she asked. "There was a voicemail?"

It was Sparks now who took a deep breath. "Nathaniel's cell phone showed that he had placed a call to Reverend Winslow's cell phone just after midnight. Your husband told me that he charged his phone, you all charge your phones every night."

Miriam looked down. "House rule," she said.

The detective waited a moment. "When we came to your house we took your husband's phone, brought it back here and listened to the message. It reinforced our conclusion that there was no foul play. It also constituted a suicide note."

Miriam closed her eyes for a moment, then opened them. "My husband never—" she began but stopped. "What did he say?" She looked at him. "What did Nathaniel say?" Then her mind seemed to sharpen its focus. "Do you have it written down? Did you make a copy?" She became more revived. Her questions pleaded. And she could see it—his eyes became softer. When he spoke, his voice conveyed as much.

"Mrs. Winslow, do you think—"

"If you have it, I want to hear it," Miriam said with quiet emphasis. "Please, let me hear it." Tears began streaming down her face as she took tissues from her purse.

Sparks stared down at his hands. Then he turned to his computer keyboard and began typing. After a moment, he stopped and leaned back in his chair.

Miriam closed her eyes as she first heard the automated voice. "One call made Sunday, May 24 at 12:07 a. m." She took a breath knowing that Nathaniel's voice would be next. "Hey...hello, Dad, this is your...this is Nathaniel..." Miriam bit on her lip as she listened, her eyes now tightly shut. "I have to...I have to commit a sin when I hang up, Dad...because...because I already committed a worse sin last Monday...I couldn't ever be a minister, Dad...there was some-one...a guy and we, uh...we did a terrible thing...Dad, I've got this demon...this demon that makes me want to be with...be with other... other guys...and commit...commit just the worst...the worst sin...I'm sorry, Dad...I am, but I don't know what else to do...I can't live like this...I hate...myself...and I know you...you would hate me...for this... everybody...would hate me if they knew...and they should."

Miriam's body began shaking as she silently wept, shaking her head, her hands covering her face.

"I know...I know I'm going to hell...it's what I deserve...I've been praying about this every night for the last I don't know how many months, no, years...I don't know...it seems like forever...and it won't go away...I know you're going to be mad and disappointed...but this is the only way...I love you, Dad...Tell Mom and Sarah Elizabeth... tell them I'm sorry...I tried, Dad...I really tried...but tonight...I know now it's real...living inside me...I just can't get that...evil out of me... This is the only way..." The call ended.

Miriam sat and sobbed, her son's voice, his hurt, his guilt, his torture now all echoing in her mind, overpowering her.

After several minutes her weeping diminished. She had not heard Detective Sparks come around the desk and sit down in the other chair beside her.

"He wasn't—he wasn't crying. I don't—" she said softly.

"We had a psychologist and two other professionals listen to it," Sparks said quietly. "They all said the same thing. Typically when someone has decided to take his own life, they are almost relieved to be able to escape what's troubling them. Oddly, there is no real sadness. They simply want to get away from their life."

Miriam closed her eyes as more tears trickled down her cheeks.

"Sarah Elizabeth is your daughter?" Sparks asked with compassion.

She nodded. "Fifteen," she said, dabbing at her eyes.

"I hope you can be there for each other."

His words rang true. "We are, especially the last three days. And we will be from now on." She looked up at him. There was a truth about him, a wisdom. "Do you have children?" she asked.

"Three. Ages two, five and eight."

"They are very fortunate." She stopped. "Love them. Please just—"

He leaned forward, his elbows on his knees. "I can't begin to imagine the anguish you must be feeling."

Miriam closed her eyes only for a moment, then opened them and slowly stood, taking a minute to be sure she was steady. "Thank you. You've been very kind and helpful."

Sparks stood with her. "Before you go." He moved back to his desk and opened a drawer. "I think you might want these. I assure you the drawing is not in any way graphic. I offered them to your husband, but he, well, he didn't take them."

Miriam stared at the DVD and the yearbook. At first, she didn't know what to do. But then decided to trust this man, this man who had been so kind to her. She reached out and took them. "Thank you. And thank you for—for everything."

Sparks moved to open the door. "Please," he said, taking a card from his shirt pocket. "If you have any further questions, don't hesitate to call."

Miriam took the card and nodded her gratitude.

Outside the warm sun bathed her and even more so as she sat in her car with the windows rolled up. She skimmed through the yearbook reading all the wonderful, caring and funny things Nathaniel's friends had written. She stopped at Jason's few sentences and read them several times before reading his senior profile with his chosen quote from the Bible. The same one from the competition. She turned and stared at the DVD case on the passenger seat and thought perhaps she was avoiding it. She remembered the morning when Sarah Elizabeth had given it to Nathaniel for his birthday. "Whoa! Thanks, Sis. Man, this is terrific," he'd said, flipping the case

244

over to read the back. "And it's autographed by all those famous players," Sarah Elizabeth informed him. He beamed. "Yeah, this is the greatest." He'd leaned over the kitchen table and kissed her on the cheek. She had rolled her eyes, but Miriam knew his gesture had meant the world to her.

Miriam reached over and picked up the case, trying to decide. Finally she opened it and removed the piece of paper and unfolded it.

At first embarrassment tried to wash over her, make her turn away, fold up the paper. But the serenity of the two faces captured her.

Nathaniel and Jason. In bed. Naked but covered by a rumpled sheet. Their eyes closed as if asleep. Holding each other. Nathaniel, his head on Jason's chest. Jason's arm around Nathaniel. "Monday afternoon. I love you, Nate. Jase."

Monday afternoon. Last week, she thought. The day he went to Jason's to return the book and was gone for so long. It was right after that he had begun to act so differently. And it was after he had gone to Jason's to study for the chemistry test that he was not himself.

As she contemplated the drawing again, she sensed the immense gentleness it portrayed. Then something else struck her. Something greater. Something she had never known.

Miriam stopped her car at the curb in front of the house. She put the gear in park and sat motionless. Why was she here? What possible good could come from this? She knew Matthew would not approve, in fact she was certain that he would be furious. Nevertheless, something was pushing her, urging her to be here. To do what? To say what? She didn't know. Maybe all she would do was— What? She took a deep breath, got out of the car and started up the walk. At the front door uncertainty still claimed her. She could turn and leave. No one would ever know. No one would ever question or even suspect. No one but her. That was what kept gnawing at her. Her own need to know.

She looked at the doorbell, then saw her finger reach out and press it. She heard the faint bong inside. After several moments, the door opened.

Claire Daniels appeared drawn, tired, her eyes blank, like opened windows into a room that was pitch-black and soulless. The two women looked at each other, stalemated.

"Hello, Claire," Miriam said finally. "May I come in?"

Claire hesitated for a moment before stepping back. Miriam went in and followed her to the living room where she sat in a side chair, Claire opposite her on the sofa. Awkward silence engulfed the room. Miriam was about to speak when Claire began.

"I'm so sorry—about Nathaniel."

Miriam nodded her appreciation. "We've both been through terrible ordeals."

Claire turned away, struggling to contain her emotion. "Carl threw him out. Disowned him." The words tumbled out unchecked. "He told him he was eighteen and, if he was—if he wanted to be one of those kind then he wished—wished—he was dead." Tears streamed down her face. "He gave him fifteen minutes to pack and get out. He took his keys to the house and his car and told him to never set foot in this house, again." She turned her head away.

Miriam moved next to her and put her arm around her.

"This is the only time I can cry because Carl has forbidden me to in front of him or—or do anything, especially to try to contact him in any way." She wiped her face with a tissue. "But you—I can't—what you've gone through. You must be devastated."

Miriam knew she could not unleash her emotions—not here. "Did you ever suspect?" she asked. "About Jason?"

Claire looked down. "I've asked myself that question a thousand times since Saturday. The signs. Did I do or not do something?" She paused as if to gather courage. "I think I always wondered—secretly, but I didn't want to believe it for so many reasons." She turned to Miriam. "Did you know?"

She nodded slowly. "The same. I just didn't think it could be possible. Not Nathaniel. I guess that's what any parent would say. 'Not my child.'" She paused. "You don't know where Jason is or how to get in touch with him?"

Claire hesitated. "He called yesterday morning because he knew Carl was at work. He gave me a phone number. He's been going to some group meeting and the person leading it found a family for him to stay with. For now. He told me that he never planned on going to Freedom. He's going to work this summer and go to Loflin Community in the fall for something in design. He wants to draw."

Miriam thought of the drawing. "He should. He's gifted." Before she was reluctant, but now she knew she could ask. "Do you think he would see me?" Then she added, "Would you trust me to see him?"

Claire turned to her. To Miriam her expression relayed surprise as well as gratitude. But then she saw a flicker. Hope or perhaps determination. "Wait here. I'll get the number."

Miriam recognized the church's name—Trinity Baptist. The pastor had been interviewed for one of the articles in the series in the newspaper. He had said he didn't see that God's word was in conflict with homosexuality, a perspective Matthew would find blasphemous. Even she had thought at the time that it seemed uncharacteristic. Bizarre, even. Yet, she was now turning into the parking lot of Trinity Baptist Church—an older church, small but with a towering, traditional steeple and cross. She saw the sign in front—Benjamin Thorton, Pastor. She recalled the name.

"Jason is still having a rough time with this," the counselor, Jim Bryles, had told her over the phone when she identified herself and her connection to Jason. "I'll have to be present if Jason agrees to meet you."

Miriam went in the side door from the parking lot. Mr. Bryles introduced himself and led her to a parlor-like room with several sofas and armchairs. Jason sat on one of the sofas, his arms folded across his chest. He stood up when they came into the room but did not meet her eyes. His face wore only one expression—intense sadness. He looked thin and drawn. Like herself, she reasoned, little or no sleep, probably not eating.

She tried to smile but was too overwhelmed by his stark appearance. She was grateful that Mr. Bryles took charge. He offered her a chair, opposite Jason. He sat to the side in another one. Jason sat back down on the sofa, still not looking at her.

"Thank you for allowing me—for seeing me." She made sure to speak with compassion and gentleness. Still, her words felt stuck inside her. She took a deep breath. "Your mother gave me—she told me how to get in touch with you."

Jason stared at the floor in front of him, arms across his chest.

"Were you at the—at the church yesterday? Up in the top row, in the dark?"

He started to speak but needed to clear his throat first. "Yes, ma'am." His voice scarcely more than a whisper. Still, he did not look at her.

Miriam saw his grief—like her own, consuming, inconsolable. From somewhere—she had no idea she would say this, it was as if another person, a force deep inside spoke it for her. But as she heard it, she knew it must be said. "You did nothing wrong, Jason."

For the first time, slowly, he turned his head and looked at her, his eyes welling.

She met them and held him firmly with her own gaze. "Nothing. Absolutely nothing."

With that, Jason leaned forward putting his crossed arms on his knees, laid his forehead on them. His shoulders shook as his grief poured out.

Miriam got up and sat beside him, her arm around him, pulling him gently to her. Jason sat up and leaned into her arms, holding on to her, his heartache and sorrow pouring out.

For a while she wanted, even pretended, that she was holding her own son, her Nathaniel, comforting him, turning back time and keeping him safe from the torment and the shame. But all too soon reality bore into her like a nail in her hand. This wasn't Nathaniel, but someone that he wanted to love but wouldn't. If she could not keep her own son safe, she wanted to do whatever she could to ensure Jason's well-being. Give him something to hold on to. To hope for. Something to weather this pit of grief and emerge, eventually thriving, being happy as he had a right to be.

After several moments, he eased back, gaining composure. Miriam dried her own eyes with a tissue. She got up and brought her purse with her as she sat again beside him.

"This is my cell phone number," she said, writing on a small pad from her purse. She tore off the page. "I would like to know what you're doing and how you're doing." She took a deep breath. "I hope you'll want to stay in touch. And if you ever need anything—anything, or just want to talk." She saw his bewildered look. "There's been enough hurt, enough shame. No more."

He took the paper and nodded. "Thank you. I will."

Again, slowly, she reached into her purse. "I think Nathaniel would want you to have this." She held out the DVD. "The drawing— You're so talented. Never give up on your dream."

Jason stared at the case as his emotions wavered, then reached out and took it. As he did, Miriam covered his hand with hers.

"And most of all, never forget Second Timothy. Never give up on yourself."

Jason could only nod.

"You will love again," she whispered. "Nathaniel would want that."

The clutch of his hand on hers tightened.

It was five-forty-five. By this time everyday, place-settings for four would have been laid out on the formal dining room table, awaiting the ritualistic six o'clock mealtime. Today, nothing lay on the classic French dark cherry surface. Only the china cabinet, the chandelier, the pictures, sconces around the room reflected in the table's mirror-like gloss. But reflections were its only contents.

Miriam sat at the table staring at its bareness, her thoughts wandering. Her morning had been long, filled with emotion—emotion that was laden with grief but was also in some mysterious way bolstered with a miniscule ray of hope. As she expected, she heard the automatic garage door open and close, signaling Matthew's arrival, followed by him entering the kitchen, then the dining room. He stood in the doorway, a look of disgruntlement on his face.

"Why isn't dinner ready?" he asked. "Why is your car still in the driveway?"

As Miriam looked at him, she told herself to remain composed and unencumbered. "You had the wrong answer for the final question at the Bible Scholar Competition."

Matthew slowly came into the room and stood on the other side of the table opposite her. He eyed her, mystified. "What are you talking about?"

She kept her voice calm, matter-of-fact, patient. "The Bible Scholar Competition. The final question. 'For God has not given you a spirit of fear and timidity, but one of power and strength and self-control.' That was the question and when Nathaniel said it was in Second Timothy 2:7, you flinched and sighed. You were subtle. I'm sure no one else noticed. But I did. You thought he'd missed it. And when Richard said he was correct, for a split second you couldn't believe it, almost as if you wanted Nathaniel's answer to be wrong, so that you could be right."

He leaned on the table, glaring at her. "What are you talking about? Why would you bring that up now? And more important, your accusation is disrespectful. Whether or not I was wrong, it's not your place to say." He had not raised his voice, but his irritation was unmistakable.

Miriam took a deep, calming breath and stood up. "Sarah Elizabeth and I have already eaten. There's ample food in the refrigerator.

I'm sure you'll find it." She picked up her purse from the floor beside her.

"What— Where are you going? What is the matter with you?" he demanded, his voice now louder. "Where is Sarah Elizabeth?"

"She's with Carolyn. They're waiting for me nearby. We're—that is Sarah Elizabeth and I—are going to Raleigh."

"Just like that? How dare you leave without my permission."

"You don't under—"

"Wait," he interrupted, holding up his hand. "What are you talking about? Carolyn and Jim left to go home yesterday."

"I called and asked Carolyn this morning to come back."

"Why would you do that?"

She fought to get the words out. She had to do this. "I asked her to help us pack—"

Matthew's eyes widened with confusion and anger as he cut her off again. "What do you mean—pack? What do—"

She paused again to gather her courage. "Pack. Suitcases. Clothes." She looked away but then directly at him. "I'm leaving. Going to Raleigh, Matthew. And I'm taking Sarah Elizabeth with me." She walked toward the foyer.

"Leaving? What do you mean 'leaving?' For how long?" Then he realized. "Raleigh. I should have known. Carolyn's behind all this, isn't she?"

Miriam did not stop. "No, Carolyn came because I called her," she said as she continued walking.

"Is she telling you to get a divorce?" he screamed. "Is she?" He moved to block the doorway.

"She is not telling me to do anything." Her voice remained calm, gaining determination. "I made this decision on my own. Totally. Completely. Leave Carolyn out of it."

"You cannot divorce me," he seethed. "It's not allowed in my church. Marriage is a sacred vow." He grabbed her forearm, causing her to drop her purse. His anger erupted on his face and in his voice. "And you're not going anywhere without my permission."

Suddenly, Miriam's forced calm abandoned her and converted into unbridled rage. With a twist of her arm she freed herself from his grasp. Reaching back, she used her entire body to wheel half way around. The force of her slap to the side of his head stunned him so much that he staggered back, his hand up to his stinging face. For a moment he stood silent, glaring at her, disbelief, contempt and fury spreading across his face.

"We've *never* had a marriage or a family," she screamed. "What we did was put on a show for your *father* and your *church*." Tears began streaming down her face, but she was not deterred. Her wrath carried her. "I talked to the detective today. I listened to the voicemail that Nathaniel sent you before he killed himself." She wiped her tears. "I saw Jason's drawing and read what he wrote and I talked to him. I know *everything*, Matthew."

"You went behind my back," he yelled.

Her eyes narrowed, studying him. "Is that all you care about?" she asked, her hands raised. "Yes, I went behind your back because I wanted the truth. For once." As she dug her eyes into his, she sensed it. She knew she was right. "You haven't even listened to it."

Matthew tried to fight back with his own silent stare.

"You haven't, have you?" He didn't answer. "You can't face the fact that Nathaniel is—was gay."

"Don't you say that!" he screamed, pointing his finger at her. "It's not true—"

"It is true," she shouted.

"Don't you dare disrespect me like this." His bitterness and rage exploded.

"And what about your disrespect for Nathaniel? He is—" She fought through her emotion. "He *was* a human being. Good and decent. And you made him feel like he was evil. You and *your almighty, sanctimonious* church."

"Don't you disrespect me. It is a sin for you to talk to me like this."

"Sin, Matthew?" she cried, her body and voice incensed. "And who are *you* to preach to anyone about sin?"

"Striking me is a sin. Talking to me like this is a *sin*." He spat out his words. "You repent this instant. Repent because Jesus Christ died for your sins."

Miriam scowled at him as she spoke through gritted teeth. "And Nathaniel died for yours."

His eyes widened. "No. Some evil has gotten into you," he clamored. "No. Not true." He crossed his arms tightly over his chest, shaking his head, denying. "I spoke only the truth of God. From the Bible."

Still boring her eyes into him, Miriam saw what she had known all along. The weakness. *His* weakness. Not only that, but his indisputable fear and cowardice, the emptiness underneath his holy armor. Again, she brushed the wetness from her face. When she spoke, her voice held no fear, only softness. "You are a very pitiful man, Matthew Winslow." Her voice and manner conveyed genuine sympathy. "You have no concept of what it means to love someone." She slowly shook her head. "Or even be loved." She picked up her purse from the floor. "I sincerely hope someday you will."

"You are not going to do this. I won't allow it. I forbid it," he yelled, attempting to command.

Miriam ignored him. As she left the room, he followed her into the foyer.

"Don't you go through that door." He yelled almost stammering. "This is a sin. You'll spend the rest of your life begging God to forgive you for this."

With total calm Miriam opened the front door and looked back at him. "No, that will be your life's work."

Tears were welling in his eyes, desperation covered his face. "Please, Miriam," he said, pleading. "Don't do this."

She said nothing but walked out.

CHAPTER FIFTEEN

THURSDAY—JUNE 4...
NINE DAYS LATER

Matthew snapped the lid closed on the bottle of Purell and dropped
it in the console of his car. He didn't think that pneumonia was contagious, but he didn't want to take any chances. As he cleansed his
hands, he glanced around the hospital parking deck. Tomorrow he
would take his shirts and suits to the laundry. Or was it dry cleaners?
He guessed they'd tell him if he was in the wrong place. And go to
the grocery store, too. He needed only a few things. He'd make a
list. He started his car, backed out of the space and drove into the
late afternoon sunshine. Estelle Caviness had looked so pitiful, lying
there scarcely breathing. Get through Sunday, he'd decided, then
he could give himself some room to do other things. He wished he
wasn't preaching this Sunday. But it was best for the congregation
to see that things were normal again. That he was strong and had
everything under control. And he had already missed being in the
pulpit two Sundays. Probably be having her funeral within the next
month at the most. She was so frail, her skin like a silk cloth draped

over bones. What grocery store should he go to? Where was the nearest one? And everyone understood about Miriam visiting her sister for a while—and Sarah Elizabeth's going with her. It was logical and it was only temporary. That night—just after she'd left—he told himself then that she would be back. She had been under a massive strain. No matter how strong she'd tried to be, she simply had broken down. She wasn't as strong as he'd thought in such a difficult crisis. That's why he felt it best not to try to call her. She needed time to grieve, to deal with the loss.

He had been fearful at first but then had turned to his Bible and read constantly, even whenever he had only a few minutes, he read. And that had been a comfort. Even though he knew hundreds of verses by heart, reading chapters and whole books gave him better insight. He hoped Miriam and Sarah Elizabeth were doing the same. Reading the Bible would bring about a true healing to all of this. When they came back from Raleigh, he would add that to the evening prayer before bedtime. More than just once a week and verifying Sarah Elizabeth and Nathan—he caught himself—Sarah Elizabeth's progress with her memorization. Yes, he would do that. A wonderful idea.

And thinking of Sarah Elizabeth, maybe he would call on the Caviness family. No, that was Richard's area. Or, no, Harry's job. What was he thinking? But then Sarah Elizabeth seemed to like the Caviness boy. So a personal call would be in order. A good, strategic move on his part to build support with a church member.

Arriving at the church he read, as always, the sign in front with his name. However, today he looked at it with a more critical eye, as if searching for spelling errors. He turned into the staff lot, parked in his space and turned the ignition off. He reached into the console for the Purell. Had he done this already? Just in case, he cleansed his hands again, at the same time wondering about the phone call from Howard Carr this morning wanting to meet at 4:30 this afternoon. He supposed it was something about this upcoming event the homosexuals were having downtown the end of the month. The church was getting everything in place to protest against it—silently, spiritually and respectfully. It had to be done this way. As he put the Purell in the console he thought he noticed his hand trembling slightly. No. It wasn't. Just a simple little flinch. Like the other times. Little jerks. Probably came from not getting enough sleep.

With his Bible he got out of the car and strode with confidence into the building, took the elevator upstairs, then went down the hall to his office. When he walked in Gwen smiled. "Good afternoon, Reverend," she said, looking up from keyboarding.

"Yes, good afternoon. Almost time for you to leave, I know, but before you do, could you make a list for the current hospital visitation? I seem to have lost mine."

"Certainly, Reverend. I'll just leave it here in your box." She gestured toward the corner of her desk.

"Thank you so much. Is Mr. Carr here yet?"

"Yes, they're waiting for you."

"They?" he asked.

"Mr. Carr and Mr. Ward," she answered.

For a moment he faltered. Why would Kenneth Ward be here? But just as quickly he saw the situation in a different light. The movement and protest. That was why he was here. This was good. The Coalition is really getting behind him. He went into his office.

"Gentlemen," he said, closing the door. Both immaculately dressed as always in their expensive navy blue suits, Howard's pinstriped. "Howard. Kenneth." He shook hands with each man as they stood. "Kenneth, I didn't know you were in town." They all sat down, Matthew behind his desk, the other two in side chairs in front of his desk. He put his Bible on his credenza. "I'm glad you're sitting in on this meeting. I'm so glad to have your support on this homosexual issue."

Kenneth Ward smiled. "It's good to see you, Matthew. Always good to see you." He turned to look at Howard Carr.

Howard Carr looked down at his manicured hands calmly clasped, lying on his crossed leg, then at Matthew. When he spoke his tone was friendly but firm. "Matthew, this meeting isn't about the homosexual movement. The—"

"Oh, my mistake" he said, smiling. "I thought you said on the phone—" His voice trailed off, not completing his sentence.

"Some information came to my attention earlier this week which, because of the gravity of the situation, I then took to the Executive Committee and then the Board of Trustees."

Matthew sat forward in his chair, clasping his own hands together—tightly in case they began flinching. "What, uh, what information is that?" Concern filled his voice. He tried to hide the uncertainty he was feeling.

"It began as a rumor which we tried to ignore, but Kenneth felt it needed to be investigated which he has done on our behalf." Howard spoke with a commanding, business-like tone, not shying away. "I'll be direct, Matthew. Your wife's absence since Tuesday a week ago—"

"She's visiting her sister in Raleigh," Matthew interrupted. "She's been under a strain as you can imagine."

Carr waited for him to finish. "According to Kenneth's report, she's not there for a visit."

Matthew stared at him. He felt a tightness in his stomach and a warmth around his shirt collar. His grip of one hand on the other became vice-like, his knuckles white. Slowly, he shook his head. "No, that's not true." He tried to sound in control, authoritative. He had to convince them. He cleared his throat. "No, she's just, uh, there just," he stammered. "It's just for a brief while." He looked at Howard. A nervous, pleading smile ignited on his face, then disappeared just as quickly. He had to convince them. Yet, he felt so helpless. He tried to gather his words. What to say. The right tone. He could do this. He had to do this. "She discussed it with me. I thought it was a good idea. Maybe not the best. I mean, I know, uh, her place is with me. But she—"

"Matthew, we know that she has spoken with an attorney in Raleigh," Howard said with evenness. "And she's taken steps to enroll your daughter in school there."

Matthew looked now at Kenneth Ward, ignoring Howard. "It's just temporary. Just until she can get her, uh, thoughts together. I know this. I've talked with her. We discussed this."

"Matthew, the Board met last night and made a very difficult decision. You know the church's stance on suicide and divorce, especially divorce, in particular if it involves a leader in the church. I know you know the bylaws set forth by your own grandfather, so I'm sure this is not coming as a surprise to you. He was right to enact such a directive because of the image it presents—an image that we cannot afford, financially and spiritually. Spiritually, being most important, of course."

"There's not going to be a divorce. Mir—my wife, I wouldn't allow her—"

Howard Carr held up his hand. "Matthew, I think—the Board thinks and Kenneth and the leaders within the Coalition concur—that in light of all the tragedy that you've had in your family in the last week or so, that it would be best for you to take early retirement from Holy Bible Fellowship. You're still a young man—"

"What? What are you saying? I can't believe this. No, please, Howard, Kenneth—don't do this." Matthew looked at both men, pleading. "I'll call Miriam, yes, I'll—right now I'll get her on the phone." He reached into his coat pocket for his cell phone. "You can hear me and we'll set up a meeting. I'll go to Raleigh. We'll talk. You'll see there's nothing to this divorce rumor."

Howard Carr shook his head. "Matthew, the Board has voted. The decision is painfully final. You have, with the generous financial help of the Coalition, a very attractive and well-earned retirement package, even health insurance for two years and—"

"But you can't do this. Please don't do this. You can make an exception in my case. My grandfather would have wanted you to take these special circumstances into consideration. He never thought— You can overlook that bylaw this once. At least give me a chance to— I mean, I'll talk to Miriam and you'll see. Howard. Kenneth. Please, how long have you known me and look at all I've done for this church. What my father did. I can't believe you're doing this. I thought we had a trusting relationship. My father baptized your children. I conducted their marriage ceremonies and baptized your grandchildren. I prayed with you in the hospital. And this is how you repay me?"

"The leader of the church has to set an example," Howard said. "If we condone your divorce, then we have to condone any other member's."

"And I'm sorry to have to say this, but the Coalition is adamant," Kenneth added. "The same is true for homosexuality."

Matthew stared at him. "There's no proof my son was one of those people."

"But rumors can do so much damage," Kenneth continued. "Damage no church can afford. The Coalition has invested a great deal in this church in the last fifteen years and has great plans for it nationally. We have to protect our investment and continue the grooming that we began." He met Matthew's gaze without backing down. "We will not be thrown off our intended course. That's why we're contributing to your retirement. You're being well compensated. In return, we expect you to do as we ask and leave quietly."

Dazed, Matthew heard the words but refused to allow them to seep in.

Howard Carr reached down to his briefcase beside his chair and took out a piece of paper. "The Board has prepared a letter to the staff and congregation. It puts you in a great light, listing your many accomplishments here and how you continued the legacy of your grandfather and father. It further states that because of the recent strain you've endured, you feel called to step aside so that God's work can continue in the greatness that has become a tradition at Holy Bible." He put the letter on the desk in front of Matthew. "Richard is going to preach this Sunday." Carr took a deep breath. "We'd like for you to collect your personal possessions and vacate your office this afternoon. The staff will be leaving in a few minutes. There will be no one but Kenneth and myself here. So you won't have to talk with anyone. No one will see you leave. There are boxes there by the door for your belongings."

Matthew glanced at the paper but did not pick it up. "You, uh, I won't, no, uh," he almost stuttered, "I'm, uh, I'm not going to let you do this to me. This is my church. I built—"

"Matthew, please, don't—" Howard began but Kenneth Ward cut him off forcefully.

"Matthew, make no mistake about it," he said. His piercing stare equaled his abrasive tone. "You do not want to take on the Coalition—legally or publicly. We have the resources to ruin you in whatever way necessary. And we won't hesitate to do so. Think long and hard before you take any action to stir things up."

The silence was deafening as Kenneth bore his eyes into Matthew. With each passing second Matthew felt himself slipping away—his dignity, his worth, his esteem, his power. All evaporating, disappearing, leaving him stranded. Helpless. Becoming smaller and smaller.

Howard had broken the silence talking about something. Matthew didn't really hear his words. He produced another piece of paper from his briefcase and put it on the desk. Matthew looked at it. The paper began with "I, Reverend Matthew Winslow..." and went on with numbers and dollar signs, and words like "insurance," "taxes," and others that he didn't try to absorb. Next were the signatures of the twelve board members with Howard Carr's name first. He saw the last two lines "Signature" and "Date." Blank. He lost track of how long he stared at them. He heard Howard say those same two words aloud. Then, he heard Kenneth repeat them.

Matthew felt like he was in a dream, being chased, hunted. The enemy, the bad person. He had no power. No defense. He had nowhere to turn. No one to turn to. Abandoned.

Still staring at the paper, he heard Kenneth's voice but not his words. The tone was harsh, demanding. He looked up and saw fury in his face. Again, he stared at the paper on the desk and tried to grasp his pen, but his hand was trembling so erratically that he had to make several attempts. He pulled the paper closer and attempted to sign, but the result more resembled indecipherable scrawl. When he finished he continued looking down.

Howard stood, collected the paper, put it in his briefcase and put a copy on the desk. He said something about the two of them waiting just down the hall in the conference room while he collected his things, that they would leave with him.

Matthew sat alone, still staring down, unable to look up. He dropped the pen as his hands now shook uncontrollably. Resting his elbows on his desk, he covered his face with his hands, fighting the emotion that threatened. He would have to come up with a plan. Somehow he would have to fight back. But how? After all his father and grandfather had done. How could Kenneth threaten him like that? He and his family had made this church the colossal power that it was. His father and grandfather would want—no, *expect* him to fight back. This was still as much their church. He took a deep breath. Maybe he would call his own attorney, someone who wasn't afraid to take on a powerful coalition. Yes, that's what he would do. Tonight when he got home. He'd look for a lawyer. Someone not in the church, of course. What was that called? Conflict of interest? Yes. A powerful attorney. Maybe someone from out of state. Someone famous. He'd do a search online. That was his plan.

Slowly he managed to stand and reluctantly began taking things from his desk and putting them in the boxes and his briefcase. From his computer he copied to a flash drive his sermons and other personal data. He wasn't stealing, he thought as if Howard and Kenneth were there reprimanding him. These were documents he'd created.

By five-thirty, before carrying out the final box, he surveyed his office. He refused to allow nostalgia to enter his mind. He would be back here—soon. Putting his keys on his desk, he simply left, saying nothing to Kenneth and Howard.

As he drove through rush hour traffic, his Bible on the passenger seat, he replayed the discussion in his office and what he wished he'd said. How he should have stood up to Kenneth Ward and Howard

Carr, especially Howard. He had no idea he was so backstabbing. Was that how he had become so successful in that bank of his? Behind the scene dealings? After today he wouldn't be surprised by any shadiness associated with Howard Carr. The audacity of the Board doing this to him. It was sinful to treat a minister this way. Who did they think they were? God? Still, Kenneth Ward's warning echoed, his voice stinging, "... do not take on the Coalition...the resources to ruin you in whatever way necessary...will not hesitate to do so...think long and hard before stirring things up."

Suddenly a silver- colored Toyota Camry cut sharply into Matthew's lane, forcing him to slam on his brakes. On the trunk lid he saw the silver outline of the Christian fish but with "Sushi" written inside the lines. A bumper stick said, "Mean people suck." Still another, "The Moral Majority is Neither."

Instantly—without warning—all reason and practicality left Matthew, including any fear. It was as if a nest of hornets had been struck by a rock; now seething, they sought revenge. Matthew began blasting his horn, not letting up. The driver put his left arm out the window and held up his middle finger. Not to be deterred, Matthew continued blowing his horn and driving close to his bumper. He did not notice all the other drivers in the lanes beside him. His sole focus was the silver Camry.

As the mass of cars approached a large intersection, the light turned red. Only when he stopped and put his Lexus in "park" did Matthew stop blowing the horn. He got out of his car, opened the trunk and took out Nathaniel's bat that had been in his Jeep Cherokee. He closed the trunk and went to the silver Camry. Ignoring the teenage driver who had rolled up the windows, frantically calling for help on his cell phone, Matthew began pounding the car's trunk lid with the bat. Over and over, again and again he hammered with the metal bat. Each pummel sent shockwaves up his arms, but he did not feel them. His jaw clenched, his eyes gaping, riveted on the silver car. With each strike he heaved a savage grunt that came from a deep rage.

Ceaselessly he attacked the car trunk. Time and time again, each blow more forceful than the previous. Loud banging, metal against metal. But Matthew did not hear any of it. Neither did he hear the other people honking their horns or the pleas of the other drivers, some of whom got out and stood at a safe distance. He did not hear the sirens or see the blue lights of the police car. Only suddenly did he see a uniformed man standing near the car, his left arm out with his hand up, his right hand on his holstered gun, his mouth moving, saying something. But Matthew did not see a policeman.

For an instant—a flash in his mind—he saw someone else. Then and only then did he stop. He lowered the bat to his side. When he did, he felt a second officer from behind him snatch it out of his hand. Immediately he turned. Something told him he had to fight. He drew back his arm, his fist ready to bash the police officer's face. Before he could move someone else had grabbed him from behind, locked his arms behind him and clicked metal around his wrists. Strong hands clamped each of his biceps and led him to a police car where he was put into the back seat. A police officer was saying something to him—something about remaining silent and questions and lawyers and a court of law.

Slowly the police car navigated its way through the traffic. He saw the silver Camry with its pummeled trunk and the people in cars and on the sidewalk staring at him. Why were they looking at— Suddenly, reality flashed before him—what he had done in front of all those people. He leaned forward, trying to hide his face. The awkward position was made all the more so by his shackled hands behind him. More reality penetrated his recall. He pressed his forehead against his knees as desolation overwhelmed him. What had he done? What had happened to him? He felt the tears on his face being absorbed by his pants. "Oh, God, what have I done?" he whispered, as he began sobbing.

Again clamped hands on his arms commanded his movement, this time into the police station where a policeman emptied his pockets and removed his belt, his hands still cuffed. He then was told to take a seat in front of a desk.

"Name," a husky officer with a voice to match asked from behind the desk.

Matthew opened his mouth to speak, but then waited a moment while he considered. "Matthew Winslow." He continued answering questions, all the while aching. The word—his title, the title he had been so proud of, the title his father had been so proud of—he could not say. He had defiled it. He had defiled himself. And now. What was going—

He stopped. A voice behind him was faintly familiar. He didn't want to turn around. Being recognized like this— No, God, please, no. He held his head down. The voices halted. Maybe he had left—whoever it was. He continued answering the officer's questions until it was over.

"All done here?" The question, directed to the officer at the desk, came from a man wearing a shirt and tie, his badge fixed to his belt. His build solid, his hair neatly tousled and blond.

"All done," replied the husky policeman at the desk.

"I'll take him from here."

"All yours," the officer said, handing him several papers.

"Reverend Winslow. I'm Detective Harry Rierson. Come with me."

The detective led him down a short hallway and ushered him into a small, drab room that contained only a table and four chairs. When Matthew saw another man in the room, he realized why the voice was familiar.

"I believe you already know Detective Sparks from the Sheriff's Department," Rierson said in a business-like manner.

Matthew only nodded as he looked at the floor.

"Reverend Winslow, do you think you're calm enough for me to remove the handcuffs?"

Matthew spoke softly, "Yes."

Rierson unlocked the cuffs and pointed toward a chair at the table. Matthew sat down, his hands in his lap, his shoulders slumped, his head bowed unable to look at either of the men.

When Rierson spoke his voice conveyed a less rigid tone. "You've had quite an afternoon, Reverend. Would you like to tell me what made you take a bat to that car?"

Matthew said nothing as he stared at the table in front of him.

Rierson looked at Sparks, then sat down opposite Matthew. When he spoke, he continued sounding sympathetic. "Reverend, you're in a bit of trouble here. Technically, you assaulted a police officer. Even though you didn't swing, drawing back as you did is considered assault." He leaned forward toward Matthew. "At the request of Detective Sparks, who told me about your son, I'm willing to help you, but I need you to talk to me. Otherwise, I have no choice but to put you in a jail cell."

Still focusing on the table, Matthew blinked his eyes. "I don't know what happened. That silver car cut in front of me and then I was just there in the street swinging the bat."

"Would you say the strain of losing your son—was that what caused you to, well, break down, lose control?"

Matthew closed his eyes, his face blank.

"Reverend?"

"They fired me," he said in a voice scarcely audible. "They fired me because my wife—because they think my wife left me and because my son committed suicide because Detective Sparks thinks he is—was a homosexual." His eyes were still shut. "In the eyes of my church those are all unacceptable. They're sins." He had heard the words, heard his voice. But they had come from someone other than him.

"Didn't your father found that church?" It was Sparks who had spoken.

"Grandfather, then my father, then me. And Nathaniel was next."

Both detectives were silent for several moments. Then, Rierson looked at Sparks as he stood up. "Reverend, Detective Sparks and I are going to step out of the room. Would you like some water, a soda, coffee? Do you need to use the bathroom?"

He hesitated for only a second. "No," he uttered in a whisper.

Matthew remained stock-still, his eyes closed as the men left the room. He listened for their voices, for some clue as to what would happen next. But he heard nothing more than the ventilation system whirring. At least here no one could see him, could see that he had been arrested. Arrested. Him. Reverend Matthew Winslow. Dragged away in public, put into a police car and put under arrest. What had happened? What had made him get out of his car and do that? Would anyone at the church find out? Even if he never went back to Holy Bible, what would they think of him? The senior minister. A Christian. But he could never go back. Not now. Not after this. That was for sure. Oh, what had he done? How was he ever going to get out of this? What if he had to go to jail? The thought caused his stomach to sour.

Over and over again, he sifted through his thoughts, his guilt, his transgressions against God. Wallowing in what he had done, then slowly shifting his attention, he began reliving his meeting with Howard and Kenneth. The way they had treated him. Like a dog. A common animal. He deserved better than that. They were the ones responsible for what he'd done this afternoon. Not him. And what about their sins? The Golden Rule. But how could he fight all this now? Endlessly he tumbled his agony around in his mind.

He had no idea how long he'd sat in the room, but for however long it was, he did not move. His hands remained in his lap, his shoulders drooped. He kept his eyes closed even when the door opened. He assumed it was Sparks or Rierson or both. He waited for one of them to speak.

"Reverend Winslow?"

Another voice. A different one. A silent panic struck him. Someone else knew that he was here. That he had been arrested. He heard a chair scrape across the floor and something being placed on the table.

"Reverend Winslow?"

Matthew opened his eyes and slowly looked up. A clean cut man, professionally dressed in a suit and tie, sat on the other side of the table. His glasses gave him a sophisticated, important appearance, yet his face gave an impression of concern as well as understanding. His briefcase lay on the table.

"I'm Dwight Overby. An attorney. The detectives said you might be in need of some legal help. I'm glad to offer my services if you'd like. If you know of someone else you'd rather work with, I'll be glad to contact them on your behalf."

Matthew stared at him, puzzled, his voice muted. "I don't really know of anyone else. Not now, anyway. I don't, I mean, as for paying you—"

"That won't be a concern if all goes well and I have a feeling we can work all this out." He glanced over the papers in his hand, then opened his briefcase and placed them inside. "Next, we're going to take you before the magistrate who will hopefully release you on your own recognizance. Then I'll talk to the prosecutor tomorrow to see if we can avoid your having to go before a judge to answer the charges against you." He paused, looking very intently at Matthew. "I have to be honest with you. I'll need to convince the magistrate that you have calmed down, that you won't repeat what happened this afternoon in any way and that you're not going to harm anyone or yourself. Do you think you can abide by all those restrictions?"

Matthew's nod was barely visible, his voice a whisper. "Yes."

"And, since we've only just met, I must ask if you trust me to represent you?"

Again, Matthew agreed verbally and with a slight nod.

"Good." He stood up and moved toward the door. "I'll go see when we can get in to see the magistrate."

"But, I mean," Matthew began, not sure of what to say.

Overby stopped. "Yes?"

"I don't understand. You don't even, uh, you don't know me. Why are you—" He couldn't finish the question.

The attorney smiled. "No, I don't. And you don't know me." He reached for the doorknob. "It just seems like the right thing to do." He left.

Again, he sat alone in the bare room with his thoughts.

Matthew followed Dwight Overby through a series of corridors and down a flight of stairs. Finally, they went into a room with rows of chairs bolted to the floor. Overby motioned toward two empty seats and sat down with his client. A glimpse around the room only added to his humiliation. Everyone had broken the law, arrested, slumped in the chairs, one bandaged, his arm in a sling, a woman with a black eye. Definitely not people he was used to being around, yet here he was in the middle of them. One of them. A policeman stood by the door. Body odor permeated the air. His urge to gag was overruled by his feeling of shame, fear and helplessness. He kept his eyes focused downward. He didn't want to make eye contact with anyone. He wanted to disappear, especially when he saw the policeman who had arrested him.

"When we go in," Overby said quietly, gesturing toward a door, "let me do all the talking. Okay?"

As Matthew nodded his agreement, a man opened the door and stepped into the room.

"Matthew David Winslow," he said loudly.

Hearing his name—having everyone in the room hear his name—felt like a knife piercing his belly. Dwight Overby tapped his arm as he stood up. Matthew stood and followed him into the room, the arresting officer coming in with them.

Inside a magistrate sat behind a formidable desk, several files lined one side. A name plate in front read Magistrate Jacob Howard. Matthew immediately thought of Howard Carr and shut his eyes trying to erase the man from his memory.

"Mr. Overby, you're working late today," Howard said, "assuming you're representing Mr. Winslow."

"Correct, Magistrate, on both counts."

The magistrate read the file. "You are the arresting officer—" He looked more closely at the file. "Officer Warren?"

Officer Warren stepped forward. "Yes, sir."

"Tell me what happened."

Hearing all the facts aloud heaped on more humiliation. Matthew tried to swallow, but his throat was caked in dryness. His chest pounded. His hands drenched with sweat. He could not bring himself to look at the man behind the desk. The man who could put him in jail.

"So there was no battery, only assault?" Howard asked when Warren had finished.

"That's correct, Magistrate."

"The charges of destruction to private property and assault but not battery on a police officer are entered into record. Mr. Overby, speak to me about your client if you will."

"Mr. Winslow is actually Reverend Winslow. This is his first offense. He owns his home, has a family and strong ties to the community. He's lived in Elmsborough his entire life. Tragically, his eighteen-year-old son committed suicide just a few short weeks ago, the strain of which is enormous, as you might imagine. He has assured me that he has calmed down and that he is not going to harm anyone or himself. Therefore, I would ask that you release him under his own recognizance."

"Sounds like a plea bargain might be in the works," Howard said as he wrote in the file.

"That is my intention."

"Mr. Winslow?" the magistrate said.

Hearing his name again sent another jolt of fear through Matthew. This time he looked directly at Howard. Overby had said he would not have to speak.

"I'm releasing you on your on recognizance. I strongly urge you to heed your attorney's advice." He closed the file and added it to the top of a stack. "And my condolences."

Matthew nodded. "Yes. Sir."

"Thank you, Mr. Howard," Overby said, taking Matthew's elbow to let him know they could leave.

It had been over in a matter of minutes, but to Matthew it had felt like hours. Out in the hallway Overby led him back to the desk where he picked up his possessions. He then drove him to the same lot where he had picked up Nathaniel's Jeep.

"I'll do my best to talk to the prosecutor tomorrow morning and call you." He gave him his business card. "Call me if you need to. Try to—try to eat something and rest. You've been through a lot, but it's not the end of the world, even though it may seem like it."

Matthew looked at the card even though it was too dark for him to read it. "Thank you," he said softly turning to his attorney.

Overby offered his hand. With subdued gratitude he shook it.

When he got into his car, he saw his Bible still on the passenger seat. He looked away from it, ashamed. As he drove he had a sick feeling—an emptiness that he wanted to vomit up, expel from his body. The turmoil of what had happened. The utter disgrace. Nearing his neighborhood, he wanted to drive in the opposite direction. He wanted to be anywhere except here. Here where people knew him. Here where people would know everything—his being fired, vandalizing a car with a baseball bat, being arrested, technically assaulting a police officer. They would know that he was a complete failure. Humiliation pummeled him as he had the Camry. Punch after merciless punch. Caving in his mind and his body, breaking every bone.

He was still several houses away when he began frantically clicking the remote to open the garage door. Finally in range, he could see it rising thanks to the street light and the house lights on the timer. Quickly, he pulled inside and immediately used the remote to close the door before getting out. He was trying to hide the fact that Miriam's car was not there.

With the garage sealed off he quickly went inside and closed all the drapes and blinds. He would keep the lights off in the front of the house as much as possible. He didn't expect anyone to come to the house, but if they did, he wouldn't answer the door.

Barricaded behind covered windows, Matthew stood in the foyer in near total darkness. What was he to do now? He had no purpose and worse, no will to search for one. He ambled to the stairs and sat down, his elbows on his knees, his face in his hands. Empty and alone. Defeated. What had he done? How was this all going to end? What was going to happen to him? What would he do with his life? He thought of his Bible. He had left it in the car. Maybe he should go get it. But he was too humiliated. Then out of the deep and dreaded silence that was confining him, the idea occurred to him. Pray. But for some strange reason, he couldn't think of how to begin, what to say. He felt so wounded. Of all the praying he had done and now nothing. Like a blind man stumbling. Helpless. He opened his mouth, trying to force words. Instead, tears slowly began to trickle down his cheeks. Then in utter despair, from somewhere simple words emerged. "Help me. Please, help me." But they seemed to go nowhere. Just echoes in his head which faded into nothingness. At first. However, that one small plea somehow nudged him to say them again. But he could only manage to whisper. "God, help me, please." In the quiet nothing happened. He felt nothing new. Just the same sledge hammer striking his insides. Over and over. Still, he muttered the words, again. "Please, God, help me."

He was surprised when the thought appeared. A reminder out of nowhere. The shoe box upstairs in his closet. Far in the back on the top shelf. Carefully hidden. Even Miriam didn't know about it. A gift from his father. He wanted to dismiss it, but it wouldn't go away. Would it even fire after all this time?

He whispered the words, again. "God, help me, please."

CHAPTER SIXTEEN

Friday—June 5

"I've received the police report on the incident yesterday," Dwight Overby said the next morning when he phoned Matthew as he had promised. "Two drivers came forward and reported that the kid was speeding and driving erratically, even dangerously, and said he looked like he was texting. Plus he already has a bad driving record. I've talked with his parents and they will not press charges against you if you pay for the damage to the car." He didn't have to wait for a response.

"Of course," Matthew said, relief evident in his somber voice.

"Good. Next." Overby took a deep breath. "I proposed to the prosecutor that you undergo—and pay for—twenty-five hours of anger management counseling. And you must also serve two hundred and fifty hours of community service. I'll get in touch with you later about this. The prosecutor felt that you should have to put in time there in light of the assault charge on a police officer. And by the way, the officer willingly agreed to let you off on that charge after Detective Rierson explained your circumstances.

"The prosecutor has agreed that if you do all of this—the counseling and community service—and have no other infractions of the law for one year, then he'll give you a deferred prosecution which means no record on the damage to private property and no assault charge. It all goes away." He paused. "Now I have scheduled an appointment for you this afternoon at four p. m. with a counselor whom the prosecutor has approved. She has agreed to work with you. Her name is Kate Thornton. Her office address is 4516-Suite C Lexington Street." He was silent, waiting for Matthew's response.

Matthew hesitated, thinking. A woman? He was supposed to talk to a woman about his—what? His anger? Still he knew he could not be overtly resistant, but neither could he not speak his mind. "I don't see what—I guess I don't understand how this is going to help."

"I think you should let her worry about that. I know her. I trust her."

"Will I have to go to court to accept this or after I've completed it all?"

"No," Overby said. "I can go for you."

He took a deep breath. "Very well."

"Were you able to get some rest?" Overby asked, his tone different, less business-like.

Matthew thought the question too invasive and probably just his being nice without genuinely caring. "Some," he answered simply.

Matthew brooded all day about his pending appointment, certain that no good could possibly come from this. He didn't believe in therapy or counseling—whatever the label. That was why he never did what the church called pastoral counseling, happy to hand that over to the associates. Let them deal with the congregants' problems. He'd had enough to take care of with preaching and larger issues.

But at ten minutes until four, he was sitting in his car in the parking lot next to the small two-story office building. The façade was ordinary—modern, red brick, smoked windows, glass entrance. What held his attention was the sign beside the front door, listing the occupants—a dentist, an attorney, a Certified Public Accountant, a massage therapist and Independent Therapists. From his car he was able to read the names of four therapists on the sign by the door, but only one mattered. Katherine Thornton. How could a therapist—a total stranger, especially a woman, probably not even a religious person, who knew nothing about him—how could she be of any help to him? But then, the magistrate's words from the night before about heeding his lawyer's advice broke into his thoughts.

Before opening the car door, he looked around to see if anyone might see him go inside. He guessed it didn't matter. He could be going to the dentist or the accountant. Walking the short distance to the building, he went into the lobby and located Suite C. He opened the door and went into the small waiting area with several chairs and a small sofa. A young woman with short, streaked hair, wearing jeans and a tank top sat with her attention on her cell phone, her fingers flying over the key pad. She ignored him, not even glancing up.

Overby had relayed Thornton's instructions about a clipboard with an information sheet on the counter. Matthew found it and sat on the opposite side of the room to fill it out. He began listing the usual information. When he came to the section on insurance, he hesitated. Would the staff at Holy Bible or the Coalition find out about this? Did the insurance company keep such matters confidential? It was against the law, wasn't it? Privacy issues? He hoped so as he filled in the information. When he arrived at the last question before signing his name, he stopped, staring at the question. "Next of kin or person to contact in case of emergency." For an instant his hand was positioned to write down Miriam's name, but then reality struck him hard. He had no one. No real next of kin. Did he know anyone who would stop what they were doing and come to his aid? He tried to think of someone from the church but dismissed each possible candidate the instant a name flashed into his mind.

He would skip it. If this Katherine Thornton woman asked, he'd simply say he would supply it later.

As he finished signing the sheet, a woman walked up the short hall and into the lobby. She wore a sleeveless, yellow blouse and flowing, chocolate brown pants. Her black hair was straight, parted neatly in the middle and reached just below her ears. Small, rectangular eyeglasses with thin black frames accented her face. A healthy tan added to her slender build. At a glance Matthew was put off by her pants. Women should not wear pants, especially not professionals. He approximated her age to be mid-forties.

"Hello," she said, smiling.

Instantly, Matthew feared she would say or ask his name so the woman who was waiting would hear but was relieved when she didn't.

"Come on back." She led the way down the hallway and stood aside for Matthew to enter one of the rooms.

A stylish, modern recliner sat next to a simple desk. Opposite it, a glass top end table separated a sofa and an over-sized easy chair. The lighting soft. The décor contemporary. Plants and an endless disarray of books lined floor to ceiling shelves which covered one entire wall.

"I'm Kate Thornton." She offered her hand.

"Matthew Winslow." They shook.

"Done with that?" She pointed to the clipboard.

"Yes," Matthew said and handed it to her.

She sat in the recliner. "Please have a seat." She pointed toward the sofa and chair. He chose the chair. She glanced at the information sheet, then swiveled in the recliner and put the clipboard on her desk. When she turned back to him, she leaned forward toward him. "First of all, I want to say that I'm very sorry for the loss of your son. You've been through an incredibly, well, *difficult* doesn't come close to describing all that's happened to you in the last two weeks." Her gentle voice and engagement surprised Matthew. Her genuine concern evident. He hadn't expected this.

He avoided her eyes as she spoke. "Thank you, Mrs. or is it Doctor Thornton?"

"Oh, very informal here. First name basis. Just Kate." She paused. "Have you ever been in therapy before?"

"No."

"The bottom line is total honesty and in exchange total confidentiality. I can't emphasize that enough. What you say in here stays in here. No reports to lawyers, police, judges, insurance companies. Nobody."

Matthew nodded as he shuffled his feet, then unconsciously began to rapidly jiggle his right leg up and down.

"So how did your evening go once you got home from the police station last night?"

The question stunned Matthew. Direct. Invasive. Too invasive. He wasn't about to tell a woman how he'd felt or what he'd done—closing all the drapes and sitting in the dark. He certainly wasn't going to tell her he had cried. If this was the way these sessions were going to be, he would say what he needed to and be done with it. Even though she was coming across as gentle and sympathetic, he was wary of her.

"Fine, I suppose," he said without meeting her eyes. At least he would sound a little unsure, not too cocky. Still, the lie didn't feel easy.

Kate nodded but said nothing for a moment. "What did you do?"

If she wasn't going to let up, he would just lie outright. "I ate dinner. It was almost nine. Just a peanut butter and jelly sandwich. And a soda." He looked at her while he spoke this time but then quickly looked away. Another lie. Half lie, really. He had had the sandwich and coke but not until that morning, after Overby's call.

"Anything else?"

An idea came to him. "I prayed."

She nodded her agreement. "Logical for anyone, but especially a minister." A longer pause. "Sleep okay?"

He waited. He had to sound plausible.

"Some trouble. Tossed and turned," he said, still jiggling his leg. "Some."

Kate was quiet for a moment, calmly watching him. "So, no problems with anything?"

Suddenly, he felt trapped. He didn't care. He didn't want to be here. Not with a woman. He would call Overby tonight and tell him to find a male therapist. "Well," he began but had no idea what to say. "It's a mess I got myself into, needless to say. And I did get myself into this." He smiled nervously but only for an instant. "Obviously."

She didn't smile but crossed her legs and clasped her hands in her lap.

In the silence Matthew glanced at her, then away. His right leg continued its perpetual up and down motion. Suddenly, he couldn't stand it anymore. "Look, I don't think this is going to work. No. This *isn't* going to work." He shrugged his shoulders. "I don't know what you want."

Kate eyed him for only a moment. "Your being here isn't about what I want. It's about you."

"It's not about you helping me?" he asked defiantly.

"Actually," she said calmly, "it's more about you ultimately becoming able to help yourself."

Matthew sat baffled at first. What did that mean? How could he help himself? This all sounded like a trap. "I just don't think I can do this with you. A woman. There I said it. I don't mean to offend you." He looked directly at her.

Kate shook her head in a matter-of-fact manner. "I'm not offended. I want you to be honest." She put her arms on the armrests of her chair. "You know people think that being a counselor would be boring and even depressing. But I don't feel that way at all. I feel honored to have people share their life stories with me and I want them to know that it's safe for them to do that."

Matthew hadn't expected that answer. He needed to recover. Maintain the upper hand. "It's just that in my church—" He hesitated for only a moment, as he fought the memory that it was no longer his church. "We believe that women, well, they don't take an active role. Not as active as men. And the same in a marriage. A wife should always defer to her husband. It's in the Bible," he said proudly. "It's what my grandfather believed when he was minister there and my father after him."

"So the minister's role at Holy Bible Fellowship—it was passed on to you? You inherited it?"

Matthew nodded.

"Are either your grandfather and father still living?"

"No, my grandfather died about twenty years ago. My father just five years ago. A massive heart attack."

"Any siblings?"

Matthew shook his head.

"What was growing up like for you?"

Matthew shifted in the chair. He didn't see what this had to do with anything, but he'd play along if that's what it took. "Constant Bible study from an early age," he said proudly. "Memorizing verses, going to school and church. Everything centered around the church. That was my father's life. The church and knowing the Bible."

"Nothing other than church?"

Matthew shook his head as his leg quivered even more. "Just memorized Bible verses."

"No sports? Ride a bike? Play cops and robbers with kids in the neighborhood?"

"I played with a few kids from school. On Saturdays and in the summer."

Kate nodded. "My father used to always throw a ball—football, baseball—with my brothers. Did you and your father do anything like that?"

Matthew merely shook his head.

"Camping trips? Scouts?"

"No. At the Academy Bible study is a requirement. It's a regular class. Each student has to keep a notebook of memorized verses beginning in the first grade. Everyone is tested in class. And there are competitions. My father wanted me to win the Bible Scholar Competition for my grade level every year. So he quizzed me constantly. There was no time for playing ball."

"Did you win?"

Matthew lowered his eyes. "Not always."

"And what was that like?"

He didn't like the question. Again, too probing. "I just worked harder for the next one. If I hadn't studied the Bible as much as I had, I could never have become a minister."

"What else? Glee Club? Band?"

He wanted to blatantly show his indignation with all this harping on his childhood but held it back. "Student government. In high school and college. My father said it was even more important in college for becoming a minister. For leadership."

"I've heard that some ministers say they experienced a calling—a feeling or a moment or a phase—when they felt they were being led to be a minister. Did anything like that happen to you?"

Matthew crossed his leg and jiggled his foot as he talked. "I just always loved the Bible. The truth that it speaks. The fact that it came from God is amazing. If more people followed the word of God, the world would be a better place. I felt that was my mission. It was my father's and grandfather's mission. That's the principle on which Holy Bible Fellowship was founded. It's the basis for everything we do there. To follow the word of God."

When he stopped talking, he had an odd feeling. Something ran through his mind, but he didn't know what it was. Like a cold shiver but in his mind, not his body. Without realizing it, he had stopped jiggling his foot. He uncrossed his legs and sat still. He tried to recapture it, but the phantom thought was too fleeting. He looked up and saw Kate watching him.

"You haven't mentioned your mother," she said.

For the first time he didn't drop his focus. "She's in a facility. She either has Alzheimer's or dementia. Maybe both. The doctors don't know for sure. It doesn't really seem to matter."

"Is she mobile?"

"Yes. She can walk, but you have to lead her, otherwise she would just stand in one spot all day. She can still do some things for herself." He paused. "They pretty much have to keep her isolated from the other folks most of the time because she swears." He was never going to tell her that she only swore when he came to see her—her own son.

"Swears?" Kate asked.

Matthew nodded. "She sounds so angry. I can only stand to stay there a few minutes."

"Do you remember her as being an angry person?"

"Oh, no. She was always calm, almost quiet, patient. Never a cross word. Never out of sorts. Besides, my father would never have allowed that."

Kate nodded. "That sometimes happens with Alzheimer's patients. It's called impulse control. When we're little we're told not to use bad words. So we learn to substitute 'damn' with 'darn.' With Alzheimer's, people lose that control and just go ahead and say 'damn.' Some therapists have wondered if the swearing stems from built up repressed anger because a patient was ordered around all his or her life. But that's just conjecture. There's no way to know for sure. Whatever the reason, Alzheimer's patients don't have the inhibition factor and so they swear without real-izing that what they're saying is offensive. Or sometimes rather than swearing they just say mean things to family and friends or their caregivers."

So maybe she wasn't mad at him or disliked him. "She never seemed angry."

"She may have suppressed it." She tucked her dark hair behind her ears with her index fingers. "I had an aunt who was diagnosed with Alzheimer's in her late sixties. At times she swore at the nurses and staff. She never married and had been very submissive all her life to her father. Not anything illegal but always made to feel less than, never really allowed to express an opinion."

Matthew wrestled with the theory. "You said *sometimes* this was the reason?" he asked. He heard a meekness in his voice which he had not intended and instantly regretted.

"Well, it's really impossible to know given the condition of the patients. Just a theory." She shifted in her chair. "What else do you remember about your mother growing up? Besides her being patient and calm."

Matthew thought for several minutes. "She always kept the house neat. Was a wonderful cook. And she loved dogs. When neighbors walked their dogs by the house, she'd watch from the window. The people who lived next door for a while had a beagle and she used to go out and pet it through the fence. The little dog was always so glad to see her." He pictured the scene in his mind. The fence that ran by the big oak tree in the back yard. "But they moved away after a few years."

"We have a dog. She thinks she's a member of the family and so do we." Kate smiled. "So, did your mother have a dog of her own?" she asked.

He had been thinking of scenes—his mother scratching the dog's ears while she talked to it. He realized Kate had asked a question. "No, my father wouldn't allow it," he answered. "He thought it was unclean to have animals in the house." More images of the beagle rose in his mind. "I think she said she had one when she was growing up."

"Do you have one?"

"No," he said. "The family is—was always on the go."

The brief silence made Matthew uncomfortable. He crossed his legs again.

"Since yesterday's incident is what brought you here, maybe we should talk about that."

Matthew squirmed, uncrossing and crossing his legs the opposite way, his foot jiggling resumed. "Not too much to tell. The teenager cut in front of me. A dangerous move. I got mad and lost my temper."

"Is that unusual for you? To lose your temper?"

"Yes. But given what had just happened, I just went berserk, I guess."

"When you say 'given what had just happened,' do you mean with your job?"

He looked down at his hands and nodded. It was the first time he'd heard someone else say it. The first time since Howard Carr had said it. But now someone else, someone outside the church had said it. "They're calling it early retirement," he said as a defense. "But they essentially fired me." He could feel his anger rekindling. "From the church my grandfather founded." His foot fidgeted even more. "And my father served there for over thirty years." He uncrossed his legs but continued to jiggle his right one. "And I've grown the church even more since I've been there. Even before I took the senior pastor's role."

"What was their reason?"

Another admission. He looked across the room at the large urn containing a plant. "They found out that my wife is—" He hesitated. "My wife says she's leaving me."

"How did they find out?"

"They said it was a rumor. She wasn't at church. People called her. I don't know exactly. But the Coalition apparently investigated and learned that she had gone to her sister's in Raleigh. They say she's hired an attorney and looked for a school for my daughter." He turned his gaze from the plant to the window.

Kate leaned forward. "Did you say 'Coalition?'"

Matthew nodded. "The Christian Coalition for Biblical Authority in America. They work with churches and universities like Freedom Bible."

She sat back. "I've never heard of them. And they investigated what your wife was doing in Raleigh?"

"Yes." He looked down.

"Do you trust what they said?"

"I don't know. I suppose. I haven't spoken with her since—since she left. Why would they lie? It was as much about that rumor as the other one."

"The other one?"

Matthew turned his gaze to the armrest and rubbed the palm of his hand over the fabric.

"Rumor. Assumption. Whatever you want to call it," he said, still staring at the armrest.

She gave him time before she spoke softly. "Rumor about what?"

He took a deep breath and exhaled, his eyes riveted on the arm of the chair. "That my son, uh, died. Killed—" The words were choking him. "Killed himself." He stopped, gathering something. Courage? "Because he is—was a homosexual." Suddenly, he realized again how vulnerable he had allowed himself to become. How could he have let this happen? He was talking too much, giving her too much information.

"And that's grounds for dismissal?" Kate asked.

"It is in my church. That and my wife leaving. Especially that." He crossed his legs again, foot in constant motion. "You've obviously talked to Overby. You already know all this. Why do we have to rehash it?" His voice had an edge as he now met her eyes with a tinge of defiance.

She nodded calmly. "In case he accidentally left anything out."

He looked away. Silent.

When Kate spoke, her voice was soft. "What do you intend to do now?"

His jaw muscle tightened. He shrugged. "I don't know." He began tapping his foot on the carpeted floor. "I guess that'll be my next move—trying to figure that out."

"Any life dreams? 'I always wanted to…' and fill in the blank?"

"Being a minister is the only thing I ever thought about." He crossed his other leg.

"So all this is going through your mind and the kid, the driver cuts in front of you. Then at the stop light you got out and started pounding the trunk of his car—"

He interrupted. "Especially that fish sign."

Her eyes narrowed. "Fish sign?"

"On the trunk. The Christian fish. The simple line." He drew the outline in the air.

"You mean you aimed for it specifically?"

He nodded. "It had the word 'sushi' written inside it." He paused. "I guess it made me angry, too. Maybe that was what started the whole thing. I hadn't remembered that until just now." He pictured the moment. "That's right. I hit it directly several times. On purpose."

"Did you make any moves toward the driver?"

He shook his head. "No. I just concentrated on the trunk."

Kate was silent. Finally he looked at her. "Does all this mean I'm a raving lunatic?" His tone sounded flippant.

"No, not crazy, insane or a lunatic. Angry maybe."

He talked more about his dismissal from the church—the exchange with Howard Carr and Kenneth Ward and the church's association with the Coalition and that they had contributed to his retirement if he would resign. What he, his father and grandfather had done for the church, how he was expecting the services to be televised, the gay pride event, the Board with the support of Howard and Kenneth jerking the rug out from under him after what he'd just been through, not to mention all he and his family had done for Holy Bible.

"So, yes, you're right. I am angry. I have a right to be," he said indignantly.

Kate nodded. "You are angry, but, you know," she said very calmly and paused, waiting.

"What?" Matthew asked.

"Do you know *why* you're angry?"

"Of course, I do." His tone was filled with indignation. "Didn't you just hear me? I just lost my church, my family, my—my son."

Kate was quiet for a moment. When she spoke her voice was soft, understanding. "Yes, those *are* good reasons," she said, leaning forward. "But I wonder if there might be others to explore."

The concept stopped him. He tried to absorb it. What did that mean? Did she even know what she was talking about?

"And I hope you'll come back so that you can do that," she said. "What do you mean?"

"You mentioned earlier that you might be more comfortable working with a male therapist. Do you want to talk with Dwight about that?"

He was still trying to take in what she had meant about the anger. He sighed. "No, I mean, I might as well stay put." He had tried to sound indifferent, disbelieving, because that's the way he felt. Besides, Overby would probably pull a lawyer's trick and say that the twenty-five sessions had to be with the same therapist.

They agreed that his appointments would be on Mondays and Thursdays at four. As they stood up for him to leave, Kate reached over to her desk and picked up a business card. "This phone number is an answering machine in case you need to call before your next appointment. I check it several times a day, every day, including weekends."

He took the card and left, relieved that no one was in the hallway to see him leave her office. Driving home he was still haunted by what she had said. Why else would he have been angry? He had just been dismissed from the church his family had founded. Of course, that was the reason he was mad. But there was that other thing—what he saw while he was flailing away at the car and the one policeman who was yelling for him to stop. It was too farfetched, but he distinctly recalled it. He had seen his father—not literally. But he came to mind when he looked up and saw the policeman. What could it mean? That his father was telling him to stop as if he were a child? He knew his father would be irate if he were alive. His grandfather, too. Probably disown him. His own embarrassment was torment enough.

It didn't seem as if he'd been in there an hour. Now that it was over he had an odd feeling. He would never admit it out loud, but talking seemed to give him some relief. He didn't think Kate Thornton had all that much to do with it. She just asked simple questions anyone could ask. But he had no one else to talk to, he thought sarcastically. Then it struck him—he'd never talked to anyone, especially a woman, about such personal matters. He rested his elbow on the car window seal and rubbed his forehead with his hand. Why had he done that? What on earth had possessed him to say all that to her? Not angry for the reasons he thought he was. Did she even know what she was talking about?

He heaved a sigh as he turned onto his street. Going home for the last week had seemed like going to his cell in a prison. Solitary confinement. No communication with the outside world.

As he neared the house he reached for the garage remote button, ready to start opening the door the second he was within range. But there was a woman wearing a floppy sunhat walking in front of his house with her dog. Then he realized. Heloise Gardner. Neighbor and church member. What would he do? He did *not* want to talk to her, listen to her go on and on, asking questions about the family, about what he was going to do in his retirement, hearing her condolences. He could circle the block and come back after she moved on, but she would still see him.

He frantically pushed the open button and thankfully the door began rising. He would drive in and just ignore her. If she were only walking away from the driveway rather than toward it. He signaled to turn but did not slow down as much as he ordinarily did. As he drove in he could see her from the corner of his eye. Even as he was driving through the door, he began pushing the close button and didn't get out of the car until it was completely shut. If she knocked on the door or rang the bell, he wasn't going to answer. The rumors were too wide-spread. He was not going to endure more humiliation. He sat in the silence for only a moment, then went inside and peeked through the blinds. Heloise had continued walking. Good. Maybe she got the message. He didn't want to be bothered.

Matthew went into the den and slumped down on the sofa, staring into nothingness. Did he want to call Overby and try to change? Kate had been— What? Maybe she could dress more like a professional. Not wear pants. She began a lot of sentences with "so."

That wasn't very professional either. And her theory about his mother and the swearing—

Suddenly, he found himself remembering the house where he grew up. How old was he when it happened? Eight? Nine? Ten-years-old? The stray, the little one that kept coming to the back door. And his mother fed it and petted it. He heard her talking to it. Scratching behind its ears, even hugging it. This went on for several days until his father arrived home unexpectedly one day and yelled at the dog, scaring it, then throwing rocks at it. One hit the little fellow causing him to yelp and hobble away. Matthew saw the look of horror on his mother's face. His father came inside. "I do not ever want to see that animal again," he yelled, his eyes wide with fury, his index finger pointed just inches from her face as he stood over her in the kitchen. Later Matthew heard her crying in the bedroom. When the dog came back the next day, she went into another part of the house so she wouldn't hear the puppy.

But that was only a theory, he told himself. Kate admitted there was no certainty as to why some elderly would swear. Still, he wasn't going to tell her that his mother only swore when he visited her, not when Miriam went. He remembered how he loved being close to her when he was a child, putting his head in her lap as she read or sang to him. He would write stories and read them to her, and she would clap and ask him to write another one. "Each one is better than the last," she always told him. After his father died, he tried to read to her when he visited. Then she got to the point where she began swearing when he came to see her. He thought again about Kate's theory. Theory or not, there was no need to tell her about any of this.

It had been quite some time since he had visited his mother. But with all that had happened, he didn't need to go just to hear her cuss at him. Maybe it was time he faced the fact that it really didn't matter whether he went or not, ever again.

He sat forward on the sofa and with the remote turned on the television. The local news and weather, followed by the national. He sat and stared at it, but none of it registered. His mind endlessly tumbled his thoughts around. A war inside his head with no hope for peace, like being entangled in barbed wire. Any movement only brought more suffering. If he could just turn off his mind.

When he realized that the news was over, he rubbed his hands over his eyes. At the same time he heard his stomach rumble and realized he was hungry. Yet the effort necessary to fix something overwhelmed him. Such had been the case ever since Miriam— He halted his thought. He didn't even want to think the words—*since Miriam left.* He thought for only a second. –since he'd been responsible for his own meals.

Reluctantly, he went into the kitchen and looked in the refrigerator. Juice and milk. Eggs. Bread. He could have a breakfast-like dinner. Nothing wrong with that. Better than ordering something to be delivered.

After some searching he found a frying pan, a bowl for scrambling the eggs, butter. He cracked the first egg into the pan, but several bits of shell ended up in the white. He went through the drawers and finally found a teaspoon. Eventually he got all the pieces out. He broke the second egg more carefully. No shell. He stirred the eggs, added some milk, stirred some more. Then he remembered his mother used to use a fork. Finally the mixture combined enough.

He placed the frying on the stove and turned it on high. He put some butter in the pan and two slices of bread in the toaster. The selector was set on light. He moved it to five and pressed the lever down. Waiting for the butter to melt and bread to toast, he noticed a strange odor. He opened the lower cabinet door where the trash can was stored. The foul smell struck him. He pulled the bag out and tied it, then carried it to the garbage can outside. When he came back the frying pan was smoking, the now brown butter sizzling and popping. He quickly removed the pan, turned the element off and the exhaust fan on over the stove. He wanted to the throw the frying pan through the window. Or take it by the handle and beat it against the counter. Or just go upstairs and get the shoebox hidden deep in his closet. Then out of nowhere, he remembered what Kate had said about his reasons for being angry and he thought he might know what she meant. You're never angry for the reason you think you are. Just then he smelled something. He looked around and saw a plume of smoke rising from the toaster.

Matthew drove around, trying to clear his head. So much had gone on. Losing everything—his church, his family, his son. How would he ever get through this? He needed solace and the only place he knew where he could feel close to God was inside Holy Bible. His church. For his whole life it had been *his* church, but especially the last ten as the senior pastor.

He turned one corner, then another. Soon he found himself on Century Street. He was able to see the towering steeple three blocks away from the sprawling campus. He turned in and stopped in front of the main entrance to the sanctuary and got out. He hurried up the sidewalk toward the massive stain glass doors. As he neared the several steps to the large slate-floored entry, a policeman opened one of the giant doors and came out and stood with his hands on his hips. He wore a thick, black vest to protect against bullets. When he saw the policeman, Matthew stopped as the two stared at each other for several moments without speaking. Finally Matthew returned to his car and began driving—

Matthew jolted awake and anxiously searched his surroundings. He was in his own house in the den on the sofa. With a deep sigh of relief, he looked at the clock on the bookshelf. A few minutes after midnight. He'd slept nearly five hours. The most since Nathaniel— He sat up and rubbed his eyes. He remembered his dream but quickly dismissed it. He should go to bed. As he climbed the stairs, he wondered if he would have trouble sleeping.

CHAPTER SEVENTEEN

SATURDAY AND
SUNDAY—JUNE 6 & 7

After his long nap on the sofa, Matthew slept only fitfully that night. Finally, at seven-thirty on Saturday morning he decided to get up. He shaved out of habit, wondering only after he'd finished why he had bothered. He wasn't going anywhere or seeing anyone. He showered and dressed casually, khakis and a Polo shirt.

Downstairs he was filling the coffee machine when the telephone rang, startling him. His stomach churned when he looked at the caller ID. Stephanie Langdon. She was one of the church members whose name he knew well. Forty-something, never married but desperate to change that, she was somewhat overweight and earnestly tried to be attractive, but poor choices in clothing, hairstyle and accessories left her defeated. He wondered if she had heard the rumor about Miriam. He closed his eyes. She had never flaunted herself, but she threw herself into church activities for the sole purpose of meeting an eligible man. Yet, a small part of him appreciated hearing from someone at his church. He just wished it was someone else. He leaned against the counter, bracing himself for her message.

"Hello, Reverend Winslow." She sounded as if she had been crying. "This is Stephanie Langdon. I was so sorry to learn about your retirement and, well, uh, all that's gone on with you and your family since Nathaniel— I mean, I just can't imagine what Holy Bible Fellowship is going to be like without you there and I just feel awful for all that you've been going through. So I've decided I'm going to call some ladies in my Sunday school class this morning and organize some meals to bring to your house later today." She sniffed back her tears. "I just felt awful when I heard about your being arrested—" He turned off the answering machine.

Instantly, his stomach churned again and his throat knotted up, almost in panic. Just like the rumors about Nathaniel and Miriam. Now this. He sat down, his elbows on the kitchen table, his face buried in his hands. How did this get out? What were people going to think of him? He could not, would not face her or anyone else from the church. The humiliation was too unbearable. He wasn't going to call her back and he certainly wasn't going to answer the door when or if she came. Nevertheless, she knew. They all knew—he had been arrested. And probably knew why. Of course, they knew why. He had demolished the trunk lid of a car with a baseball bat in front of how many people? Dozens. Road rage.

He stood up and paced back and forth from one end of the kitchen to the other, like a caged animal. He had been—he was a minister. And he had lost it. Gone berserk. Scenes rose up in his mind of only two days ago. And everybody—*everybody* knew. People who'd heard him preach God's word knew. The near seven or eight thousand that heard him every Sunday—they knew. He closed his eyes.

Suddenly, the issue of his anger popped into his mind. Why was he angry? He couldn't deal with that now. He sat down at the table again, thinking. He wanted to do something, but there was nothing he could do. Nothing except sit here, barricaded in his house behind closed blinds and drapes. Lights off at night, signaling that no one was here. And with that thought came a meager wave of comfort. As long as he didn't have to see or talk to anyone he could survive. He would go out only at night. And yet, there was Stephanie going out of her way to be nice to him. While that felt good, he just couldn't endure being around her or anyone, pretending to be nice, listening to them prattle on about whatever. A wave of guilt intruded. That the women would go to all that trouble. Surely she would call before she came over and when she didn't get an answer she would drop the whole thing. But a second thought reminded him that this was Stephanie. He could expect a knock on the door at any moment.

He took a deep breath and let it out. The aroma of the coffee got his attention. He looked at the filled pot steaming. He was safe here. Fighting a nagging "why bother" attitude, he stood up and poured a cup of coffee. Only a splash of milk remained in the carton. A scant amount of sugar was in the bowl. He remembered that he had planned to go to the grocery store on Thursday before his entire world came crashing down on him. He searched the refrigerator, pantry and cabinets but found nothing to eat—no cereal, oatmeal, bacon, eggs. Only two slices of bread and some jelly. And coffee. He was used to more, but he could make do. He stood over the toaster, watching to make sure he didn't waste bread as he had last night. When it popped up, he immediately ate both pieces, trying to convince himself that he was satisfied. He would make a list. But when would he go? Not during the day. Not when he might see a church member. He'd have to wait until late. Very late. Find one that was open twenty-four hours a day. He could go after midnight. No one he knew would be there then. But what would he eat in the meantime? Maybe he would order a pizza. No. Some student from school might work at the very place he called or worse be the one to deliver it. Same would be true if he went to a fast food drive-thru. He sipped some coffee. He had just felt safe in his house from the outside world. And now he felt like a prisoner. When would all this end? More importantly, how?

Exasperated, he went to the front door and looked out for the newspaper. It wasn't on the porch near the door as it usually was. He opened the door further and saw it in the middle of the front yard. A reconnaissance up and down the street revealed that Steve Earls was washing his car in the driveway across the street and down several houses. He could also hear a lawnmower but couldn't decipher where it was. He wished he knew what kind of car Stephanie drove.

Quickly he went out and grabbed up the paper, at the same time realizing how high the grass had gotten. Since Nathaniel—he stopped his thoughts—he had paid one of the maintenance men from the church to come out to cut it. He'd have to hire someone he didn't know and who didn't know him. He could do it himself, he supposed. He had done it enough while growing up, but he couldn't risk having to face anyone. If he went out, he knew the whole neighborhood would be watching him.

Sitting down in the kitchen with his coffee, he fought the images that were trying to break into his mind. The grass. That was something he had never had to worry about. Nathaniel had always taken care of the yard. The picture of his son pushing the mower, sweat staining his t-shirt. Trimming the shrubbery, edging the sidewalk and driveway. Nathaniel. He grappled with the memories. Baseball. That perfect night when he won the Bible Scholar Competition. The Senior Banquet Awards. And underneath it all was the unrelenting, choking reminder—the voicemail on his cell phone. He wouldn't think— Not about that.

He drank some more coffee and removed the newspaper from the plastic bag. He spread open the paper on the table and began a cursory scan of the headlines for each article, reading many and offering his customary opinion. *Obama's Supreme Court nominee Sonia Sotomayor and GOP threatening to filibuster*, as well they should, he thought. *The Obamas have a date night in Paris.* He was sick of reading about this president. *Shelters for the homeless.* Let them get jobs, then they wouldn't be homeless. *U. S. military deaths in Afghanistan had reached 621.* He hoped that war would be over soon. *California man sentenced to death in five arson murders.* What he deserved. An eye for an eye.

He even tried to read the sports page. *Maria Sharapova announced she would play at Wimbledon after losing in the French Open ladies' final* with a picture of her in that skimpy tennis outfit. No self respect, he thought. He turned the page and found nothing but baseball. Too many reminders. He went on to another section.

When he finished with the paper, he straightened up the kitchen and began making his grocery list. Coffee, bread, eggs—other staples. But what about main dishes? Things he liked to eat. Things Miriam and Sarah Elizabeth had cooked. Chicken. Roast. Steaks. How much to buy? What about vegetables? Which ones? In a can? How to fix them? What did Miriam do? Were there recipes? In the middle of it, he thought he'd heard a knock on the door. No, Stephanie or anyone would ring the bell.

He closed his eyes. He had to focus. He looked at his list. Maybe he would just eat sandwiches. He could do that. No cooking. But he could heat up things from a can. Didn't peas come in a can? Corn and beans? Frozen items. He was sure there were frozen things he could put in the oven or microwave. The list grew, but as it did Matthew's enthusiasm waned. He wasn't meant to cook. It wasn't his place. That chore belonged to women. He surveyed the list which had grown longer than he'd expected. It was enough.

Still annoyed at having to do this for himself, he stood in the kitchen. What would he do now? He went into his study and sat at his desk. Nothing to do. Absolutely nothing. No sermon to work on. Glancing around the room he saw the notebooks on the shelf. The ones he had filled over the course of his twelve years of school when he was a student in the academy at Holy Bible. From first grade on. He counted them, knowing full well there were twelve and, as he did, he recalled what he had told Kate—learning verses, creating the notebooks. But what he didn't tell her—the memories deeply embedded in his mind that came with them.

"All right, young Brother Matthew, I want to hear you recite the books of the Bible," his grandfather ordered him. He was six-years-old. His grandparents and mother and father were all gathered in the living room on Sunday. This was to become a weekly occurrence—to hear him recite verses with the audience of four. "That will be the first thing you'll have to do when you begin schooling in the fall. I was able to do this when I was five in no time flat because the Lord was guiding me. Now let's hear you, son, starting with the Old Testament. Remember, speak up, like a preacher." Matthew took his place in front of the fireplace and cleared his throat. He felt his stomach flutter and his knees go weak, like they might collapse. "Genesis, Exodus, Leviticus, Numbers, Deuteronomy, Joshua, Judges, Ruth, First Kings—" "No, no," his grandfather thundered, slapping his own leg, startling Matthew. "First and Second Samuel are after Ruth, then First and Second Kings." He shook his head. "If you can't do any better than that, you'll never be the head of my church." He got up and left the room.

His father had made him write the books over and over, that very afternoon until bedtime. He had promised to take him to the circus that week, but because he had forgotten the books, he told him he would have to study so he could try again the following Sunday. And he succeeded—proudly—but the circus had already moved on. "Well, you passed the test," his grandfather declared the following Sunday, "this time," he added with a warning. "But you better study a lot more in the future. You won't always get a second chance."

Matthew rested his elbow on the leather covered armrest. He'd been embarrassed. Grandfather always expected so much. And so had his father.

Just then, another memory floated to the surface—the ninth grade Bible Scholar Competition.

The old sanctuary was nearly full and he could feel all eyes were on him. All but five of the ninth graders had been eliminated. Even though he was nervous, Matthew had known every question—his and everyone else's. "Matthew Winslow, where in the Bible is this often recited verse found, "...nor will people say, 'Here it is,' or 'There it is,' because the kingdom of God is within you." Matthew recognized it instantly. His father had quizzed him on it repeatedly. "Mark 21:17," he responded confidently. Immediately he heard the audience stir, enough to unsettle him. "I'm sorry. The correct answer is Luke 17:21." Instinctively he looked from the stage down to the front row where he saw his father calmly sitting, smiling, trying not to appear disappointed but brave and supportive. But as he took his seat, he could feel his father's shame and knew the silent treatment that was to come.

The humiliation had been torturous. All eyes still on him, burning through him, watching him. The pastor's son, the founder's grandson had missed. Failed. Afterwards his father congratulated the eventual winner but said nothing to Matthew. The ride home was in total silence. When they went into the house, his father simply said, "I'm just glad your grandfather wasn't alive to witness this." He never mentioned the competition, again. However, the next day he gave Matthew a rigorous schedule of study, intended to last the entire summer. He would recopy every verse in his notebook—nine volumes in all, ten verses a week for the past nine years. His father would quiz him every night. And that was the summer that he saw the new kids—brothers who had moved in across the street—riding bikes, playing ball with their dad in the evening, making friends around the neighborhood, having so much fun.

Matthew continued to stare at the notebooks as more memories gouged his mind. His father making him write sermons and "preach" them to him and his mother, learning to gesture with his Bible. *"Point your finger at the congregation and talk loud one minute, then soft the next. Bring them to the edge of their seats. Make them sit up and strain to hear you as you whisper the truth, because you have a secret from God that you're going to tell them."* The books his father told him to read, even after he graduated from Freedom Bible School of Divinity, all of them about what he should believe—the place of women in the church, loving the sinner but hating the sin, tithing, war— He stopped. And homosexuality.

Suddenly he realized what day it was. He swiveled his chair around so he could not look at the notebooks. It was as if a ghost had walked into the room. Two weeks ago. Two weeks ago today. Detective Sparks was right here in this room, telling him that Nathaniel— He looked down at his desk. His cell phone, there in front of him. He picked it up with one hand and with his other hand he opened a desk drawer. He started to put it inside. Today, especially today, he wanted it out of his sight. But just as quickly he questioned that decision. What if Miriam called? Or Sarah Elizabeth? What if she had changed her mind? Wanted to come home? No, he would keep it with him, just as he had been doing since the night she left. But he couldn't stay in this room. Not today.

He got up from behind his desk and went out into the foyer. He stood there. What should he do? What needed doing? He had to keep doing something. If he didn't, he was going to lose his mind. The house hadn't been cleaned since— Since that night. Clothes washed. But that wasn't something he should have to do. He wasn't a maid. Even so, he had to do something. Change the sheets on the bed. That hadn't been done in almost two weeks. He supposed there was more than one set. He went upstairs to the linen closet and found a set that looked familiar. He took them to the bedroom, stripped the bed and put on the fresh ones. Stepping back, he admired his accomplishment. Still, it wasn't his place to do this.

What then to do with the dirty sheets? Maybe wash them. His own clothes as well. A gathering process ensued and, after nearly fifteen minutes he had deciphered how to operate the washing machine. He was only doing this because of self-preservation of his mind, he told himself. And the simple fact that the blinds and drapes were closed and no one could see how he was spending his day. He supposed he could hire someone to come in and do this work. But where would he find such a person? How would he go about it? No. He didn't want some stranger in his house poking around.

The larger question still loomed—what was he going to do? What kind of job? If he was going to be a minister, would he have to move some place where nobody knew him? Another state? But anywhere he went they would want to know about his past. How could he tell them? And if he tried to conceal it, that would just make it worse if they ever found out, even if it didn't remain on his record. But first—what was he going to do? Not only that, what else did he know besides being a minister? His mind blanked. Nothing. He couldn't just sit in this house all day, everyday for the rest of his life.

He went into the den and stood in the middle of the room for several minutes. The room seemed just like the last one. Void. Nothing happening. Even though the house was full of furniture, it felt so empty. What was there for him? Finally, he sat down. He had to find his life. What he was going to do? He thought about his future, Kate's question about his calling to the ministry came to mind. And he remembered his answer—distinctly. *He loved the Bible. Always had. It speaks the truth because it came from God. We'd all be better off if people did what the Bible said. It was the word of God. That was his mission and his father's and grandfather's. It's why Holy Bible Fellowship was founded, the foundation for everything that goes on there. To follow the word of God.* And that was when he had that odd feeling. A memory? Something? He still couldn't describe it. But the words themselves—they had sounded familiar. So familiar that it seemed he had said them without thinking. Not exactly in that order. Not even precisely the same words. But the same idea. The same intention. He *had* said them without thinking. They had just fallen out of his mouth. Just the way his father and grandfather used to say how they had been called to the ministry.

Unsettled frustration leaked into his mind. Irritated, he got up and walked into the kitchen, as the speech ran through his mind, again. Questions kept prodding him. Questions he felt guilty and ashamed that he was even thinking. Of course, he knew what the words meant. He wasn't an imbecile. But, what had that feeling been about? Was he doubting his beliefs? How could he? He was the minister. The very question itself felt blasphemous. Of course, he believed in God and the Bible. How could he *not* believe in both?

How could anyone not believe in them? He never had understood atheists and agnostics.

He drank a glass of water even though he wasn't thirsty and went into the darkened living room and sat back down on the sofa, his right leg jiggling up and down. The whole thing was ridiculous. He believed just as he always had. His objective was to decide what to do with his life. He closed his eyes to think and as he was thinking he realized he hadn't prayed. Not since Thursday night when he was so—should he dare say it? When he was so lost. So completely undone. His life a wreck. And he was so scared. He had prayed then.

He cleared his throat. "Dear Father God—" He stopped. His usual manner, the same format, the way he'd always stated what needed to be said—all of it wanted to come out, just like the formula for his "calling." But something stopped him. Something was urging him to find another way. Other words. Other phrases than the ones he had always used. "I don't know what to say," he whispered. "I don't know what I'm *supposed* to say." He was beginning to feel the same way he did last Thursday night, sitting on the stairs in the dark. Lost. Lost and alone.

Still feeling compelled to pray something, he leaned forward, his elbows on his thighs. "Help me," he said softly. "I don't know what to do." He took a deep breath as tears squeezed through his closed eyelids.

Matthew sat in his car in the near empty parking lot of the twenty-four hour Horace Hughes Groceries. It was just after midnight. He had found an old baseball cap, hoping to disguise himself. He looked in the rearview mirror and pulled it lower down over his forehead. Maybe this was deceptive enough. He'd thought about sunglasses, too—anything to conceal his identity now that the whole church probably knew about his arrest—but decided against that.

After ten minutes of watching, he noticed the few patrons who went in were college age, or slightly older, and leaving with beer. He decided he could go in, buy the items on his list, go through checkout and leave without seeing anyone he knew. With his list in hand, he got out of the car and went in the entrance where all the carts were racked. He pulled one free and entered the store.

Immediately he searched the area for people he might know. Seeing no one other than an employee sweeping the floor, he breathed more easily. The sheer size of the store and the brilliant fluorescent lights overwhelmed him. He drew in a deep breath of frustration and began. Produce was first. He had no produce on his list, but he saw apples and bananas, strawberries, melons, tomatoes—was all of it ripe? How could he tell? Nevertheless, he put some of each into his buggy. Lettuce. An idea ran through his head. Salads. He would get some salad dressing. Moving on, carefully searching, wary of familiar faces, he found a loaf of bread, then meat. A package of steak. He could freeze what he didn't eat right away. The same for chicken breasts. Cans of vegetables—beans, corn, green peas, black-eyed peas, beets. He stumbled across the salad dressing. What kind did Miriam always get? He searched what appeared to be an endless variety. He recognized a vinaigrette and added a bottle to his cart. Tuna. He liked tuna. He also found packages of lunch meats—turkey, ham for sandwiches. Next aisle. Cereal. He saw sugar. A small bag. Milk. Juice. Then the frozen food section. Bags of vegetables he could put right in the microwave for steaming. And they were on special. Better than the canned. He'd put those back. On and on he shopped, searching for items on his list, examining and buying many that weren't. All the while, wary of the few people he saw.

Finally, he wheeled his purchases into the only open checkout. He liked not having to wait. He realized, too, that he had bought a lot things not on his list.

"Do you have your SSC card?" The young girl at the checkout counter could scarcely reach into the cart, she was so short and thin as a rail, but her breasts were enormous. Her bleach-blond hair, also short and straight, drooped just to her heavily pierced earlobes. Straight, long bangs covered her eyebrows. She punctuated her question with a yawn.

"My what?" Matthew asked nervously.

She looked up at him as if he must be from a foreign country. "SSC card." Her name tag said her name was Twila.

"I don't know what that is." He shook his head helplessly.

She began taking items from his cart at the same time giving him a well rehearsed but uninspired speech. "SSC stands for 'Super-Savings Card.' You go online, register for a card, they mail it to you and you bring it with you to the store and save money on weekly specials."

"Reverend Winslow?"

Panic engulfed him. Matthew jerked around to find a woman, probably in her thirties, in line behind him. He had no clue as to her name. He tried to speak but stumbled over his words. "Yes, uh, I mean, hello."

"Do you need a SSC card?"

"Yes, with this cart full as it is, he sure does." Twila took charge, moving around him to take the card from the woman.

Completely bewildered, Matthew, again, tried to speak but with little or no success. "Uh, yes, thank you. Very kind."

"I know you don't know me. I'm Natalie Simpson." She extended her hand.

Matthew quickly shook her hand. Please. He was terrified that she was going to say she was in Stephanie Langdon's Sunday school class.

"I was so sorry to hear about your loss. Your son," she said quietly so that Twila could not hear.

No more. Please be somebody who hasn't heard the rumors, he thought. "Thank you, uh, I appreciate that."

"Like this melon," Twila interrupted, hoisting it from the lowest part of the cart and cradling it in her ample bosom while she punched in the produce code. "Saved a buck fifty with her card."

"I'll check into it," Matthew said, grateful for the butting in. "Thank you, again." He moved toward the checkout counter.

"Saved a bunch," Twila responded. "Comes to two hundred and five dollars and fifteen cents."

Matthew gasped. "What?"

"I'm tellin' ya, hon, that card saved you thirty-six dollars." Twila began putting his groceries into plastic bags and the bags into the cart.

"Thank you, again," he said to the woman.

He dropped his protest and quickly swiped his credit card, vowing he would check his order for accuracy when he got home.

"Sorry," Twila said not so privately. "That card's been declined." She read the information on her register.

Matthew could feel his face redden with humiliation. He looked at the card. Holy Bible Fellowship. He had used the wrong one. Nervously he smiled. "Wrong one. Expired." He swiped another one.

"There we go," Twila chirped. She handed him the slip to sign, then his register tape. "Thank you for shopping at Horace Hughes. Have a good evening."

As he began wheeling his cart away, he looked back at the woman.

"See you in the morning," she said pleasantly.

Matthew smiled at her as he walked away. She didn't know, but soon enough, she would. Then she would be telling everyone about his credit card.

His salad and turkey sandwich had filled him. He felt somewhat better. Incredulous, he sat at the kitchen table, looking at the register tape from the grocery store. He had no idea food cost so much. But he had bought a lot. Stocked up. He wouldn't have to go back next week, maybe even two weeks, except for staples. More fruit perhaps.

But that Natalie whoever she was—she had saved him money. He wondered how she would feel when she found out. Glad she had helped or wished she hadn't? He would never know now. And what about Stephanie? She hadn't called or come over. Unless.

He got up and went to the front door and looked out on the porch. No food containers. Nothing. He closed the door and stood in the foyer. She cared this morning, but had that changed during the day sometime? Had the other women refused to help? Had they advised her not to contact him? As much as he didn't want to see or be bothered by anyone, a part of him felt betrayed by the congregation. An outcast.

He switched on the stairway light. He didn't care, he tried to convince himself. He felt safe. He was in his home. He had everything he needed to survive. He would figure out the house cleaning next week. It was the food issue that had worried him. Now that was taken care of.

He looked at his watch. Nearly one-thirty. He heaved a sigh. Past time for bed. But he wasn't sleepy. He had catnapped off and on most of the day. He listened. The house was quiet. Empty. Everything was empty. He had just eaten a meal. But he was empty.

When Matthew opened his eyes the next morning, he was lying on his side, face to face with his alarm clock. Remembering it was Sunday, he forgot for a fraction of a second that he would not be going to church. The moment of habit passed so quickly that his body did not even have time to bolt. But when reality struck him, the impact transported him back to Thursday afternoon—being dismissed by Howard Carr and Kenneth Ward, beating the car with the bat, getting arrested. Now for the first Sunday in his entire life, even as a child, he would not be going to church on a Sunday. Not participating in the worship services. Not standing up and preaching twice in one morning. Not bringing the word of God to some seven thousand people as he had every Sunday for the past five years.

He rolled over away from the clock and recalled what he had thought about the day before. He pictured himself flooded by the bright lights in the sanctuary, holding up his Bible, proclaiming, gesturing.

"Wonderful sermon, Reverend...You've inspired me as you do every week...What a gift you have...You're a blessing to us...We're so lucky to have you..." and on and on the comments rolled. So many hands to shake. Yet he was able to call so very few by name. He had convinced himself that names weren't important. Bringing them to the Holy Bible and Jesus was his mission. His purpose. Now, if that were still his mission, he had no idea how to go about fulfilling it.

He thought about staying in bed all day. Forget Sunday. Then just as quickly, a wave of guilt shot through him. He shouldn't think that way about the Lord's day. But it wasn't the Lord's day that he was at odds with. It was Howard Carr and Kenneth Ward, the Board of Trustees and the Christian Coalition for Biblical Authority in America. They were the culprits. They were the ones who had forced him out. Forced him to lose control of his senses. Suggested to the congregation that they not contact him. And in the midst of it all he had been dealing with his family.

He threw back the covers with hostility. He was tired of thinking about it. Tired of it eating at him.

After shaving he showered and dressed in khaki pants and a shirt. In the kitchen he started the coffee machine, poured himself juice and made toast. Still nothing more than that. He wasn't going to do anything today. Nothing except wait for tomorrow. That seemed to be his whole existence—wait for tomorrow. And the tomorrow after that tomorrow.

Retrieving the morning paper, which gratefully was on the porch today, he returned to the kitchen just as the toast was on the verge of turning from dark brown to black. Saved by only seconds, he changed the control dial to a lower notch. He spread jelly on each slice and glanced at the front page.

"Senatorial Candidate to Speak at Gay Rally." He didn't want to read the article, but he had to know. What candidate would be so stupid as to speak at a public gay rally and still expect to get elected? Rather than skim the story, he read it. Keith Frosavich. State senate, not Congress. Well, good for him. Never heard of him and probably never would again after the election. He remembered all the plans he had put into place. The press conference. His sermon. The meeting with the other ministers in town.

He turned to the rest of the newspaper. Enough of that topic. He thumbed through the sections until he came to "Concepts and Opinions" and opened it to the Letters to the Editor. Reading the teasers for each letter, one halted him. "I support my daughter." A mother wanted to let everyone know that she stood behind her lesbian daughter. "She's a good person. I ought to know. I raised her. I'm so blessed that she's mine. I don't care who she loves." Another person wrote an opposing view. "In Leviticus...." Matthew closed the paper. No more. He couldn't read another word. Not today.

He carried the newspaper and a second cup of coffee into the den. By the time he had finished reading the newspaper, it was nearly eleven o'clock. The main service at Holy Bible was about to begin. The simulcast online.

He went into his office and found the web site for his church. With the downloading complete, the picture opened to the sanctuary. A strange feeling washed over him at he watched Richard Newland lead the ministers onto the stage and stood in front of their designated ornate chairs. Only there were three chairs instead of four. A knife of anger mixed with sadness and regret stabbed him. *He* should be sitting there. This was *his* church.

The orchestra and organ began the music as the choir led the congregation in a hymn. The greeting and announcements were next. He wondered if they would say anything about him and his so-called retirement. Harry Borkin came to the pulpit. Would they include him in the prayer? Would the rumors be too much for them to risk sounding compassionate? Or would they attempt to sound compassionate just to look good? He went on for several minutes but said nothing about him. Matthew smirked. Howard probably told them not to say anything. Howard and Kenneth.

They sang two more hymns, recited the creed his grandfather had written, read the scripture. The choir sang an anthem. The ushers took up an offering. As Howard had said Richard would be preaching.

The tall man came to the pulpit. The lights dimmed in the sanctuary as spotlights flooded Richard from all sides as they had Matthew every Sunday.   Richard perched his reader glasses on the end of his nose.

"Genesis 2:24-25 says, '*Therefore shall a man leave his father and his mother, and shall cleave unto his wife: and they shall be one flesh. And they were both naked, the man and his wife, and were not ashamed.*' Hebrew 13:4 says, '*Marriage is honorable in all, and the bed undefiled: but whoremongers and adulterers God will judge.*'"

"Why didn't you recite it from memory?" Matthew asked aloud. "This is Holy Bible Fellowship. You're supposed to recite it when you preach."

"In three weeks the so-called Gay Pride event will take place in Elmsborough where hundreds of sinners will gather to take pride in their sinful ways. Right here, flaunting it in our faces. They even want to be given the legal status of marriage. But as you have just heard in God's words, sexual acts such as prostitution, adultery, promiscuity and especially homosexuality are not part of marriage, in no way can they fall under the label of marriage, and are therefore a sin in the eyes of God. Even Saint Paul says that adulterers and whoremongers shall not inherit the kingdom of heaven. He calls this effeminate, soft men."

Matthew shifted in his chair and at the same time saw the photograph on his desk of his family. He looked at Nathaniel as

Richard's words echoed in his head—not inherit the kingdom of heaven, effeminate, soft men. He tried to look away from his son, but he couldn't. As Richard droned on, the image of Nathaniel hanging in a tree— And the detective here in the study— The photograph with the marks around his neck—

He turned off his computer and went back into the den and sat down on the sofa. He scrubbed his hands over his face. He was falling deeper into the mess that made up his existence—a sinkhole that had no bottom. As he leaned back, his eyes fell on another family picture on the mantle over the fireplace. Miriam, Sarah Elizabeth, Nathaniel, himself. His family. All gone. Helpless to stop it, his gaze again lingered on Nathaniel. His son. Miriam's words broke through—good and decent. Relentless, the image of him hanging in a tree out in the county drummed into his mind. And the voicemail. When would this torture ever end?

He closed his eyes as he remembered the shoebox in his closet and at the same time the business card Kate had given him.

CHAPTER EIGHTEEN

MONDAY—JUNE 8

"Are you okay?" Kate asked as she closed the door to her office. Matthew had come in, scarcely spoken and sat in the chair opposite her recliner. Kate sat down but leaned forward, watching him.

Matthew took a deep breath and let it out. "I'm irate," he said with more calm than his words indicated. "I drove by my church on the way over here. I don't know why exactly. I guess because yesterday was the first Sunday I wasn't there when I was supposed to be. I mean, I was never sick and never took a Sunday off." His fisted hands lay on the armrests. "They've removed my grandfather's name as founder from the sign in front and mine as well." He shook his head. "I can't believe it. MY name, maybe. But not my grandfather's. It's...not...Christian." He emphasized the three words by patting both armrests with his hands for each of the three words. "And when I get home I'm going to the web site to see if they've changed that." He reminded her again of his grandfather's place in the church's history. "I'm seriously thinking of talking to Dwight Overby about taking legal steps to get my position back."

"That's a fairly bold move. Did you sign anything in that final meeting?"

Matthew nodded but didn't meet her eyes. Why did she have to remind him of that? "Yes, but it's still not just."

Kate thought for a moment before speaking calmly. "I'm not suggesting that you should or shouldn't take legal action, but I wonder what kind of atmosphere you'd be working in if you had to force them to give you your job back."

Memories of the meeting with Kenneth Ward and Howard Carr and their veiled threats ran through his mind. "I think the office staff might be fine to work with."

"And what about the governing body and that other organization that's influential—"

"The Christian Coalition For Biblical Authority in America," he interrupted. Just saying the name sent a cold shudder through him.

"How possible would it be to reconcile with that segment of people?"

He thought about potential meetings with other committee chairmen besides Howard, including the three associate ministers. "I don't know," he said reluctantly.

"Has any of the staff contacted you or reached out to you since last Thursday?"

An uneasy embarrassment swarmed over him. He merely shook his head.

"Nobody?" she asked softly but with surprise.

Matthew shook his head, again without looking up. He sensed her leaning forward.

"Any members of the church?"

He hated this. He kept his eyes on the armrest. He didn't have to tell her. "A woman left a message. She was upset about all that had happened and said she was organizing her Sunday school class to bring food over. That was Saturday but nobody brought anything. Not yet anyway." He finally looked up at her. "I'm sure somebody told them not to do that or at least strongly discouraged them."

Kate met his eyes.

"How does that make you feel?"

For a brief moment, he didn't answer. His father had always taught him to keep certain things private. Certainly expressing feelings fell into that category. Still, the question held a yearning deep inside him, like water on parched, cracked soil. However, his upbringing forbade him, told him to push it away immediately. Too risky. Too personal.

"They probably sent word out that I wanted my privacy." He continued looking at her. "The Board of Trustees strongly suggests that when they think it best not to become involved with people who leave the church abruptly." He crossed his legs, his foot jiggling, and looked away. The silence was unbearable. After a moment, he turned back to her, his eyebrows raised. "I don't know what you want me to say."

Kate's voice remained kind but unflinching. "Can you tell me how it feels?"

Matthew uncrossed his legs, shuffled his feet and shifted himself on the chair's cushion. He took a deep breath. "I guess I never really thought about it." Maybe that will satisfy her, he thought, proud he'd found a way out of being cornered.

"Okay," Kate said quietly. "I want to give you some homework. I would like for you to think about that between now and Thursday."

Reprieve coursed through him. She was letting go of the question. For now, at least.

She leaned back in her chair. "How was your weekend?"

He wasn't going to get trapped again. "Uneventful, I suppose," he said confidently.

"Go anywhere? Movie? Concert? A walk?"

"No, I didn't feel like getting out. I read some and, oh, yes, I went to the grocery store." He didn't want to sound too happy and satisfied, but neither did he want to give away how difficult it had been. And he definitely wasn't going to reveal that he had burned food, gone to the store after midnight, and all the other things.

"Are you a cook?"

"I guess you could say I know my way around the kitchen enough not to starve."

Kate smiled. "That's good. How about dreams? Have any?"

Surprised, he answered right away, before he had given any thought to where this might lead. "Actually, yes." He described the scene with the policeman in front of the church but made no mention that he had had the same one last night as well.

"And was he the same policeman who arrested you on Thursday?"

The words stung him. *The policeman who arrested you.* A cold, hurtful reminder, but he refused to show it. "No, it was neither of them. Just a policeman. He had on one of those vests. Bullet proof, I guess."

"And did the policemen have those on last Thursday?"

He thought for a minute. "Yes."

"And that's all? Did either of you say anything in the dream? Or did you ask him to move out of your way?"

"We stared at each other for a few seconds and I turned and walked away."

Kate nodded. "So what do you think that means?"

He shrugged. "I don't know that it means anything. It was just a dream."

"Not into symbolism or interpretation?"

He shook his head. "I don't really believe in all that. What do *you* think it means?" he asked.

"I'm interested in dream interpretation. In this one, the policeman might represent authority and he's blocking you from entering the church. Is there usually security at the church?"

"Just to direct traffic on Sundays but not around the buildings and certainly not at the front door."

Kate folded her arms. "So there's a policeman wearing protective gear in a place—the main entrance—where there usually isn't one. I guess I would wonder why he needs the protection—the vest." Matthew still jiggled his leg. His curiosity was piqued. "There's never been any violence at your church? Protestors? Disruptions from outsiders?"

"No."

"I guess what intrigues me the most is that you don't challenge him to let you go into the church. Given your anger and hurt over the dismissal, I would think that you would demand to be allowed inside. But you don't. You just walk away."

Matthew instantly felt a surge of anger. "That's just a little insulting and ridiculous. It sounds like you're saying that I couldn't or wouldn't stand up for myself."

"No. More like maybe you no longer want to be a part of the church."

The idea stunned him and for only a single heartbeat it resonated with him. But with the next pulse in his chest, he rejected the thought. How dare anyone even suggest such a thing. "No. That could never be," he said. He tried to sound emphatic but did not look at her. His leg moved more rapidly now. "Impossible." He shook his head. "No. Not possible. That's just not true. Holy Bible Fellowship has been my whole life."

"That's exactly what I mean," she said.

Silence fell in the room and weighed heavily on him. Still not looking at her, Matthew continued his protest. "No. Church work is all I know. I have no purpose otherwise." He wished he hadn't said that. He wished he hadn't gotten himself into all this trouble. He wished he didn't have to be here.

"Why would you say that you have no purpose outside the church?"

For an instant he considered just getting up and walking out, but that would mean facing Overby and the law. He shifted in the chair and shrugged. He had to come up with an acceptable answer so that she couldn't trap him again. "The church is where I belong. It's all I know."

"I want to be sure that you hear me. I'm not saying that you shouldn't be a part of church work. Okay?"

"I understand that." He still wanted to get up and walk out.

"And secondly, I firmly believe that everyone has a purpose. Yours may involve a church or not, but you do have a purpose. You may have to stumble around some before you find it, but you will find it. I sincerely believe that."

He glanced at his watch, then focused on the plant in the urn across the room in a corner. Nearly thirty more minutes before this torture would end. He heaved an internal, irritated sigh.

Driving home Matthew could not rid Kate's idea from his mind. It just proved that she didn't know a thing about him. Not being at Holy Bible. Absurd. Leaving there was what had hurt him the most. Where his whole life had been. How could he not want to go back? And that dream and her parting assignment—to think about why the policeman was in front of the church and was wearing the vest. Even more ridiculous. And the fact that he had not confronted the cop. Good thing he hadn't told her that he'd had the dream two nights in a row. All this along with how he felt when no one from the church came by to see him and Stephanie hadn't called back or brought food. She still might do that. But no matter. He didn't want to see anyone from the church. Suddenly, he heard himself. *He didn't want to see anyone from the church.* But that was because he was too embarrassed. Too hurt by the church. He stopped again. *Too hurt by the church.* He slammed his fist on the steering wheel. "Stop thinking about it," he muttered through a clenched jaw. "Assignments or no assignments." He knew what he meant and he knew how he felt. He didn't have to say it out loud.

But worst of all, he wished he hadn't slipped up and told her about his father walking out on that competition that he lost in the ninth grade. And naturally that led to, *And how did that make you feel?* This time the question really clawed at his mind. Worse than the first time she'd asked it.

"How do you think it made me feel?" he said out loud in the privacy of his car. "It made me feel like—" He tried to keep it back, but it pushed too hard against his mind. "It made me feel like nobody liked me," he said. Then, louder. "It made me feel like nobody liked me!" And even louder. "IT MADE ME FEEL LIKE NOBODY LOVED ME!!" And again. "IT MADE ME—"

Suddenly he realized that the traffic light at the intersection he was approaching at forty-five miles per hour was red. He slammed on his brakes, skidding to a stop just short of half-way through it. Horns blew as approaching cross traffic on both sides of him slammed on their brakes. Fortunately the driver behind him had stopped far enough back, leaving him room to back up. Matthew waved his gratitude as embarrassment washed over him. Messed up again, he heard a loud but silent voice say. He also heard Kate's question, yet again. "It makes me feel angry, embarrassed." He paused, thinking of labels. How did he feel? "Inadequate. Stupid." He searched his mind. "Not perfect." His own words stung him, like a bullet to his heart. Bullet. Bullet proof vest. He wanted to scream. Again.

As he walked into the kitchen from the garage, Matthew heard the phone ringing. Immediately he thought of Stephanie as a mix of panic and relief ran through his mind—someone from church was reaching out to him but not anyone he wanted to see. Or maybe it was Miriam or Sarah Elizabeth. He read the caller ID on the handset. Dwight Overby. What did he want? He hoped he wouldn't ask how the therapy was going. If he did, he just might let him know he wasn't too happy about the arrangement.

"I've set up your community service," Overby said after they exchanged brief, customary pleasantries. "You'll be at Elmsborough Outreach Ministry at the corner of Eden and Sampson. Roger Gooden is the person to ask for. You'll be working the lunch shift six days a week, Monday through Saturday, from ten until two. He wants you to begin tomorrow. Will any of this interfere with your schedule with Kate Thornton?"

Matthew felt a knot in his stomach. Not only because of hearing Kate's name but about EOM. Not in the best part of town and the people that it served— Why had he gotten himself into all this? "No, it won't interfere," he said, trying to hide his exasperation and the urge to sound sarcastic. "Did you say tomorrow?" He couldn't believe he had dropped this on him so suddenly. Not even a full day's notice. Inconsiderate.

"Yes, tomorrow at ten. Problem?"

"No. I suppose not." Did he have to thank him, too, he wondered. "What will I be doing?" he asked hesitantly, fearful of the answer.

"Not sure. Roger said that lunch is when they serve the largest number. So they need more people than for breakfast and dinner. Any other questions?"

The idea of taking legal action to get his job back. Should he ask? At least get his advice? He remembered the points Kate had made. Having to deal with Howard and Kenneth. Would all this get in the paper and be on the news? Did he want all the publicity? "No." He closed his eyes. Why not just bring it up?

"I hope everything is going a little better for you, I mean, since last Thursday."

Matthew thought Overby's voice had changed, like it had on Friday when they talked. A different tone than when he talked about the community service. Maybe he was sincere. "Yes, it is." He attempted to sound genuine. Again, the notion of thanking him passed through his mind, but for some reason he could not form the two simple words.

"Good. I'm glad to hear that. Call me if you need me."

Matthew stood holding the handset for several moments. Why couldn't he say those two simple words? Thank. You. Why was that so difficult? He had said them a million or more times when people complimented him on his sermon or something else he'd done at the church. Why not now? Why wouldn't the words come out of his mouth? At least Overby hadn't asked about therapy. And what would he have told him? What a bad situation this was? How he questioned Kate Thornton's competency? No need to go there now. The conversation was done.

He put the phone down. Tomorrow. Ten until two. At least he would have something to do besides sit around here all day.

After the evening news which held no interest for him, Matthew went into the kitchen to prepare his dinner. He plugged in the countertop grill and retrieved the chicken breast from the refrigerator that had been thawing all day. When the grill had heated up, he carefully placed the chicken on it and closed the lid. He microwaved the two bags—frozen mixed vegetables and frozen brown rice. While that was happening he filled a glass with ice and water and put a simple setting on the kitchen table and checked the chicken. Almost done, the brown stripes just beginning to show. He nearly burned his fingers opening the two plastic bags and spooning some of the contents from each onto his plate. Chicken done.

He sat down at the table. It wasn't gourmet, but, as he had told Kate, he wouldn't starve. He cut into the chicken breast, hungry for golden brown poultry. Very tender. Delicious. He cut, again. This time he saw raw—not fully cooked in the middle. He cut into another place. Even more raw. Why hadn't it cooked all the way through? Then he realized it was thicker in the middle than the outer edges. He shook his head—annoyed. When Miriam or Sarah Elizabeth had grilled anything it was perfect. Always. Golden brown, fully cooked. He fought the wave of emotion that was threatening—self-pity, sadness. He looked at the places where everyone else in the family always sat at the table, especially Nathaniel. He closed his eyes. He wasn't going to let this happen to him. He wasn't going to fall deeper into that pit.

He got up and found a sharp knife and slit the chicken breast open, exposing the raw center. He put both pieces on the grill and watched it carefully to be sure that it didn't burn. After only several minutes, the meat was ready. He would remember that in the future. Cut the breast in half. Make the thickness uniform.

At the table he cut another piece and ate it. No thinking of the empty places around the table, he ordered himself. Or that he was alone. No. He took a bite of rice and vegetables. He then realized he had not blessed his food. Had he forgotten? That had never happened. Never. Even in restaurants, home, picnics—he or somebody had always blessed the food. Kate's words shot into his mind. "Maybe you don't want to be part of the church anymore." He put down his fork. Suddenly, a burst of rage caught him and he pounded both fists on the table, once and only once. "NO," he shouted, his fork and plate rattling with the vibration. He did want to be part of the church. His church. Holy Bible Fellowship.

Then he remembered. The web site. He left his dinner and went to his study. He switched on the computer and pulled up the site. His name was gone from the home page, too. Just like on the sign in front. So was his grandfather's. Only the three associates were listed. He went to the church's history. That had been abbreviated. Much less inclusive of the Winslow family. How long each of them had served as pastor and how the physical church and membership had grown under each—gone. Even the tab for "Recent Sermons" had been removed. It was as if they had erased him. Deleted him like a mistake.

He leaned back in his chair and stared at the screen as Kate's suggestion haunted him. All that he had given. Deleted. Time, effort, commitment—deleted. He turned off the computer and returned to the kitchen. Standing in the doorway he stared at his plate on the table. One plate. One fork. One knife. One glass of water. All alone. Just like Stephanie Langdon, he realized. He sat down and closed his eyes. Try to be thankful. Try.

"Lord," he whispered. "Thank you that—" He stopped, searching. "Thank you that I have this food, that I was able to figure out how to fix it, that it's hot and it's good." More thought. "Thank you for this house." He remembered something else Kate had said. Did he dare say it? Did he want to admit that she might be right? Again. Did he want to admit that— He squeezed his eyes tightly closed. Tight because he didn't want the idea, even the possibility to go any further than the inside of his head. He wouldn't—couldn't say it out loud. Thank you for showing me my purpose—whatever it may be.

Alone Matthew walked up the sidewalk toward the giant front doors to Holy Bible. As he neared the entrance, the policeman came out and stood in front of the door, his hands on his hips. He looked at Matthew but said nothing. Matthew made no attempt to enter the church and did not speak to him. He turned and—

Matthew woke up and rolled over in the bed. He looked at the clock. Three-twenty-one. Then he realized that he had had the dream again. His mind cleared somewhat. Nothing different about it. Same details. Church. Policeman. Vest. His groggy thoughts dissipated even more. His assignment. Why was the dream so important? He closed his eyes. Now was not the time. He tried to fall asleep, but it was useless. His mind was tumbling with thoughts. What could the vest mean? How did it feel that nobody from church had reached out? It had now been three days since Stephanie Langdon had called. He felt betrayed by his congregation. That's how he felt. The very people he had helped, had walked with through their crises. He turned over and punched his pillow, then nestled his head in it, trying to get comfortable. All he had done for them. And Kate saying maybe he didn't want to be a minist— Suddenly, a memory plowed into his head, causing him to be wide awake. He opened his eyes and stared at the shadows in the room. What Miriam said about them never having had a marriage or a family. A show, she called it. A show for his father and the church.

He didn't have to roll over to realize the emptiness in the other side of the bed. He thought of the sex he and Miriam had had and how long it had been since the last time. Several weeks. Maybe.

Had that been a show, too? Had it meant anything to her? The other question surfaced fast. Had it meant anything to him? And what was it supposed to mean? Love, of course. Anyone knew that. Questions kept prodding and goading him relentlessly. Had he loved Miriam?

The question slammed into him causing him to instantly swing his legs out and sit up on the side of the bed. What was happening to him? Suddenly all matter of memories began attacking him—his father walking out on the competition, the policeman's vest, nobody reaching out to him, getting fired, Miriam leaving— He leaned forward with his elbows on his thighs, his head between his fists when the next question seized him. It was Kate's voice in his head. *How did it feel?*

He wrapped his arms across his abdomen as if it ached. In the glow of the alarm clock on the nightstand, he saw his cell phone. Instantly, the image of Nathaniel standing beside a tree burst into his mind. In one hand he was holding a bungee cord and in the other his cell phone up to his ear, saying over and over "homosexual."

CHAPTER NINETEEN

TUESDAY & WEDNESDAY — JUNE 9 & 10

Drug dealers, murderers, prostitutes, Matthew thought as he drove down Eden Street, a major thoroughfare through the seedy side of Elmsborough. Turn off of Eden onto any street and you found yourself in an unsavory neighborhood. Every single one a high crime zone. And yet, here he was, being forced to head right into the thick of it. All of his car windows were up and the AC on. Again he clicked the lock button near his door handle.

At the intersection with Lexington Avenue, he stopped at a light, the Elmsborough Outreach Ministry just two blocks away. While he waited for the light, he saw a homeless man on the curb holding a sign. Wants a handout, Matthew thought. Because he was wearing his sunglasses, he could cut his eyes to read the sign without the man knowing. "Vietnam veteran. Can do light work." His camouflage pants were torn at one knee, his boots battered, his long sleeve white shirt dirty, the sleeves too short for his arms. A floppy military hat covered his stringy hair. His scraggly beard was mostly gray. A large, dirty backpack stuffed full lay on the sidewalk nearby under a tree. Next to it lay a dog. Immediately Matthew's attention shifted to what resembled a yellow Lab but smaller. Mixed breed. It rested its head on an outstretched paw, constantly eyeing its master.

Matthew realized that the man was staring at him, but he turned back to watch the light. If he had to beg for food, how could he care for a dog? Why didn't he go to the Veterans' Administration if he was a veteran? They ought to be able to help him. That was what taxes were for. And if he could do light work, why wasn't he doing it instead of begging?

When the light changed, Matthew drove on, not looking at the man or dog again. Two blocks further as he approached Sampson he began searching for the entrance to EOM.

The large brick building gave the appearance of an ordinary two story office building. The large parking lot in front seemed unrealistic for an establishment which served the homeless. The main entrance, labeled as such, was in the center. An entry on the right side was marked for donations—food and clothing. The sign over the door on the left side said "Food Services." Matthew supposed that was where he would be working.

Once in the parking lot, he saw the sign "Deliveries and Staff Parking," leading to the back of the building down its left side. The driveway—large enough for trucks—led to the back of the building where there were ramps for hand trucks and a small loading dock for bigger vehicles behind the food service end of the building. Beyond that was parking for perhaps fifteen to twenty cars. Only ten were occupied.

Matthew chose a space, turned off the ignition and looked again at the name Overby had mentioned. Roger Gooden. He took a deep breath. "I can do this," he said aloud, convincing himself. He got out and used the remote to lock his car but tested it to be sure. Wouldn't be surprised to come back and find the windows smashed, he thought.

At the far end of the building he saw a sign which read, "Night Entrance." Must be for the ones who sleep here, he thought. In the center he saw the door he had been told to go to—"Staff Entrance." He climbed the half dozen steps to the center porch and opened the door. Immediately he found himself in a room containing metal benches with backs. A window with a sliding glass door separated him from a stout security guard.

The black man, whose ID badge on a lanyard around his neck identified him as Beck, slid the glass panel open. "Help you?"

Matthew stated briefly his business—only that he had an appointment with Gooden.

After Beck checked his name on a clipboard and phoned Gooden, he pressed a button underneath the counter which caused a buzzer to sound. At the same time he simply pointed with his other hand to a door. "Through there and down the hall to your left," he said without looking up. Matthew opened it and stepped into a hallway. Even though the building appeared new, its interior showed use. The vinyl flooring was stained. The paneling on the walls dull.

After he had passed several office doors, a man stepped out. "Matthew?" he asked. Thin, clean-shaven, thick, curly blond hair, wearing plain shirt and pants, Gooden extended his hand.

"Yes." Matthew completed the greeting.

"Nice to meet you. Roger Gooden. Come in." They sat in the small office which was laden with stacks of paper and pamphlets in the window sills, on top of file cabinets and on the floor. "Welcome to the EOM. We can certainly use your help here although I'm sorry about the circumstances that brought you here, uh, that Dwight mentioned," he stammered. "Hopefully, being here will help take your mind off of it for a while."

Matthew simply nodded. It seemed everyone knew his "circumstances." What about privacy? Exactly how much had Overby told him? He heaved a silent sigh as Gooden discussed his duties.

"You'll work in the kitchen and eating area during the lunch time. The person in charge of the mid-day meals, Evangeline Mays, will be your boss. And she will be very glad to see you. Her assistant quit last week and she's been running the show all by herself for the last few days. She'll keep a time sheet that you both will sign each day. Oh, and make sure you pronounce her name 'Evange-line' like drawing a 'line.' Not Evange-leen' and not 'Evange-lin.' She's not exactly touchy about it, but she will correct you." He smiled at his own attempt at humor, then became serious. "We're very proud of her. She's one of our success stories. She lost her home and her job about ten years ago. Single mother, one child. She was on the street. No money. No skills. Nowhere and nobody to turn to. Even so she never fell prey to the bad side of the homeless—drugs, addictions. Always helping out around here and when the cook left five years ago, she talked us into giving her a try. Scrimped and saved and got a small house that Habitat for Humanity built. She's one of our most dependable staff members. Respected and admired. All this to say that she might come across a little harsh at first, but that's the street sense talking. She's really a great person." He placed his hands flat on his desk. "Any questions?"

Matthew cleared his throat. "Actually, I do have one. Would there ever be a time when I'd have to be here while outside groups serve mornings and evenings?" He thought about explaining why he was asking but since Gooden already knew so much, maybe it wasn't necessary.

"No, we have a crew to handle that."

Relief washed over Matthew although he was careful not to show it.

After giving him an ID badge on a lanyard to wear around his neck, Gooden led Matthew through more dingy hallways and into the eating area. Even though Holy Bible served here once a month, Matthew had never participated. He was somewhat surprised but also impressed by the arrangement—small metal tables with four attached seats, all one piece, all bolted to the floor. Everything was situated with easy access to and from the serving line at the far end of the large room. Large trash cans sat along the wall near the exit.

Roger Gooden led him through a door into the kitchen where everything was commercial-sized—the stove with six burners, several ovens, the refrigerator, food preparation tables, counters. The serving window resembled any public cafeteria, with glass between the people in line and the food. All the plates of food would have to be placed on the shelf above the glass for the person to pick up.

At the stove Evangeline Mays was stirring a large pot of steaming soup with one hand. The other was propped on her stout hip. She put the long-handled metal spoon down as Gooden introduced Matthew to her.

"How you do, Matthew?" she said, putting out her hand. Her quick smile revealed a large gap between her front teeth—all brilliantly white in contrast to her dark brown skin. Gray filled her close cropped hair, leading him to speculate she might be in her mid-fifties. Her stature was medium, her hips wide, the flesh of her upper arms flabby, her prominent, ample breasts filled her white plastic bib apron. Her glasses sat on the end of her nose, reminding Matthew of Richard Newland.

Awkwardly he shook hands with her, detecting her thick, calloused palm. "Hello," he said simply.

"I've explained everything to Matthew," Roger said. "Hours and time sheet. He knows you're the boss and will give him his duties." He turned to Matthew. "Any questions beyond that, you know where to find me. Welcome and good luck." He offered his hand, after which he left.

"Okay, Matthew," Evangeline said, stepping to a nearby cabinet. She pulled a white plastic apron from a box and handed it to him. "You have to wear a apron anytime you workin' in the kitchen. Put your ID badge behind it so it don't get in the food." She took a pair of clear plastic gloves from a box on a nearby counter. "You have to wear these here anytime you handlin' any kinda food. First, you gotta wash your hands." She pointed to a sink on the far side of the kitchen. "Use soap and don't touch nothin' til you put the gloves on. Go on and do that," she said with a shooing motion as she returned to stir the soup.

Matthew didn't move for a moment. He had never been ordered around by a woman and certainly not an African-American woman.

He toyed with the idea of walking out of the kitchen and back to Roger whatever-his-name-was and telling him this wasn't going to work. Then, he'd go back to Overby and ask for another assignment.

"Somethin' wrong?" Evangeline asked as she stirred, her eyebrows raised.

Matthew fought the urge to smirk, to display his disdain but went to the sink and washed his hands without any overt expression. When he finished he put on the apron and gloves.

"Okay, we havin' vegetable soup and ham and cheese sandwich today," Evangeline said, leading him to a stainless steel table across the room. "You goin' to start makin' the sandwiches." She retrieved large containers of pre-sliced lunchmeat ham and cheese from the commercial refrigerator along with mayonnaise and mustard. "Now, bread's over yonder." She pointed across the room to metal shelving with dozens of loaves of bread. "One slice a cheese, one slice a ham, mayonnaise on one piece a bread, mustard on the other. Cut it in two from the corners and stack 'em in this." She reached to a shelf underneath the table and pulled up a deep metal pan. From a drawer she retrieved a knife. "Okay, we got little over a hour and a half. No time to lollygag around. I got to make cookies and keep a eye on my soup." She walked away.

Again, Matthew hesitated. How could his life have deteriorated to this? Making sandwiches in a shelter for homeless people. He stared at the table with the cheese and ham. His church had contributed to EOM, probably even paid for a lot of this food and even some of this equipment. And sent money to foreign missions as well. He had seen to it. That was his job as senior minister—to oversee, not spread mayonnaise and mustard on slices of bread. Harry Borkin was in charge of community ministry. This was incredible. As he walked to the shelf, got several loaves of bread and began his assigned menial task, he desperately hoped no one would ever see him here.

Later, when he had almost filled one pan, Evangeline came over to check on him. She took a knife from the drawer. "You not ever done too much kitchen work, have ya?" she said, pulling up a stool and began smearing a slice of bread with mayonnaise.

"No," he said.

"Well, don't worry. You'll catch on soon 'nough."

He quickly saw that she was able to make two sandwiches to his one and talk all the while.

"I 'spect Roger told you how you best not say my name wrong, now didn't he?"

Matthew kept working without looking up. "Yes. He said you would get upset if I mispronounced it."

"How'd he tell you to say it?" She sounded serious.

"Evangeline, like clothesline."

"Well, least he didn't tell you wrong on purpose like he done some folk." She then broke into a smile. "He such a mess. Don't know what I'm gonna do with him." She put a slice of ham and one of cheese on the bread. "Since you here in the middle of the day, you out of work? 'Cause I know you too young a man to be retired."

He didn't like her probing. He just wanted to do the work and leave. "Actually, I am retired." He wasn't about to tell her it was early retirement. Let her think what she wants to.

She stopped spreading mayonnaise for an instant and looked at him. "You way too young for that. What kinda work did you do?"

Maybe she didn't know about his "circumstances" like everyone else seemed to. "I am—was a minister." He hated using past tense.

"That so? Well, that just is fine. What church did you reverend at?"

"Holy Bible Fellowship," he said proudly.

"That right?" Evangeline exclaimed without halting her work. "I heard of it. I declare. That just is fine. Well, I'm just so proud you workin' in here with us. Means a lot, 'specially you bein' a reverend and all. We need more folk in here who know how to see the face of Jesus in these poor folk that come in here that don't have nothin' hardly but the clothes on they back." She cut a sandwich corner to corner and placed the two halves in the pan. "Too many folk too busy lookin' to see how others so different from theyselves when they oughta be lookin' to see how we all alike." She finished making another sandwich and stood up from the stool. "Got to check on my soup and cookies," she said absent-mindedly, moving to the stove. "Don't want nothin' to burn."

When the fifth pan was full of sandwiches, she declared they had enough and told him to close up the unused ingredients and put them in the refrigerator. At that moment he heard a door open. Instantly, he worried that it might be somebody he knew. But he didn't know the three people—two women and a man, all three African-Americans. He wondered if they would want to know all about him, too. It didn't matter if they did. He would never see them again once he had served his time here.

"Matthew, this is Crystal, Frannie and Robert. They work in the food bank and clothing store and in here at lunch. Y'all, this is Matthew."

They all approached him and shook hands, welcoming him. Matthew felt awkward and was relieved when they immediately set to work without instructions—filling cups with ice, tea and water, setting out plastic eating utensils, napkins, bowls for soup, plates for sandwiches. All disposable. Activity shifted into a flurry mode when a security guard came in and asked Evangeline if she was ready.

"Two minutes," she said. "Matthew, I need you to carry this pot of soup to the serving window," she said, pointing. "Then get one of them pans of sandwiches and put it here." She designated a place next to the soup. "Robert, I need you to put a pan of cookies right here." Robert complied. "Matthew, I want you and Robert to stand back here ready to bring us more soup and whatever else whenever things runs out. May even have to make more sandwiches if these not 'nough." She turned to the serving table and began directing Frannie and Crystal.

Just then, the first people in line began entering through an outside door to the large eating area. Roger Gooden's voice came over the speaker system, that reached both the inside and the outside waiting area where the line continued.

"Let us pray. Father, God, thank you for this food and for the people who have worked to prepare it. Bless each one here and sustain each one with this meal. Help each of us to be peaceful and loving to one another everyday, no matter where we might be or what we might have. Thank you, God, for hope and change. Amen."

Matthew was surprised by the short prayer. Needed more praise of God, more punch, maybe even a hint of getting these people to work.

The security guard then gave the signal for the line to move to the serving window where each man and woman picked up food and drink. Matthew watched as the people shuffled by. A few spoke. Some mumbled a thank you. Most wore tattered clothes. A few attempted to appear well dressed in worn suits and scuffed shoes. Most men were unshaven. Some of the people had bruises or small cuts, some bandaged, others not. Hair hadn't been washed. Most women had no makeup, although Matthew noted two had on too much which went along with their skimpy clothes. He thought of what Evangeline had said—the face of Jesus and looking to see how we're more alike than we are different. He wanted to disagree—vehemently, even.

Everyone sat at the bolted down tables with attached seats for four. He observed that manners were lacking as they ate quickly while slumped over their food guardedly. Most used their hands for wiping their mouths rather than the paper napkin.

The line continued, on and on—at least several hundred—among them Matthew spotted the Vietnam veteran, his jammed backpack slung on his shoulder. He wondered where his dog was.

For over an hour the kitchen was a flurry of activity, all five workers moving constantly between tasks. Matthew and Robert replenished the soup pots, the pans of sandwiches, cups, pitchers of tea and water.

"Okay," Evangeline said when the last person had gone through the line and the entrance to the dining area was closed. "We got extra. Frannie, how 'bout you fillin' some bowls with soup and Robert and Crystal put the bowls on a tray and carry 'em around to see who wants more. Matthew, you take this pan of sandwiches out there and see who wants another one. But just one. And get on some plastic gloves. You put the sandwich on the plate. Don't let nobody reach in and get one."

The thought of leaving the safety of the kitchen and mingling among those people—he wanted to refuse but knew he couldn't. He put on the gloves and picked up the large pan holding it with one arm. He walked up and down the aisle between the tables. "Another sandwich?" he asked at each table. Some of the people nodded or shook their heads. Some raised their hand and began gobbling it immediately. He saw the grime on their hands, under their nails, the rough, calloused skin, the gnarled or missing teeth. The smell of sweat from the summer heat overpowered the aroma of the food.

"Would you like another sandwich?" Matthew said dutifully to the veteran sitting at a table by himself.

The man looked up at him from his soup. "Yes, thank you." His deep voice was calm. His teeth were dinghy, two missing from his lower gum. Matthew detected only minor odor.

He handed him a sandwich and moved on. Probably not even a veteran, but at least he did express his gratitude, he thought.

As he walked away he saw the man take a plastic bag from his pants pocket and put the sandwich in it. Probably for his dog.

After he had asked all those still eating if they wanted another sandwich, he saw the veteran was still there. Remembering the dog that had come to their door for food—the one his father threw rocks at—he wondered if he should give this man more for his dog. What if Evangeline saw him or another person saw him and made a scene? But he had asked everyone. He wandered across the room. Others who'd been nearby had left. Without asking, Matthew placed two more whole sandwiches on his plate. The man stared at them.

"For your dog," Matthew said quietly.

The veteran looked up at him, mild surprise covered his face. "Thank you, sir." He spoke softly. "Thank you very much."

Matthew said nothing but made his way back to the kitchen.

After another few minutes the eating area was empty again, the door locked by the guard. In the kitchen, Evangeline had placed five bowls of soup, a plate of sandwiches and another with cookies around one of the large stainless steel preparation tables. Robert brought up five stools and placed them around the table.

"Whew, big crowd today, y'all," Evangeline said, hefting herself onto a stool and reaching for a sandwich. Crystal, Frannie and Robert also sat down.

"Not as many as usual," Frannie said.

Matthew stood back and looked at them.

"Aint' you hungry?" Robert asked, eyeing him.

He considered declining. More than anything he wanted to finish and leave. "What else do I have to do?" he asked Evangeline but made no move toward the table.

"Wipe down the tables and seats and sweep the floor out there and in here, pots and pans, and trash. But you come on over here and eat first. No need to hurry with all that." She began eating her soup.

Reluctantly, Matthew sat down on the stool and picked up the plastic spoon. The aroma called to mind soups that Miriam had made. The taste just as good. He took another bite.

"I know Evangeline's glad to have you in here helpin', Matthew," Frannie said as she tore her sandwich in half.

"Sure 'nough am," Evangeline nodded, just before reaching for a sandwich. Matthew nodded as he chewed. "Y'all not gonna believe it, cause he looks so young, but Matthew here is retired from bein' a reverend."

At first Matthew cringed being the center of their conversation but politely smiled at their compliments. They asked the same questions as Evangeline. When he had satisfied their courteous curiosity, he was glad they turned to other topics.

"They were some nasty smellin' people through here today," Crystal said. "I gave out some clothes to a woman this mornin' and, my heavenly days, I wanted to show her to the showers. Felt bad for her in all this heat. Not hardly any way not to smell bad." She ate a bite of her sandwich.

"I thank Jesus everyday for my job and house," Robert said.

"Amen to that," Evangeline said.

As they all ate in silence for a moment, Matthew imagined himself addressing them on what the Bible said about the poor, quoting some scripture. It might make up for Gooden's short blessing. These were surely willing listeners. All attended a church, but not his. No, no mini-sermons. He just wanted to do his work and leave. Besides, he just wasn't in the mood.

"Evangeline Mays, you sure know how to make good soup," Robert said. The others agreed. Evangeline smiled.

The soup and sandwich began to fill Matthew up but didn't make him want to converse. After sweeping the floor, wiping down all the tables, washing the pots and pans, and carrying out the large bags of trash to the dumpsters it was two o'clock. From a cubby hole of an office, Evangeline brought out a manila folder and a time sheet. Using one of the work tables, she filled in the date and hours, then wrote her initials beside it and let Matthew do the same. She wrote his name on the folder's tab but made no reference as to why they had to do this meticulous paperwork.

"You did a very good job today. I appreciate it more than I can say to you," she said, smiling as she closed the folder. "And I'll see you tomorrow."

She must already know his "circumstances" about his arrest, he surmised as he walked to his car and drove out of the parking area. Just as well. At least she had the decency not to ask him about it or offer any advice. Just do the work and leave. All he could think about was the last day he'd be driving out of this parking lot and never have to return. His time and talents could be used in much better ways than here, if only he knew where and how. This was not his calling. But he was going to have to put up with it for the next—he tried to figure how many weeks he was going to have to be there. Six days a week times four hours a day was twenty-four. Divide two hundred and fifty hours by twenty-four. That was ten or eleven weeks roughly. Almost the end of August, he realized. He sighed deeply. No mistaking that he would be going home and taking a shower everyday before he did anything else.

A few blocks down Eden Street he saw the veteran walking along the sidewalk, his dog tagging along beside him, its tail wagging. He was impressed how obedient the dog was—no leash, no wandering away. He was amazed that the man was willing to give up part of his lunch for his four-legged companion. He can't feed himself, much less an animal. Why would any homeless person want a dog? What if it got sick? What about in the winter when it was so bitterly cold? Not his concern, he told himself, as he continued on his way.

At home he drove quickly into the garage as usual but noticed how high the grass was getting. He was glad he had called a lawn service to take care of the yard. They would send him a bill, he'd pay it and never even have to see them. Perfect.

Later as he was in the midst of preparing his dinner—the same three things he'd had the night before—he thought about how well off he was. And he should be better off, he decided. He had worked hard his whole life. He deserved the comfort he enjoyed. But then, he remembered some of the people he had seen that day. Where would they eat tonight? Where would they sleep? And Evangeline's words—seeing the face of Jesus in those people. Just as quickly as the image appeared, it evaporated. He had served his four hours, he thought, splitting the chicken breast in half to insure thorough cooking. He wondered about some barbeque sauce, maybe for dipping. He would add that to his grocery list.

"We havin' Sloppy Joe's, pork-n-beans and peaches for dessert," Evangeline told him the next day. "So I need you to go back to the pantry and get four cans of the Sloppy mix and I'm gonna get the ground beef started."

Matthew put on his plastic bib apron and did as he was told. When he had brought out the cans, Evangeline instructed him to open them and pour the contents into several large flat pans. As he worked he noted the process and what Evangeline was doing. Maybe he could make Sloppy Joe's at home, he thought. Next he opened large cans of peaches and poured them into pans. Sooner than he expected, Frannie and Crystal appeared to work, again setting up cups for water and tea.

Matthew was about to ask about Robert when all three women saw another man walk in from the outside and spoke to him warmly. He looked vaguely familiar which sent a surge of fear through Matthew. Somebody from Holy Bible? Maybe. No, that didn't feel right. His salt and pepper hair was neatly tousled. His wore tennis shoes, faded jeans and a Polo shirt that filled up by his well defined slender but muscular frame. Matthew gauged him to be his age—late forties. After warmly greeting the ladies with a wave, he walked over to Matthew as he stood next to his pans of peaches at the preparation table.

"Ben Thornton," he said, smiling as he extended his hand.

Matthew took his hand and fought the wave of disdainful thoughts that immediately began to race through his mind. Ben Thornton. Minister of Trinity Baptist Church. Quoted in the paper as saying that homosexuality was not contrary to God's and Jesus' teachings. And worse. Thornton. Was he related to Kate? Could she be his wife? Did he know his "circumstances"—either through his wife or the ministerial grapevine? If he told him his name, would he launch into what he had read about him in the newspaper—his letters to the editor about that ridiculous gay pride event? Again he wanted to walk out. Say nothing. Take off the plastic apron and leave.

"Matthew," he said simply and left it at that.

"Glad to meet you." He took a plastic apron from the box. "I don't think I've ever seen you here before. Did you just start?"

"Yesterday," Matthew said. He carried a pan of peaches to the service window, hoping he would leave him alone.

"Matthew here is a reverend, also," Evangeline announced to Ben. "And he retired."

"Really? What church?" Ben inquired, tying the apron behind him but keenly interested.

Matthew fought the urge to leave. Just turn and walk out. "Holy Bible Fellowship," he said, his spine stiffening for a confrontation. "I'm Matthew Winslow." He looked Thornton in the eye, watching for a smirk, waiting for a comment. He saw a flicker of recognition as if puzzle pieces were going into place.

"That's a very large church. You must miss being with your congregation."

Matthew tried to hide his surprise. He hadn't expected such a thoughtful response. "Yes, I do," he managed to say without measuring whether it was true or not.

Just then Evangeline told Ben she wanted him to serve at the window with her and Frannie. Crystal would manage tea and water. Matthew would keep watch on what any of them needed and bring it to keep the line moving.

He was glad to have the distance between himself and Thornton. All he wanted was to work and leave. No more. No less.

While Matthew was thinking about how to avoid Thornton, he almost missed seeing the veteran come through the line. He had seen him that morning on the street as he drove to EOM. His dog walking dutifully along. He wore the same clothes as yesterday, same backpack, unshaven. He thanked the servers and took a seat in the same area as the day before. When the line finally closed, Evangeline took the leftovers and prepared eight or nine more Sloppy Joe's and cut them in half and put them in a pan.

"Matthew, take these out there and see if anybody wants more. Just give them a half to start with." She called to Crystal and Ben and told them to put the extra beans in bowls and offer them to the people.

Matthew made his way through the dining area, being sure to stay away from Crystal and Ben. As he handed out the surplus sandwiches, he purposefully made the veteran his last stop.

"An extra half sandwich?" he asked.

The veteran looked up. "Please, sir."

Matthew was able to place two halves on his plate without anyone noticing.

"You're very kind."

"One for you and one for your dog, or however you want to do it," he said softly.

"I'll probably give her both."

Again, he remembered the two dogs from his childhood. "What's her name?"

"Sadie."

Matthew nodded. He didn't know what else to say, so he went back to the kitchen.

They had done some preliminary cleaning up in the kitchen, waiting until the last person had left the dining area, when Evangeline called the workers to sit down and eat. Matthew sat as far away as he could from Ben and said little. The conversation made it clear to Matthew that Evangeline, Crystal and Frannie held Ben Thornton in high regard, asking about his family and a recent trip he'd made to the Holy Land. Ben told several funny stories and had more than just a passing interest in their families and events in their lives. He fit in, like one of them, as if he'd been working there a long time. He got along, was accepted like an old friend. *Beware of false prophets*, he silently quoted Matthew 7:15 to himself, *who come to you in sheep's clothing but inwardly are ravenous wolves.*

Matthew ate quickly then went out to the dining area to wipe down the tables.

"Need some help?"

Ben's voice startled him. Before he could answer, the minister took the spray bottle and tore some paper towels from the roll and began cleaning a table. Matthew didn't want to respond. This was going to be awkward. "You come every week?" Matthew asked after he could no longer tolerate the silence.

"Yeah, Robert has to leave on Wednesdays so I come in and help out."

"Every Wednesday?" Matthew asked.

"Except when I have unforeseen conflicts." He dried off one of the seats. "How about you?"

Matthew didn't know what to say. "Just volunteering," he managed but quickly added, "temporarily."

"Since you're retired do you do any volunteering besides here?"

Matthew tried to hold his irritation in check. Too nosey. Was he trying to be his friend like he was with the others? He kept wiping the table and didn't look up. "No. I'm here everyday except Sunday. Apparently, Evangeline's assistant quit suddenly. So I'm filling in." He tried to make his tone sound flat, hoping to convey that it was none of his business.

"I'm sure she's very grateful. It takes a very special person to do what she does." Thornton moved on to another table but said nothing more until all the tables had been wiped down. He handed Matthew the spray bottle. "I do want to tell you that I'm so very sorry for your loss. I can't imagine what that must be like."

Matthew was stunned. Another one—and how much did this one know about his "circumstances"? Probably just trying to be nice and didn't really mean it. "Thank you. I appreciate that."

"And you'll always be welcomed at our Sunday service, too, if ever you want to."

Again, Matthew was struck. This man couldn't be so ignorant as to not know that they were opposites in every way. Matthew simply nodded. Why would he say that if he didn't already know he could no longer go to his own church?

Later, as Evangeline had Matthew initial his time sheet, he casually asked, "So Ben comes in every week?"

"Yessiree, every Wednesday," she said. "That Ben, he's a special reverend. They love him at his church. You know he's the one that said it first—that coming over here reminds him to look for the face of Jesus in these poor people. You know, he's just a wonderful soul."

Yes, a saint, he thought but held back his sarcasm. "That's very commendable."

All the way home, he fought the war in his mind. The rumor mill was obviously running in high gear. There was no stopping that, he supposed. But more important—was Kate Thornton Ben's wife? And if she was, did she talk to him about the people who came to her? Did Overby tell Kate where he was serving his community time? And did she then tell her husband? He said he'd been volunteering there every Wednesday. So maybe it was all coincidence. And Evangeline giving him credit for that line about seeing the face of Jesus in the poor. Did he really come up with that?

He stopped himself. Maybe he was getting a little crazy. Kate had practically sworn that whatever was said in her office was completely confidential. He was going to ask her anyway.

He sighed as he pulled away from a traffic light. His life just kept getting more and more complicated.

At home, the lawn service company had cut the grass, edged the sidewalks and driveway, even trimmed some of the hedges. It looked immaculate. Worth every penny, he thought. Now he wouldn't have to step foot out in the yard.

Inside, as he had vowed and done the last two days after getting home from EOM, he took a shower. While standing in the warm water, he realized that none of the people he had helped to feed that day had this luxury. None of them had a yard. None of them had any of the things he had. But he remembered his rationale. He had worked all his life for this. He deserved it. But just then, Evangeline's voice echoed in his head and he remembered the faces he'd seen—sad, dull eyes, unshaven, bruised, sores, rotten teeth. Hopeless. Abandoned. Forgotten. Alone. Suddenly it struck him how those four words described— As the warm water cascaded down his body, he crossed his arms over his chest and realized something. The four words described how he felt.

CHAPTER TWENTY

THURSDAY & FRIDAY— JUNE 11 & 12

As Matthew meticulously combed his hair in the bathroom mirror, he remembered that it was Thursday. That realization also brought to mind that exactly one week ago his whole life had changed—changed even more than it already had. One week ago he had been fired, temporarily lost his sanity in traffic and been arrested—all within the span of a few hours. Now just a mere seven days later, he was in therapy for anger and working in a facility for the homeless. From leading a congregation of thousands to feeding lunch to several hundred destitute vagrants six days a week. From working with three highly educated ministers to working with four African-Americans, one of whom had authority over him. He stared at himself in the mirror. How could all this have happened? Just as quickly another thought struck him. He had thought about his job first—before thinking of Nathaniel. May 23. He closed his eyes. No. He didn't want to think about it. Not now. But it was there. It was always there—in his head. He took a deep breath, let it out and opened his eyes. Move on, he told himself.

Thursday also meant that he had a standing appointment with his barber. Eleven o'clock, always just after his hospital visitations. But did he want to go? Could he face those men? They knew about Nathaniel and had been very sympathetic, but what about his arrest? Did they know about that? He hadn't seen it in the newspaper. The question was—did any of them have a connection with the rumor mill from church? Could Frank and the other barbers possibly not know that he had lost his job? It didn't matter. He couldn't go at his usual time at eleven. He should call and cancel his appointment anyway and not make Frank miss taking another client. Did he want to go later today? Could he chance that? Or just start all over with another barber somewhere else in town?

He leaned closer to the mirror and examined the few sprigs of gray on his temples. He thought of what had happened at the grocery store after midnight on Saturday. He didn't want to go through that again—especially not at the barbershop. He'd call and cancel before he went to EOM. Maybe look for another barbershop and go tomorrow or Saturday. He took in a deep frustrated breath and exhaled. Would there ever come a time when he could just do things like he always had?

"Crystal had to go home just while ago," Frannie announced as she and Robert came into the kitchen.

"Her mama again?" Evangeline asked.

"Second time this month," Frannie answered, shaking her head. "Her daughter's not payin' close enough attention."

Matthew listened but said nothing as he continued carrying pans to the serving window— turkey hash, green beans, slices of bread. The small ice cream bars would have to be brought out a few at a time, Evangeline had told him.

"Okay, then, Matthew I'm gonna put you servin' beans on the line," Evangeline ordered. "Robert, you put the bread and dessert on and, Frannie, you do water and tea. We'll all just have to get stuff when we run out. But we'll be fine. Won't make that bigga difference."

Everyone went to work and within a few minutes the doors opened. Evangeline showed Matthew the serving size of the uncut string beans using a pair of tongs. He glanced up at most of the people—some who said they didn't want beans and a few asking for more. When the veteran passed through near the end of the line, he did not look up at Matthew although Matthew looked at him. At first he thought the tattered man was snubbing him, but then realized that maybe he was fearful of raising suspicion about the extra food Matthew had been giving him.

As usual after the line closed Evangeline sent him and Robert out to serve extra turkey hash and ice cream bars. Matthew volunteered to take out bowls of hash. The veteran gratefully accepted the additional serving. When all had been offered a second helping, Matthew gave the man a third. He noticed that he put the disposable bowls in the plastic bag and left right away.

After serving, as the four ate their lunch in the kitchen, Matthew asked, "Is Crystal's mother sick?"

"Alzheimer's," Frannie answered. "She lives with Crystal and her daughter supposed to look after her."

"But her daughter's only fourteen and—well, I just best shut my mouth," Evangeline said. She plopped a spoonful of hash in her mouth and ate with a disgruntled look.

Immediately Matthew thought of his mother in the facility. Her swearing. Don't think about it, he told himself.

"How's your daughter?" Evangeline asked Robert.

"She had a good treatment yesterday. Doctor said he thought he had a donor but turned out he didn't. Wrong blood type."

"What's wrong with her?" Matthew asked before he caught himself. He really shouldn't be prying.

"She's on dialysis. Has to go twice a week. I take her on Wednesdays. My wife takes her on the other day." Robert stopped eating and stared at his plate. "We just prayin' for a donor and hopin' somebody don't have to die so my child can live."

"God's got a plan," Evangeline said. "And He's in charge. You know that, Robert." She leaned over the table toward him. "You just tryin' to hurry Him along and He hears you. Remember He's got the whole world in His hands." She patted his hand.

Robert sniffed back his emotion. "Thank you, Evangeline. I needed to hear that."

"Well, we got us a reverend right here that tell you it's true. Right, Matthew?"

Matthew saw that all three people were now looking to him for wisdom. God's wisdom. He wanted to quote an appropriate Bible verse, but oddly his mind was tumbling, taking in what Evangeline had said. So simple, yet her truth stunned him. "I don't think I could say it any better," he said. "I'll—" He stopped. The three were still watching him. "I'll keep her in my prayers," he said. He had said that so many other times before—probably thousands of times—but this time it felt different.

After he had finished all of his duties, he and Evangeline signed his time sheet.

"That was very fine what you said to Robert. I know he appreciated it. His daughter is so beautiful and can sing up a storm."

Matthew remembered his words. "I hope she'll be well soon."

Evangeline nodded and put the time sheet in his folder. "And before you go," she began, getting up from her stool and going to the refrigerator. "I have a little something for you." She took out a brown paper bag, holding it level. "It's just a chicken pie I made last night. You can heat up a servin' in the microwave. Should last you several dinners."

Matthew was stunned.

Evangeline sat back down on the stool. When she spoke her voice was soft and gentle. "I know what it means to lose a child." She smiled courageously as her eyes brimmed with tears. "My Darius was killed in Iraq over a year ago. I thought I'd never get over it."

She wiped her wet face with a paper napkin. "Don't guess I ever will." She slid the paper bag toward Matthew. "Reverend Ben told me yesterday about your son. So I just wanted to give you a little comfort food cause I know—" She shook her head. "I know they's no words nobody can say can help you." She smiled. "But you bein' a reverend and all, you know how that is, I'm sure."

He stared at the paper bag as a hollowness overtook him. He had no words. It was almost as if he could not comprehend what was happening. He looked at Evangeline, drying her eyes and smiling at him, the gap between her white teeth ever present. "I'm so sorry about your son," he managed to utter. Evangeline nodded. "And thank you so much for this."

Later, Matthew sat in his car, the chicken pie carefully placed in the passenger seat beside him. He stared at the package and heard Evangeline's words over and over. *Lose a child...my Darius...killed... never get over it...never will...your son...comfort food...no words can help.* Her voice swam over him like a gentle shower, yet he resisted any such cleansing power. Instead, he started his car and began his drive home.

Several blocks later he had to stop for a red light. He glanced down the intersecting street. There sitting on the curb a short distance away next to a fire hydrant was the Vietnam veteran, beside him Sadie gobbling her two bowls of turkey hash. When she finished, she sat down next to the veteran. He hugged her to him, scratching behind her ears and petting her side. Sadie stretched her head up and licked his smiling, scruffy face. The scene engulfed Matthew, so much so that he didn't hear the first honk of the car horn behind him. With the second blast, he realized that the light was now green. The raucous, impatient horn also caught the veteran's attention. He saw Matthew and smiled slightly as he continued hugging Sadie.

As he drove away Matthew felt the same feeling he had about Evangeline and her making the chicken pie for him. A feeling he had to hold back. He didn't know why. He simply knew he had to. It was the right thing to do.

"I need to ask you if you're related to Ben Thornton," Matthew asked as soon as he sat down in Kate's office later that afternoon. Immediately he began jiggling his leg up and down.

She smiled. "He's my brother-in-law. Do you know him?"

He felt some relief, that maybe his privacy had not been betrayed. He told her about his assignment to Elmsborough Outreach Ministry and Thornton's volunteering every Wednesday.

"I know he is a big supporter of EOM, but I didn't know he helped out on such a regular basis," Kate said.

"He said that Evangeline—she's the head of the kitchen staff—told him I'm a retired minister from Holy Bible Fellowship, he put it all together and expressed his sympathy. Since he knows that, he must know the rest of it—that I'm not exactly retired, got arrested and that my wife left me. I guess the grapevine is yielding a great harvest," he said sarcastically.

"I want to repeat my stand on confidentiality and reassure you. Even if Ben were my husband, I would never discuss my clients with him." She raised her eyebrows. "Okay?"

Matthew nodded. "After all that's happened, it's hard to know who to trust."

"I fully appreciate that, but I hope you won't let the past cloud your view of new people coming into your life. You could have spent time in jail if people hadn't been sympathetic to your situation."

"Pity," he asked somewhat timidly.

"No. Caring, helping, reaching out, expressing feelings. People saying 'I know what it's like to hurt.' It's empathy."

Matthew focused on the arm of the chair. As he had in every other session, he rubbed his hand across it, sensing the texture of the fabric. His leg no longer moved. He wondered if he should tell her, knowing where it would lead.

"Evangeline gave me a chicken pie she made last night. She said she lost her son in Iraq and wanted to give me some comfort food because there were no words—" He stopped. He was in that hollow place. He could feel it.

Kate leaned forward. "And?"

He took a deep breath and spoke softly. "I know you want to know how that made me feel. I tried to figure it out. It's difficult. I guess that sounds dumb."

"No, not really. Although I'm very glad you're aware of it." They sat quietly for several moments. "It's ironic that someone you've only known a few days—actually only a few hours—is the only person who has reached out to you. She's got lots of empathy."

Matthew continued staring at the armrest as he remembered Stephanie Langdon's phone message. Kate was right, but he wasn't going to tell her about his near wreck on Monday—yelling about how he felt when no one from his church had contacted him.

"I dare say she might even understand your hitting the car with the bat. She probably felt like doing that."

Matthew thought about this being the day to go to the barbershop. How he didn't want to face those men or think about them talking about him behind his back after he left. Did he want to go into that with Kate?

"I wonder if the men at the barbershop are capable of empathy." He blurted it out before he had a chance to think about what he was saying.

"An all male situation like a barbershop might feel a little daunting. Self-conscious maybe. Feeling judged by other males. But, do you think all of them have perfect lives, never been burned in a work situation? Some may even have been arrested. Who knows?"

He hadn't thought about that. Actually, he did remember hearing that one of them had had a run-in with the law. Still, he was the one they would all look at when he walked in.

"Nobody really likes to change barbers if they've been going to the same one for a long time and like him," Kate said matter-of-factly.

He told her more about his experience at EOM even though he knew she would probably ask him how it felt to be dealing with the destitute. He also mentioned the Vietnam veteran but said nothing about Sadie.

"He's probably not even a veteran," he said. "I'd like to think he is. That he's not just using that to gain sympathy." He looked up at her. "And being around those people in general makes me feel sorry for them and grateful that I've got all that I have." He turned his gaze toward the armrest.

After several moments, Kate broke their silence. "Any more dreams?"

Matthew immediately looked away from her and took a deep breath. "The same one. The policeman in front of the church."

"How often have you had it?"

"I guess several nights. Maybe."

"And you didn't talk to him?"

"No."

"Is he still wearing the bullet proof vest?"

He nodded. "And I haven't had any ideas about what that means." He thought he'd save her the trouble of asking.

"Keep thinking about it."

Out in the parking lot, Matthew sat for a several minutes trying to decide. He had a good barber. He liked him. He liked the privacy his cubicle provided. He'd only have to go through the room when he got there and when he left. Otherwise, no one would know he was there. If a church member happened to show up, he'd just greet him, ask about his family—as he usually did—and leave. If they talked about him, then they would just talk about him. He called on his cell phone and spoke to Frank. He'd had a cancellation at 5:30.

"I'm close by. I can be there easily."

"Good. See you in a few," Frank said cheerfully.

He arrived at the strip mall and sat out in front of the barbershop waiting until five-thirty before going in. All four of the barbers greeted him warmly as he followed Frank to the cubicle near the back. Once behind the partition he relaxed somewhat. He talked less than usual and Frank seemed to follow his lead and not make conversation.

Just as Frank was finishing up, Matthew heard someone come in. Instantly he recognized the unmistakable voice. Near panic seized him. Kenneth Ward. He must not be a regular since he had to ask which barber was Bill. He could hear him go to the chair and begin telling him how he wanted his hair cut. Matthew wanted to go out the back door but knew that asking would be more embarrassing. He had no choice. He would walk out with Frank, pay and leave, completely ignoring Kenneth. He was certain that the man from the Coalition would not speak to him.

After examining and praising Frank's work, they walked from behind the partition. Walking through the opening between the other chairs to the cash register was like walking a gauntlet, his heart pounding. Matthew looked straight ahead of him the whole time. When he got his change, he gave Frank a slightly larger tip than usual.

"Thanks, Matthew," Frank said. "Here, take a couple of tomatoes from Bill's garden."

"Yeah, help yourself, Matthew," Bill said, standing behind Kenneth combing his hair.

"Thanks, Bill." Matthew forced himself to look at the other barber. What he saw took him by surprise. He had forgotten about Kenneth's obvious comb-over. All of his long hair now draped over one ear almost down to his shoulder, exposing the slick, pale skin on the top of his head. "That's very kind of you," he added, noting that Kenneth stared straight ahead.

"Don't tell him that," Chris, another barber, said. "We've got to work with him everyday." Everyone laughed, including Matthew.

"Good thing you can work here instead of trying to make a living playing golf," Fletcher, yet another barber, chimed in.

The jovial exchange gave Matthew confidence as he noticed Kenneth's sour, unsmiling countenance. He picked up two tomatoes. "See you next time," he said to Frank and offered his hand.

As he walked to his car, he thought of the irony of bumping into Kenneth and seeing what his hair really looked like. He doubted he'd ever see him again in that barbershop. Driving out of the parking lot, he decided he'd call Frank tomorrow and try to set up a standing 5:30 appointment every Thursday, right after his session with Kate.

Matthew pressed the buttons on the microwave to heat a serving of Evangeline's chicken pie slowly rather than blasting it and possibly destroying its flavor. Next he heated some broccoli and corn, both of which he had steamed in their own bags the night before.

Sitting down with his dinner on the plate in front of him, all that had happened that day tumbled gently through his mind. He put his elbows on the table, clasped his hands and rested his chin on them.

"Oh, God," he began softly, "thank you for this food and all my blessings. I pray that you will watch over Evangeline, Robert and his daughter, and Crystal and her mother. Look after, too, the homeless veteran and Sadie." He sat for a moment with his eyes closed. "Especially care for Miriam and Sarah Elizabeth." The emptiness in him rose up but he pushed it away. "Amen."

As he ate the chicken pie, he recalled how Evangeline talked about her son. Darius. She probably had made him many such pies over the years. In an odd way he felt like he was sharing this meal with him, that he was there, sitting at the table, talking about his mother.

Matthew put down his fork and stared at his food. He had so much, yet he felt so— He wrestled with the thought. He felt so— Homeless. Even with this four bedroom house, he was as homeless as the people who came through the shelter everyday. Unconnected. With nothing. Nobody. The emptiness reared up again. No, he said, picking up his fork and eating. He was grateful and he would enjoy it.

Evangeline's chicken pie had given him an idea. After cleaning up the kitchen he opened the drawer where he'd seen some of Miriam's recipes. He took out a folder and thumbed through a collection. Casseroles of all kinds, dishes that he loved—squash, corn, bean, chili con carne, pork tenderloin, roast beef. And there were desserts—pies, cakes, cookies. He read through the recipes. They didn't sound all that difficult. If he had all the ingredients, he could make some of these. And then he saw the cookbook with recipes for the slow cooker on the counter and noted the various buttons—four hours, six hours, eight hours, warm. He read some of those recipes. He guessed it was safe to leave it turned on all day. Miriam did that. Still, it seemed risky. He could cook it all day on Sunday. When he would be home to keep an eye on it. He read the recipe for a roast and wrote down what he would need from the store.

On Friday as he signed his time sheet with Evangeline, he thanked her again for the chicken pie and took the opportunity to ask about leaving a slow cooker on all day unattended.

"Oh, I do that all the time," she said. "Specially a roast. Tell you what, too. Buy you a box of plastic liners to go inside the cooker. That way they's no cleanup. Just do it like the picture on the box shows."

The thought of having a roast cooking and ready for Saturday night caused him to alter his plan. He'd go to the store late tonight. Maybe not as late as he had the week before, since he had to be at EOM by ten on Saturday. Needing only a few things, he'd wait until ten-thirty or eleven p. m. Going an hour earlier couldn't make that much difference in who was there.

For dinner he heated another portion of the chicken pie and some vegetables, priding himself on his healthy eating and domestic ability. Eating at the kitchen table, he noticed a ball of dust in the corner under a cabinet. He guessed he should probably do some cleaning. He'd see what supplies were in the closet. A big house, he thought. He could break it down into upstairs and downstairs. Downstairs tonight. Upstairs tomorrow after he got home from EOM. And it was time to wash, again. He sighed thinking of the number of things needing to be done. And he had wondered what he would do with all his time. More irony.

After dinner he opened the closet in the laundry room. Vacuum cleaner. Mops. Bottles and cloths. Was all of this necessary? he wondered. He began reading labels. A box with disposable dusting things, not exactly cloth, that according to the instructions, were supposed to slide onto a plastic handle. He looked around and found the wand that matched the picture on the box. He sighed as he tried to push back avoiding feeling overwhelmed.

He knew how to use the vacuum cleaner so he ran that all over the downstairs. Next he used the odd dusting apparatus. Finally he mopped the kitchen floor and half-bath off the hallway. He noticed a ring around the water's edge in the toilet. How could that be? No one used this. He found the bowl cleaner in the laundry closet and used the brush in the stand beside the toilet. The downstairs was clean.

Feeling like he had conquered one hurdle, he drove to the grocery store shortly before eleven as planned. He picked up a hand basket rather than a cart at the door and went on his mission, carefully watching for familiar faces. He chose a plump lean roast, picked up the cream of mushroom soup and dry onion soup mix, then went in search of the liners Evangeline had told him about. One of the few clerks wandering the store pointed him to aisle seven, on the left. "Across from the pet food," he told him. Matthew made his way over and began searching. Trash bags, wax paper—

"Reverend Winslow?"

His entire being cowered. The voice belonged to a young female. He jerked his head. Martha Davies. He said nothing at first. The two stared at each other in silence for several seconds. Even though there was some distance between them, he could see her eyes beginning to brim. Finally, Matthew found his voice. "Hello, Martha. How are you?"

She bit her lower lip. "I'm—" She said nothing more but walked toward him, tears now running down her cheeks. When she got to him she reached out her arms and embraced him.

Matthew was completely stunned. For a moment he did not react physically. Finally, he put his arm around her in a feeble attempt to console her as she cried.

"I miss Nathaniel so much," she said quietly. "Even if he was gay."

Matthew's demeanor stiffened as he released his embrace. "Nathaniel wasn't— He wasn't that way." He steeled himself against the turmoil and anger that was beginning inside him. "But—and we all do miss him," he said blandly.

Martha stepped back, staring at Matthew. "You're wrong," she whispered. "He was."

"Martha." The young male voice was gentle but the inflection unmistakably hinted of command.

Matthew had surmised she was not alone. Not this time of night. He recognized Billy French and Andrew Perryman but not the girl with them, all three standing at the end of the aisle. Martha stepped back from Matthew, drying her eyes with the back of her hand. She sniffed in her emotions. "It was nice seeing you, Reverend," she said quietly enough that her companions could not hear. "Take care." She walked up the aisle to her friends.

All the events of the last few weeks traveled through his mind as he stood as still as a statue, staring at the shelf of aluminum foil but seeing only what his mind's eye wanted him to see.

"Sir, did you find the liners?"

He looked up at the young clerk. "What?"

The slender twenty-something-year-old had only a few whiskers which he proudly displayed on his chin. "Here they are." He pointed.

Matthew followed his finger. The young man distinguished between the shapes and sizes of the slow cooker. Matthew continued to stare at the shelf.

"Sir, are you okay?"

"What? Yes. Sorry." He choose one of the boxes. "Thank you."

At the checkout counter someone other than Twila gave him the same speech about the advantages of having a SSC card, but he heard nothing of what she said.

As he drove home Martha's words echoed relentlessly in his mind. What did she know? She was a girl in high school for crying out loud. What kind of credibility could she possibly have? Just then Miriam's words broke into his mind—her words and the voicemail. No. He slammed his hand on the steering wheel. It wasn't the truth. They were wrong. All of them were wrong.

When he got home he put the roast in the refrigerator and left the other things on the counter. He wasn't going to let this or anything spoil his plan to cook his roast. He turned out the light. He needed to get to bed.

He climbed the stairs and went down the hallway. When he got to Nathaniel's room, he refused to even look at the door just as he had every other time he passed it. He blocked it out. As if it weren't there. But tonight Martha Davies made it real. Too real.

He went into his own bedroom and undressed. Emptying his pockets he took out his cell phone. He checked the battery. It didn't need charging. He stared at it. *You're wrong.* He turned it off and put it on the nightstand. He would not let this keep him awake. He wouldn't. He would control his mind enough not to let this hamper his sleeping.

CHAPTER TWENTY-ONE

SATURDAY—JUNE 13

Matthew spread the plastic liner into the bottom of the oval shaped slow cooker and pulled the top edges over its rim. He put the raw roast in the center and poured the soup mixture over it, then shifted the beef back and forth to be sure the thick liquid was underneath the meat. It seemed so simple to be so good. And nothing to clean up. He put the glass lid on and moved it to the center of the counter away from the back wall and overhead cabinets. Not too close to anything for safety reasons. He set the timer and immediately peered through the glass cover, half expecting something to be happening. The ringing of the phone startled him. He hoped it wasn't Stephanie Langdon. He picked up the handset and looked at the caller ID.

"Miriam?" he said anxiously, putting it to his ear.

"No, Matthew. This is Carolyn."

"Is something wrong with Miriam or Sarah Elizabeth?"

"No, nothing like that. This isn't an emergency," Carolyn said calmly.

"Oh, it's just that I wasn't expecting— So they're both all right?"

"Yes, please don't worry," she reassured, again. "Sorry to alarm you. I am calling for Miriam. There are some things, personal things—clothing, some toiletries, pictures, small items—she's asked me and Jim to come and pick up for her. And a few things of Sarah Elizabeth's, too. At your convenience, of course."

The request stung him. Further evidence that Miriam was not only gone, but the likelihood that she might come back had grown even more remote. What was he to say? No, she could never step foot in this house again? Everything that she left she was no longer entitled to? He didn't know why, but he knew he couldn't say either of those. Maybe it was about practicality.

"Yes, I wouldn't— That would be okay. Wouldn't it be better if she came herself? Or with you?"

"No, she'd rather not."

Matthew closed his eyes and felt the impact of the words. First seeing Martha last night, now this. Would the hurt ever end?

"When would you like to come?"

"Would this afternoon be a convenient time, say between two and three?"

Silently, he sighed. "Closer to three would be better," he said reluctantly. "I'll be out until about that time."

"Okay. That will work for us. We'll see you then. Thank you."

Even though she sounded pleasant enough, there was no mistaking her business-like tone. Knowing Carolyn as he did, she was probably looking forward to taking his wife and daughter's possessions out of the house right under his nose. But what would he do with any of their personal items? They might as well have them. Still, keeping them, letting them stay here in the house—it gave him hope. Hope that she would want to come back, try to mend their relationship. He heaved a deep sigh and exhaled. Why did he have to go to EOM today? Saturday.

He looked at the clock on the stove. Nine-thirty. He was glad he'd already made the bed and that he had cleaned the downstairs yesterday. He wondered what Carolyn would think about that. He didn't care. Let her come in and do whatever she had to do and go back to Raleigh.

With one final worrisome check on the slow cooker, he left.

All during his drive to the shelter he thought about the impending appointment. Too, he wondered if somehow Miriam had learned about him losing the church—the almighty, sanctimonious church, as she had referred to it that last night he saw her. And his arrest. Had she found out about that? Had the people investigating the rumors on behalf of the Coalition actually talked to her? Approached her?

After the serving line at the ministry closed and he was offering the left over food to the last ones there, he approached the veteran who was alone as always and gave him two extra hamburgers with buns.

"What will you do tomorrow for food for Sadie?" he asked quietly.

"The servers on the weekends give out the extra food same as you," the veteran said. "Appreciate all you do for us. I mean, everybody here." He gestured with his head toward the entire room. "Specially for Sadie."

Matthew nodded. He wanted to say more, but he was at a loss as to what he should or could say. He gave a quick half-smile and returned to the kitchen.

Rushing home after finishing his work, he wanted to at least get the blinds and drapes open. He didn't want Carolyn and Jim to think he was walling himself off, even though he was.

He turned down his street and reached up for the garage door button. However, before he arrived he saw their van parked in front of the house. He glanced at the clock on the dashboard. Two-fifteen. They were early. Very early. He turned into the driveway and into the garage but didn't close the door behind him. He saw that the grass had been cut and the yard edged. Maybe they would think he'd done it himself. He got out, pressed the button inside the garage door and stood outside as it closed. Carolyn and Jim walked up the driveway carrying several empty boxes and two suitcases.

"Hello, Matthew," Jim said pleasantly. He wore a five o'clock heavy shadow of a salt and pepper beard. His avid play of golf and tennis kept him trim. They both wore shorts and sandals. Carolyn's blond hair, like Miriam's, was touched up but still appeared natural.

"Hello," he responded cordially but not offering his hand to his brother-in-law. "Jim. Carolyn."

"Matthew." Carolyn's voice sounded colder, but that held no surprise.

"Well, let's go inside."

He led the way to the front door all the while wishing he could have at least arrived before they had. When he opened the door, the aroma of the roast had permeated the entire house and caught him off guard for a moment. As he stood back from the door to let them in, he could see that Carolyn was taken by surprise as well.

"You're cooking," she said evenly, trying to hide her shock and not convey a compliment.

"A roast in the slow cooker," he answered, closing the door. "I hope you weren't planning on taking it." He gave a very weak smile, more to be polite than humorous.

"No, there's nothing on the list from the kitchen," Carolyn said, choosing politeness over any minimal humor.

He moved toward the living room and began opening the drapes. "I had to leave in a hurry this morning. I didn't have time to open up." When he finished, he returned to the foyer. He stood awkwardly for a moment, the emptiness colliding with itself inside him. He looked at Carolyn. "How are they—Miriam and Sarah Elizabeth?" The somberness in his voice stunned him.

Carolyn gave a smile which disappeared instantly. "They're fine."

Matthew nodded. "Please tell them I asked about them." He saw Carolyn eyeing him. Maybe she wasn't expecting him to ask.

"I will." There was a whisper of genuineness in her voice.

He sighed slightly and nodded as he felt an awkwardness growing. "Where would you like to start?"

"Most of the things are in the bedroom," Carolyn said. "Hers and Sarah Elizabeth's."

"Do you know which of the bedrooms is which?" he asked.

"I'm not really sure."

He turned to the stairs and led them to the second story. As he walked down the hall he opened a door. "This is Sarah Elizabeth's room." He went inside and quickly opened the blinds. Returning to the hall he went toward the open door at the far end. "And this is—" What was he to say? Our bedroom. Miriam's bedroom. It was neither. "This is the master." He also walked to the windows to open the blinds, then went back to the door and stopped. He didn't want to ask because he feared the answer, but he had to know. "Do you need anything—" He would have to say it. He bolstered courage from somewhere within him. "Do you need anything from Nathaniel's room?" His insides cringed as he waited for the answer. Please say no, he thought. Please.

"There's nothing on the list," Carolyn said.

He thought he heard a sympathetic tone. Matthew wasn't certain he had hidden his relief. He exhaled and nodded. "I'll be downstairs if you have any questions or need anything."

"We'd like for you to stay with us," Jim said, first looking at Carolyn, then back to him.

Matthew hesitated, considering. "I don't really feel the need to be present. Thank you though for offering."

Again, he thought he saw an odd look appear on Carolyn's face before he left the room. He supposed she expected him not to trust her. That probably would confuse Carolyn, now that he thought about it. It wasn't about trust. Not with this. Watching them pick up items from the room and put them in suitcases and boxes would be too— He couldn't watch that happening right in front of his eyes—robbing him of any hope and at the same time confirming the truth he didn't want to face.

Downstairs he opened the blinds in the den and the drapes in his study and dining room. When he went into the kitchen the aroma of the roast was twice as strong. He peered through the steam-coated glass cover. Small bubbles rose to the surface of the gravy ever so often. Evangeline had told him to freeze what he wouldn't eat right away, so none of it would go bad and he wouldn't have to eat roast every night for a week.

He sat down at the table and tried to skim over the newspaper but nothing he read registered. Clearly his mind was upstairs. Even though he wasn't with them, he still wondered what Carolyn and Jim were thinking about him—how he was coping with living by himself. He often wondered about that himself. He realized he was not putting on a front for them. He had already started the roast when Carolyn called. And he'd already cleaned the house. He was coping. Somehow. Everyday he was getting by reasonably well. Still the emptiness was always lurking inside his mind, ready to seize his soul. Threatening—always threatening, and more and more often. Even now he had to shove it back. No, he would not—could not deal with that now. He got up and took a can of soda from the refrigerator. Maybe he should offer them something to drink. He thought again. No. Too familiar. Given all that had happened, he had to maintain a certain distance. Respectful but distant. He put some ice in a glass and popped open the can. Waiting for the fizz to settle, he heard Carolyn and Jim moving around upstairs. It sounded as if they were Sarah Elizabeth's room now. He really didn't care what they took, but he didn't want them to go into— Into the other bedroom. Not without him there. He began to listen more intently to try to discern where they were.

He couldn't decide if this was only a means to find out what he was doing. Had Miriam really forgotten to take certain items? And Sarah Elizabeth, too? But would she be interested in snooping around to find out how his life was going? Now? He was still glad he had done the cleaning yesterday. He doubted that Carolyn or Miriam would believe he had done it himself. They'd probably think he had hired someone, maybe a maid service. Not to mention cooking a roast that makes the house smell delicious. He took a sip of soda. But he knew deep down this wasn't some underhanded trick to spy on him. Not Miriam. She was beyond that.

Suddenly, it struck him that the neighbors would see Carolyn and Jim carrying out all the boxes and filled up suitcases. In broad open daylight. He stood up and paced to the counter and back, again. They had probably seen Miriam doing that several weeks ago when she left. Might as well film it and show it on the news, he thought sarcastically. But everyone in the neighborhood and the church already knew by now. Still, this felt like another slap in the face. He stopped cold. That night and the whole right side of his head stinging after Miriam had hit him. He reached up and touched the side of his face. So humiliating. He sat down, his elbows on the table, his face buried in his open hands. When was this ever going to end? How—

"Matthew?"

Even though Carolyn had spoken softly, he jerked his head up and stood, tipping the chair over, causing a clamoring on the ceramic tile floor. "Yes. I didn't hear you come downstairs."

"I'm sorry. I didn't mean to startle you," she said, still standing in the doorway.

He righted the chair. "No, uh, it's fine. I was just having something to drink. A soda. Can I offer you all something?" he asked before thinking not to say this. He picked up the can as an example.

"No, no thank you. I just came to tell you we have everything except a picture. Miriam said it's in the den."

"Picture?" He put the soda can on the table and led the way out the other kitchen door to the den. "Which one?"

Carolyn looked at the list, then up at the pictures. "I think it must be this one." She walked toward the mantle and pointed.

He stared at it. A picture of Nathaniel and Sarah Elizabeth. His children. Their children. Of all their family photos it was the most recent. Taken just three months ago. There were others, but they were a year old. Sensing that Carolyn was staring at him, he walked over and gently lifted it off the wall. He held it for only a moment, looking at it, willing the sickening feeling inside him to stop tormenting him. He extended it to Carolyn.

For a moment she didn't take it. She looked down at it, then up at him. She seemed to be studying him. "She said if you'd rather keep this one, she has others."

He forced a weak smile and nodded. "Thank you. It's so recent. I can call the photographer the church hired and see if I can get a copy. If I can, I'll—"

"That's fine. Very fair." She smiled, warmly, he thought. More so than he ever remembered.

She turned and walked to the foyer with him following her. The suitcases were by the door, along with the boxes filled but not brimming with somewhat larger items—a blanket, shoes, a desk lamp, Sarah Elizabeth's stuffed animals.

Jim took out the suitcases. Carolyn followed with one of the boxes. Matthew supposed he should offer to help but couldn't bring himself to express it. He watched from the window in the living room and saw Eloise Gardner walking by with her dog just as Carolyn and Jim got to the car. She stopped to speak to them. Matthew crossed his arms over his chest. Please don't come up to the door, he thought. I don't want to talk to you. Thankfully, Carolyn didn't allow the conversation to drag on. She and Jim both came up the driveway for the second and final load while Eloise continued down the street.

Carolyn sighed heavily. "Well, I guess this will do it. Thank you, Matthew. I hope we didn't inconvenience you." Again, she sounded genuine.

He shook his head. "Not at all." He hesitated. He looked down for a moment, then up at Carolyn. "Are they doing all right?" His voice was soft, sincere.

She nodded, hesitating for only a moment. "I think Sarah Elizabeth was really hurt when the boy here that she liked wouldn't respond to her calls and messages. But she's made some new friends, all of whom are very understanding of what's happened. She has a new interest—a boy. He's a great kid. Very considerate. We've known the family for years. They seem to really like each other. She still has a lot of sadness, but she's getting stronger."

Matthew hesitated again, an even longer pause. "And Miriam?"

"It's been very difficult. Lots of tears, but she's taking one day at a time." She nodded. "But she'll get there. Eventually."

He looked at the last two boxes, then met her eyes. "Please be sure to tell them I asked about them."

"I will. For sure."

They picked up the boxes and left. Matthew closed the door as Eloise Gardner was passing by, again, this time returning home.

He meandered to the stairs and sat down as he had the night he came home after being arrested. Please tell them— Please tell them— Tell them what? He leaned forward, resting his elbows on his knees, and put in his hands over his face. He couldn't let this get to him, pull him down. He had to stay on top of it all, no matter how much Kate wanted him to figure out what he was feeling. Feeling. He shook his head. He just wanted all the—the pressure to go away. And the ugliness, too. Having to think about himself. Answering questions about—about life. His past. Feelings. And dreams. He slid his hands up on top of his head and pressed hard, as if he was trying to hold everything together.

CHAPTER TWENTY-TWO

MONDAY & TUESDAY— JUNE 15 & 16

"I cooked a roast in the slow cooker," Matthew told Kate on Monday afternoon in answer to her usual question about his weekend. "On Saturday morning my sister-in-law called and asked if she and her husband could come by and pick up some things for my wife," he added with an edge of sarcasm.

"How long has your wife been gone?"

Matthew did not have to think. "Three weeks tomorrow."

"And no communication between the two of you?"

He shook his head. "After she left I had thought I would give her some time to grieve, hopefully become less angry. A week or so. Then the mess at the church— And everything fell apart. I suppose I could email or call, but since she sent her sister to get her things— I don't know now."

"Would it hurt to try?"

"I suppose not," he said but without hope.

"Do you have a good relationship with your sister-in-law and her husband?"

He smirked. "Not really, but this time went okay. There was expected awkwardness." He crossed his leg and jiggled his foot. "I didn't like that the whole neighborhood could see them carrying out things—like a big sign saying 'Matthew Winslow's wife left him.'" He stared at the footstool next to the chair.

"Aside from what the neighbors might think, what else went through your mind while this was going on?"

"You mean, how did it make me feel?" he said, proud that he had caught her.

Kate did not react. "How *did* it make you feel?"

He took a deep breath. "Like the chances that this—what? Separation?—might end and my wife and daughter would come back were less likely."

"And?"

He looked at her, then away. What could he say to satisfy her? "Sick to my stomach." He thought for a moment. "Loss of hope." She was watching him. He looked back at her. "I'll work on it," he said, hoping to sound sincere.

Kate nodded. "Okay. So, did they take furniture?"

"No, clothes, shoes. Some of Sarah Elizabeth's stuffed animals."

"Sarah Elizabeth is your daughter?" Kate asked. Matthew nodded. "Wonderful southern double name."

"It's Biblical," he responded with automatic authority. "Sarah was Abraham's wife. Isaac was her son. My wife wanted 'Elizabeth' after her grandmother. But it's also Biblical. Everyone in our family has a Biblical name."

Kate gave a single nod but nothing more. "How old is Sarah Elizabeth?"

"Fifteen."

"That's the first time you've mentioned her. Tell me about her."

Matthew continued eyeing the ottoman and shaking his foot as he talked. "Smart, I suppose. I would like for her to make A's, but she's more of a solid B student. She's her mother's daughter which is the way it should be. That's what we—the church—promote."

"That's how your church regards women?" Kate asked.

Matthew did not have to think. "Yes. It's not different when they're young. That is, we start instilling in them the woman's role in the family very early." He paused. "You're probably opposed to that."

Kate did not react.

"I don't think her brother agreed with it. I don't think he ever treated her— She's very—" He stopped, closed his eyes, opened them and began again. "I always got the feeling that they were very close."

"Big brother looking out for younger sister and younger sister looking up to older brother?"

"I suppose that would be one way of putting it."

"What was your son's name?" Her tone was compassionate.

Matthew instantly looked down. He uncrossed his legs but kept the one in perpetual motion. For a several moments he said nothing as he stared down.

Kate leaned forward. "I don't think you've ever told me."

He could do this. He could hold back that horrible dark emptiness. "Nathaniel."

"Would you tell me about him?"

Matthew drew in a long inaudible breath and let it out. He knew that eventually she would do this. She would bring up Nathaniel and that whole— The entire mess.

"An athlete and scholar. He played several sports but liked baseball the most. Wildly popular with his peers. Good-looking, all American, boy-next-door type. Straight A's since the first grade. The only person in the history of Holy Bible Academy to win the Bible Scholar Competition for his grade level every year. He is a—" He stopped. "He *was* a phenomenal young man with a full scholarship—four years—to Freedom Bible University. Poised to become a minister and eventually take over as the head of my church after I retired. His grandfather idolized him."

He stopped talking. He had said enough, but he knew she would have questions. She wasn't done.

"Were the two of you close?"

"Of course, we were. He was my son," he said, not hiding his indignation.

"What things did you do together?"

He looked down. "Bible study. I heard his recitations every week since he was in the first grade. I went to every one of his baseball games at school. Whenever he did anything, I was there."

"That's wonderful that you showed so much support. But did you do anything together—just the two of you?"

Matthew jiggled his leg, then crossed it, jiggling his foot. "I had dinner with my family every night. It was our time." His anger was growing. She was cornering him again. "Family time was for the whole family."

"I know you said you didn't play sports, but did you and Nathaniel go to football or baseball games together?"

He wanted to scream but instead only shook his head.

Kate was silent for a moment. "I'm sure this is difficult to talk about, but I want you to try."

Matthew uncrossed his leg as if preparing for the challenge while hiding his irritation. "I think he was probably closer to his mother, especially when he was younger. As he got older it was necessary to take on a more adult role. As a man. That's my church's stance." He eyed her directly. "To cut the apron strings." When Kate didn't respond, he began fidgeting again. "And about him being gay like the police said— I don't believe it. I won't believe it. I'd have to hear him say that." He gritted his teeth. "And since that's not possible, then I'm not believing it. I will never believe it." He was going to stand his ground on this. "I don't care what the sheriff's detectives said or my wife, for that matter. And I certainly don't trust that boy from school or Nathaniel's girlfriend. He had a girlfriend, even though I don't trust her," he said emphatically. "How could he be a homosexual if he had a girlfriend?" Martha's words bored in his mind as he spoke.

"What do you mean you don't trust her?"

He looked at her, angry with himself as he realized what he'd just said. It didn't matter. He was not going to give in. "I saw her at the grocery store last Friday. She said something about missing him even though he was gay. But it's not true." He looked down at the armrest. "It's not."

Kate's voice did not threaten him. "It sounds like you're the only one who thinks that. What are the police and your wife basing this on?"

Matthew closed his eyes for a moment. He had known this was going to happen. That he would have to tell her. But that didn't mean he had to listen to it. No matter what she said. "There was— He— Nathaniel left a voicemail." He folded his arms across his chest. "For me. On my cell phone. That night— When he— When he died. The police took my phone the next day and listened to it. My wife went down there and listened to it the day after the funeral."

Kate said nothing for a moment. "And what did you think when you listened to it?"

He pulled his arms in closer to himself and did not look at her. He crossed his legs, his foot nervously shaking. "I haven't— I haven't listened to it."

Kate sat stock-still as silence filled the room. "Have you deleted it?"

He stared down. "No."

Kate sat silently. "If you haven't deleted it," she said, "are you planning to listen to it at some point?"

Matthew said nothing but stared at nothing across the room. When he didn't respond, Kate posed another question that was scarcely above a whisper.

"Would you like to listen to it now?"

For several minutes Matthew remained quiet. No thoughts raced through his mind. Then, he sensed an odd feeling. A mixture of fear but with a whispered twinge of courage. At the same moment a struggle began within him. A familiar sense told him not to reach into his pocket for his cell phone. Another impulse—a foreign but gentle yet strong force—urged him to trust. To trust that he was safe.

He shook his head. "No," he said. "I don't want to do that." He wanted to wait. He didn't know why. He looked across the room. "Not now."

"Okay. That's fine," she said soothingly. "Just know that when you do, I'm here to help you."

Matthew simply nodded as the image of the shoebox in his closet came into focus.

On Tuesday Matthew took off his lanyard ID and walked toward the staff parking lot behind EOM. Lunch had been chicken salad sandwiches, green beans and potatoes. This was his second week and he had learned the basic routine. Evangeline didn't have to tell him as much what to do everyday. He wouldn't admit it to anyone, including Kate, but the work was going well. It wasn't that he enjoyed it, but it had become routine. And he was recognizing some of the people and even knew who liked what and who wanted seconds when he passed them out afterwards.

Walking to his car, he realized how hot the day had become. He wondered how these people were able to survive in this scorching, unmerciful heat. Being out in the cold in the winter was probably worse. Again, he noted to himself his good fortune.

As he slowly drove toward the parking lot exit, he heard a dull flapping sound, he thought, from the front of the car. Please, not a flat. But then he noticed that the front right of the car seemed lower than the left. He stopped, got out and went around. When he saw the pancaked bottom of the tire, he let out a sigh of disgust. He put his hands on his hips. Too low to try to drive somewhere to get it fixed. He would have to call the garage and have them come out and fix it or have it towed. Exasperated, he started back to get in the car where it was cool. Had he run over some trash? A board with a nail in it? Whatever the cause, it didn't matter. A flat was a flat and a real inconvenience.

"Trouble?"

He turned around toward the exit gate and saw the veteran with Sadie obediently beside him. The dog was favoring her right front paw. "Flat tire." He motioned toward the other side.

"Got a jack and tire tool?"

"I'm just going to call someone."

"No need to do that." He approached and looked at the tire. "Glad to change it for you. Won't take a minute. Probably be more than a half hour before anybody can get here." His voice was gently unassuming. "Besides, it's the least I can do for the extra food for Sadie." He looked down at the dog who had found a small spot of shade just off the curb and lay down, her tongue alternating between licking her front paw and simply hanging out as she panted heavily.

The veteran didn't appear strong enough to change a tire. "I couldn't ask you to do that."

The man half smiled. "You didn't ask. I offered." He set down his large backpack beside Sadie and started toward the rear of the car. As he walked, he removed his floppy hat and combed his fingers through his greasy, long, gray strands of hair.

Matthew hesitated. Was this safe? After all, the parking lot had a chain-link fence around it for a reason. And sometimes jobless hoodlums hung out at nearby empty buildings. He didn't know if this man had a record. More importantly, he didn't want to feel obligated in the future. He had some cash he could pay him. He reached in and turned off the ignition and at the same time popped open the trunk.

"I think it's in here," he said, lifting a side panel.

The veteran lifted out the spare and rolled it to the front of the Lexus, carrying the jack and tire tool, and began jacking the car up. Matthew stood back a few steps over near Sadie. He looked down at the dog who was looking up at him, her ears half-pricked, her tail wagging intermittently in the grass. Immediately, memories of his mother and her fondness for dogs surfaced. She appeared to be more lab than anything, except for her small size.

"Does Sadie like people?" he asked.

"Oh, yeah." He looked over his shoulder as he loosened the lugs. "She's good with people. Just put out your hand and let her smell it before you pet her."

Matthew hesitated, but even with her seeming affable nature he held back. She had to be filthy. How could she get a bath living this way? Slowly, she made a crawling motion, mere inches, toward him. Torn between ignoring her and giving in to the obvious invitation, he leaned over and put out his hand. Sadie craned her neck upward to the extended hand, her nostrils minutely flaring as she registered his scent. After a moment Matthew eased his hand slowly closer. Her quiet, soothing whimper lured him. He had the hand sanitizing gel in his car, he reasoned. With that assurance he fully lowered himself to a stooped position and scratched her behind the ears.

"She's been kinda quiet last day or so. Not too hungry. I think it might be the heat."

"How long has she been limping?" he asked.

The veteran turned. "Since yesterday. Piece of glass somehow got in the bottom of her paw. Cut it. Bled a lot. She keeps licking it."

As he continued to scratch her, Sadie occasionally licked his hand and wagged her tail, a good sign.

"How long have you had her?"

The veteran lifted the flat off and replaced it with the spare. "About five months. I think somebody hurt her. Her hind leg was really sore. She was limping then, too. She had chewed through the rope that was around her neck and was hobbling some when I found her or she found me. Not sure which. Couldn't stand thinking somebody might be hurting her."

"She seems pretty loyal."

"Yeah, she's my family." Sadie looked up at Matthew and reached out with her left paw as he continued to scratch her.

"Do they let you bring her into the shelter at night?"

"No," he said simply.

"What does she do? Wait for you until you come out the next morning?"

He tightened the lugs on the tire. "I don't stay in the shelter. Not since I found her."

Matthew was incredulous. "Where do you sleep?"

"Mostly I camp out in the woods. Sometimes under a bridge. Like to move around."

"What did you do before? I mean, in the way of work? After the army and the war?"

"Taught school before I went in. Nam made a mess of me. Too many nightmares about killing people. Drugs to get rid of the nightmares. In and out of rehab. Never could get rid of the war in my head. Lost my ambition. Lost any purpose. Pretty much lost everything." He stood up and gave the lugs a final tightening. "Including my family. They wrote me off because they couldn't abide a dirty, lazy, lowdown bum. Strict, narrow-minded folks. Go to a big church, call themselves Christians, but you have to wonder," he shook his head, "if you don't see God their way, believe what they believe, you're a heathen. Didn't have it in me to give in to them." He jacked the car down. "That's the great thing about Sadie. She doesn't judge me. Do you, girl?" Sadie looked at him, gave a slight bark, then licked her right paw, again. "Dogs could teach the world how to love unconditionally. Especially Sadie. She's a lot better at it than my family or the church, if you ask me."

Matthew stopped scratching Sadie as the veteran's words about loving unconditionally slammed into him.

"Okay. All done. Here's your problem." He rolled the old tire over, pointing to a nail. Matthew leaned over to examine it. "They can plug it at a tire store and you can use it as a spare or ask them to switch it out for you." He picked up the jack and tire tool and wheeled the tire to the trunk and with some difficulty hoisted it all in, then closed the lid.

"I'm going to pay you," Matthew said, reaching for his billfold.

"No, no," the man said, holding up his hands and backing away.

Matthew thought for a moment. Why was he doing this? "Will you wait here fifteen or twenty minutes while I go get something from a drugstore for Sadie's paw? Just some alcohol or something to keep it from getting infected."

The man looked down at Sadie who was sitting up now, first panting, then licking her paw. He went over to her and stooped down, rubbing her head as she tried to lick his hand. "I think she'll be okay," he said, unable to meet Matthew's eyes.

Matthew shook his head. This was so awkward. It was probably that he had no money. He moved toward the driver's side of his car. "I'll be right back." He got in his car and turned on the air conditioning.

Driving down Eden Street he used some Purell and at the same time realized how involved he was getting with this man. Giving him extra food for his dog, talking to him even. Why was he getting so wrapped up in this one individual? Especially a homeless person. He hoped he hadn't started something that was going to cause a problem at the shelter, especially other homeless people asking him for favors. What would Roger Gooden say if he knew he was doing this? He might even have seen him changing the tire if he'd been looking out his office window. He already had enough to worry about. Why was he giving his time to this man? But then the two words echoed in his mind—unconditional love.

He saw a Walgreens store and pulled in. Not likely to see anyone from church in this neighborhood. When he found the alcohol, he also saw Peroxide and remembered how his mother had put than on cuts when he was a child—keep it from getting infected, she always said. But which one? He picked up both and some cotton. On his way to pay he saw a small plastic bowl and added it to his purchases. At a small grocery store across the street, he bought several single-serving cans of dog food with pull-top lids and four bottles of water. He wanted to put a twenty dollar bill into the bag, but knew he shouldn't. He might waste it on drugs—probably the reason he wore a long sleeve shirt. To hide the needle marks.

When he drove into the parking lot at EOM, the veteran was sitting on the ground in the shade, scratching Sadie's chest.

He parked his car and took out his supplies. "Let's try one of these," he said, showing the man the Peroxide and the alcohol. "Maybe do the Peroxide first, then wash it off with the alcohol." He was nodding agreement as Matthew showed him the bottles.

"Okay. She's probably not going to like this, so I better hold her," the veteran said, "just in case she might try to bite."

While the veteran held Sadie on his lap and her injured paw extended, Matthew poured a small amount on her foot. She whined and struggled to free herself, but when she saw that there was no pain, she settled down. Next he poured on some alcohol to wash away the foamy Peroxide. Sadie barked and wiggled, then finally settled down with whimpers and whines. He handed some cotton to the veteran to dry it off. Sadie sniffed her paw.

"Do this maybe twice a day and see how she does," he said, scratching Sadie's chest. He handed him the bag with the dog food and water without explanation and stood up.

The veteran put Sadie on the grass, stood up and looked inside the bag. He nodded his head. "Thank you," he said. "You're a good man." He nodded. "Decent. My idea of a real Christian."

The two words stunned Matthew, but he quickly hid any hint of a reaction. "Thank you, again," he said simply, "for changing my tire." He almost put out his hand to shake, but then thought better of it and awkwardly waved.

The homeless man tipped his floppy hat.

As he drove away, he balanced his driving with another application of Purell. The man's story replayed itself in his mind—his college background, teaching, his family, killing in Vietnam, drugs. And how he had referred to him—good and decent, a true Christian. But more important was another voice—Miriam's. She had described Nathaniel the night she walked out using the same two words—*good and decent.*

CHAPTER TWENTY-THREE

WEDNESDAY & THURSDAY— JUNE 17 & 18

On Wednesday as he drove to EOM, Matthew began preparing himself for being around Ben Thornton. He had not forgotten the minister's expression of sympathy. The gesture was nice, kind even. But that was all it was. A gesture. That claim about seeing the face of Jesus in the homeless people—was he sincere or just being a preacher, trying to impress Evangeline? He had seen him interacting with some of the people last week out in the eating area. He acted so normal with them, earnest, and they all did seem to respond, some of them smiling. It didn't matter. Why would he ever want to associate with Thornton? His beliefs were too progressive, to the point of— He wasn't sure what to call it. He was just different. Radical even. And his jeans. So unprofessional. And his so-called charm. No. It would be best to be pleasant but avoid anything more.

When Thornton arrived, Matthew kept to his plan, did his job and stayed focused. When they were done with all the serving, Crystal and Frannie began setting up for the five of them to eat in the kitchen. He waited until Ben sat down, then filled his plate and sat at the opposite end of the table and ate quietly. He wished he could disappear into the wall and not be noticed.

"How's Pauline doing?" Ben asked Crystal. Matthew wondered who Pauline was.

"Getting worse," Crystal said, looking down at her stew and biscuit. "Had to go home last week and help find her when she got out. More and more now she forgets our names. I call her 'Mama' and she looks at me like I'm a stranger. Forgets where she is. Forgets her way around the house. She puts things in places and we can't find them. Put her toothbrush in the mailbox. She's getting to where she's soiling herself some. Not everyday but at least once a week." She shook her head. "Don't know what I'm going to do. My husband thinks she'd be better off in a place where they look after folks with Alzheimer's. But I just don't know if I can do that."

Ben stopped eating, put down his fork and devoted all of his attention to her. "How's the rest of your family doing with this?" he asked gently.

Crystal sighed deeply as her eyes began brimming with tears. "We don't have much of a home life because we're always having to watch out for her. Can't get anybody to sit with her so we can go to a ball game even. My daughter resents having to stay there all the time when I'm at work. We're fighting way too much."

As Crystal talked, Matthew noticed Ben Thornton's complete concern for the middle-aged African-American woman sitting across the table from him. He never took his eyes from her, not even to eat. A nod of his head, furrowing of his brow, a slight shake of his head. Then he talked about the feelings of abandonment and guilt he had gone through when he had to put his father in an assisted living facility. "It's hard to keep your faith when you're going through something like this." As he gently laid his hand out on the table toward her, Matthew sensed his caring.

"I try to remember to pray," Crystal said with exasperation. "But I don't know." She picked up her napkin.

"Praying helps, but we all forget about that. I don't pray enough myself, not that I don't believe. Life just gets in the way." Ben paused. "I think if there's one thing God doesn't know how to do, it's abandon us. It's just not how His love works. Whether we pray or not."

Evangeline said nothing but put her arm around her friend.

Crystal wiped away a tear. "Thank all y'all for listening to me go on. Lord have mercy, I didn't mean to get so carried away."

Frannie reached over and patted her shoulder. "It's what we do for each other. You know that. Remember how y'all listened to me lay my burdens out last month about my brother, don't ya?" She picked up her glass of tea. "Well, today's your turn."

While Matthew finished his lunch, he said nothing about his own mother's illness and being in a facility. Maybe some day he'd tell them about her, but not about her always swearing at him. He didn't want anyone to know about that. But he knew how Crystal felt, and Thornton, too. Putting your parent in a place—lost and alone in their emptiness. He remembered Kate's word—empathy. Was that what this was?

As he went about his daily cleanup, he could not rid Ben Thornton's words from his mind, and especially his total concentration on Crystal and her problems with her mother, letting her reveal as much as she felt comfortable. But most of all, he treated her as if she were the only other person in the world at that moment.

As he was wiping off the bolted tables and seats, Matthew noticed that Ben had come out of the kitchen with a push broom and begun sweeping the floor. He wanted to tell him to stop. It was his job. He didn't need help. Besides, *he* had a church and congregation to go take care of. He sprayed the top of a table and began swabbing it more vigorously than necessary, then rubbed a spot of dried ketchup from the edge of a seat. Shouldn't he be taking care of his own business? Don't say anything, he told himself. Just keep on cleaning the tables. Mind your own business. But in only a few minutes the Wednesday volunteer had made his way to the same area.

For Matthew the silence felt awkward, uncomfortable. This—This person. This minister with his know-it-all attitude about God. A minister who admitted he didn't pray enough. He was in his space. He was doing his job. Without anybody asking him to. Suddenly, he turned and looked directly at Ben as words shot out of his mouth.

"What you said in the kitchen to Crystal," he blurted. "About God never abandoning us. Even when we sin, I mean, when a person sins? What makes you think—" He stopped, caught himself. "Why do you think that?" He felt his face getting warm, probably red. Where was this coming from? What had made him do this? All of a sudden he wanted to crawl into a hole.

Unfazed Ben stopped sweeping, rested his hands on the end of the broom stick and spoke calmly. "I think God's love is too great to do otherwise." He thought for a moment. "I believe that God is closest to us when we're alone and afraid, especially," he said, "right before we die and at the moment of death—kind of catching us and taking us home to eternal life. Like a doctor catching a newborn and welcoming it to life. And just like with the newborn, there are no sins. They're all forgiven." He paused for a moment, looked down, then back up at Matthew. "Even those who take their own life."

Matthew felt his words—newborn, welcoming to eternal life, sin, forgiven—felt them swirl around him, trying to break through, but he pushed them away. He had to. Instead, he latched on to the last bit. The personal reference. This man whom he scarcely knew—that he would be so bold to talk about what had happened in a family he didn't know. He wanted to be angry, to pummel him like he did that car. "And what about God accepting homosexuals? Leviticus 18, verse 22: 'You shall not lie with a man as with a woman. It is an abomination,'" he challenged, his voice rising, his tone defiant. "And granting those people eternal life?" He would win this one. He knew what the Bible said.

When Thornton spoke, Matthew heard the same caring he'd heard him express to Crystal. "No difference. We're all God's children and His love is unconditional."

His last word shook Matthew. Unconditional. It was the second time in two days that he'd heard it, and for one second, one miniscule tick of a clock, he also wanted to believe it. Believe this rogue minister. Believe that what Nathaniel had done was not a sin. But then that imaginary, thought-stomping clock ticked to the next second and the trapped feeling engulfed him. He wanted to yell, tell him he was wrong, that *he, Ben Thornton,* maybe he was the sinner.

Just as Matthew drew in a deep breath, Ben's cell phone rang, but he unhooked it from his belt and attempted to turn it off. Matthew was relieved. "Better answer that. It might be important," he said.

"Maybe, but so are you," Ben responded sympathetically but quickly.

"No. Take your call. Please. I've got to finish here and then I have an appointment I have to go to right away," he said simply but with authority, returning to his work and ignoring Ben.

Matthew raced through cleaning the remaining three tables and their seats, all the while quickly putting distance between him and the other minister. Ben was still on the phone when Matthew returned to the kitchen where Evangeline was taking inventory.

"See you tomorrow," he said, not stopping to sign his time sheet nor waiting for her okay.

Driving home and throughout that night his mind was bombarded with Ben's words. *Like welcoming a newborn to eternal life... All sins are forgiven...Even those who take their own life.* As he ate the slow-cooked roast beef, he tasted none of it because bits of their conversation repeatedly stormed through his mind. *At the moment of death, catching us, taking us home to eternal life.* This was Ben Thornton. The polar opposite of what he believed. He would not be taken in by this man. This "so-called" minister. He would not. But even after he went to bed, his words were there. *God is closest to us when we're alone and afraid.*

After tossing and turning, he eventually fell asleep, but the following morning the droning continued. At EOM he did his work but had little to say to Evangeline and the others. They seemed to give him plenty of space. He wondered what Evangeline had thought of him running out so quickly the day before. He didn't care.

By the time he went for his appointment with Kate on Thursday afternoon, he had carefully considered whether or not to tell her about his conversation with her brother-in-law. He didn't want to be trapped and, if it turned to that, he would just stop talking. Somehow. Get up and leave if necessary. As he remembered her offer to help him with the voicemail, something told him that walking out— He wouldn't have to do that.

"And how did you respond," Kate asked.

"We were interrupted. His cell phone rang."

"But have you thought about it?"

Matthew nodded as he shifted nervously in the chair, then crossed his leg and jiggled his foot—all without looking at her.

"By chance did your father and grandfather enter into your thoughts?"

Matthew looked at the armrest as he lightly traced one of the large threads back and forth several inches. "My father would never have approved of me even having a conversation with a man like Ben Thornton. I doubt he would have considered him a minister. I know my grandfather wouldn't have."

"I suppose you never disagreed or contradicted your father or grandfather, but did you ever want to ask if they would consider another point of view?"

He shook his head and almost laughed. "No, never. In my church you're not supposed to question a parent. Ever. It's a commandment."

"Does disagreeing mean dishonoring?"

"Almost the same as blaspheming, especially if you're disagreeing with a minister about something in the Bible."

"So let's get back to Ben's statement. Did you feel like he was putting you on the spot?"

Matthew stared at the armrest, his finger still tracing the thread pattern. He took a deep breath and let it out. "Pretty much," he said, trying to sound convincing but said nothing more.

Kate stared at him for several moments before speaking. Matthew shifted in the chair. "I'm going to pose his question a little differently and directly." She held out her right hand. "On one hand you've got the God your father and grandfather introduced you to—the one who judges, condemns and is authoritarian." She held out her left hand. "And on the other there's the God, let's say that Ben talks about—the one who loves and accepts everyone unconditionally."

Her words pushed and prodded him. He felt the makings of entrapment looming over him and thoughts of running away crept into his mind. But even as his mind was telling him to escape this—this interrogation, this being put on the spot which he hated with all his being—something else was prodding him to listen.

"I wonder," Kate said, "if one of the questions you've come here to answer is 'which God?'"

Matthew uncrossed his legs and sat perfectly still as he stared down at the floor.

"Having to make that choice might be part of the reason you were so angry." Her voice remained calm.

Without lifting his eyes he asked the question that had garnered considerable curiosity since his first session. "That we're never angry for the reason we think we are?"

"Yes," she said with quiet comfort. "Anger, maybe feeling like you've been trapped."

That word—trapped—the very word he'd used so often. "Trapped?" he asked, intrigue evident in his voice. His own voice was soft. "So when I was smashing the trunk of that car, it wasn't about losing the church or—" He stopped. He didn't want to say it. "Or my wife leaving?" And he couldn't—he wouldn't say the rest. "And the other?"

"I think it's a distinct possibility."

Matthew tried to absorb it all. So much. How could he be sure? Could he trust Kate to be telling him the truth?

"Could we talk about your recurring dream with the policeman?"

Matthew looked up at her, both surprised and uncertain. With reluctant curiosity he nodded.

Kate sat back and crossed her legs. "Policemen wear those vests to protect themselves from bullets. But there's no violence connected with your church—no guns and bullets. So why a vest? What makes a vest necessary? If we assume for the moment that the policeman represents your church, what's he protecting himself from?"

Matthew was listening intently. He searched, but nothing occurred to him. He drew in a breath to tell her he had no idea, but at that same time a glimmer of a thought skimmed the edge of his mind. He kneaded it for a moment. No. Too ridiculous. He shook his head.

"What?" Kate asked.

Again, he shook his head. "No, it's nothing." He looked away but continued attempting to give substance to what had come to him. With a tone of uncertainty, he asked, "Beliefs?"

Kate sat forward. "Say more."

"I don't know."

"Beliefs about what?"

Matthew sighed heavily. "I don't—" Suddenly, he stopped as the glimmer became an avalanche of understanding. He turned to Kate, his eyes wide with questions. This couldn't be.

"What?" she asked.

He shook his head. "No, I'm wrong."

Her tone was calm but also reassuringly firm. "Nothing bad is going to happen to you for thinking on your own."

Without realizing it, rather than tracing the fabric on the armrest, Matthew was now pinching it. "Belief that—" He stopped. How could he say it? What if Kate was wrong? What if this wasn't right? None of it? "That God loves— That God doesn't reject— Doesn't reject— That homosexuality isn't a— Isn't a sin."

"Yes," Kate said softly and after a moment added, "Or that divorce is not a sin."

Inside, Matthew steeled himself. He wasn't going to let that emptiness get out. No. Even if she was right, he wasn't going—

"Or taking one's own life," Kate said.

Matthew closed his eyes. He wasn't going to do this. He wasn't. He would think about this later. Deal with it later. He knew Kate was watching him, waiting on him to react. No. Not now. It was too much. Too much to take in. Too much to think about.

"And at the very end of your dream," she asked, "what do you do?"

Matthew opened his eyes and stared at nothing. "I walk away," he said in a whisper. Complete silence reigned over the room, but Matthew could not hear it for the ricocheting of thoughts in his mind. Glimpses of his past—his father and grandfather grilling him with verse after verse, their belittlement, Bible competitions, his sermons—surfacing, one after the other. The only thing outside his head which commanded his attention was Kate's voice—soft, gentle, honest.

"Many, if not most of us, grow up believing what our parents believed. At some point some of us come to realize that their beliefs don't fit for us—for whatever reason. And when we let go of those beliefs we feel like we're disappointing or displeasing our parents, even if they're no longer with us. Some people don't ever let go. It's too hard to change. Too much work. For many it's too much fear."

Matthew continued staring at nothing. When he spoke, he didn't stop to measure his words. "My father made me start writing sermons when I entered the upper school at the Academy. He always told me that my grandfather said a preacher had failed if he didn't put the fear of God in his listeners every Sunday."

Kate slowly nodded. "I don't believe it's healthy to live in fear of anyone, and certainly not a parent. But it's especially not healthy to believe that God wants us to live in fear of Him."

She leaned toward him and spoke sincerely. "I know this is a lot, but as you process this, I want you to keep in mind one passage in the Bible that might give you some peace and comfort. It's where

Jesus says that the Kingdom isn't in churches or other places. It's within."

"Luke 17:21," Matthew said as he closed his eyes and his mind raced back to the Bible Scholar Competition when he was in the ninth grade. The memory punched him hard in the gut. "It's the question that I missed," he told her. "The question that caused my father to shun me for a week." Without even thinking, he added, "That really hurt."

The session with Kate caused memory after memory to flood Matthew's mind. Even as he drove home he continued trying to fit all the pieces of the puzzle together, to bring about order of his mental chaos. Every question that popped into his head resulted in another one charging to the front, begging for attention. His turmoil so consumed him that he forgot about his appointment with Frank at the barbershop.

Instead, he went home and tried to distract himself. He went into the den and turned on the television to hear the news, and although he stared at the screen, nothing on the program registered. *If you can't remember the books in the Holy Bible, you'll never be a minister...Unconditional love...An abomination...Hanging from a tree....*

Mired in his thoughts, he lost all track of time. When he finally realized his surroundings, he saw that the day was about to become night. He reached over and turned on a lamp and clicked off the television with the remote. Maybe he would eat something. Even though he wasn't particularly hungry, he made his way to the kitchen and opened the refrigerator. Maybe a roast beef sandwich, he thought. Anything to distract— *Our marriage has been nothing but a show for your father and the church...We think it would be best for you to take early retirement...You don't want to cross the Coalition....*

He sat at the kitchen table, staring at the sandwich and the coke. After a few bites he resigned himself to the fact that he had no appetite. Maybe later, he told himself as he put the plate in the refrigerator without wrapping it or covering it. *The kingdom is within... Which God?...Living in fear of God...Homosexuality isn't a sin....*

In the den he sat down and picked up the newspaper, but his total lack of attention forced him to put it down. He sat and stared into nothingness as his mind was besieged with whirling thoughts. All time escaped him as he mentally waded through them, achieving nothing. *It's not about memorizing words. It's about what they mean...Divorce isn't a sin...The policeman represents your church; what's he protecting himself from?*

As the evening grew later he knew he would need to sleep, especially since he had not slept so well the night before. He looked down at the couch. Why not just sleep here tonight? he thought. He'd be just as comfortable. But then, something was tugging him to go upstairs. To his own bedroom. Where he belonged.

He turned off the lights and reluctantly started up the stairs. As he went down the hallway, memories of the nightly family prayer circle sprang up. A coldness overtook him, but he tried to ignore it just as he had all the past weeks since Miriam—since Miriam left.

As he forced himself toward the master bedroom, he saw the closed door to Nathaniel's room. He had passed the door dozens of times since that night. Why was he noticing it tonight? This was no special day. Still, it was as if something was blocking him from continuing down the hall, as if something was beckoning him to open the door and go inside. Why should he? What was there to gain? To learn? Nothing. Not one thing, he tried to assure himself. Still, the pull was too great.

Slowly he reached out his hand and took the doorknob. The coolness of the metal surprised him. Should it be that cool? Why was he thinking about that? A distraction? He released it. Maybe he would talk about this with Kate before he did it. What was the hurry? Then without any explanation, as if he was ignoring himself, his hand turned the knob and gently pushed the door open. Light from the hallway pooled across the carpet, making him feel both safe and apprehensive.

Matthew stared through the dimness, remembering the room. Like an inventory he listed mentally what he was seeing—the bed, the bathroom door, the closet, the desk, the books, the— He stopped. He wasn't saying it. He couldn't bring himself to say it. His name. It wasn't *the* bed. It was— He took a breath. "Nathaniel's bed," he whispered. "Nathaniel's closet. Nathaniel's desk. Nathaniel's bathroom. Nathaniel's books," he continued whispering.

He took a step into the room. Then another. His tuxedo still lay neatly on the bed. The closet door stood open. Inside was his graduation gown, the cap on the bookcase. Pictures on the shelf— Martha Davies, Nathaniel and Sarah Elizabeth, Nathaniel in his baseball uniform. Also on a shelf of the bookcase he saw Nathaniel's notebooks of Bible verses. A twinge of angst poured through him as he remembered listening to him recite. Always perfectly. Always. Every week of his young life.

He looked toward his desk—all his awards and plaques from the banquet still there just as he had left them. The standing ovations. That night surged into his mind—so many trophies and accolades, almost more than he could carry. Matthew had been so proud. His son had done it all. He looked at his laptop and next to it some papers. He moved closer and in the gray light could see it. The speech he was to give at graduation, urging his classmates to go out and serve God. More angst seeped into him. Taking several steps he stood next to Nathaniel's bed and on the nightstand, he saw his Bible.

Matthew stood in the empty room and felt his own emptiness. The darkness he had feared so long—now he was at its center. This was where his son lived and slept. This was his part of the house. His private space.

Matthew knew his cell phone was in his left pants pocket. He pressed his hand against the outside and felt the small rectangle. He reached in the pocket and took out the silver phone. He stared at the time and date. He didn't have to do this. It could wait. Like turning the doorknob, the decision didn't seem to be his completely. He saw that he had turned on the phone and was pressing numbers and codes to retrieve messages. One last button to press. One more and he would hear Nathaniel's voice. His last words spoken on earth. And they would be for him. And that was the moment Matthew realized. This was what he never wanted to have to live through. The voicemail. Since the moment the detective had told him Nathaniel had left him a message, he had found excuse after excuse—never did he want to hear it.

He pressed the button and put the phone to his ear.

"One call saved Sunday, May 24, 12:07 a. m." Matthew closed his eyes, knowing he was going to hear Nathaniel's voice. It wasn't too late. He could turn it—"Hey...hello, Dad, this is your...this is Nathaniel..." Matthew closed his eyes. "I have to...I have to commit a sin when I hang up, Dad...because...because I already committed a worse sin last Monday...I couldn't ever be a minister, Dad...there was someone...a guy and we, uh...we did a terrible thing...Dad, I've got this demon...this demon that makes me want to be with...be with other...other guys...and commit...commit just the worst...the worst sin...I'm sorry, Dad...I am, but I don't know what else to do...I can't live like this...I hate...myself...and I know you...you would hate me...for this...everybody...would hate me if they knew...and they should....I know...I know I'm going to hell... it's what I deserve...I've been praying about this every night for the last I don't know how many months, no, years...I don't know...it seems like forever...and it won't go away...I know you're going to be mad and disappointed...but this is the only way...I love you, Dad... Tell Mom and Sarah Elizabeth...tell them I'm sorry...I tried, Dad...I really tried...but tonight...I know now it's real...living inside me...I just can't get that...evil out of me...This is the only way...End of saved messages."

Matthew stood numb. His boy. His son. *Sin...demon...hate...* The words knifed through him, screaming at him, taunting him.

Words he had used in that sermon. Oh, God, no. And it was Nathaniel's voice. *Sin...demon...hate...*

He squeezed his eyes closed, as tightly as he could. But it didn't help. It wasn't outside. It wasn't inside. Had he done this? Was he guilty? Had he killed his own son? Killed him as if he had had been there and put the bungee cord around his neck and pushed him out of the tree? Miriam's accusation punched him in the gut.

Matthew crumbled onto Nathaniel's bed, his arms wrapped across his chest. He rolled onto his side and drew his knees to his stomach. The emptiness—that dark, vast black hole of agony inside him—began erupting. And he was helpless to stop it.

Tears streamed from his eyes. "I did it," he wailed. "Oh, God, I killed him."

As he wept and writhed in his torture, spit spilled from the corner of his mouth along with the endless confession. The confession he had known was his and his alone. He had sinned in the worst possible way. He was responsible for his own son's death. He was the demon. The monster.

He could not battle this. He stood, walked out of the room and down the hall into his bedroom. Tears pouring from his eyes, snot oozing from his nose. He opened his closet door and reached up for the hidden shoebox deep in the back on the top shelf.

CHAPTER TWENTY-FOUR

FRIDAY—JUNE 19

All night Matthew lay on Nathaniel's bed in the fetal position, crying while clutching his cell phone in his left hand next to his chest. He had listened to the voicemail a dozen times throughout the night, tortured by the sound of Nathaniel's voice—his pain, his fear, his shame. As if trying to bring his son back to life, he fought to find something to cling to—that he wasn't dead, that all this was a bad dream. His right hand held his gun, present but detached, a threat but a sure and desperate way out. He cried, wrestling with the torture that consumed him.

The darkness in the room had eventually given way to a dim gray. Now early rays of sunlight sliced through the blinds bringing color and definition to the objects in the room. Through watery eyes he looked at Nathaniel's clock on the nightstand. Seven-twenty. Another whimpering sob uncontrollably escaped as his agony once again gutted him. He felt as if a murderous madman had maliciously carved up his insides, sparing none of him, least of all his soul. And why not? Had he not done the same to his Nathaniel every time he talked about—about homosexuals? Branding him, demeaning him. Oh, God—

His cell phone ringing interrupted him. Without letting go of the gun, he pressed the button with one hand. Desperation filled him.

"Kate?"

"Yes, Matthew. I got your—"

He cut her off. "I have to see you." More tears began streaming from his eyes.

"What's happened?"

He squeezed his eyes closed as he tried to speak. "Voicemail." It was the only word he could get out before he began sobbing again.

"Okay. Can you get to the office by eight?"

He clung to her voice. "Yes."

"I'll see you then. And Matthew? You can and will get through this," she reassured.

He could not respond.

"I'll see you in a little while," she said.

Matthew turned off his phone, holding on to her words. *You can and will get through this.* Could she be right? How? How could he move from this bed? He wanted to spend the rest of his life right there, never having to leave this bed, this room. It was the only way he could survive. He had told her he could get to the office, but now he wasn't sure.

More tears seeped from his eyes. He stared at the gun inches from his face. He could smell the metal, the years of old oil. Like a paralyzed person trying to will his limbs to function, he ordered his hand to let go of the cold weapon. He would leave it right here on the bed. No one would bother it. He watched as his fingers slowly loosened their grip, leaving the gun alone, detached from him for the first time in hours. He slid it a few inches away from his face. It would stay here, waiting for him when he came back.

He inhaled heavily and slowly stretched out his legs, each movement a feeling that he was leaving safety, that he had to stay here—here where nothing could harm him but would change nothing. Still clinging to his phone, he pushed himself up and sat on the edge of the bed. His head felt light as he tightly crossed his arms over his chest. As he began to look around the room, memories of Nathaniel charged toward him like starving, raging beasts—baseball, his glove and bat, trophies, awards, posters of athletes. Matthew closed his eyes. He couldn't take it. He wanted to lie back down and just stay there. He opened his eyes and looked at the gun. It wasn't going anywhere. It would be here. But he would get to Kate first.

Another deep breath and he stood up, his arms still tight across his chest. He walked to the door, down the stairs, through the kitchen, to the garage. As he started his car, he thought about not opening the garage door. No, not now. Not this way.

Driving while still clutching his phone, he arrived at Kate's office at ten minutes before eight. He wiped his eyes and got out. The door to her office was still locked. He stood with his back turned to the main part of the hallway, waiting and trying to control his emotions, his arms folded as if protecting himself.

The wait dragged by. With each sound of footsteps he prayed they belonged to Kate.

"Matthew." Her calm voice offered only mild relief. "Come in." She unlocked the door and led the way to her office.

Matthew went immediately to his usual place and sat down, unable to hold back his tears. "I killed him," he said, his arms around his abdomen. "I killed my son. It's my fault. All that talk." He slowly shook his head. "I drove him to it."

Kate sat down on the edge of her chair and leaned toward him. "Okay. You've listened to the voicemail?" she asked. He nodded. "May I hear it?"

Through bleary eyes Matthew punched in the numbers and password. He pressed a button on the side, opening the speaker phone. With his eyes closed and tears running down his face, he listened once again to Nathaniel's voice.

"I'm sure that your pain is beyond description, but I think you were also very courageous."

He wiped his eyes and looked at her completely dumbfounded. "Courageous? How? What did I do?" Anger but with some glimmer of hope rose in his voice.

"You listened to it. You listened to your son's voice. I think you've known all along what was on there." She pointed to his phone. "You could have deleted it and continued with your life. But you didn't."

"So I wanted to accept the blame? Is that what you're saying?"

"Maybe you decided you were strong enough to live with whatever you were going to feel after hearing it."

He would not let her words make him pause. Not this time. "But I *am* to blame. It is my fault. Miriam was right. I am guilty."

"You did not set out to drive him to do anything."

"But if I had known—"

"You were doing what you thought was right. What you believed."

He stopped and wiped his eyes again. "What my father believed. And grandfather," he added.

"Yes, but let's stay focused on you."

"I don't want to. It hurts too much."

"That what happens in this process of getting well. It isn't easy."

"'Well' is not how I feel."

"But you are feeling. Feeling those things that you wouldn't let yourself feel before."

"Guilt is the only thing I feel," he said with disgust.

"I'm sure. The question is, how do you live with it?"

Should he say it? Should he tell her about the gun? And the car running in the garage? "I'm not sure I can," he said quietly, looking down. "Live with it."

"I think you can," she said softly. "There will be days when you'll hurt like hell and think you can't take it anymore. Days when you'll feel like taking a baseball bat to a car and beating it to a pulp. But you won't. Instead, you'll go on."

"What makes you so sure?"

"You're here."

Her words stopped him.

"You called. You asked for help."

He closed his eyes.

"And when those hard days hit, you'll call again until the day comes when you won't need to. When you can deal with the guilt and feelings on your own. You take one minute, one hour, one day at a time. And you tell yourself you will go on to the next one."

Matthew opened his eyes and stared at nothing in the middle of the room, allowing Kate's words to mingle with the harshness—the memories, the reminders of all he'd done, his part in bringing to pass all that had happened. Like pouring something good into bitterness, hope into despair.

"I don't know if I can ever forgive myself," he said, almost whispering.

"Forgiving ourselves is the most difficult of all," she said.

They sat in the quiet for several moments. Finally, Kate gently broke the silence. "You haven't said anything about where you are with God in this."

Pictures of his family suddenly came into his mind. "I had it all—a wife, a son, a daughter." Slowly he shook his head. "I'd say God is pretty fed up with me."

"What about grace?"

Matthew stopped moving his head but did not look up as Kate's words took hold of him.

"It's similar to what Ben said. If God can love you unconditionally, can't you do as much for yourself?"

Matthew dropped his cell phone into his lap, covered his face with his hands and wept.

"Matthew," Evangeline said with concern. "You all right?"

He had scarcely walked into the kitchen. When she posed the question, he stopped and stared at nothing. He should have gone home and called Roger Gooden to say he was sick. But Kate had encouraged him to go to work. Evangeline's question made him realize that he hadn't showered or shaved. Nor had he slept. He was still wearing what he'd worn yesterday. Better that he not look into a mirror, he thought. But not because of his appearance. He didn't want to see the face of a man who had killed his son. He turned and looked at her. What should he say to her? Tell her the whole truth? Tell her a lie?

"I had a very—" He stopped, looking down, trying to think. She was only being kind. "I had a very emotional night and did not sleep well," he managed softly. "I'm sorry about how I look."

"I'm not worried about how you look," she said, walking toward him. "Do you need to take the day to rest?"

He shook his head. "No. Thank you, though." He moved to the drawer where the plastic aprons were housed, pulled one from the box and put it on.

"Okay," Evangeline said, walking slowly back to the stove. Concern as well as doubt were evident in the two-syllable word. "We havin' turkey sandwiches. You start makin' those."

Matthew worked mechanically, not keeping track of the time nor the number of sandwiches. He did not speak, but his mind continued its silent scream as he battled his torment.

"Whoa," Evangeline said gently an hour later. "I think you got enough."

Matthew looked at the five pans of sandwiches. It seemed he had just started.

When Crystal, Frannie and Robert came in they greeted him. He spoke but kept busy, ignoring them, not wanting to talk, and especially he did not want to break down. Not here.

The lunch, the people, the food—all were routine. It wasn't until Matthew walked through offering extra food did he notice that the veteran was not there. Had he been there earlier and left? Had he moved on somewhere else? Another city? He didn't know and gave no further thought to it. He would come back when he came back, he thought. He gave out his last sandwich and returned to the kitchen. When he saw that the last person had left the dining area, he immediately went out and began wiping down the tables and sweeping without eating. By the time he'd finished, Robert, Frannie and Crystal had left the kitchen to go back to their other EOM jobs.

"I fixed you a plate," Evangeline said as he put away the broom.

He was about to shake his head, but her kindness humbled him. He caught the emotion in his throat as it tried to escape.

"Please. You need your strength." Her voice was gentle.

Matthew stood still for only a moment. Finally, he nodded and went to the sink to wash his hands.

As he sat down, Evangeline went about her usual after-lunch chores. He was glad she was ignoring him. He didn't want any attention. He picked up his turkey sandwich and began eating. The taste of food almost seemed foreign to him. He had to concentrate to remember when he had eaten. Not breakfast that morning. Only a bite or two of the roast beef sandwich the night before. He hadn't thought he was hungry, but as he ate, his body sent him a message for more. The green peas and rice tasted good.

When he finished, he put down his fork and sat staring at his plate.

"I'd say you musta been some kinda hungry," Evangeline said, walking up to the table as she dried a large plastic bowl.

Matthew looked up. He had wanted to be ignored and he had been. He looked at her dark brown face, half-smiling, kindness and understanding pouring from her eyes.

"I hadn't eaten hardly anything," he began slowly and softly. Evangeline listened standing on the other side of the table from him. "Not since lunch yesterday." He paused. Was it safe? Safe to tell? It was as if the question was unnecessary. He already knew the answer.

"My son—the one who—" He stopped but only for a moment as he put his hand over his cell phone in his left front pocket. "The one who committed suicide. He was—" Again, he had to catch his breath. "He was gay. My wife left me and took our daughter with her and my church fired me because they believe divorce is a sin. And they believe the same about homosexuality." He had said it. Not nearly everything but enough. He inhaled deeply and let it out. "I just had a very bad night." He looked up at her across the table.

She sat down on a stool opposite him and slid the bowl and drying cloth to the side. Resting her forearms on the table, she clasped her hands and stared at them. She shook her head as she began speaking softly. "I just don't understand these churches that ain't read they Bible where it say in Matthew 7:1, 'Judge not.' Yet all they do is go 'round judgin' everybody. That ain't Christian. Life's messy. So's people. Can't everything and everybody be all tied up with a pretty little bow on it all the time. Like I done told you before—people spend too much time lookin' for how people is different than how they's alike." She looked up at him. "Sounds like to me your church lettin' you go was a good thing for you. Turnin' their back on you, after all that happen to you—shame on them. That ain't what Jesus woulda done." She took a deep breath. "You know seein' the face of Jesus in these folks that come in here is good. But sometimes we need to look in the mirror and see Him in ourself, too. I don't know you too good, Matthew Winslow. But I 'spect you a good man. I 'spect you got a good heart." She leaned toward him. "You just don't know it yet. But you will. You got some mess goin' on in your life right now. But you gonna be all right."

Matthew nodded his appreciation because he was afraid to speak. Afraid even to look at her as his emotions threatened.

"'Sides, anybody give a homeless man food for his dog—he a good man."

Matthew looked up surprised.

"Don't you think Evangeline Mays don't know what goes on in her kitchen and dinin' room?" She smiled.

* * *

394

As he drove away from EOM, Evangeline's words and her goodness echoed in his mind, but in the quiet emptiness of his car, so did Nathaniel's voicemail. All too quickly, he remembered that his gun was still on his son's bed. Kate had been right. Going to work that morning had been good. It had busied him. But now there was nothing. No one. No where to go. And his self-loathing was taking hold once again.

Approaching the intersection with Eden and Trademark Streets, he decided to turn. There was one place. As he thought about it, he felt his emotions rising. Maybe he would feel some relief, if only for a moment. Anything would be welcomed.

Ten minutes later, he parked his car in front of Woodfield Haven, walked up the gently sloping sidewalk to the automatic sliding glass doors. Mr. McDuffie greeted him warmly. Matthew nodded, proceeded to the elevators and pressed the up arrow. When the doors opened to the third floor, he walked down the hallway to 304.

As he turned to walk in, a nurse was coming out. "Oh, Reverend Winslow." He didn't speak nor try to read her nameplate. "Uh, I'll, uh, just close the door so you can have some privacy." She forced a quick smile as she hurriedly shut the door behind him.

Ruth Winslow sat on half of the small sofa. She wore a dark blue skirt and a powdery pink blouse with wide cuffs; her hair neatly combed in waves of white. She turned her attention from the small television and looked up at her son.

"Hello, Mama," Matthew said, fighting back his tears.

"Son of a bitch." Her small voice was almost squeaky.

Matthew moved toward her. His mother now stared not at him but straight ahead into some far off place.

"Shit," she said without expression.

Matthew sat down slowly next to her.

"Fuck." She remained perfectly still as she spoke.

Matthew took a deep breath. "Fuck," he repeated.

"Bastard."

He hesitated only a moment. "Bastard."

"Asshole."

Tears began streaming down his face. "Asshole."

"Go to hell."

"Go to hell."

"Motherfucker."

He sobbed. "Motherfucker."

"Piss on you."

Matthew continued crying. "Piss on you."

"Damn you."

"Damn you." Slowly he leaned next to her, then forward as he put his head in her lap.

"Shit, fuck, damn," she said.

"Shit, fuck, damn," he repeated.

As he cried, his mother ceased her litany of foul language and became silent. After a moment he felt her hand on the side of his head, stroking his temple gently. He felt her other hand on his shoulder, again, soothing strokes. Her gentleness made him weep all the more.

"Jesus loves you this I know. For the Bible tells you so. Little one to him belong. You are weak, but He is strong."

He had been only a boy. She had sung it to him at night as she tucked him into bed, changing the words just for him.

"Yes, Jesus loves you. Yes, Jesus loves you. Yes, Jesus loves you. The Bible tells you so."

Every night she sang her own version—directed to him. Every night until his father made her stop. Amid his anguish he heard her end it the way she had decades ago.

"Jesus loves you and so do I."

CHAPTER TWENTY-FIVE

SATURDAY & SUNDAY— JUNE 20 & 21

On Friday Matthew had gone home but did not follow Evangeline's orders to go to bed. Instead, he immediately went to Nathaniel's room. Standing in the doorway for several minutes, he focused on the gun—the all-night gut wrenching on Thursday etched in his mind, along with listening to Nathaniel's voicemail. Finally, he sat down on the bed and looked around the room, mindlessly seeing the contents, remembering conversations they'd had. Then followed Miriam's accusations, Martha's correction *You're wrong*, Kate's words about forgiving himself, Ben Thornton's take on God and unconditional love.

He had stared at the gun for several moments as Evangeline's perception of him wafted through his mind. *A good man. A good heart.* He picked up the gun and slowly walked down the hall toward his own bedroom. As he passed Sarah Elizabeth's room, he opened the door and looked inside. He noticed the empty shelves of the overly bright orange, purple, green and yellow bookcase which used to be the home to her stuffed animal collection that Carolyn had taken. Her colorfully modern desk and chair. When he saw her Bible verses notebooks on another shelf, his stomach knotted. He tried to push it out of his mind. So seldom had he ever been inside his daughter's room. Memories of her ran through his mind—programs in grade school, piano recitals, glee club concerts, Bible verse competitions. But what did he remember about her outside of school? What did she like to do? Did she have a favorite book? Music? He shook his head sadly. He scarcely knew her. His own daughter. He gripped the handle of the gun. He closed the door and continued up the hall.

He had carefully unloaded the gun, put it and the bullets in the shoebox, then returned it to the dark recesses on the closet shelf. As he was about to close the door, he saw again, as he had everyday since she'd been gone, the emptiness of Miriam's half of the walk-in. But today the thought struck him that his half was still there. He was, in fact, still present. Still alive. Some part of him wasn't certain that he wanted to be. Nevertheless, he was living and breathing, walking around. He felt like— The image of his mother shot into his mind. "I feel like shit," he had said softly, disbelieving his language had erupted so easily.

Looking in the mirror on Saturday morning he was surprised how much gray was in the day-old growth of his beard. It was then that he realized he hadn't gone to his weekly appointment at the barbershop on Thursday. He examined the gray hair around his temples. Considerable. Then he stared at his face as Evangeline's words pressed into the forefront of his mind. He searched for Jesus and realized he didn't know what he was looking for.

Later he sat at the kitchen table, his hands cupped around his coffee mug, feeling its warmth as he stared into the brownish liquid. Saturday, he realized. June 20. Exactly one month to the day since Detective Sparks came to the front door." He took a deep breath. Hard to believe. In some ways it seemed like years had passed. Yet on some level, it could have been yesterday.

As thoughts were trailing through his mind, he realized the time. He needed to get to EOM, but Evangeline would probably understand even though she might not show it.

"Well, you do look better today," she said when he walked in. "Did you get some good rest like I told you?"

He nodded. "I slept better," he said and with some degree of timidity he added, "and thank you for the things you said yesterday."

"Well, I meant ever word." She punctuated her sentence with raised eyebrows. "So you ready to get to work?"

He smiled slightly. "Yes ma'am."

"Ham, macaroni and cheese, roll, mixed fruit cup. Put me on two big pots of water to boil and then get 'bout five of those big cans of fruit from the pantry."

Matthew set to work, grateful that he had this to occupy his mind. He realized, too, that he and this African-American woman worked well together. Something else that surprised him.

Around eleven with preparations well underway, Roger Gooden came into the kitchen with someone that Matthew recognized.

"Evangeline Mays and Matthew Winslow," Roger said, pointing to each of them. "This is Detective Rierson of the Elmsborough Police. He wanted to ask you all a few questions."

Being arrested was not one of the things Matthew had revealed to Evangeline. He wondered if Gooden knew.

"Good morning, folks," Rierson said in a friendly tone but without smiling. "Sorry to interrupt your work, but I need to ask if either of you recognize the man in this photo." He reached into a large envelope but stopped before removing its contents. "I should warn you that the man is deceased." He held out the picture.

"Oh, no," Matthew gasped, seeing the empty face. "The veteran."

"Veteran?" Rierson asked.

"I saw him on the corner out on Eden and he had a sign that said he was a Vietnam veteran and had cancer. Where's his dog?"

"He had a dog?"

Matthew held up his hands to estimate Sadie's size. "About this big. Tan coat. No single breed I don't think."

"Did this man come in here?"

"Yes, for lunch. Everyday."

"What in the world happened to him?" Evangeline asked.

"Some kids found his body in some woods where a lot of the homeless camp in the summer. The good thing is there doesn't appear to be any foul play. The medical examiner said it was natural causes. Maybe even related to the cancer." He nodded toward Matthew. "But he had no identification. We don't know his name or where he's from. Relatives. Nothing. I was hoping you all might know something. At least a name."

"What about his backpack?" Matthew asked.

"What backpack, Mr. Winslow?" Rierson said.

"He always had a backpack crammed full. I don't know what was in it."

"Can you describe it?"

"Kind of ragged army-green. Looked like it was pretty old. Maybe the one he had in Vietnam. I don't know. But it was full."

"That's very helpful. If we happen to find that it could lead us to an ID. Anything else?"

"He wasn't here yesterday," Evangeline said. "But he was on Thursday."

"What about his dog?" Matthew asked. "I mean, if she's out there loose somewhere."

"Depends on how resourceful she is," Rierson answered. "She might get picked up by Animal Control and put in the county shelter. If she's got an ID chip implanted, they can find the owners possibly." He returned the photo to the folder.

Gooden told Rierson he could stay and ask the people as they came in for lunch if they knew the deceased man. Gooden returned to his office and Evangeline went to the pantry for something, leaving Matthew alone in the kitchen with Rierson.

"How are things going, Reverend?" he asked quietly as he had that night at the station—not his police-voice but his reaching out tone.

Matthew made eye contact briefly but looked away shyly as he spoke. "Fairly well, I guess."

"I'm glad to hear that. I hope they continue for you." He turned to walk away.

Matthew's expression was a mix of humility and embarrassment talking with the man to whom he had confessed everything. "Detective?" His voice was soft, uncertain. Rierson turned back. Matthew, still not looking at him, put out his hand. "Thank you," he said.

Rierson took his hand and shook firmly. "You're very welcome."

After Rierson went out to wait for the people, Matthew gathered himself emotionally and returned to his duties. However, he kept thinking about the veteran—especially the day he changed his tire. He felt badly that he didn't know his name. Why had he never asked? Such a simple thing. And what about Sadie? Would another homeless person take her and be good to her.

That afternoon as he was driving away from EOM, he knew he needed to continue keeping himself occupied. Too much thinking would not be good. He'd done enough of that. The answer came almost immediately. Cleaning.

When he got home he started with a load of laundry, then the kitchen, followed by his bathroom. He also dusted his bedroom and ran the vacuum. Next week vacuum and dust the downstairs. As he was about to put away the vacuum cleaner in the upstairs hall closet, he thought about Nathaniel's and Sarah Elizabeth's rooms. He had done no cleaning in either of them. His stomach queased as he tried to decide. Maybe he could at least try to vacuum. If that went well, maybe more.

Running the vacuum cleaner in his daughter's room he pictured her phoning friends, doing homework. Next dusting. In the bathroom he found some empty bottles of toiletries in the trashcan. Could it be that she was so close to being a grown woman that she used a pale lipstick and jars of creams? Had he missed that much of her life? He sighed as a sinking feeling took hold of him.

In the hallway he looked at Nathaniel's door. Could he do this? He walked slowly to the door and opened it. He took a deep breath and pushed the vacuum cleaner inside. At first he tried not to dwell on the details. He'd already done that. Dusting with a disposable cloth he could not avoid the minutia that confronted him. He handled everything carefully as if it were fragile. His notebooks of Bible verses. Matthew shut his eyes fighting back the emotion, edged on by anger.

In the bathroom he saw the remnants of a man—razor, shaving cream, aftershave lotion, deodorant. A man. Nathaniel would have been a— He stopped. "He would have been a good and decent man," he whispered, tears escaping from his eyes.

Sunday morning Matthew rolled over and looked at his alarm clock. Eight-seventeen. He had slept more than eight hours. He closed his eyes. He had not set the alarm, planning to sleep until he woke up since he didn't have to work. As groggy sleep cleared from his head, he rolled onto his other side, the events of the last several days replaying in his mind's eye. It was only a few minutes until all the thinking and analyzing made him fully awake. He might as well get up. He threw back the top sheet and sat on the side of the bed. Eight-thirty. He stretched his arms and stood. A long day of nothing to do, he thought.

He showered and shaved. As he applied his aftershave lotion, he leaned closer to the mirror and examined his face closely. Suddenly that phrase—*the face of Jesus*—sifted into his mind, again. Surprised—as if someone had tapped him on the shoulder—he stood back. With that thought, he began looking at his face differently. Not missed spots or nicks with his razor. But something more. After several minutes frustration began swooping in. What was he supposed to see? What was he looking for? Then, *unconditional* entered his head. He thought of the veteran and the other homeless. And Nathaniel. As his eyes once again filled with tears, he looked at himself. Broken. Twisted. Guilty of everything it seemed. Yet, could he be accepted? Loved, even? Could he love himself? Unconditionally? Him? The person responsible for his own son's death? He placed his hands on the vanity next to the lavatory and hung his head.

While he fixed and ate breakfast and began reading the newspaper, an idea struck him and lingered to the point of nagging him. He tried to dismiss it. Ridiculous. Still the prodding continued, offset by his endless doubts. He took a deep breath. Was this a half-baked idea? Maybe not even baked at all. Maybe insane. That's what it felt like. He could always walk out. If anyone made him feel unwelcome, he would simply leave. Finally, he gave in and found himself again standing in front of a mirror, but this one was the full-length one on the back of the closet door and he was checking his tie. It was the first time he'd worn one in several weeks. Up until everything had happened, he'd worn a suit and tie almost everyday.

He put on his suit jacket and examined himself in the mirror. "This is crazy," he said to the image before him. "A month ago you'd never even thought—" This was more than crazy. "Insane," he said aloud. He reached up and took hold of the jacket's lapels to take it off. Why shouldn't he go? Why should he? He closed his eyes, wanting to scream at the decision ricocheting in his head. "Go. Don't go." he growled aloud through gritted teeth. Suddenly, he released the lapels and stormed downstairs and drove off. The whole time he was telling himself he was doing the wrong thing. He didn't want to call attention to himself. He'd go in just as the service started and sit in the back. That way he wouldn't have to talk to anyone. He could slip out early.

After the ten minute drive he sat in his car in the parking lot nervously checking his tie again and the time. Two minutes before the hour. Drive home or go inside? He growled again, then grabbed the door handle. He got out of his car and walked the short distance to the steps leading up to the large colonial-style porch with its four massive white columns. Just inside the door an usher welcomed him and handed him a bulletin. He thanked him with a nod and kept moving, avoiding any conversation.

The sanctuary was plainly decorated. White pews. Probably seated four hundred. The windows clear-paned. The walls a neutral off-white. The carpet a deep blue. The pulpit and choir loft unadorned. Typical basic decor, he thought. No special lighting. No huge symbols or sculptures or drapes. Oddly, no American or Christian flags. Just church.

Even as Matthew took a seat in the last row his uneasiness and vulnerability grew. Immediately he noticed that most of the men were not wearing suits or ties but Polo shirts or casual regular shirts instead. He was overdressed. This was all a mistake. Just then the organist began playing and the choir and ministers entered. One was a woman. Disbelief immediately rose up in him. This was so alien. He didn't know if he could sit through it. This wasn't what he expected. Suddenly he felt a hand on his shoulder. Startled he turned.

"Welcome," Kate whispered, leaning down to him. "I'm glad you're here." She smiled. "I'll see you afterwards."

"Thank you." Matthew forced a smile as his face cooled. He supposed it was logical that she would be a member.

The lady preacher announced upcoming events and concerns and celebrations—a church-wide picnic, some kind of Frisbee event, illnesses, surgeries, one lady had just turned ninety-five. Everyone applauded her when she stood. This would never have happened at Holy Bible, he told himself.

"And, of course, we want to wish all the fathers a very Happy Father's Day—"

Matthew heard no more of what the female minister said. He hadn't realized. The last thought on his mind was celebrating the fact

that he was a father. He closed his eyes. Suddenly Evangeline's procla-
mation rang out in his mind: *Life's messy.* That was for sure. But was
being here making his life all the messier? He felt so helpless. Stay or
leave? He didn't know. The dream had him going to his church—what
an idiotic thing to base his decision on. Yet, here he was, thinking he
should probably leave, especially since it was Father's Day. He felt so
out of place already. Entombed. Buried alive. Or was he alive? Maybe
he was dead. Dead and in some kind of hell. He took a deep breath.
Maybe this was a dream? He opened his eyes and looked up and that's
when he saw the back of a head that looked vaguely familiar. The man
was seated halfway down the aisle with a family—three small children
between him and his wife. When the man turned to look down at one
of his children, Matthew almost gasped. Detective Sparks.

Matthew turned his eyes downward. Why was this happening to
him? Why had he come here? He looked back up, wanting to shake
his head but instead sat still as a statue.

As the service continued he noted several interracial couples,
Asians, Hispanics, one or two others wearing some kind of native
dress—definitely not American. When the children came to the
front for their brief sermon, the diversity was astounding. So different from what he was accustomed to. Then another familiar face
appeared. Detective Rierson took his child down to the front for the
five minute story. Who else? he wondered.

Ben Thornton stepped up to the pulpit without fanfare, without
spotlights and closed-circuit TV cameras, no mammoth screens
to project his face on. Ben read the scripture. The parable of the
Prodigal Son. Matthew winced. Forgiveness. It would be all about
forgiveness. Now he really wanted to leave. He almost felt he had
to. But people would turn and look. Could he endure this? Could
he keep his emotions under control? He crossed his arms over his
chest and kept himself directly behind the person in front of him so
Ben could not see him.

Thornton began by telling stories about grudges, vengeance,
hurt, anger and bitterness between friends and family members.

He recounted scripture—Peter's question of how many times to forgive. "Jesus' point?" Ben said. "There is no limit to forgiveness—for God or us. And another famous story is of the woman who was an adulteress. The people said by law they should stone her to death. 'Let him who is without sin cast the first stone,' Jesus wisely challenged them and they all dropped the stones they had picked up and walked away.

"So who do you know that is without sin? Are you without sin? I'm not. Far from it. There are no perfect people. Obviously, that was Jesus' point. We're all in this together. For me not to forgive you and vice versa— That seems to be the bottom line, isn't it? We've all done our share of sinning but we're reluctant to forgive.

"Some of you know that my father walked out on my mother, brother and sister and me when I was ten-years-old. The man who had taught me to ride a bicycle, throw a football and play baseball, who was teaching me about becoming a man, came home at lunch one summer day, packed a suitcase, told my mother he didn't love her or us and left. I happened to be standing in the next room and heard him. I ran after him as he went to his car, tears streaming down my face, begging him not to leave. Even as he backed out of the driveway and drove off, I chased after him, screaming for him to come back. He never did.

"It took a long time—years—to go through all the stages—disbelief that he'd really left, hurt, anger, rage even, bitterness, feeling abandoned. There was shame with it, too. Shame in my friends knowing. And the hurt when other fathers were at school events and mine wasn't. But one day it just got to be too much to carry around and I had to either forgive him or I'd be fighting an uphill battle everyday for the rest of my life. And if you think your baggage doesn't affect those close to you, think again. It eats away at you from the inside out. Even though I never saw him again, even if he were dead, I still had to forgive him."

Ben took a deep breath and looked out at the congregation. "Who do you need to forgive? And who do you want to ask to forgive you?" He stepped back from the pulpit and sat down.

During the moment of silence that the service allowed, Matthew sat stunned by what he'd just heard. Never before had he heard a minister speak about his own private life. Never had he heard such honesty, such baring of a soul. Never before had he heard a range of feelings that so closely resembled his own.

Just then the organist began playing the introduction to the next hymn. The congregation rose and sang. Matthew stood but did not sing. His mind was still trying to grasp what he'd heard. When the hymn was over, a prayer was said for the offering. The people sat. As Matthew reached for his wallet, he saw someone else he knew. One of the people in the aisle passing the offering plate was Dwight Overby. When the young lawyer came to Matthew's pew, he smiled and extended his hand. As Matthew shook hands with him he thought he noticed that the younger man's eyes were slightly bleary, as if he'd been crying.

As the church members sang the doxology, the ushers brought the offering plates to the front then returned to their pews. Matthew watched to see where Overby went. He thought it was odd that he stood with three other men. He then noticed that he was standing close to the one next to him, so close that their bare arms were touching. Just then the other man put his arm around Overby's shoulder and hugged him closer as if he were consoling him. Overby then put his arm around the man's waist.

Matthew was shocked. But then everything seemed to fall into place. All the people who had helped him—Sparks, Rierson, Overby—they were all members of this church. His lawyer. A homosexual? Just then, Dwight's words came back to him. He'd asked that night at the police station why he was helping him. "Seems like the right thing to do," he'd said. A gay man had worked to keep him out of jail.

After the doxology Ben Thornton came down from the pulpit to stand on the floor before the congregation. "Please be seated for a moment," he said. When he said that, the two men next to Overby and his friend—both very tanned, athletic, maybe mid to late thirties—walked to the front of the sanctuary to stand with Ben. "We welcome two who come today to join our community of faith," Ben continued as the men turned and faced the congregation. "Jeff Brown and his partner, Ed Thomas have been attending for several weeks and participating in our Wednesday night fellowship. They've especially been active in our Ultimate Frisbee pickup games on Monday nights in the park. Jeff is a vice president at First Citizens bank and Ed is a chemist at Nesco Research. They make their home on West Oak Drive. Both Ed and Jeff are avid sportsmen. Besides Frisbee, they also play competitive softball in the city leagues. Since Jeff went to Carolina and Ed attended Duke, I would think that fact alone makes them prime candidates for working in the diplomatic corps in Washington."

The congregation laughed, then joined Thornton in reading a pledge printed in the bulletin to support and care for these new members.

Matthew, however, heard nothing more. Thoughts of Nathaniel swept through his head, relentless reminders of how his life might have been if only—

When the rest of the congregation stood for the benediction, Matthew could not move. He put his elbows on his knees and covered his face to hide the emotion that silently came pouring out of him. He gave no thought to embarrassment. He had no power to stop what was happening to him or to leave.

As the people began stirring and leaving, he soon felt someone sit down beside him. He heard Kate whisper something to him as she put her hand on his back and simply sat with him. After several minutes he was able to gain some control of himself. Slowly, he removed his hands from his face and took a Kleenex from the small pack that Kate held out to him. After wiping his eyes, he leaned back in the pew without speaking. When he glanced up, most of the people had left the sanctuary. Only a few remained talking quietly—one of them, a young man with a man and a woman on the opposite side of the sanctuary, were watching him. His arms were folded tightly over his chest in an embrace of himself. Matthew blinked to clear the blur in his own eyes. He wanted to be sure. He was right. Jason Daniels. He was crying.

CHAPTER TWENTY-SIX

MONDAY & TUESDAY— JUNE 22 & 23

As he drove to EOM on Monday morning Matthew still remained consumed by what had happened at the church service. Thornton's openness about his father to the whole congregation. Sparks and Rierson. Dwight Overby apparently being gay. The two men—the couple—joining the church and being accepted like anyone else. And Jason Daniels. Matthew couldn't get him out of his mind. In the world without a family. Without anyone. And the other. He didn't want to think about it, but it was there. Right in the middle of his head—Jason was without Nathaniel. Even from across the expanse of the sanctuary, he could see his grief. His loss. Even though he tried to block it, thoughts about Nathaniel joining a church with another man had sifted into his processing throughout Sunday afternoon and evening. Nathaniel and another man. Maybe with Jason. Maybe not. Nevertheless, a couple. Living together in the same house. Making it a home. The two men yesterday had seemed so normal. Then it struck him. Nathaniel had seemed so normal. And instantly he'd corrected himself—Nathaniel *was* normal. And Jason? He *seemed* normal. So much to take in. But Jason was— He stopped. Jason was alive even though he was alone.

But so was he, he realized. Neither of them had a family. He wondered if Jason had tried to call his father yesterday for Father's Day. Knowing Carl Daniels as he did, and after hearing how he had blown up and thrown Jason out of the house, he doubted it. Just as Sarah Elizabeth had not called him. And he'd kept his cell phone with him all day—hoping one minute that she would, then an instant later hoping she wouldn't. Why should she? What would he say to her? He had not been a good father. He had always expected too much from her. He didn't deserve to hear from her. He'd thought several times he would call her and tell her just that. Now he wished he had. Now that the day had passed, it was too late. Her birthday would be coming up—but that wouldn't be for another six months. Why wait for a special day? Still, maybe it would be best not to. Not yet anyway. He had derailed all their lives and for that reason Miriam might not allow her to take the call.

He heaved a deep sigh as he pulled into the EOM staff parking lot, got out of his car, went inside and began his routine duties for lunch. And it was routine. No surprises. Nothing different. He wondered more about what Wednesday would bring when Ben Thornton made his weekly visit. He hadn't come up to him at church as he sat crying. He'd let Kate handle that.

At two o'clock, he signed his time card with Evangeline and went outside into the blistering hot afternoon. As he walked toward his car, he looked to the other side of the parking lot and saw her. She was watching him—sheepishly, uncertain, her tail tucked between her legs. As he walked toward her, she began walking toward him— slowly, head down, exercising great caution. Her tongue was hanging out. Probably thirsty as well as hungry, he thought. Matthew knelt down and held out his hand. Sadie stopped, then inched closer. After only a quick sniff to be sure, she took the final few steps and allowed him to pet her. Making a pitiful whimpering sound, she almost fell over as if she were too weak to stand.

Matthew rubbed her head. He'd never dealt with a dog before, but he couldn't just drive off and leave her. Carefully he picked her up and carried her to the landing near the staff entrance. He put her on the cool cement in the shade and rubbed her head again. Beck, the security guard, saw him and came out to help. While he stayed with Sadie, Matthew went inside to the kitchen and told Evangeline about his find.

"Get a bowl and run some water in it," she told him while she went to the refrigerator and retrieved some leftover stew.

Out on the landing the three of them watched Sadie gobble up her food and lap at her water.

"What you gonna do now?" Evangeline asked him.

Matthew sighed. "I don't know. I couldn't just leave her."

"No, but don't think she just gonna lick your hand like she thankin' you and then trot off on her merry way neither."

Matthew stared at Sadie as she lapped up the last drop of the stew and then the water. "Do either of you want a dog?"

"Not me," Beck said. "I got one already."

"Seems to me you the only one around here who need a dog," Evangeline said, her eyebrows raised and her hands on her hips.

Matthew remembered what the veteran had said about dogs and unconditional love. He tried to picture himself with a dog. Clueless, he thought, as he stooped down and scratched her behind her ears. At the same time she was trying to lick his other hand.

"You either take her or Animal Control likely to pick her up like that police-man said. Then they take her to the shelter and if nobody get her, well, then they might put her to sleep."

"She might have one of them chips they put in dogs and cats just under the skin. Tells who they belong to," Beck said. "But only a vet can tell you that. Or maybe the people at the shelter."

Matthew sighed. "Okay, I'll take her to a veterinarian and see what they say."

By now Sadie seemed to have more energy. Matthew picked up the two empty bowls.

"I'll take those" Evangeline said, holding out her hand. "You got to take care of your dog."

Sadie willingly got into Matthew's car and immediately lay down on an old blanket he took from the trunk and put on the back seat. He remembered there was a veterinarian office near where he went to the grocery store. For an instant, he thought about someone from Holy Bible Fellowship being there, but he dismissed it. What concerned him more was how Sadie might react going to a strange place and a doctor. He had no leash. She might bolt from the car and run off when they got there.

Surprisingly, when he opened the door she still lay on the seat and just looked up at him, her tongue panting. She allowed him to scoop her up and carry her into the office. The assistant led him to the examining room where he laid her on the stainless steel table. He told Doctor Tim Dean everything he knew and, with reluctance, about the possibility of an ID chip. After the doctor told him what they should do to check out her condition, Matthew agreed to pay.

"Sadie could use a bath," Doctor Dean added, stroking her back. "We could take her to the groomer next door if she checks out okay."

Matthew looked at Sadie for only a second before agreeing.

As he drove home the thought of keeping her hammered away at him. What would he do with her when he went to EOM everyday? He'd have to walk her and that meant he'd see Eloise Gardner and other neighbors. He did have a large fenced backyard for her to run around in. She did seem very loyal. But dogs were expensive. What if she got sick? And throughout it all he kept hearing the words that had come to haunt him—*unconditional love.*

When he drove into the driveway, a small post office truck was parked in front of his house, the mailman standing at the front door. Matthew stopped in the driveway and got out.

The mailman read the label on the envelope as he approached him. "Afternoon. Are you Matthew Winslow?"

"Yes, I am."

"I need your signature to verify delivery, please, sir."

Matthew signed the card and handed back the small clipboard.

"Thank you, sir. Have a nice afternoon." He gave Matthew the envelope.

"You, too," Matthew replied. When he read the return address, he felt an ache in his gut.

"It was from a lawyer in Raleigh representing Miriam," he told Kate an hour later when he went for his session. "She's establishing notice of separation as of three weeks ago. So I guess according to North Carolina law a year from now we'll be divorced."

"And how are you with that?"

"It hurts, but if I'm honest and realistic, I can't say that I'm surprised or even—" He hesitated. "Or that I blame her. The night she left she said we didn't have a marriage. A show for my father and for the church, she said. She was right." He was silent for a moment, listening to his own truth.

"Not any romance, even early in your marriage? Maybe in college?" Kate asked.

Matthew stared out the window, thinking. "I don't suppose I've ever known what romance is like," he said. "Miriam probably hasn't either."

"Was this the first communication with your wife since her sister was here?"

Matthew merely nodded.

"And your daughter?"

Matthew looked down and shook his head. "I was hoping she would call yesterday on Father's Day, but I'm not surprised she didn't." He was quiet for a moment. "The letter also covers financial support for her and my daughter, especially the private school she'll be going to."

"Are you okay with that?"

"Yes," he said, not hesitating.

"Have you thought about contacting them? A letter?"

Matthew shook his head. "I've thought about it, even tried composing a letter, but I just couldn't, especially not after last week."

"Do you think you'll ever tell them about all that's been going on with you?"

He stared off into the distance. "Maybe some day. Right now, everything—there are still so many unexpected things popping up. Like what happened at your church yesterday." He paused. "Sparks, Rierson, Overby. And you." He fidgeted with the armrest. "The last time I talked with Sparks I wasn't very nice to him. And yet he intervened that night at the police station and got Rierson involved. Then one of them called Dwight Overby who sent me to you. I never thought a gay lawyer would go out of his way to help me." He looked up at her. "So much compassion," he almost whispered, his voice threatening to break. "I've just never known—" He waited a moment, trying to gain control. "That night I came home from the police station, I was so lost. I prayed—I asked God to—" He stopped and reached for a Kleenex.

Kate gave him a moment. "Grace," she said softly. "Even before you asked."

Matthew nodded as he struggled to accept what she'd said.

"It must be a very special church."

"It's a very caring community of faith that is always reaching out."

"And Jason Daniels. Does he go there?"

"He's been coming to the youth group for a while," Kate explained.

"I'm glad he had somewhere to turn."

Kate merely nodded.

After a few moments he told her about the Vietnam veteran and Sadie.

"And if the vet doesn't find an ID chip are you going to keep her?" she asked with an upbeat tone.

Matthew looked at her knowingly. "I don't know the first thing about taking care of a dog."

"There's nothing wrong with trying it out for a few days. See how she does. How she likes being indoors. How the two of you get along. Then if it's not working, you can put an ad in the paper or as a last resort take her to the shelter and hope someone will adopt her. Nothing's etched in stone." She shifted in her chair. "I think this might be another of those surprises you mentioned a minute ago. You know, taking care of a pet has all the elements of a relationship—commitment, mutual respect, compassion. In a lot of cases a dog becomes as much a member of the family as anyone."

Matthew nodded. "Unconditional love. That's what the veteran said. Dogs were put here to teach humans about unconditional love."

"I couldn't agree more," Kate said. "And about connecting."

"Connecting?" he asked.

"Allowing other people into your life. Genuinely caring about someone else."

"I don't guess I've ever done that," he said.

"But you're getting there."

"You have a gem of a dog here," Dr. Dean told Matthew.

Ever since he'd left Kate's office, Matthew had fought himself about what to do with Sadie. Part of him was hoping to return her to a good home. But another part was praying that she wouldn't have an ID chip and he could give keeping her a try.

"She's obviously house broken," the doctor continued. "We asked her if she needed to go out and she barked once and stood up. She's very gentle and loving. Although I think she was abused at some point but not recently." He leafed through some papers in a folder. "She was dehydrated and undernourished a little, I'd say because she hasn't had a decent meal in several days. Blood work looked good, considering her condition. You just found her, right?" Matthew nodded. "Well, she has no ID chip, so if you want her, I'd say you've found a great friend, Mr. Winslow. See how it works out and we can put in a chip anytime."

Matthew felt a lump in his throat. "I've never had a dog. I don't know how to take care of her," he said.

"Well, we have the solution for that," he said cheerfully. "I'll have my assistant give you two booklets on that very subject. It's not as hard as you might think and in the case of Sadie, the rewards will far outweigh any drawbacks." He smiled. "The groomer next door has everything you'll need to start off. I'd say she's got enough lab in her that she loves to fetch and it would be good for her to run and be exercised. But I'd wait a day or two. Give her some time to get her strength back."

Matthew paid the bill, then with his "how-to" booklet went next door to the groomer. When the assistant brought her out, she immediately trotted to Matthew, her tail wagging so fast it was a blur. When he knelt down, she wanted to lick his face. He scratched her ears and petted her. She smelled so clean and acted perky, her coat gleaming.

"Man, she sure loves you," said the teenage helper.

The young man's unbiased observation wasn't lost on Matthew. Someone loved him. For the first time he realized, he was smiling. Before leaving he had bought—with Sadie's approval—a leash, collar, treats, a chew toy, food and water bowls, some very nutritious dog food and a bed.

Sadie willingly allowed him to put on the collar he'd picked out and she even didn't mind the leash. In the car she sat on the back seat for a while but then lay down. In the house she sniffed around in every nook and cranny. When Matthew took her outside in the backyard, she looked at him as if she couldn't believe this was to be her playground. She roamed every corner, and marked every bush and tree while he sat on the top step of the patio devouring the booklet on caring for dogs. He didn't want to make any mistakes. After a short while, Sadie came up on the patio, lapped some water from her new bowl, then sat next to him. Matthew put down the booklet and rubbed her head and scratched behind her ears.

"Welcome home, Sadie," he said, looking at her. Sadie responded with a half bark. "I believe you're the first female member of the Winslow family whose name is not in the Bible." Sadie reached up and licked the side of his face. Matthew didn't pull away and he didn't reach for his Purell. Instead he smiled—again. As he continued to pet her, Sadie lay beside him, her head against his leg, and within a few minutes she was asleep.

Later while he fixed dinner he talked to her and she watched his every move, her ears pricked not for conversation but in anticipation of her own meal. Afterwards, he allowed her onto the couch beside him while he read the paper and watched some television. When he got up to go to bed, Sadie jumped down onto the floor and stretched her front legs out.

The booklet said to establish a pattern. So before bed, Matthew took her outside. Back inside he told her to follow him upstairs. In his bedroom she watched him put her bed across the room from his. When he pointed to it and told her to lie down, she sniffed and nudged and circled the soft pad before obeying. He rewarded her with a scratch on the head. Lying in bed he heard her stir a few times before settling down.

In the dark the reality of what he'd done finally set in. He owned a dog. That act was so alien to everything he'd ever believed about himself. But he also realized that having Sadie there, in his life, had made the evening go by very quickly. More importantly, she had made receiving the letter from Miriam's lawyer easier. He supposed, in a way, he had lost one family but had gained another. That fact alone made him feel very blessed. Suddenly, he realized what he'd just thought. That last word stunned him. Blessed. He could hear Kate. Grace. And how all the events of the last few weeks had played out to this day, especially meeting the Vietnam veteran and him changing his tire and both of them treating Sadie's paw.

All at once Matthew found himself crying. When life had seemed so brutal, he'd been blessed. Just then, he realized Sadie had gotten up and come to him, her front paws up on the edge of the bed. She whimpered. He got up and sat down on the floor in the dark, hugging his dog as he cried.

The next morning Matthew noticed Sadie acting strange. She sat beside her bed but seemed not to want to move. When he swung his legs out of bed and put his feet on the carpet, he felt the dampness and then the odd odor hit him. As he dried his feet with a sock, disappointment filled him, but Sadie's countenance appeared so remorseful. When he told her to follow him downstairs, she obeyed. He opened the back door and she went out immediately. He got some paper towels and cleaner from the closet. Upstairs, he got down on his knees and blotted the pee, then sprayed a cleaner on it and blotted some more. The booklet had said that being in a strange place might bring this on, but it was usually only temporary. She was probably used to going whenever she wanted, living with the veteran outdoors. Maybe if he left a light on in the hallway.

As he showered, especially his hands and feet, the thought of giving up on her loomed. No. She was so loving. Unconditionally. He felt his emotions stir. *Life's messy.* Evangeline's words haunted him. A perfect fit? He wondered. Shaving, he looked in the mirror and smiled faintly, at the same time blinking back his tears.

Downstairs he found Sadie lying on the patio in the sun. When he opened the door, she looked up at him, her head down but did not come to him. She knew, he thought. And now she's afraid I'm mad. He went toward her with his hand out. He sat down next to her, stroking her head, scratching her ears. When she sat up, he hugged her and she wagged her tail with fury.

"I'm not mad," he said. "I don't think I ever could be."

Later, however, he was riddled with guilt over having to leave her alone while he went to EOM. He made sure he did everything possible so that she would be okay until he got home. He filled her bowl with fresh water and put it on the patio overlooking the backyard. The patio provided ample shade and cover in case of bad weather. The temperature was mild enough not to be a factor. Having been with the veteran, she was used to being outdoors. Still, he worried. What if she thought he wasn't coming back and got out somehow? The fence had a gap at the bottom all the way around. What if she dug underneath it and ran away? What if something happened to her? What if someone took her? Just before leaving he gave her a treat, but that did nothing to ease his conscience.

When he walked into the kitchen at EOM, Evangeline asked about Sadie before offering any greeting. When he told her what he'd done, she put down the large spoon she was using to stir the soup and clapped her hands.

"Meant to be," she almost sang. "Meant to be. I could feel it in my bones." She picked up the spoon and continued to stir. "Yessiree."

After serving lunch the five workers gathered around the stainless steel work table, eating soup and sandwich. Evangeline asked for their attention.

"Matthew here has a new friend," she announced. "He 'dopted that veteran man's dog."

Crystal, Robert and Frannie all congratulated him at once.

"I thought you were actin' different today," Robert said.

"Yeah, I noticed that, too," Crystal added.

Evangeline nodded. "And I think this is the first time you smiled since you been here, too."

Matthew realized she was right.

Driving home, all of his fears of what could happen to Sadie plagued him, causing him to imagine the worst. When he arrived, he didn't even bother with the garage door, parking instead in the driveway and rushing to the patio door. Sadie had heard him drive in and had her nose at the edge of the door, waiting for him to open it. Her tail was flying back and forth, and she was whimpering with excitement. Matthew knelt down and hugged her as she put her front paws on his leg and licked his cheek.

After feeding her he decided to act on an idea he'd had driving home. He got her leash and put her in the car. Fifteen minutes later they went into the assisted living residence, with Sadie sniffing all the way down the hall. When they entered his mother's room, she was sitting on the sofa, looking at the television with her usual blank stare. However, when she saw Sadie, a spark of life ignited on Ruth's face.

"Molly," she exclaimed as she held out her arms.

Matthew then remembered. Molly was the next door neighbor's beagle some forty years ago.

Sadie lowered her head a bit cautious as she slowly walked over to the elderly lady. Ruth stroked her head and then her back. Sadie put one paw up on the edge of the sofa and when Ruth patted the seat next to her, Sadie needed no coaxing. She hopped up and lay down beside her as her new friend petted her and even talked to her.

Matthew smiled as he sat in a nearby chair. No more swearing, he thought. And in an odd and very private way, he was somewhat sorry.

CHAPTER TWENTY-SEVEN

SATURDAY—JUNE 27

Matthew did not have lunch with his co-workers but instead immediately began tending to all his after-lunch chores, telling Evangeline he needed to be somewhere by one o'clock. He would make up the time somehow, even work an extra day if necessary. She had asked no questions. "You go right on," she said simply.

Now at fifteen minutes before one, sitting in his car in the staff parking lot behind EOM, he felt his stomach begin to knot as all forms of uncertainty tried to dissuade him. He wouldn't be gone any longer than usual, so Sadie would be fine. What else was there truly to worry about?

On Thursday he had finally confessed to Kate about not going places, even going to the grocery store late at night to avoid people he might possibly see from his church. They had discussed his fear in terms of his emotional power and self-confidence. Her question still echoed in his head. "How long are you going to give away your power to other people?" It had stopped him cold. This was bigger and more important than what people thought of him. Much bigger.

He started his car and drove downtown toward the vicinity of Elmsborough's Governmental Plaza. He thought it was an odd place to hold a rally and begin and end a parade, but it was in the heart of the city and the main steps to the building provided a good stage for speeches. Maybe the organizers thought it would be safer, less likely to have any disruptions if they staged it on government property which also housed the police department.

As he parked his car and got out he tried to quiet the clamor and misgivings in his head. It served no good purpose. He checked his watch. Just now one o'clock. As he neared the plaza, he saw that people had already begun gathering along the street, waiting for the parade to begin.

Standing on the sidewalk in front of a gift shop, Matthew observed the spectators. It wasn't the first time he'd seen young people with tattoos, body piercings, overly exposed body parts, strange haircuts and colors, low-slung pants on some of the boys. Most, however, were dressed in what he considered normal clothes—caps, t-shirts, shorts, sandals. The ages of the onlookers ranged from younger to older with a fair representation of all. One elderly gentleman steered his special motorized chair up the sidewalk and to the curb. He was tethered to an oxygen tank below his seat. On the back he had attached a long, flexible pole with a rainbow flag on it. Some men seemed not so masculine in their mannerisms, some of the women not so feminine in theirs. Several people had brought their dogs, some even sporting rainbow collars and leashes. He thought of Sadie and how she might have fared in this crowd.

Matthew fought his urge to condemn the odd sights he saw. He even remembered what Evangeline said about judging others. Still, all he could think about was how this wasn't who Nathaniel was. He didn't wear strange clothes, nor act in an odd way. He was normal. Normal in every way. He wanted to turn around and leave. Go home and play fetch with Sadie. Take her out somewhere and allow her to run. But just then, he heard applause up the street in the next block. When he looked, he saw that the parade was nearing. He folded his arms across his chest. He had made it this far. Might as well stay.

Slowly, the lead car made its way down the street. Its occupant, according to the sign on the convertible's door, was the Grand Marshall. A former soap opera star—handsome, deeply tanned, his shirt open, heavy-shadowed beard—he sat up on the back, waving to the people. Next was a small band playing music that Matthew didn't recognize. A pickup truck serving as a float had a sign that read "Elmsborough Support Foundation." The people on the back tossed out wrapped candy to the crowd. Others walked along and handed out cards and condoms. Matthew took a card. "Elmsborough Support Foundation, non-profit fundraising to support gay, lesbian, bi-sexual, transgender causes through grants." Bi-sexual, transgender, Matthew noted, not expecting so much diversity. A tractor carried in its front loader an overweight man badly dressed as a woman. Even from a distance Matthew could see that his makeup was caked on. Streamers of all colors adorned the large mechanical scoop as he sat regally on its lip. Several other men dressed in women's clothes walked along with the tractor. Several cleverly decorated flatbed trucks passed—one with the Elmsborough Gay Mens' Chorus singing and waving to the crowd, another with men dressed in western garb, another with men dressed in skimpy swimsuits. A pickup truck sponsored by the After Hours Club followed with decorations and a DJ in back playing music.

The next group apparently was not affiliated with any organization. They carried banners and posters of various sizes, memorializing people—loved ones, partners, brothers, a few even said "lover." As the crowd read the posters, polite applause rose up. Suddenly, the parade slowed to a complete halt and Matthew saw him. He held the center of the seven to eight foot long PVC pipe from which hung a banner. He alternated carrying it first with one hand, then the other, needing to rest his arms. Matthew read it. "In Loving Memory of Nate Winslow." Around the words were drawings of Nathaniel. Playing baseball and basketball. Studying. Laughing. Being serious.

When Jason Daniels turned to survey the crowd, Matthew stepped back behind other people so that Jason would not see him.

But something within him—a whisper of courage—took hold of him and made him move back where he had been standing, that he was exactly where he was supposed to be at that moment.

When Jason saw him, they stared at each other for several moments. Matthew had no thought. He merely stood on the sidewalk and was himself. When he saw Jason gesture with the pole, offering for him to help carry the banner, he could not move. Him, Matthew Winslow, in front of all these people, marching in a Gay Pride parade. Was this why he had felt compelled to be here? Was *this* another act of grace? *How long are you going to give away your power?*

Suddenly he defied all questions, all hesitations, all doubts. He felt his feet moving. He was no longer on the sidewalk. He was in the street, standing beside Jason Daniels, a gay man. He was carrying a banner memorializing his son. His son, a gay man.

He and Jason did not speak as the parade began its slow pace again, nor as it continued. As they walked, he heard the applause from the onlookers and he felt good. He wasn't protesting, nor repenting, nor asking to be forgiven. As Dwight Overby had said—it seemed like the right thing to do.

Several blocks later they arrived at the point where the silent protestors from all the churches lined one side of the street with their posters. Nervousness stirred in Matthew's stomach. He took a deep breath.

"Are you okay with this?" Jason said to him, nodding to the side of the street up ahead.

Matthew surveyed the line of congregants. After only a moment he nodded. "I am," he said with a quiet confidence. He eyed the protestors once more, then looked back at Jason. "In fact, let's make sure they don't miss us." With that he swung ahead of Jason so that the banner directly faced the protestors. He looked back at Jason who nodded his approval.

Matthew began reading the posters— *Homosexuality = Abomination...Gays Spend Eternity in Hell...God Hates Gays...Stop Spreading AIDS....*

When he saw his former colleagues—Richard Newland, Harry Borkin and William Josephs—all lined up together, he noticed that their posters all had quotes from the Bible. He didn't read them or any others. He did find the courage to look directly at each of them, but none of them acknowledged him. It was difficult to tell since all three were wearing sunglasses and caps. Were they trying to disguise themselves? he wondered.

As he continued walking, Matthew heard several protestors gasp. Were they members of his church shocked at seeing him?

"You'll burn in Hell," one woman said, not loudly but loud enough for him to hear.

"Sinner," a man's voice.

"Traitor to God," another said.

"Blasphemer," one woman said, pointing at him.

Each one stirred the feeling growing inside of him. He realized he was proud. Proud that he was doing this for his son. Also proud because he knew in his heart he was doing the right thing.

In the next block a woman in her mid-twenties standing with the church protestors held a poster which simply read, *Leviticus 18:22.* He tensed. Suddenly she stepped off the curb and walked into the street toward him. Was she going to quote the Bible to him? Curse him? Try to damage the banner? Panic was about to seize him when he saw that her lower lip was quivering as she battled back tears. She was obviously nervous, frightened even.

"Reverend Winslow," she said, her voice breaking. "May I walk with you?"

Matthew was so stunned that he could only think of one question—a question which made no sense. "Do you go to Holy Bible Fellowship?"

She wiped away a tear. "Not after today." She then tore her poster into four parts and dropped it on the street.

Matthew smiled and then, after a moment of hesitation, put out his hand to her.

Later that afternoon he drove to the cemetery for the first time since the day of the funeral. With Sadie on her leash, they walked to Nathaniel's grave. As he approached, he felt his emotions rising up, but he did not try to hold them back. He placed a single red rose on top of the granite stone, then cleaned away some twigs and dead leaves that had blown in. He stepped back to read the dates of his son's life. The beginning and the end. Eighteen years and five months. He took his handkerchief from his back pocket and dried his eyes. When he sat down on the ground underneath a tree, Sadie sat down next to him and put her paw on his leg. He scratched her head and hugged her.

Hi, son. This is Sadie. She's my new family. She's very special. You would love her and she would love you. Yesterday when we played fetch in the backyard, I kept thinking about how much you'd love doing that with her. I'm sorry we never had a dog. It might have brought all of us a little closer together.

He closed his eyes and took a deep breath. What to say? How to say it? Be real, he heard from somewhere inside. Real and honest.

I'm sorry about so many things. Things that I can't correct because you're gone. But I'm trying to—trying to figure out everything. I feel like I'm starting my life all over again, but I'm having to carry all this guilt around. I hurt you. All the times I talked about homosexuality and sin. I wish—I wish I hadn't done that. It was—I was wrong.

I didn't come here to ask you to forgive me. I don't deserve that. I just want to talk to you. Talk in a way I should have talked to you all along. Honestly. Had a relationship with you. Treated you like a son. Loved you like a son. I didn't know how because of my own father and grandfather. And I did the same thing to you. I thought I was doing the right thing, but I wasn't. That regret and emptiness will never go away.

He tried to think of things he had discussed with Kate.

I think I understand now—about you being gay. I mean, I'm working on it. I know it wasn't a choice you made—or anyone makes. My counselor said it's about how we're all wired. Everybody's wired in some way. I just never thought about God making anyone feel differently than the way I feel. I wish I had thought about it, known that. Why would you ever have chosen to go through what you must have?

Matthew felt his emotions rising. He lowered his head as tears trickled down his cheeks. After a few minutes he sighed and closed his eyes.

I saw Jason today. We carried a banner he made in that Gay Pride parade—if you can believe that I actually did that. We talked afterward. Turns out he's getting counseling from the same lady I'm going to. He's living with a family in a kind of apartment in their house. He's working and going to school this fall at the community college. He's been going to a liberal Baptist church. Sounds like an oxymoron, doesn't it? But it's true. I went there last Sunday. I'll go again. But you probably already know all about him. He says he comes here often.

He sat quietly for a several minutes, listening to nature—birds singing and calling to each other. Had he ever done that before? Had he ever noticed birds singing? Then he realized the trees and the sound they made as the breeze wafted through the leaves. Something rustled in the tall grass and weeds nearby. Sadie lifted her head up, her ears pointing skyward like radar. Matthew smiled and rubbed her back.

Well, Sadie and I have to go, but we'll be back. I promise.

He stood up and so did Sadie. She looked up at him, but Matthew was staring at his son's grave.

I love you, Nathaniel—Nate.

Epilogue

Thursday—October 22... Four Months Later

"I still don't know what to write," Matthew told Kate. "I've started so many letters and every time I wind up deleting it all. And no, I'm only composing on the computer. When I finally decide what to write, I'll copy it on paper and mail it." He crossed his legs—ankle over knee—and clasped his hands in front of his chest.

"You still don't know if they've heard about what's gone on with you?" Kate asked.

"No, and I'm not going through a litany of—of everything."

Kate said nothing but raised her eyebrows which Matthew took as disagreement.

"Dear Miriam," he began, "After you left I was fired, got mad, attacked the trunk of a car with Nathaniel's baseball bat and got arrested."

"Couldn't you tell them that you're now working at Elmsborough Outreach Ministry as assistant to the head of food services and that recently, you had to run the whole show for two days while your boss was out sick?" Kate asked. "You wouldn't have to say what brought you there."

Matthew heaved a huge sigh as he avoided her eyes.

"Or that you helped Jason Daniels carry his banner that celebrated Nathaniel's life in the Gay Pride parade? Or that you're going to Ben Thornton's church? Or that you're in therapy?" She raised her eyebrows. "None of that?"

"No," he said. "It would sound like I was saying, 'Look at all these great things I've done. I'm now the greatest husband and dad in the world. Won't you please forgive me and come back?'"

"What do you think you can write to let them know that you aren't the same person they've always known?"

Matthew did not respond.

"You know we've talked about connecting with other people. And to do that you have to open up. I wonder if it's time for you to consider being vulnerable with your wife and daughter. Truly be yourself. Like when you walked in the Gay Pride parade in June."

Matthew shook his head. "That was different. Somehow. Guilt, maybe. I'm still baffled that I did that." He looked away in frustration with himself. "I don't know who I am."

"That makes you just like everybody else." She leaned forward. "If you're waiting until you know who you are, until you have all the answers—" She stopped and merely looked at him.

Matthew gave the kitchen countertops and the table where he'd eaten a final wipe down and draped the damp dishrag over the handle of the oven door. After Sadie lapped some water from her bowl, he turned off the light and the two of them went to his office. He sat down at his desk and smiled as Sadie went through her routine of circling her spot before lying down and drifting off to sleep. So peaceful, he thought. So loving. So—so ready and willing to connect. "Your life is so simple," he said softly. "Lucky you."

Even though he had received no important emails other than spam in months, he checked just in case. When he found nothing, he sat staring at the blank screen as he replayed Kate's words. He took a deep breath and opened a Word document. He stared at the new screen. Finally, thoughts began trickling through his mind.

Dear Miriam:

I've tried countless times to do this—write to you—but the words would not happen. I still don't know what to say or how to say it. Right or wrong, however, I want to make the attempt.

You should know that the money I sent for Sarah Elizabeth's school did not come out of her college savings fund. That will remain untouched until she goes. I found her new school online. It appears to be a wonderful facility with exceptional programs and teachers. I suspect this is the same school that Carolyn and Jim's kids attend which will also be good for her in terms of making new friends more quickly. I sincerely hope that the money requested in your attorney's letter has been enough for yours and Sarah Elizabeth's living expenses. Please know that I will always meet that responsibility.

I will be putting the house on the market probably next spring since I don't need all this room. I'll let you know the time frame so that we can discuss furniture and other items without having to rush.

I am no longer a part of Holy Bible Fellowship which has turned out to be a blessing and quite a journey, but I know that doesn't change the past.

In June when Carolyn and Jim were here, Carolyn said that you're taking one day at a time, so I hope you have been able to find more and more peace each day. Easier said than done, I know.

Suffice it to say that you were right about everything you said the night you left. I think of Nathaniel constantly and the negative impact I had on his life. I've come to understand that his sexual ori-

entation was not a choice. Add to that my outspokenness— My guilt knows no end or depth. The same is true for the way I treated you, going back as far as college. With all the hurt and anger you must feel raw. I'm not asking that you forgive me, but I am asking to be allowed to keep up with Sarah Elizabeth if she is agreeable. Please give her the enclosed letter which you, of course, may also read.

If you need anything, do not hesitate to ask.

Matthew

He read what he had written. It wasn't what he wanted to say, not exactly. But he didn't know how he could ever accomplish that. Was he being vulnerable? Was he trying to connect? Maybe. Did he have a right to ask for that? He didn't know. He just knew he had to get this out of him. Now. Before it might be too late. He scrolled down to the next page and locked his eyes on its blankness. This one would be more difficult. He sat for a long time before he was able to begin.

Dear Sarah Elizabeth:

For me to say that I'm sorry for shattering our family's world—well, "I'm sorry" is not now or ever will be enough to repair the damage. I know how close you were to Nathaniel, how much you loved him. That my beliefs pushed him to do what he did is a hell that I will live in for the rest of my life.

I was not a good father to you. I hurt you in so many ways and so many times. I hope that some day you will be able to forgive me for how I treated you and allow me to be a part of your life—exchange of emails, phone calls and hopefully visits, maybe even go out to eat. I never told you before that you're a beautiful young lady and I'm very proud to call you my daughter. So I'm telling you now from my heart. I hope you'll give me a chance to say that many more times in person.

I'm also so very sorry for the way you were shunned by your classmates at school here, especially Mike. That was just wrong. You're better off away from that environment.

I've seen your new school online. It looks like a terrific place with a lot of opportunities and extracurricular activities. I hope you're taking advantage of as many of them as you can without foregoing your studies. I know that you'll be an asset to the student body, making lots of new friends. Carolyn told me in June that there's already someone special—well, kind of. That's great. He's very lucky.

If you ever need me or just want to say "hi," please write or call. I will always love hearing from you.

Much love,
Dad

P. S. Believe it or not, I have a dog. Her name is Sadie. She's great, loves to play fetch in the backyard. I think you'd like her. I hope some day you can meet her.

He thought for a moment before adding one more line.

(Her first night here she had an accident—

He stopped and thought for only a minute, then pressed the delete key.

--she peed on the carpet in the bedroom, but only the one time. Don't tell your mother.)

He read both letters several times, and each time he started to make changes but didn't. Maybe it was best just to write. He opened a drawer and took out some blank paper and began copying them in long-hand.

With the long metal poker Matthew lifted the screen cover off of the fire pit which he'd moved to the edge of the patio. He poked around in the ashes to be sure all the pages were burned as the fire was dying out. Then he placed the last six notebooks into the small flame, stirred them around and watched as the blaze came to life again. He eased the screen back over the pit and sat down on the glider beside Sadie on the other side of the patio away from the heat.

When he started he hadn't stopped to add up how many he had. His grandfather's, his father's, Sarah Elizabeth's, Nathaniel's and his own. Each had twelve notebooks of Bible verses, except his grandfather who had only ten. A total of fifty-eight. No wonder it had taken so long to burn them. He stroked Sadie's head as she watched the fire with him, her ears pricked up.

"A lot of ashes to put in the trash tomorrow, huh, girl?" he said softly.

Sadie looked up at him, whimpered, then rested her muzzle on his leg.

When the idea had come to him, he had wondered if it was wrong to burn something about the Bible. But he had reasoned he wasn't burning the Bible. Nor was he blaspheming God. Memorized verses didn't make him or anyone a better Christian.

"It's not what's in your head," he whispered. "It's what's in your heart." Sadie looked up at him, then yawned and put her head down again. "Unconditional love," he said, scratching behind her ears.

As he watched the smoke rise from the pit, he reached into his pocket and took out his cell phone. He stared at it for a moment. After pressing several keys, he put it to his ear and listened to Nathaniel's message. Tears filled his eyes.

"End of message," said the automated voice. "To delete this message, press seven. To save it in the archives, press nine."

TO THE READER

The Kingdom is self-published. Therefore, I am relying on my readers to tell your family and friends about it. Either direct them to Amazon.com, my web site (tomhardinbooks.com) or my Facebook page (Tom Hardin Books). It is available both as a book and an ebook at Amazon.com. Also, please "Like" and "Share" my web site on Facebook. And feel free to write a customer review on my Amazon page.

Recommended reading:

YOUTH IN CRISIS: 40 Stories Revealing the Personal, Social, and Religious Pain and Trauma of Growing Up Gay in America. Edited by Mitchell Gold with Mindy Drucker. Forward by Martin Navratilova. (www.FaithInAmerica.com)

IF THE CHURCH WERE CHRISTIAN: Rediscovering the Values of Jesus by Rev. Philip Gulley.

If you are struggling with your sexual orientation, please seek help. YOU ARE NOT ALONE. Here are just three of a multitude of organizations to which you can turn:

GLBT Hotline

(888) 843-4564

email: glnh@GLBTNationalHelpCenter

GLBT National Youth Talkline

(800) 246-7743 [(800) 246-PRIDE]

Human Rights Campaign (HRC)
1640 Rhode Island Avenue NW
Washington, D. C. 20036
(202) 628-4160
www.hrc.org

Made in the USA
Charleston, SC
25 January 2013